A SEVEN CITIES NOVEL
BOOK ONE

A Concealed Pursuit

Michaela Bryan

Contents

Prologue

The fugitive threw on his long, black coat and took up his briefcase. Aside from his special package, tucked away safely, he had no need to pack anything besides what he already had stuffed in his coat pockets. The Lumerians had found him again and would be headed to collect him any second; he had to move quickly.

Leaving the key behind, he exited his apartment and began walking down the dark hallway.

The down button on the elevator—the only light in the corridor—glowed with a dim yellow light and gave off the faintest hum. Soon, the sound of spinning wheels and sliding metal grew more distinguishable as the elevator drew near in its shaft. The man looked left and right, staring down into a long, dark hall. When morning came, his neighbors likely wouldn't notice the stranger beside them was gone—the odd man who offered little more than a nod in greeting before retreating back into the security of his apartment.

A red down arrow appeared with a *ding* and the doors slid open.

Where to go now, I wonder. He stepped inside. *Not Italy again. Perhaps a third world country. Who would be able to locate me there? No. I have to finish my work. I have to stay in the country.*

He stepped out of the elevator and headed through the empty lobby to the doors. The room smelled as if the fireplace had recently been put out, as the sweet aroma of burning wood still lingered in the air. Wide windows reflected the streetlight on both sides of him, the silhouette of a man outlined against the glass as he sat comfortably on a sidewalk bench, apparently reading. The emptiness in the room felt comfortable with the tranquility that the night carried seeping in through the illuminated glass.

Except for the man outside on the bench. There was something peculiar about him. The moment the fugitive realized this, he stiffened.

No wonder. He turned and stared at the man outside the window, who looked as if he were oblivious to the fugitive who stood just behind the glass. *They've been following me.*

He pushed open the door and headed along the sidewalk to where the reading man sat on the bench. Setting down his case, the fugitive rested on the same bench, busying himself with the matter of getting comfortable.

"Good evening," the reading man spoke with a nod.

The fugitive had seen this man before. He had seen his face through several windows, though he had always ignored the faint alarm of recognition. He had seen too many faces over too many years to even begin to compare one to another. They all began to look the same after a while. *This* man, on the other hand, had a face the fugitive knew.

"Good evening, sir," he replied with a grin. "It's a beautiful night."

The other man nodded.

"Are you out to enjoy it, or has your book got you too intrigued to move from your spot?" The fugitive tried for a friendly smile.

"Both, I suppose," the other man replied. "And what brings you out here?"

The fugitive turned his face to the sky. "Oh, the night is something to take advantage of, I suppose." He looked at the man. "Do you know which place is exceptionally beautiful at night?"

The man raised his eyebrows.

"The Arc City," the fugitive said.

The other man's face darkened as his facade began to dissolve.

The fugitive went on. "You've been there, haven't you? I can't imagine why you'd leave. Unless, of course, you are looking for someone."

The act fell.

"I'm here to make you answer for the lives you've taken," the man responded darkly.

There he is. The fugitive relished the audible shift from polite friendliness to cold honesty. However, this man was picking at a wound in the fugitive's thick skin, which would not do.

"Killing those men"—the fugitive sat forward, resting his elbows on his knees as he folded his hands out in front of him—"would not have been my first call. By then, they were in too deep and, if anything, I was sparing them from what was to come."

The other man laughed. "So you did them a favor?"

"You, like them, are after something that is out of your reach. Look how they ended up. Do you want to suffer the same fate?"

"You can't run forever," he warned.

"Actually, I can," the fugitive said before the other man could go on. "And where I'm going, neither you nor your council will be able to find me again. I would tell you to consider that your warning, but I'm afraid you'll have nowhere to carry my message."

"Are you going to kill me now?" the unfazed man taunted. "Add to the pile of bodies that died by your hand?"

"Eventually, yes," the fugitive answered. "But The Way will open soon. In fact, it will only be a matter of years now. I cannot kill you right this moment, not here, but I can show you."

"Show me what, exactly?"

"Why I do what I do." He opened his case, removing a small, shimmering blue rod about six inches long with a metal cap on the bottom end. Blue mist circled within the narrow cylinder, from which a faint glow radiated.

The man eyed the rod suspiciously. "Where does that go?"

"I don't know exactly," the fugitive responded, inspecting the rod in his hand. "I made it only today using the fibers I took from an English museum. It will take us to wherever The Way opens."

"*Us?*"

The fugitive raised an eyebrow. "You'd rather I kill you now and make a mess on the bench?"

The man stood. "My name is Agent Levile Portute, and I'm placing you under arrest by order of the Lumerian Council for the murder of ten officers and obstruction of justice."

The fugitive hardly flinched. With a quick, simple movement, he tossed the rod at the man. The moment the rod hit Agent Portute, it burst into a thin-banded hole in the air, which expanded in a split second to a large window. On the other side of its glowing circumference, a suburban street strung together a line of dark houses.

The portal opened around Portute and he was immediately pulled through, left stumbling down the new road.

The fugitive stood, closed his case, and stepped through the portal, shutting it behind him so once again the cold, glowing rod lay in his gentle fingers. "So," he said, looking up. "This is the place."

Bewildered, Levile turned in circles until he found the street sign, which had been bent diagonally in the middle of its post. *King Avenue.* "There is nothing here," he said. "There has been too much renovation. It is buried."

"But it's not gone," the fugitive replied, continuing down the street. "So now, I wait."

"You plan to live here?" Levile said, turning around to follow.

"It seems logical."

The agent looked around. "How do you plan to find it?"

"I have a nose for the old and valuable," the fugitive replied as he walked on. "And I have something you don't."

"Old and valuable, yeah." Agent Portute snorted.

"Obtaining enough information was difficult, but what I can do with it once I have it makes it worth the effort," he went on, ignoring Levile.

"Well, look where it got you," the agent responded. "Ten are dead and you're a wanted man. You'll spend the rest of your life on the run."

The fugitive smiled. "There is so little you know for sure." Then he paused, right at the driveway of dark house. "I found it," he said.

"What?" Levile looked at the old house. "It's here?"

The fugitive took a small package from his pocket, wrapped in brown cloth and tied with a string. "Do you know what else I have that you don't?" he continued as he pulled the string loose and slipped a golden knife from its cloth cover. "Legacy."

Levile's eyes widened. *"Bane?"* He hissed. "That knife belongs—"

"To me," the fugitive said. "Consider it an honor that you died with such an artifact."

Portute's muscles flexed as he tried to spring back, but the fugitive was quicker. The knife pierced the man's neck, digging all the way into his skin, cutting into his throat. Agent Portute froze, his terrified eyes locked onto his killer. Blood splattered across the fugitive's face, but he was unfazed by its warm touch. The dying agent sank to the ground, pulling himself away from the knife.

The fugitive looked down on the body. Though he was very familiar with death, it pained him each time his hand was forced into killing. He wiped the knife clean with the cloth. Hopefully, that would be the last time he had to take a life. His work was almost completed and, until then, he would remain here.

CHAPTER ONE

The First Tower

It started with a tower. A tower and a level of curiosity that wouldn't have existed if Elise Montason wasn't so damn bored with herself. This particular tower wasn't the normal, modern American kind but looked to be built entirely of poorly cut stones, in a place just out of reach but not quite out of sight, where Elise had never seen anything out of the ordinary before this night.

Not many lights remained on at this hour of night on King Avenue. Elise Montason, perched by her bedroom window, was well aware of the fact that any onlooker would think her behavior to be doglike. She had been staring out the window for a count of three minutes now, waiting for something to happen. Now was about the time Hank Martinez came over, and he always came with something to do that was worth doing. Of course, Elise could be working on her English essay, but sitting by the window doing nothing seemed far preferable.

Finally, she turned away and elected to pursue the easier solution she had been putting off since she began her wait. She trudged down the stairs and poked her head into her mother's office.

"Is Marty coming over tonight?" she asked.

"If he wants to," Eleanor replied without looking up. "Elise, I'm busy. Please keep the door closed."

On 8742 King Avenue, Elise Montason, along with her mother, Eleanor, and her brother, Percy, lived quietly. Across the street stood an even quieter house, owned by a man named Hank Martinez, who used it not as a place of living but for storing, building, tinkering with, and otherwise messing with his various projects. Mr. Martinez, despite living in an apartment in the city, happened to be in that house when the Montasons moved in eleven years ago and had welcomed their arrival warmly, marking the beginning of a long and strange friendship. Since they had moved in, then five-year-old Elise had asked the same question almost daily, especially the first year or so.

"Can Mr. Marty come over?" young Elise asked many times a week.

"No, Mr. Martinez is at work right now," irritable Eleanor would reply.

It had become a fast tradition for "Marty" to come over each night to please Elise and keep Eleanor company.

Everyone on King Avenue loved Mr. Martinez and his frequent visits. He was an engineer—a charming, polite, tall, and handsome one. He lived alone, for his wife, Maria, divorced him a long time ago, taking their daughter with her. So he said.

Hank became like a father to Elise, since her own father had been divorced by Eleanor soon after Elise's birth, when Eleanor found out her husband had gotten another woman pregnant. It was a messy situation; they didn't talk about it much. Hank's closeness with the Montasons soon led to Hank meeting Elise's birth father, Lucious Ataliarma, and, without the knowledge of Eleanor, the men developed an odd, unlikely friendship.

Lucious had left the Montasons for the other woman, remaining with her for the birth of their daughter, whom they named Laleitha, before leaving them once again for God-knows-where, returning only to visit both his families on occasion. At first, Elise had a hard time warming up to her half-sister—the result of her father's betrayal—but when school started for both, she and her half-sister became very closely bonded.

Their friendship began out of their favoritism of the familiar in such a new environment.

Elise had walked into a full classroom, immediately scanning the crowd for a face she recognized. Laleitha had been the only one, so she had had to do. Consequently, they grew up side by side, much to Eleanor's disdain. Elise never bothered to consider her mother's thoughts on the matter, however, as Elise enjoyed Laleitha's company immensely. They only grew closer as the years passed, Laleitha often accompanying Elise to Marty's house, which was how he first encountered the girls' birth father. Of course Eleanor eventually made her thoughts known to Elise, that Laleitha belonged to a dishonest family and a psychotic mother, who, even though she lived a city over, sent her daughter to the same school as Elise, which Eleanor was certain she did just to spite her. Elise wasn't so sure, being that she and Laleitha discussed in length that they were essentially in the same situation.

When Elise discovered the friendship between Hank Martinez and Lucious Ataliarma, she decidedly kept it to herself. The revelation had come gradually to her through small hints in her casual conversations with Marty. She didn't like it, but she didn't see anything she could do to stop it. Life couldn't be anything but messy when it came to her father.

Now, Elise still anticipated the company of Mr. Martinez each night. His presence was an effective distraction to the fact that she didn't really have a father—and often didn't have a mother either.

"Honestly, Mom, why didn't you just go to college after high school?" Elise demanded, ignoring her mother's request to close the door.

"I *did* initially, then I became pregnant with Percy. Now *please* leave me be."

Elise scoffed and left the doorway to her mother's office, allowing her to return to her college education. She grabbed *The Hound of the Baskervilles* from the bookshelf and curled up on the sofa in the dim living room.

The messiness of life perhaps affected Eleanor more than her children, who had known nothing else. Her mother's face had hardly been seen by Elise or Percy most days. She always locked herself in her study and never even made them a meal or went to their sporting events. This hardly bothered Elise though. What really brought about the frown on her face was her mother's foolishness. Eleanor was so fragile, so dependent. She waited too long for others to pick her up before she even tried to pick herself up. *I don't want to be like that.* And to that Elise had held true.

Elise closed her book. Usually, she marveled to hear the deductions of the world's greatest detective, but Sherlock Holmes was not holding her interest this night. This night, she couldn't seem to focus.

"Mom?" she called without getting up.

"*What?*" her mother snapped in reply.

"Where is Percy?"

"He is at the Dennises. I suggest you find somewhere to be as well."

Elise set aside Sherlock Holmes and bounced up the stairs to her bedroom. She grabbed a drawstring bag that hung on the edge of her bed and stuffed in her phone and a different book. Out the front door she went and down the sparsely lit King Avenue.

When King Avenue split into a T intersection, she crossed into the field in front of her, headed to Wellington Park, where she spent much of her time.

The park was empty at that time of evening. Elise stepped into the gravel and made her way across the playground, past the swings and back into the grass. She crossed through the trees until she found the perfect one for climbing that sat right next to the lake's edge.

She hoisted herself onto the lowest branch and worked her way between and around the rest of them until she got as far up as her nerves permitted. Making herself comfortable in a wedge of branches, she took out the contents of her bag, turned on her phone's flashlight, and buried her face in the pages of the book.

She had made four chapters into it before she heard a familiar voice from below.

"Aw, man, you took my spot!"

Elise shined her flashlight into the squinting face of her half-sister.

"Mine now," she replied.

"Ugh." Laleitha pulled herself up onto the first branch. "Be like that then."

"What are you doing here this late?" Elise asked.

"Me? What are *you* doing here?" Laleitha fired back, sitting down next to her sister.

"I'm always here."

"Not *here* here. I'm *here* just about every minute of the day. I see you around here; you just never see me."

Elise cast her sister a sideways glance. *Why on earth does she spend her time hiding in trees?* "You always find the best hiding spots," she said. "But that's pretty much where your sense of subtlety ends."

Laleitha ignored the comment, turning her attention to the book Elise was reading. "You're really reading a book about *engineering*? What kind of nerd are you?" Laleitha snatched the book from her.

"Shut *up*," Elise replied as she snatched her book back and stuffed it in her bag. "I'm determined to finish my pressurized water reactor project, and in order to do so, I need some background knowledge."

Laleitha rolled her eyes "You already have *some* background knowledge. You don't need a master's degree. And you've been working on that project forever. How many times have you had to dismantle it again?"

"Did you hear the company Marty works for is starting an energy project?" Elise asked, changing the subject to avoid the question. "Marty says he's working on a nuclear reactor that should allow his facility to be self-sustaining for an entire week!"

"God, *why* do you care about nuclear reactors, Mont?"

"Marty's engineering fascinates me," Elise replied, waving her hand. She had given up protesting Laleitha's cringeworthy nickname for her years ago.

"No, you're totally bored with yourself again. You just need another project."

She shrugged. "I like to build things."

The corner of Laleitha's lip rose upward. "I noticed that after a few years of being your sister."

Elise grinned, not bothering to think of a response.

Laleitha had their father's look, much to her disdain. Brown hair—but with her mother's intense curls—hazel eyes, and a splattering of freckles. It always surprised Elise how different the two of them looked, despite sharing a father. Elise's hair was platinum blonde and wavy to the point of always looking messy, and her eyes were a deep brown that never shined like Lalietha's. She stood a few inches taller than Lalietha, and her frame was slimmer and straighter, while Lalietha had wide hips and a somewhat stout frame.

"Have you seen Dad in a while?" Elise asked after a minute. It had been over a year since he'd visited the Montasons, and Elise couldn't help but be curious.

"Still away. Things haven't been good," Laleitha said, looking away, out toward the lake. "He's been visiting us less and less. We don't know where he is."

Elise bit her inner lip. "When was the last time you talked to him?"

"Two months ago—I think he called my mom."

"When was the last time *you* talked to him?"

"Last year some time."

Elise winced.

Laleitha refused to meet her sister's eyes. "Has he talked to you guys at all?" she asked her older sister.

"Mom has been pretending he doesn't exist ever since she went back to college. She's been doing the same with your mom, too, and a little bit with you."

"She's like that still?"

"She's always like that, Lee." Elise sighed in reply. "I've just stopped getting mad because I don't expect anything different. Anyway, as far as we care, Marty is just about the closest thing to a father I have."

They sat for a moment, searching for something else to talk about. The topic of their father never lasted over two minutes before the girls moved on to a more lighthearted subject. The transition usually happened abruptly, as if they were momentarily pretending the issue did not exist.

"So, how's Percy?" Laleitha asked after a while. "I haven't seen him in forever."

"He's no less annoying," Elise replied with a smile. "Hopefully the navy will beat him into shape."

"He's going to the *navy*?" Laleitha gawked.

"Yeah, where have you been?"

"Why didn't you tell me?"

"I thought he told you."

"I hardly talk to Percy."

"Why not?"

"I don't live with him," Laleitha pointed out. "And I don't see him at school every day like I do with you."

Elise shrugged. "I guess I can't really blame Mom for the lack of communication on that one, either, because she hates half the people on *her* side, let alone Dad's."

"That sure sounds like your mom," Laleitha agreed.

"Yeah. Whatever, though—it's not like Mom will be able to control me much longer."

"See? That's what I've been telling you for years!"

Elise laughed. "Well, it hasn't worked out very well for you yet, has it?"

Her sister began to reply before Elise's hand shot up, motioning her to stop.

"Did you see that?"

"See what?" Laleitha asked, obviously lacking the interest that shone in Elise's voice.

"That flash of light?"

"You think you saw a shooting star?"

"No, it was green," Elise answered, her eyes searching the horizon. "It was green and looked like a firework, but then it faded as fast as it appeared."

"Your mind is just playing tricks on you, Elise. There was nothing."

"Look!" Elise jabbed a finger toward the forest at the other end of the lake. "It came from there. Do you see that?"

"That's a private reserve. Nobody goes over there. Nobody *can*—the fence is twelve feet tall and electric. I know because I tried to climb it!"

"But do you see that?" Elise's finger did not lower, decidedly ignoring the fact that her sister once tried to climb an electric fence.

"See what?"

"Th-that . . . *thing*. Right where I'm pointing."

"Oh, the thing? Really descriptive there, Mont."

"The circular thing. It looks like the top of a small tower or building or something."

Laleitha squinted. "Oh my gosh, there is something out there," she murmured on catching sight of it. "How did I not see that before?"

"I guess I'm not the only unobservant one here," Elise said with a smirk.

"Shut up," Laleitha said, punching her sister.

)(

The tower top did not leave Elise's mind when she went home that night. When she walked through the door, the first thing that left her mouth was a question. "Hey, Mom? Do you have any idea who owns the reserve on the other side of Wellington?"

"The government," her mother replied, bluntly. "Why are you up this late? We have church tomorrow morning."

"I know. I just wasn't tired," Elise replied as she headed up the stairs, skipping a few steps with every bound.

Her bag slipped from her shoulder when she entered her bedroom, and she tossed it aside. Order and cleanliness were not priorities in Elise's bedroom. One wall was dominated by bookshelves, which were overflowing, and her laptop sat closed on the neat desk across from her bed. Her desk was the only thing in the room that was neatly organized. Her dresser had scattered knickknacks and keepsakes all over it due to Elise's unwillingness to throw anything away or box it up where she would never see it. Her closet door was always closed to hide things from her mother, her stash of sweets that she had stolen from the kitchen concealed behind the hangars. Despite the messiness, her room was built on pure sentiment. She had photos all around the frame of her mirror and a few posters from her favorite books hanging by her bed, and soccer medals from before high school dangled from a tie hanger in the corner.

Elise leapt onto her bed and plopped down hard, the tower top still in her mind. *What use could they possibly have for that land? Nobody lives there or anywhere near there, they haven't been building anything, there aren't any already existing facilities, and it is too small to be a nature reserve. So what could it be?*

Elise sat up to flip off the lights. "Whatever. I'll figure it out tomorrow." She gave the string next to her bed a tug, triggering the contraption she had built last year to turn off the lights—which she designed out of boredom and used out of laziness. Regardless of her sudden exhaustion, Elise remained awake for hours, staring up at the ceiling, occasionally tossing and turning.

Finally fed up with her restlessness, she flung off her covers and slipped from the mattress. With careful and silent feet, she stepped down her ladder and onto the floor. She slid into her chair before opening her laptop. Blinding light poured from the screen, forcing Elise to squint until her eyes adjusted.

"I can't believe I'm doing this," she muttered to herself as she pulled up a map of the area. "I'll figure this out and then what? Would I be satisfied enough to sleep? Of course not."

She had found Wellington Lake and was now scanning the area on the other side of the park, zooming in on every area in search of an address or some indication something was there.

Nothing. Her gaze traced the road to the borderline of the labeled *9551 West*—there it stopped, and there were only trees. No roads, no facilities, no indication there ever were any.

After nearly an hour of googling property records, she found it. The property at 9551 West was owned by Hank Martinez.

⅍

Mornings at the Montason house were tumultuous affairs.

Percy sat at the table in the midst of a heated argument with Eleanor, who shouted at him for not being home by his midnight curfew. Something on the stove was burning—probably Eleanor's breakfast, which went unnoticed on account of the argument.

Elise poured herself a bowl of cereal and sat down on one of the stools by the counter, completely unnoticed by her family as they shouted at each other.

Their mother had finally grown too agitated to argue and stormed off without a word to her daughter, slamming the door to her office a few seconds later.

"Good morning," Elise said simply when her brother had finally taken notice of her.

He said nothing but turned back to his breakfast.

She couldn't wait to visit Marty today.

✕

"Are you clairvoyant or something?" Marty asked when he answered the door. "I was just about to request your help in repairing an old computer I found in my basement."

Elise smiled.

Marty led her to the workspace—also known as the basement—and set her to work.

"So how has Eleanor been lately?" Marty asked while they worked.

"College work is basically consuming her. Her books are scattered all over the house. I tried to read a chapter of one, but I got too bored to focus."

"I thought you loved books, especially books of theory."

"Not when it has 'philosophy and religious studies' written across the spine. Of all the topics to pick, why philosophy?"

"She seems like the type that would do well in the field."

"Really? I don't see that."

"Well, being her daughter, you've only seen the one side of her. As her friend, I've seen more. She'll never strike you as a philosopher because you only know her as your less-than-philosophical mother."

She nodded, not convinced.

"I hear Percy is going to the navy in a few weeks. Is he excited or nervous?" Marty said, reaching across the table for the screwdriver.

"A bit of both. He likes a challenge."

"Yet he doesn't like it at home?"

Elise snickered. "Not any kind of challenge Mom will give him. Though she definitely has been getting him in shape for it, with all the yelling that goes on in the house."

"Oh, I bet."

"It'll be strange for him, though, being somebody else's toy soldier for once. When we were young, he'd always play general and I'd be the private he shouts at. He'd always been into that sort of thing, combat and whatnot."

"Ah, yes, didn't he do karate at that age as well?"

Elise nodded. "Kempo. I was his test dummy."

"I'm guessing that's how you broke your arm when you were seven?"

"Nah, he pushed me out of a tree."

"He pushed you out of a *tree*?"

Elise laughed as she recalled the memory. "Yeah, Laleitha and I had a 'tree house' that wasn't exactly a house so much as it was a few blankets and baskets hung on the branches, and we didn't want him in it, so we got into a bit of a fight. When he tells the story, he says I slipped, but in truth, he pushed me off the branch."

"Of course he'd say that. Now I haven't heard from Laleitha in a while . . ."

Elise toyed with the wires in front of her, not doing anything in particular with them. "She's kinda fragile right now; her family is going through a rough patch. She spends most of her time at Wellington."

"Like another girl I know."

Elise shook her head. "It's different with Lee. Usually she can't be contained in one place for over an hour, but now she spends almost every minute of her free time there. I'm worried about her."

Marty sighed. "I fear things are going to get worse for them for a while. Your father will be returning soon, and I expect both your mothers will have things to say about it."

"Really?" Elise exclaimed, dropping the wires in her hand and looking up at him with wide eyes. "Why have you been in contact with him?"

Marty pursed his lips, setting down the screwdriver and reaching for a spool of wire. "I neglected to tell you because I didn't think you'd like it. But I like being able to contact him so I can prepare for when he returns, being that it's always a mess."

Elise deflated. "I'm not stupid, Marty. I would have understood," she mumbled. "I would have liked to at least know you were talking though."

Marty sent her a stern look. "Would you have told your mother?"

"Of course not."

He gave a wry chuckle. "She would have found out if you knew. Your mother has a knack for that."

※

Elise nearly forgot to ask. She brought it up as she was perched on the counter in his kitchen, happily eating the bowl of ramen noodles he served her. "Do you own the private reserve by Wellington?"

Marty nodded as he scrubbed the pan in the sink. "I do, although I haven't used it for the last ten years," he answered.

"What is it used for? I mean, back when you did use it?" Elise inquired on.

"Testing some of my larger projects," he replied simply. "Why the sudden interest in that area?"

Elise shrugged. "Last night, I was in a tree with Lee, and we saw something on the other side of the lake in that private reserve. It looked like the top of a building."

"I don't remember there being a building—nothing that anyone could see from the other end of the lake. I made sure of that."

"Why did you stop using it?"

"There are lots of dangerous areas in that reserve, especially after some tests gone wrong. I wanted to keep using it, but the people in my team backed out after one of them fell in a crater and broke their leg."

Elise frowned. "What do you mean dangerous areas? Like, life-threatening?"

He almost laughed as he answered. "Sometimes, actually, there was quite a risk working there. It was probably better that my team backed out."

"And you wanted to keep working there?" Marty didn't seem like the type to take those kinds of risks, especially not with other people's safety.

Marty shrugged. "I believed in what we were working on. Most are frightened by the possibility of death or pain, no matter how slim the possibility is. We all have to go in some way, don't we? It's either going to be poetic or ironic or mundane—always for a purpose though."

Elise studied him carefully, trying to work out a root to these words. Did he really believe in his project so much he'd let people *die* working on it? The way he talked about death kind of scared her, but at the same time, she felt an overwhelming desire to see this place.

"Will you take me to see it?" she asked.

Marty considered this for a long moment before finally turning back to her and saying, "I'll take you tomorrow. Don't tell your mother."

CHAPTER TWO

A Sudden Departure

The fourth period lecture came to a pause when the phone rang. "One moment," the teacher said as he went to answer it. Elise set her pen down, looking back over her notes to find that she didn't understand a thing she'd written down.

"Oh, yes, I see," the teacher said quietly into the phone. The class was stirring now, people striking up conversations and moving from their seats, but the teacher didn't seem to notice. His hand seemed to move in slow motion as he placed the phone back on the receiver. "Elise Montason, your mother is waiting in the office to take you home."

All eyes turned to Elise as her head lifted. Confused and caught by surprise, she closed her notebook. She wordlessly collected her stuff and hugged it tightly to her chest as she stood up and walked out of the classroom.

What happened? Mom would never pull me out of school unless something serious has sprung up. Are we in danger? Has someone died? Is someone dying? Is it Dad? Please tell me it's not Dad . . .

She had reached her locker by now and shoved her books into her bag. *Mom never schedules appointments during school hours. Whatever, I'm sure it's nothing. Nothing to worry about, anyway. I'm getting ahead of myself . . .*

When she reached the office and saw her mother, Elise's heart dropped. Eleanor's cheeks were streaked with tears, and her hands were clasped in a tight ball on her lap as she sat on one of the worn, and obviously mistreated, chairs in the corner.

"Mom?" Elise said as she approached her mother.

Eleanor looked up at her daughter and sprang to her feet. "Oh, Elise!" She threw her arms around her daughter and began sobbing on her shoulder.

Confused, Elise awkwardly patted her mother on the back, struggling through the tight embrace.

"Y-your . . ."

Elise couldn't pick up anything else from her mother's incoherent babbling.

"I-it's going to be okay," Elise guessed.

"Marty, he—" Eleanor said.

Oh.

"He's *gone*, Elise. He's . . ." Her voice began to fail her again and she just continued to cry.

Then Elise realized what her mom meant.

"Oh," Elise whispered, closing her eyes.

Her mother continued to sob, but Elise didn't shed a tear. In fact, she hardly reacted at all.

Percy arrived minutes later, and the process began all over again. Wordlessly, Elise and her brother ushered their mother out of the office, all the way to her car. By then, her mother had run out of tears to cry and sat at the steering wheel just as silent as Elise.

Elise refused to speak the entire car ride. There was no way Marty had died. This was some sort of mistake. She'd just seen him yesterday and he was healthy as ever. It had to be a mistake.

It has to be a mistake.

✕

"How did it happen?" she asked quietly, her head rested against the window of the back seat.

"I don't know. They didn't tell me," Eleanor said, gripping the steering wheel with white knuckles.

You didn't ask? Elise wanted to say, but now wasn't the time for starting fights with her mother. Instead, she nodded and looked out the window.

"Where are we going?" Percy asked after a minute from the passenger seat.

"Chicago," Eleanor replied. "The investigators want to talk to us."

"What do you mean *the investigators?*" Elise demanded, raising her head in alarm. "What happened to Marty?"

Her mother let out a sharp breath through her nose.

"Do you mean they think he's been *murdered*?" Elise mind jumped to the darkest possible place first.

She wanted more than anything for her mother to tell her she was wrong. She waited for several long, painful seconds that felt like hours for her mother to say no. With each subsequent beat, her heart began to sink.

Finally, her mother gave a stiff nod.

Elise stared out the window. *Who would want him dead? No. There's no way he's dead. Nobody would ever want to kill him. There must be some mistake. Marty wasn't killed; it's not possible.*

Finally, once they had driven into the district with tall towers that loomed over the crowded city streets and navigated a dim parking garage, they stepped out of their car into the chilly outdoors.

Elise floated like a ghost behind her mother and brother as they entered the building, passing the desks and doorways without a single thought to her surroundings, trapped in some sort of absentminded daze. Her mother engaged in a quiet discussion with one or two men in suits before they ushered her and Elise to a conference room. Elise sat by the window, gazing down at the cars below. Nausea churned in her stomach. She swallowed down her discomfort with difficulty.

A detective entered the room. "Ms. Montason, may I speak to you and your son first?"

Eleanor nodded, and she and Percy stood. Then, without looking at Elise, they left the room, the detective closing the door behind them.

Elise sat anxiously alone, picking her sleeve to pieces until there were hardly any loose threads to pull at. She tried to imagine the rest of her life in Marty's absence. She pictured several scenarios but found each one feeling emptier than the last. When the tears almost came again, she forced the thoughts away.

Soon after, the detective entered again and asked to speak with her.

A knot formed in her stomach as she stood and approached the detective, still self-conscious of the tears she just barely held back. He was a large man dressed in a spotless black suit. His thick, sausage-like fingers gripped a case file as he waited for Elise to step out the door.

Elise finally let the detective slip from her glance as she exited into the hallway.

The door shut behind her and the detective said, "Right over here, Miss Montason."

They entered another room. Elise speculated it belonged to the detective. It looked messy, with papers scattered all across the broad desk, family pictures strung up on the wall in random places, and desk toys shoved to one corner of the table.

"You can sit down," he said gently. He spoke quietly, as if he expected her to shatter if he talked too loud.

Elise did as she was told. Her gaze fell to the papers in front of the detective. At the upper right corner of the top one, the small image of a tree was encircled, all in blue ink. She briefly stared at the unfamiliar symbol, wondering to what company the seal belonged.

Her attention was drawn back to the detective when he cleared his throat. "You were close to Mr. Martinez?"

"Yes."

"I'm sorry for your loss."

Elise nodded and an uncomfortable pause ensued.

"Did he ever talk to you about his personal life?" the detective asked after a moment.

Elise's eyes rose to meet his. "Don't you usually ask these questions to all of us? Not just individually?"

"Not under these circumstances. Did he ever talk to you about his personal life?" he repeated.

"Yes, but why are you talking to me individually?" Elise asked again, letting a bit of agitation into her voice.

The detective leaned forward, folding his hands on his desk. "Did you two have any codes or special signals between the two of you?" he asked.

"Huh?" Taken aback by this unusual question but seeing his complete seriousness, she answered, "No."

Before she could say anything else, he moved on. "Did you often talk about languages, other cultures, or any form of mythology?"

"No." She opened her mouth to ask another question before she was interrupted again.

"Did he take any interest in runes or dead languages?" the detective inquired.

"No," Elise replied. "May I ask a question?"

"Yes."

"These are not normal questions."

"That was a statement," he pointed out before she could go on.

"But it demands an explanation," Elise said, trying to harden her voice.

The detective said nothing but took out a plastic bag from the case file. Within the bag was a letter, and he placed it in front of her. It was not written in any language she recognized. Strange characters were scrawled across the page in black pen, forming multiple paragraphs of odd symbols.

Elise blinked, looking up at the detective and back down at the paper in front of her.

"Notice"—the detective pointed to the top of the letter—"it is addressed to you."

Sure enough, at the top of the paper, her name was scrawled in Marty's messy handwriting. At the very bottom of the letter, "the way is closed" was scribbled in English and underlined.

Why would Marty write me a letter that he knows *I can't read?* The answer hit her immediately. *He wants to send a message to me. Only me. He doesn't want the cops to find out. That means he* did *use a code, which means there is a key, meaning I have to find the key.*

"Miss Montason?"

Elise looked back up at the detective.

"Do you know what this says?"

"What does this have to do with anything?" Elise asked.

"Do you know what it says?" he repeated gravely.

"What does this have to do with it?" Elise said a little stronger.

He sighed. "He was holding it when he died," the detective answered. "The message is unfinished because we think he died while he was writing it."

Elise could hardly take it all in. This letter must have something to do with his sudden death. She took in a shaking breath and asked, "When did he die? Was it this morning?"

"Last night, ten o'clock," he informed her. "Miss Montason, if you know something important, it is *crucial* that you tell us."

Elise swallowed, trying to arrange her words. *I have to lie. I have to sell it.* She closed her eyes, letting herself draw in a long, slow breath.

She opened her eyes. "We did have a code a long time ago. I don't remember it, but I will try to. It must be secretive if he is bringing it up again. I forgot all about those days, but he is obviously trying to tell me something. Do you think I could take a picture of this? I think if I stare at it enough, I may be able to make out a few words."

He shifted, looking uncomfortable. "Miss Montason, I'm not sure you can do that."

"I want answers just as much as you do, sir. I will try my best to decode this and then bring the message back to you. Please," she begged.

He sighed once again. "No."

She swallowed and nodded; she had anticipated this answer. Taking another breath, she attempted to keep the hurricane in her stomach from being reflected on her face. "Will that be it?"

"Not quite," he responded, giving her a stern and suspicious look. "Were you aware of any enemies that Mr. Martinez had?" the detective asked, moving the plastic bag to the side.

Elise's gaze followed the plastic bag as he pushed it away, her mind still on the letter. At the top right corner of the bag, the same blue seal she had seen on the paper was present. The small, navy tree enclosed in a circle was almost as enticing as the strange letter.

The detective cleared his throat and repeated his question. This time, he had Elise's attention.

She shook her head. "Not that I know of," she answered truthfully.

She had been under the impression nearly everybody loved him. Internally, she was rather comforted by the fact that they had moved on to the basic, more traditional questions.

His list of inquiries continued, wherein Elise gave brief and honest answers.

"One last thing," he said finally. "When was the last time you spoke to your father?"

Elise lowered her eyebrows. "My father?"

The detective nodded.

What does my dad have to do with this? Elise wondered as she felt her heart begin to beat against her ribcage. "I haven't seen him in a year."

"Do you know what his relationship is to Mr. Martinez?"

"They . . . are friends," she answered slowly.

"Have they been in contact with each other recently?"

Elise nodded. "What does my dad have to do with this?"

"He is missing."

Elise had never been in an autopsy room before. Nor had she even seen a dead body, but this particular, dreadful day, she was able to do both. She assumed this was also a first for her mother and brother, who seemed equally as anxious as she. She was prepared, eager almost, to see the body, perhaps to find some sort of indication that it wasn't him and this was all some sort of mistake.

The room was wide, white, and looked about as cold as it felt. The body that laid on the table, naked with a white sheet laid over it, was none but Hank Bolivar William Martinez, pale, still, lifeless.

Elise almost choked on all of her inner organs that leapt into her throat when the medical examiner pulled the sheet back to reveal Marty's head and chest. This was not some cruel mistake. It was really Marty in front of her.

His face was so familiar but so strange at the same time. His features were exactly the same, but his veins shone purple through the pale, almost transparent skin. He seemed chunkier and undignified, not lean and comfortable like he always was when he'd been alive. His eyes were closed, and his eyelashes lay like spider legs on his cheeks. His lips were closed and protruded from his face oddly, not stretched into their usual smile.

At his chest, his skin was deformed and pink, a terrible burn mark.

"Wh-what is that?" Elise asked, pointing at the burn.

"He was burned. It was not the cause of death, but it happened before he died," the ME explained.

The burn was oddly shaped, like a symbol of some type—none she had ever seen before, but it definitely did not take that shape by accident.

She had heard some killers left some sort of signature, whether it was how they killed, a mark inscribed on the body, or where they dumped the body. She immediately wondered how many other bodies had been found in the past with this same burn mark.

Elise was the first to turn away from her friend's body, followed by Percy.

The siblings walked wordlessly out of the autopsy room and waited at the elevator for their mother.

It was several minutes before Eleanor left her friend, and she returned to the elevator to find Percy holding his sister, who cried on his chest.

CHAPTER THREE

The Way Is Closed

Both of her fathers had vanished from her life, leaving nothing in their wake except for the note Elise couldn't read.

When she came home that day, she perched atop her bed, cross-legged and still. Wild theories formed in her mind as to where her biological father could possibly be, hidden from the eyes of the law. Among this confusion was, expectedly, pain. It came in the form of tiredness constantly washing over her, sometimes coupled with brief, tear-inducing stings that seemed to stab her at random times. Other times, it was a sickly sort of ache that stirred quietly, ever present in the back of her mind.

Elise was almost angry with herself. She bitterly regarded this pain she felt, a bad taste forming in her throat as she recovered from each breakdown. She had never felt pain like this before but had made a silent oath that when she would face such hurt, she wouldn't let it destroy her—unlike her mother, who retreated into her endless studies, unwilling to confront the trauma of her husband's infidelity. Elise had always expected some sort of family catastrophe to ensue eventually, but she didn't expect it to be caused by Marty's death. She had always thought it would be her father, or maybe Eleanor and Percy would push each other to the point of snapping and the family would then collapse in on itself. Apparently that would have to wait. So, here Elise was, attempting desperately to regather herself as one of the most important people in her life dropped from it without warning.

She hated that she'd had to cling to Percy earlier. Never in her life had she felt more vulnerable, like she could not stand on her own feet and endure the pain like she had always promised herself she would.

When night rolled around, she finally exited her room and sat down on her stool in the kitchen. The windows remained open, but the night sky provided no light. Instead, the warm yellow glow from the fixtures above them illuminated the room, as well as casting bright streaks across the lawn outside. Eleanor stood at the counter, making sandwiches for herself and Percy, but seemed to be moving in slow motion. Percy had crashed in the living room and was snoozing soundly.

When she was finished spreading butter on a slice of bread, she set down her knife and cast her gaze in her daughter's direction. "Do you want to talk about it?" she asked quietly.

Elise looked up at her mother, startled. Upon realizing Eleanor was completely sincere, Elise considered it. "No," she answered honestly. The idea of having a meaningful conversation with her mother sent cold and sickening sensations crawling under Elise's skin.

Eleanor huffed angrily, tossing the knife into the sink and snatching up a sandwich to take to Percy.

"Uh . . ." Elise nearly jumped from her seat. "Do *you* want to talk about it?" she asked abruptly.

Eleanor turned around, looking her daughter in the face. Elise could not tell if her mother was touched or annoyed.

"No," she replied and turned to enter the living room with the sandwich.

Elise plopped dejectedly back down onto her stool.

Percy stirred on the couch, groaning softly as he awakened. He accepted his meal promptly and demolished half the sandwich in a single, absentminded chomp.

When Eleanor reentered the kitchen, she paused in the doorway, studying her daughter again as if considering something. The action was brief but prompted Elise to shift in her spot. Eleanor continued on past her and sat down at the dining table behind Elise and began chewing her dinner. Elise could *feel* her mother's eyes trace to her back on occasion.

Swallowing, Elise spoke tentatively. "Marty had a note in his hand when he died."

The feeling of Eleanor's eyes on Elise's back intensified. "What did it say?" she asked.

"I don't know," Elise answered.

"You *don't know*?" Eleanor repeated. "Did you not *ask* about it?"

"I saw it," Elise responded, refusing to turn around and look at her mother. "But it wasn't written in English."

"What was it written in, then?"

"I don't know," she said again. "I didn't recognize the characters. There were only two things written in English. The only thing I could read was 'the way is closed.'"

"What was the second thing?" Eleanor pressed.

Elise hesitated. "My name."

Eleanor didn't respond immediately, but her emotions radiated. Her gaze nearly burned holes in Elise's skin.

"Why?" Eleanor's voice was strained. "Why would he write your name in his note?"

"Because it was addressed to me."

This time there was no response. Curiosity finally outweighed Elise's apprehension and she dared to turn around.

She found Eleanor crying silently with her head in her hands. Her chest heaved with every soundless gasp; her tears were beginning to dampen the sleeves that her head rested on.

A terrible feeling of illness stirred in Elise's stomach, heating her skin and causing her throat to constrict. The discomfort became overwhelming. Elise wanted nothing more than to flee back to the safety of her room, but it felt wrong to turn away from her mother while she sobbed. To escape to her room would entail regripping the control that felt to be slipping from her grasp, but she apparently couldn't bring herself to leave. Instead, she only sat there with a war of emotions raging inside of her.

She had never seen Eleanor like this. Eleanor cried, Elise knew, but never openly and especially not in public like she had when she picked Elise up from school. Elise forced down a painful swallow as the observation sank in.

"You loved him." Her own words sounded disjointed to her.

Eleanor sniffled and looked up at her daughter. The woman's eyes were surrounded with a puffy pinkness and her nose shined a cherry red. The sight disturbed Elise's stomach.

Eleanor's eyes closed as more tears slipped from their corners, and she nodded.

Elise finally stood and took Eleanor's plate. Her mom had resumed crying as her daughter cleaned off the remains of her food and slipped the platter into the dishwasher.

"W-why don't you go sleep, Mom," Elise said, walking around the counter to stand next to her chair. Elise didn't touch her mother, but Elise's presence was enough to coax Eleanor from her seat.

"I love you, Elise," she said between sniffles.

"Yeah, Mom, love you too. Go get some sleep. You'll feel better," Elise replied.

Eleanor began making her way upstairs. "Don't parent me," the woman muttered.

Elise ignored her mother's words and turned away. She almost wished she *had* dashed to her room, just to avoid any possible meaningful encounter with Eleanor. Percy and Elise tended to remain within their own worlds while leaving Eleanor in hers, where she wanted to be. Many kids consoled their parents during tough times, but neither Percy nor Elise were very fond of that idea. Eleanor was perfectly comfortable in believing her children had no problems in their life that required counsel, so it seemed. Elise sometimes had the suspicion Eleanor had picked up on this and intended to alter their relationship, thinking a closer family would be a healthy one. Elise, on the other hand, had concluded a long time ago that the family operated best when everybody kept the things that mattered to them to themselves.

She remained standing in the kitchen for a few moments, deciding she wanted to do something but having no idea what. She reached up to wipe a stray tear from her face and, feeling the hotness of it, resolved to step outside and feel the chill of night air. When she did, however, her gaze landed upon 8741 King Avenue across from them, the home of Hank Martinez, now lined closely with police tape. She stared at the house, compelled to walk toward it, to enter it, to see what it was without Marty. A bead of sweat ran down her face as the thoughts flashed through her mind. It was illegal to enter a crime scene, but the desire tugged at her like a mad dog on a leash. She reached up to wipe the sweat from her face, realizing this was counterproductive to her reason for exiting the house.

Sighing, she turned away, leaving another emotional war to fight itself to the death.

※

It was noon when she awoke the next day and found Laleitha in the kitchen—for some reason—burning a grilled cheese sandwich. Elise stopped in the hall, leaning against the wall to watch her sister.

"You forgot to lock the door," Laleitha said without looking at her sister. "And you have no food in this house. I was going to make myself a baked potato or something but I had to settle for grilled cheese."

"Which you are destroying," Elise added.

Laleitha said nothing but kept her attention focused on the blackening bread.

After a long pause, Elise said, "I want to go to Marty's house."

"Can't," Laleitha said. "It's a crime scene."

"I know," Elise sighed.

It wasn't long before Percy entered the kitchen from the living room, looking drowsy. "Hey," he grunted in greeting. "Why is Lee here?"

"Why don't you ask her yourself?" Laleitha snorted.

Elise shrugged. "Both good questions."

Percy looked at his half-sister, who gave an exaggerated shrug.

"I got into a fight with my mom. She's been a real bitch about the whole thing with our dad being missing."

"Ah," Percy said. "Seriously, Lee, that thing is going to go up in flames." He nodded to the grilled cheese.

"That's the idea," she replied nonchalantly.

"He left me a note," Elise blurted.

Both of her siblings looked at her, confused.

She shifted her weight. "Marty died holding a note that was addressed to me, written in a language I've never seen. I think he was trying to tell me something that he couldn't let anybody else know. That means he had to have also left a key, a Rosetta stone of some sort, for me to find. I think it might be in his house."

Both siblings continued to stare. Percy seemed to be in deep thought, but Lee just seemed to be waiting for somebody to say something.

"You want to go to his house," Percy stated, not even bothering to form a question with his words.

Elise nodded.

"I don't think that's a good idea."

"Of course you don't." She sighed. "But I feel like I have to. I *have* to find out what that note says, Perce. He meant for me to find out and I owe it to him to at least try."

Laleitha cast a sideways glance to her sister. "What could that note possibly say? It may not even be important, Elise."

"Or it could be essential," Percy added. "It could provide some sort of clue as to why or how he died."

"Why would he code it then?" Laleitha pointed out. "If something were so important, he'd want us to be able to read it."

Elise strode toward her sister, turning off the stove and getting out a plate for her to put her charred sandwich on. "I wondered that too," she said. "But I think he coded it because he only wanted *us* to be able to read it. Which means he hid a key for only *us* to find, and I can't imagine any other place it would be."

"I can," Lee said.

Elise and Percy paused to look at her. She met both of their gazes before shrugging. "He knows we spend a lot of time at Wellington. He probably hid it there."

"A public park?" Elise said skeptically.

"I think," Percy began, "that you both bring up good points, but we should try to think of *any other place* and search there before we search the active crime scene."

Elise shrugged. "That sounds reasonable."

Laleitha agreed.

"We'll start tonight then," Percy said.

With that, Lee bit into her blackened sandwich before grimacing, spitting it out, and ejecting the grilled cheese into the trash.

"I should also tell you," Elise said after a minute, "at the bottom of the note, 'the way is closed' was written in English. Any ideas as to what that could mean?"

Laleitha grunted. "Well, it's a little vague."

"You're an observant one."

"*The way is closed.*" Percy hummed. "I have no idea."

When evening rolled around, the siblings exited their house without a word to Eleanor and headed toward Wellington. Laleitha was already there when they arrived and waited for them in a tree.

After hours of searching under every leaf, scaling every tree up and down, and scavenging across the ground, they finally admitted defeat. They arrived home at midnight with dirt covering their hands and their faces solemn with disappointment.

Thus, Elise was given something to focus on for the remainder of that week. Eleanor had permitted their absence from school, on the agreement they would always be home for a family dinner. Many nights, however, when the aggravated and very introverted children refused to provide their mother with proficient conversation, she ended up snapping at them angrily then retreating to her office. It was then they were given the opportunity to escape their house and set their minds to their task.

They tried their school, the forest in which their "tree house" used to remain suspended in the branches of a willow tree, and even the gates surrounding the property of 9551 West. Each night they came home empty-handed.

After dinner that Saturday, Elise found Percy sitting on the front step, looking tiredly at 8741 King Avenue. As she sat down next to him, she became aware of Laleitha's presence on the porch swing as well. Laleitha always seemed to appear and disappear to and from the Montason house as she pleased.

When Elise's eyes settled on the house across the street, she spoke. "We're going there tonight, Perce."

Her brother's jaw tensed.

"We agreed."

He sighed. "Let's make this quick."

With that, the siblings and their half-sister arose from their seats and crossed the street to the empty home.

The eeriness of a dark and vacated house made Elise's skin prickle unpleasantly as she stepped inside. They entered through the side door into the living room, one Marty never locked. It was like walking into an empty school—a place usually so bright and bursting with exciting opportunity and possibility—now still, quiet, and dark.

"Where do we start?" Percy wondered aloud.

"Bedroom," the girls replied together.

"Probably," Elise added.

The siblings tiptoed upstairs and took a right into the master bedroom. The bedroom was wide with navy blue walls, a large walk-in closet, and curtains that were still drawn back, letting moonlight spill into the empty room. The bed sat against the far wall, rarely touched, and a small dresser stood beside it, but otherwise, the room was void of decoration and furniture, given that Marty didn't actually use this house for a place of living. Everything was still and deathly quiet, intensifying Elise's feeling that she didn't belong here.

"All right, so, look for a paper, or a notebook, or something," Elise said as they spread out and began their search.

Marty had no books in his bedroom. *He may have kept a diary. It might be hidden somewhere.* She opened the top drawer to his dresser and found nothing but a few folded shirts she hadn't seen him wear in months.

"The detectives have already been through here to collect evidence," Percy said. "So there's nothing for us to find that they haven't already found and are examining right as we speak."

"But we know Marty; they don't. We understand how he thinks," Elise pointed out. "Knowing him, if there was something he wanted to tell us and not the authorities, he would have made sure they didn't find the answer before us."

"This place smells," Laleitha remarked with a sniff.

She was right. The room did carry faint traces of the stench of death with it, but Elise was too intent on the search to care. She ignored Lee and continued to open drawers.

After minutes of searching, there was a small crash and a sharp grunt from Laleitha. Elise stood and turned to find her sister standing at Marty's dresser, slamming a picture frame against the wooden surface.

"What the hell are you doing, Lee?" Percy demanded, striding over and ripping the frame from her.

"This," Laleitha said, reaching into the puzzle of shards and removing one.

Elise peeked over her sister's shoulder to catch a glimpse of what was so important.

Inscribed on one side of the glass were nine characters of the same language that the letter was written in, while on the other side, in Marty's handwriting, four words were carved into the surface:

The Way Is Closed

"This man is sneaky," Laleitha mused. "But he still isn't giving us much to work with."

"I think this is a key of some type—maybe part of one," Percy speculated.

"What do you mean?" the youngest inquired.

"He thinks these nine characters spell out 'the way is closed' in the code," Elise explained, running her fingers along the symbols. "Or language, or whatever it is."

Lee nodded. "That makes sense."

"Definitely sounds like something he would do," Percy added.

The siblings looked at each other. "So what do we do now?"

"Take it home and study it," the oldest answered. "We'll figure out which characters correspond to which letter."

The girls nodded. "Right."

It was then Elise noticed the picture that the shard had once protected. In the shattered frame was a photo of Eleanor, Percy, and Elise all gathered on the steps of 8742 King Avenue with large grins on their faces. Elise only vaguely remembered when the photo was taken, but Marty had had it sitting in this bedroom for years.

She refused to let herself comprehend the sentiment behind that.

Finally, somewhat satisfied, the trio exited the Martinez house. Lee said a quiet goodbye to Percy and Elise before walking back down the dim road to find a way home.

After crossing the street, Elise slowly and silently opened the door to her house as Percy peered in behind her. If they could creep through the house quietly enough, perhaps their mother would never know how late they had been.

They stepped into the mudroom, tiptoeing past the washing machine and dryer and into the hallway. The door to Eleanor's study was still open and she lay draped on her desk, her arms sprawled over her papers and books.

The siblings relaxed.

"She's asleep," Percy whispered. "In the morning, if she asks, say we were home by eleven."

Elise nodded and the two of them crept up the stairs to their bedrooms, where they spent a long night getting well-earned sleep.

CHAPTER FOUR

The Will of Hank Bolivar William Martinez

Elise and her brother made eye contact several times the next morning, yet not a word was uttered between them. Eleanor quietly hummed a tense tune to herself as she ate her cereal—just because she didn't like the silence—with the newspaper laid out in front of her on the table. Elise found her mother's soft melody somewhat peaceful, almost fearing the silence that would sweep over the house if it stopped. It seemed that even her thoughts began to echo when the Montason house was silent.

A loud knock at the door jolted wakefulness into the group, prompting Percy to remark that it was probably Lee and Elise to offer to answer the door, decidedly ignoring Eleanor's huff of contempt.

When the girl opened the door, however, she found two men in suits looking down at her.

"Is Eleanor Montason home?" the first asked. He was taller than his partner, and significantly slimmer, his features hard and his expression stern.

"Yeah," Elise replied. "Is this about Hank Martinez?"

Both men nodded. "Yes. If we could speak with . . ." the tall man began.

"Did you find out how he died?" Elise interrupted earnestly.

"May we speak to your mother, please?" the shorter man asked pointedly, his annoyed tone betraying his polite phrasing.

Elise was about to turn to fetch Eleanor, but the woman appeared at her side, greeting the men respectfully. Percy had also arisen from his breakfast but lingered in the back of the hall.

"My name is Detective Dawson, and I'm here to inform you that Hank Martinez has been found to have died of a heart condition that went undetected prior to his death," the taller and thinner man said.

There was a brief moment of silence.

"That doesn't explain the burn marks," Eleanor stated wryly.

"The angle suggests he did them himself," the detective explained shortly.

Elise cast a glance over her shoulder to meet Percy's eyes. He looked from his sister to the detective, suspicion gleaming in his blue irises.

"His body is being transferred to the local mortuary, where his funeral will be arranged. His last will and testament will be opened after," the man continued.

Eleanor forced a tense smile. "Thank you, Detective Dawson."

"Why would he burn himself?" Elise asked him, almost challengingly.

"We don't know."

"Did you ever decrypt the note?" the girl pressed.

The taller man shook his head. "It is currently being studied by nationally renowned cipher clerks. The message should be worked out soon enough."

Elise nodded. "Thank you," she said. Though she meant it sincerely, it sounded rather dry.

The detectives nodded and turned away.

Elise closed the door, leaving it open just a crack. She refused to believe the detectives. There was obviously much more to the story, something that was so out of place they decided to push it aside.

Elise slid past her mother as the woman made her way back to the kitchen. She peered through the window at the detective. The tall one stooped to remove a strand of grass from the lawn as the big one waddled back to their car. They appeared to be exchanging words as they did so. Detective Dawson was talking to the other, who was looking at him sternly. Elise strained her ears to hear what he was saying.

"I am sure she is it," he said.

"You have to be positive," the other said. "Or Reighba will kill us."

✕

The black dress was warm and comfortable—a winning combo when going to a funeral. Despite her physical comfort, nothing could still the churning in her stomach. Elise was not ready to honor Hank Martinez's death yet. A funeral implied closure, yet she was in the midst of a sea of questions. Everything that had happened in the past two weeks seemed to be causeless effects, as if she were capable of looking only at a small portion of the big picture. She sat silently through the music, the eulogy, everything, her head down, not listening to a word.

※

When the Montasons were finally called in, they sat down across from the lawyer silently.

"Eleanor Montason?" the man asked.

Eleanor nodded.

"Hank Martinez leaves you this letter and a number of his investments." He held out two envelopes, and Eleanor took them. "The information can be found here."

"Elise Montason?" the man went on.

Elise did not respond but waited expectantly for him to continue.

"Mr. Martinez left you his diary, with no message. Unfortunately, his diary is missing. The minute it is found, it will be given to you."

Elise nodded, disappointed. Her eyes trailed downward before the man spoke again. "He also left you the property of 9551 West. Though officially it will have to go to your mother for now, it will be written under your name when you are of age."

Elise's head snapped back up and she stared at the man with wide eyes. "W-what?"

"He has left you the property of 9551 West. He made that change to his will the night before he died."

CHAPTER FIVE

Sar Prague, The Hunter

"I'm going out with some friends for drinks," Eleanor told her children. "Macy will be driving me home. You remember her—right?"

They nodded.

"Good. I won't be long." She kissed Elise on the head. "See you." And with that, she left the house.

This is new. Her mother was going out in public, in the evening, and telling her kids what she was up to. *Strange but pleasant.*

While normally she would invite Lee over or go to Wellington or work on a project, Elise couldn't find the energy to do anything but trudge upstairs and crawl in bed. She fell asleep quickly, despite the early hour.

Hours later, she awoke to a loud *crack*. Her eyes flew open and she stared into the darkness of her room, heart beating rapidly.

A bump sounded from downstairs, followed by hushed voices. Elise's heart rate spiked. *There is someone in the house!*

She was the stillest thing in the room by then, and her lungs strained as she refused to breathe. There were definitely people downstairs, at least two. *Maybe it's Mom, or maybe Percy has friends over.* She looked at the clock, which read 3:27 a.m.

Finally, Elise found the courage to step out of bed and silently walk down her ladder and to the door. She picked up a T-shirt from the floor and slipped it on, as well as some dirty leggings.

She paused before trying to leave her room, running all the possible scenarios through her head. With a deep breath, she turned the knob and cracked the door open. The hall was no brighter than her room, allowing not even a silhouette of anything to take form.

She scanned the entire hall until her gaze settled on the area where the staircase was situated. Suddenly, her blood turned to ice. There, standing on the top step, a dark figure lurked, the gleam in his eyes making them the brightest objects in the room.

Elise heard movement but couldn't see in the blackness. The man drew out a glowing yellow rod. The cylinder provided enough illumination to confirm that Elise really was staring into the eyes of a man; her fear was not the work of dream-dancing hallucinations in her paranoid yet exhausted state. The light from the strange rod also fell on the metallic object in his other hand, which appeared to be a handgun.

A scream swelled in her chest. The moment she moved just one of her muscles, the man lunged at her with terrifying speed. She had hardly let out a squeak before he grabbed her and forcefully silenced her, letting her choke on his sleeve in her attempt to scream. His occupied hands had no impact on the efficiency or effectiveness of his attack, as it took him only a second to encircle her, trapping and silencing her with his arms.

Terror gripped her and she squirmed relentlessly, screaming against his sleeve, trying to escape his grip. His left hand grasped her wrist, inadvertently pressing the yellow rod against her skin. Cold radiated from it, but she had little time to take note of its features before her attacker twisted her arm behind her back. She tried to cry out in pain but ended up gasping into his arm that still covered her mouth.

Her heart pounded against her ribs. She couldn't see the man, but she felt his every move. A thousand possibilities of what would come flashed through her head, each one more terrible than the next. She struggled harder and his grip tightened. This method wasn't working. A new technique would be required if she wanted to escape, but not a single idea came to mind.

Another man came up the stairs now.

What the hell do they want with me? She wanted to cry. As the thought shook her skull, a disturbing idea slowly closed its nasty fingers around her mind. This craziness had been unleashed the day Hank Martinez died—her biological father's absence, Marty's encrypted note, the suspicious exchange between the detectives, these intruders—leading Elise to believe they all shared a common denominator. Where she fit into the equation was still unclear, but Elise felt dangerously confident in the assumption that these men were responsible for the death of her friend.

Elise stopped struggling as another man came into sight from the stairs. The gears spun inside her head. *Why would they come for* me *now?* Her chest heaved. *What do Marty and I have in common?*

The realization hit her like a slap to the face.

9551 West.

"This is her?" the second man said.

Focused now, Elise's fear drove her like nothing had before. It was too dark to make out either of the men's features as the rod the first man held between the fingers that gripped Elise's wrist gave off the only eerie, unsettling light.

"Yeah," the first man replied. "She doesn't know it though."

The second man nodded in approval. There was a pause before he spoke again, this time in a commanding tone. "Give me the rod. We take her to Second Reighba."

The man took the glowing device from the one who held Elise. The moment it left Elise's skin, warmer air blanketed the chilly area the rod had left.

The man turned his back to Elise and her attacker and tossed the rod in front of him. It should have fallen all the way back down the stairs, but instead there was a small *crack* and the rod burst open, suspended in air.

A large, glowing hole had appeared in front of them. Looking into it was like looking into a window. The inside of a building shone within it, an empty room, illuminated only by moonlight, where a dark figure sat in the corner.

Elise did not believe her eyes. *A . . . portal?*

"Release her," the man commanded.

The grip on Elise's arms loosened and the hand on her mouth was removed. She stumbled away from him, falling to the ground but too terrified to make any other movement.

The man nodded toward the portal. "Jump through."

"W-what?" Elise's voice was hardly a squeak.

The man threw up his hands. "You're really going to make us throw you through? Jump in there. Now."

Elise backed away. "What is that? What did you do?" she sputtered, her voice carrying almost as much horror as her face.

The man sighed. "Dawson?"

Detective Dawson?

The first man grabbed her again. She struggled in an attempt to rip her arms out of his grip, but he lifted her off her feet.

She thrashed and kicked in a mad, frightened scramble to be released. But before she knew it, the man had tossed her.

She had expected to feel something as she passed through the hole, perhaps the kind of feeling one experienced when breaking the surface of water, but she felt nothing. The world just seemed to change around her when she passed through, just like walking through a door.

Elise landed with a thud and scrambled to her feet. The dark figure who sat in the corner did not stir, not even to look at her. The room had one wall that was lined in windows, revealing a city below that glowed brightly in the night. The room was part of an office building and almost reminded her of a conference room. It was long and sparsely decorated but held no table or chairs.

She looked back at the hole and found herself peering back into her familiar hallway.

The commanding man leapt through, followed by her attacker, Dawson, who grabbed something that hung at the top of the hole—the rod he had tossed. In a split second, as he passed through with the rod, the walls of the portal seemed to follow him, folding inward until it snapped closed. Dawson looked back down at the rod in his hand as a white mist stirred inside of its yellow glow.

"Which one is this?" the man in the corner asked without looking up.

His voice was neither deep nor strong, but the ice beneath the words struck fear in Elise all the same.

"I'm not sure. Once I get the others, we'll find out," the second man said.

The others?

The man in the corner turned, extending another glowing rod. This one was white. "Go then."

Elise's captor took the white rod and exchanged it for the yellow one. He nodded to Dawson and then threw it. With another *crack*, it opened a different portal. The man and Dawson jumped through, closing it behind them by grabbing the rod.

Elise had backed into a corner by then, staring at the other man, who seemed to take no notice of her. Covering his face was a mask, white and blue, that protected his entire head like a helmet. On his sleeve, Elise managed to make out the same seal of a blue tree that she had seen at the detective's office.

Minutes later, another *crack* sounded. And the two men emerged from the hole, this time with another captive. They brought with them a Hispanic-looking boy with loosely curling black hair, a built frame, and dark brown eyes. He didn't look much older than Elise.

He was struggling like mad, and Dawson was having trouble restraining him. Finally, Dawson tossed the boy aside, and he stumbled into the middle of the floor. Dawson extended the white rod to the man, who exchanged it for one that was a darker shade of yellow than the first. They set off again to an unknown place.

Elise sank to the floor, trembling. She was still trying to make sense of the portal-rod things. She had no idea who these people were, why they would want her, or what they planned to do to her.

The boy looked at the man, then looked to Elise, then looked back to the man. "Who are you?" he asked accusingly. "Why did you bring me here?"

The man turned to face them. He said nothing, only staring at the boy, his eyes hidden under the helmet.

From the opposite end of the room, a portal snapped open, and the two men flew in with another captive.

Elise squeezed her eyes shut, trying to make sense of the madness so maybe she could plan her escape. Her mind, however, flew about in a panicked rush, and she couldn't think of any course of action that could get her out of this.

The capturers bounced in and out of the room, bringing captive after captive. Not until the last one did Elise open her eyes again when she heard a familiar voice.

"Lee!" Elise cried, jumping to her feet and rushing to her sister as the men wrestled her through the portal. *Not Lee too!* Tears came to Elise's eyes as she looked at Lee, and Lee looked right back at her, terrified.

"Elise, what's going on?" Lee asked, her voice trembling.

"Line up," the man in the mask commanded.

Dawson and the man grabbed two by the necks and shoved them to the center. Elise and Lee slowly turned to face the man, still shaking together.

"Kneel," the next order came.

Not knowing what else to do, the six captives kneeled.

"Sar Prague," the masked man said, holding out his hand to the other man.

The one called Sar Prague handed him the handgun.

"If you are wrong about them—any of them—you will die as well," the masked man warned Sar Prague. He approached the captive on the right side of the line, a short, black-haired boy who was thin as a broom. "What is your name?" he asked.

The boy whimpered a few incoherent syllables, but the masked man seemed to have interpreted them better than Elise.

He used a gloved finger to raise the whimpering boy's chin up then set the pistol to his forehead.

The boy let out a little cry, then the masked man pulled the trigger.

There was a bang and a few shocked cries. Elise and the others trembled in fear, but when they looked over, the boy was still there, alive, not bruised but confused.

The masked man moved on.

The next person in line was the boy who was brought in after Elise. He didn't tremble like the first but stared up at the masked man in fear.

"And you?" the man asked.

"Gerald Rodum," he replied, obviously trying to hide the tremble in his voice.

The gun pressed against his head and he closed his eyes. There was another *bang* and the clatter of a squashed bullet falling to the floor. The boy opened his eyes. His stare remained fixed on his captor, even after he had moved on.

The man came next to a small girl.

She didn't wait to give her name. "Amy Tarhower," she said, quivering.

The man pressed the gun against her head, Elise daring to watch this time. He pulled the trigger slowly, and the bullet shot out from the barrel. This time, however, it did not bounce to the ground.

Elise thrust her head back, away from the awful scene, horrified. The body thumped to the floor, prompting Elise's chest to heave and tears to fill her eyes. *That girl just died. That girl just died. What if that is me next? Or worse, Lee.* Her body trembled again. The image repeated itself over and over again in her head. Her back locked in an arch, and her hands strangled each other behind her back. *Don't look that way,* she told herself as her eyes flew to the masked man again. *Don't look that way. The dead girl is that way.*

Sar Prague's eyes were wide now, and his cool, composed smirk had faded as he stared at the masked man in fright.

The masked man turned toward Sar, pausing for a moment before lifting his gun and firing two shots at him. He let out a small grunt and flopped to the floor.

Elise stared, wide-eyed, at the body. She was, at first, confused, before she remembered the masked man's promise. *If you are wrong about them—any of them—you will die as well.*

Elise soon ripped her thoughts away from the fate of Sar Prague, as the next person the masked man came to was Lee.

The anticipation tormented Elise as the masked man towered over her sister. Elise's body ached with the fear of what she could possibly see next as the *thump* of the last girl's body hitting the floor echoed in her ears.

He stood above Lee expectantly, but she remained silent and unnaturally still. "Your name?"

She did not answer.

"Jane Doe." He stepped forward and placed the gun at her forehead. "Either Lumerian or dead." He pulled the trigger.

Elise's eyes snapped shut at the *bang*, but she couldn't stop herself from picturing terrible images of Lee on the floor next to the Amy girl.

A small whimper coaxed Elise's eyes back open. Laleitha was alive and unharmed. The stress swelling within Elise eased the slightest bit.

Now the man moved on to the person next to Elise, a blond boy whose jawline quivered the slightest bit as he kneeled with his eyes closed.

"And who is this?"

"What the hell do you want from me, man?" His panicked but angry response burst forth.

"Depends on what you have," the man replied. "Give me your name and, if you are to die, it will be painless."

The boy hesitated but soon realized he had no other options. "Darren Nosia." He gave in, frustrated.

"Nosia . . ." the masked man mused. "I know that name. I know enough . . ."

Without bothering to put the gun to his head, the masked man moved on.

Elise's heart dropped as he slid in front of her, looking down on her, peering through the eyes of his mask so curiously. "And who are you?"

It took two swallows to find her voice, but when she spoke, it came out stronger than she had anticipated. "Elise Montason."

He tilted his head, studying her as she refused to look at his mask.

He didn't even bother putting the gun to her head, but there was an alarming *bang* as a bullet flew at her with no warning. She gave a small yelp but felt only a small piece of metal bouncing off her face. She opened her eyes, confused, for the moment it touched her skin, a strange sensation had shot through her body. Something foreign in her had stirred, something she couldn't identify.

She had survived.

The masked man took a few steps back and looked upon the terrified and bewildered survivors. "So he found them then," he said. "He found the last Five Majors."

CHAPTER SIX

387 Identical Passages

Elise couldn't help but turn her gaze to the two men in the corner. Sar Prague, her capturer, bleeding out, and Dawson frantically but silently rushing to stop the blood from gushing out of his leader. It felt as if a steel fist had clenched her throat; she had just witnessed a girl younger than her get shot in the head and a man receive two bullets in the stomach. It had become clear by then the only real threat in this room was the man in the mask.

"Dawson," the masked man said.

Dawson looked up from bandaging his master, his eyes filled with panic. Sweat poured from his forehead.

"Prepare the transportation."

The man nodded and stood, working quickly with the glowing rods.

"Where are you taking us?" the boy next to Elise asked.

The masked man did not answer.

"Where are we now?" the boy named Gerald asked.

"Silver Industries," the masked man replied.

That's where Marty works!

"The only place in this world that is blocked from the view of the Council of Orphia." The masked man turned to Elise. "Do you know why that is?"

"I don't know what you're talking about." Elise shook her head, trying to pull herself together. "But I know that you were involved in the death of Hank Martinez and—" She swallowed hard. "I want to know why."

She wasn't sure how she could back up such a claim, but being taken to Silver Industries by her captor secured the link between Hank Martinez and her current situation. She had yet to understand how, but the less the masked man knew about what she knew, the better.

Lee shot her sister a panicked look as the connection crashed over her.

"Where are we?" the first boy asked. He had a slight Russian accent.

"Hank Martinez was not the man you knew," the masked man told Elise, disregarding the other boy's question.

She shook her head frantically. "I don't believe you!" she cried.

"And," the masked man went on, "he is responsible for this hidden sanctuary. But I did not kill him, nor do I know who did."

"What do you mean 'hidden sanctuary'?" Gerald asked. "You said there was a Council of Orphia. Where? I've never heard of it."

The masked man turned back around, firing off his explanation as he did so. "The Council of Orphia predates any other rule or government that you are familiar with. And has been a secret to your people ever since it was established."

"Our people?" Lee repeated.

It seemed this man spoke only in gibberish. Elise understood his words, but his sentences were disjointed and made no sense to her, like she was missing something.

Suddenly, there was a loud *bang*, and Dawson went up in flames. He screamed horrifically as Elise and the other captives scrambled backward, all except for the first boy with the dark hair and Russian accent. Elise's jaw hung open, her eyes wide as the fire cast inverted shadows dancing across her skin. The orange and yellow resonated throughout the dark room with an aura of fierceness, heat pulsing from the man as he fell to his knees. They sat paralyzed in surprise and dreadful awe as the scene unraveled before them.

The floor in front of the masked man abruptly burst into another fiery explosion, circling him in flames.

Gerald snapped back to his senses first. "Come on! Out that door! We have to go!" he exclaimed.

Elise scrambled up and followed him as he hoisted the boy named Darren to his feet. Her eyes never left the fiery mess behind them, even as her body traveled forward. In no more than a second, all five had dashed out the door and slammed it behind them, only to find themselves standing on a narrow bridge that overlooked an enormous factory below.

"Oh, God." Darren breathed as he stared over the railing.

"This place is bigger than I thought," Elise remarked as they ran along the overpass, her voice shrill.

Suddenly, the masked man burst from the room at the end of the bridge.

"Go!" Gerald cried, frantically trying to urge them on faster.

The masked man struck the bridge's right support, sending that side lurching downward as the left support hardly held it up. The passage abruptly bent underneath them, throwing them toward the ground below as the entire structure helplessly submitted to the will of gravity. The metal screamed as they fell into the railing, holding on to the cold steel in an attempt to regain their balance.

There was another *crack* as the left support was struck by the masked man. The platform lurched downward, threatening to drop from its wall fixtures at any second. The five let out loud cries as the bridge lurched once again.

Elise yelled, "Who designed this?"

"We have to jump!" Gerald shouted. "Aim for the highest point closest to you!"

"Well, do you think we're going to aim for the lowest point, furthest away?" Darren responded scathingly.

Before they could jump, the masked man leapt over the railing and fell gracefully to the ground, landing with a thud but seemingly unaffected by his fall.

"Bad idea!" Elise cried and, in a chance move, began scrambling back up the bending bridge. The metal finally gave way and the cord holding the platform together snapped, sending Elise and the others tumbling down.

There was a millisecond of utter silence when the bridge fell, as if the room itself held its breath to brace for impact, before an enormous *crash* sounded as it hit the floor. Machines tumbled and burst to pieces underneath it, some even exploding into a spray of sparks. The bedlam was so catastrophic, the five hardly processed that their bodies were hitting the ground as well.

When the impact hit, it sent buzzing pain through Elise's bones, suddenly forcing her to regain awareness of what she was doing and what had just happened. Her mind was alert, but the world around her seemed fuzzy and distant. The only thing she heard was her own heartbeat pulsing in her ears as she clambered painfully back to her feet, every limb aching. Remembering the man, she turned in a quick circle, trying to locate her masked pursuer, but she was dizzied by the blurry world around her.

"Elise, *run!*" Lee shouted as she dashed past her sister.

Elise turned in a panic and charged after her, desperately attempting to navigate through a spinning world. They ran down a large hallway, accompanied only by the dark-haired Russian boy, with no idea where the others went and no intention to stop and find out.

The hallway opened again into another circular passage like the one they had just come from. Wide, complex machinery was everywhere, even stretching above their heads. Windows lined the very top of the wall, at least three stories high judging by two narrow bridges protruding from the walls above, letting the slightest bit of eerie moonlight spill into the long, dark cylinder. The three stopped and took to the wall, keeping out of the sight of any eyes that could be staring down the halls.

"This room . . . is exactly . . . the same . . . as the last," the boy noticed between pants, his gaze tracing the equipment.

They all were breathing heavily, Elise staring down at the floor as she tried to gather herself. She closed her eyes and took one more breath before saying, "We have to find a phone."

"We have to hide," the boy contradicted.

"And then do what?" Elise argued. "We have to get authorities over here before this guy gets away with the others."

"What did he even want with us?" Lee asked, her cheeks just as flushed as Elise's.

Lee leaned against the wall, her eyes occasionally darting back to the hall they had entered from, as if expecting the masked man to appear.

"Right now," the boy said, "I don't care. Let's just get out of this horror movie."

Suddenly, something else caught Elise's attention. A machine in the center of the room glimmered, glowing faintly in the darkness.

"Is that—"

"What are you doing, Mont?" Laleitha asked in the most exasperated tone she could muster.

There was something different about this machine; the glow was so strange. It was round and several components of its inner workings remained visible on the outside surfaces. Much of it was black or gray, but a ring that encircled the upper portion glowed with a whitish-purple light.

"I thought it was supposed to be a nuclear reactor . . ." Elise mused.

"Oh, my God, Elise, *now*? We're being chased by a madman, and you want to stop and look at a reactor?" her sister scoffed.

"Something is wrong here." Elise turned to face her sister, conviction filling her voice. "That is supposed to be a nuclear reactor core, but it's not. Marty told me all about the reactor he was developing and that *thing* over there looks a lot like a reactor but *isn't*."

"Elise, I don't care," Lalietha stressed.

"Look at it!" Elise exclaimed. "What does it remind you of?"

"The portals," the boy said, his green eyes fixed on the machine's glow. "They're somehow using the same energy source that created the portals."

Lee looked at the machine with wide, shocked eyes. "We have to get out of here," she concluded.

Suddenly, the voice of the masked man sounded. "Try."

The three snapped around, spying the masked man standing in the corner adjacent to theirs. Elise stared, eyes wide, chest heaving, slowly stepping backward.

The masked man moved forward, "How do you think your friend was able to keep this place hidden? Keep *you* hidden. And your sister."

Elise and Lee exchanged terrified glances. How did he know they were sisters?

"Why do you think he wanted to?" he went on. "Come with me now, and I'll show you what he's kept from you."

"What do you want with us?" Elise demanded, fighting to keep the fear out of her voice.

"To help you."

"By shooting me in the head?"

"That was only a verification process. We had to ensure that the people Sar Prague brought me were the ones we were looking for. Our operations are centered around secrecy."

Confused at first, his meaning dawned on Elise. *He wants only the bulletproof ones, and anyone else who had already seen him couldn't be left to report them.* She shuddered at the twistedness of this man's "operations."

"We?" Laleitha repeated. "Who's we?"

"Would you like to find out?"

She shook her head. "Not by whatever you had in mind."

Suddenly, a window smashed somewhere and alarms began blaring. Lights blinked from every direction as a loud wail erupted from widely scattered speakers, echoing through the halls.

Elise didn't wait to see what had happened. She turned to her sister and the Russian boy and followed them as they dashed away.

They ducked under a looming machine and charged through the first dark and blank hallway they found, not daring to look back, until another man stepped out from behind one of the corners, stopping the three in their tracks. He wore a black and navy blue outfit, something that appeared to be a uniform, with a white circle on the left breast wherein a navy tree stretched its branches. That same symbol again. He held a blade in his hand that shimmered oddly, gleaming like a moonlit mirror. Elise found herself staring right at the edge before turning and sprinting for her life down the hallway to her right. It would have been much more comforting to see a gun in his hand; at least she could—apparently—defend against one of those.

This hallway was much shorter and before she knew it, she was in another identical passage with her companions on her heels. This time, the boy quickly located a set of narrow steps that took them to a higher platform in the chamber. Lee and Mont followed suit. They were beginning to recognize the layout of the passages; the main hallway entered on one side of the cylinder and continued on the exact other side. Lining the edges were smaller workstations and metallic steps up to the higher platforms, some of which circled the entire perimeter of the room and some of which had doorways to smaller halls or rooms. At the top level, a narrow bridge ran across the diameter of the passage, connecting two doorways. This was the setup of every passage they had been in so far, and likely the setup of every other passage they had yet to enter.

Elise's rapid heartbeat pounded in her chest as her eyes traced the room. Fear tingled in her spine while she stood, waiting in anticipation for another attacker to emerge from the shadows that littered the floor of the facility. Suddenly, her sister's hand took a vice-like grip on Elise's arm. Elise's head jerked in Laleitha's direction. Her face tilted toward the ceiling, her eyes fixed on something on the bridge above them. Elise followed her gaze then inhaled sharply when her eyes locked on a figure.

A female wore the same uniform as the man before, holding a dual pair of the same shimmering knives. Her dark hair was pulled into a ponytail that whipped behind her as she hoisted herself over the railing and launched herself to a lower platform.

Elise wasted no time in turning and darting away, yanking her sister in the same direction. She flew down the steps and headed for the large main hall before another man emerged, blocking their escape.

The pair skidded to a stop, bolting back up the stairs. The other boy was out of sight, which hopefully meant he had safely escaped. Elise and Lee scrambled back up to the platform, searching frantically for a new method of evasion.

"Up here. Go," Laleitha instructed, pushing Elise toward another set of steps that would take them to a higher level.

Elise's eyes traced upward as she climbed, locating the woman, who was approaching quickly by jumping from platform to platform. At the platform ahead, an open door frame could be spotted. *We'll escape them there.*

Their female pursuer landed on their platform just as the pair reached it, immediately launching herself at Laleitha. Elise yelped when their bodies crashed, sending all three tumbling. Their attacker's nails dug into Laleitha's arms as the girl attempted to rip away; meanwhile, Elise scrambled away from the scuffle out of instinct. Their attacker's blades had clattered to the ground when she lunged, and one of them had fallen back to the ground level.

Elise was preparing to use the blade before a fourth body flew at them. The man who had blocked their escape through the hall had followed them up the steps and now soared at Elise with his blade bared. She let out a cry as she ducked away, before realizing she had rolled under the rails and right off the platform. Her body crashed onto a ledge, the impact rippling through her muscles. She sat up immediately to gaze upward, forgetting to process the pain.

It seemed the entrance of the man had surprised his female colleague, as well, and Laleitha finally managed to shake herself from the woman's grasp at her moment of stupefaction.

"Lee, run!" Elise shrieked as she began to scramble to her feet.

Laleitha bolted through the doorway they had initially aimed for, sprinting down the hall to who-knew-where.

"You go for her," the man muttered to the woman, who soon took off after Lee.

He turned his attention to Elise, who was still a level below him due to her fall. Her eyes fixed on him, her chin turned upward as she took slow, careful steps backward. As she backed away below, the man crept to the edge of the ledge like a cat preparing to pounce on prey.

Elise didn't breathe. She briefly considered fighting back before deciding she stood no chance. But the thought persisted in her mind. Running had proven ineffective, and in order to escape the situation, she had to switch methods.

As a result of her thoughts, when the culmination of the encounter was finally reached and the man lunged toward her, she found herself paralyzed with indecision. Miraculously, instinct took over and she threw her arms above her head. That was when something within her pulsed, something she had never felt before. Then she heard a cry, followed by a thud, as the man landed on the platform.

Elise slowly removed her arms to peek down at the man, her mouth hanging half open in bewilderment. His black clothes were sizzling, flames beginning to grow at his collar and below his sleeves. His body was shaking and thrashing as he writhed, yelling in agony as his body slowly became engulfed in scorching fire. His flesh began to shrivel and stiffen, peeling and cracking as it did so. Through these cracks, sickening bulbs of melting fat began to pour, warping the man's skin. She could do nothing but watch, her eyes wide and mouth agape. Eventually, the man's screams were cut off and his body went limp. The flames continued to crackle softly as they slowly ate at his shirt and pants. Elise's hand flew to her mouth and she stumbled a few feet backward. *What did I just do?*

Elise watched the flames sway with her heart in her throat, her hands trembling as they went to her hair. "What did I just do?" her quivering voice repeated. Vomit pitched up her throat, just narrowly stopped by her clenched jaw and protective hand clasped over her lips.

Before she could accomplish anything else, something moved beneath her. The strange pulse in her forehead had intensified into a throb. When she looked down, she found the metal platform on which she stood was beginning to dissolve into a steaming silver liquid. The floor melted beneath her, slowly at first, dripping down to the ground level in chunks, but by the time she realized what was happening, she was falling.

Her head snapped downward and dizziness overcame her as she plummeted to the ever-approaching floor. Letting out a small cry, she threw out her hands as if to stop her fall or cushion her landing.

Then everything stopped.

She stared at the floor not even three feet away from her face. Her fingers could nearly stroke the tiles as she hung there. A cold, fear-driven tear ran down her nose, lingering there for a few seconds, then plopped onto the floor. Elise stared at it, trying to comprehend what had just happened—what *was* happening.

A shine in the corner of her view caught her eye, and she soon found herself staring at a blob of liquid that had once been the platform she stood on, now solidifying again.

At the shift of her attention, her suspension released. Just like that, she thudded to the floor, a mess of limbs, the cold tile suddenly smashing into her. She lifted her head, flexing her hands against the very real surface of the ground beneath her. *What the hell is happening here?*

She pushed herself upward and staggered to her feet, still dizzy. Her gaze wandered across the floor until she came to the deformed body of the man who had attacked her. Instinctively, she jerked in the other direction, ripping away from the product of whatever she had done—whatever horrible thing that stopped the bullet, killed this man, and melted the platform.

She began to run, headed for the hallway, too confused to do anything but flee. No point in trying to make sense of all this; she just wanted to get out of this nightmare.

Suddenly, she found herself face to face with the boy named Gerald. Both jumped, Elise letting out a small shriek.

"Where is he?" Gerald asked.

"Who?"

"The guy with the mask."

"I don't know. He's not following me," Elise answered, trying to catch her breath. "But there is something seriously wrong here."

He nodded. "I know. We need to hide."

Elise also nodded, following him as he passed her. They found themselves in a passage identical to the last three, ducking behind pieces of machinery until they were well concealed.

"I think I just killed a man . . ." Elise murmured, still breathing hard.

"What?" Gerald asked. "What happened?"

Elise shook her head. "I don't know. He flew at me. I panicked. I felt something in my forehead, and then he burst into flames," she blurted. "And then I think I melted the thing I was standing on, and I fell but then I put out my hands . . . and I stopped in midair."

Gerald stared at her blankly.

She looked back at him, certain her terror showed in her gaze. "And I saw a machine that Marty told me was supposed to be a nuclear reactor, but I swear it was using the same substance that opened the portals that brought us here," she rambled on.

"I don't know what you're talking about," he said.

"We have to find my sister," she said, setting aside her recollections.

"We need to stay here until the authorities arrive. You can hear the sirens now," Gerald argued.

"Elise!"

She turned toward the nearest hall to see Laleitha and the boy named Darren approaching them quickly, the one with the Russian accent still nowhere to be found.

Elise rushed to meet them, tempted to hug her sister but afraid she might send her into flames. "Are you okay?"

"Yeah, I'm fine," Lee answered.

"They're coming," Gerald said from behind them.

"Which means we have to go," Darren, who was lined with sweat, added. "Does anyone know the way out?"

The dark-haired boy from earlier then emerged from the shadows, causing them to jump when they noticed him. "I do," he said. "But it's being blocked by four of them."

"Then our best bet is the emergency exits," Gerald said. "Which are either on the roof or the edges of the building."

"Let's go then," Darren said, hastily headed for the stairs.

There was an abrupt crash in the distance, followed by raised voices.

"What was that?" Darren asked, turning back around slowly to look over at the four others, who were returning his shocked look.

There was more distant running and crashes.

"There's someone else," Elise said. "Get to the walls!"

Before they could do anything else, four black-clad attackers emerged from the hallways, blocking off their exits. The kids huddled together in the middle, staring back at their enemies.

Unexpectedly, one of the men let out a small cry before falling forward, revealing a tall dark-skinned man standing over him. Two of the other men lunged at him, but the man, wielding only a small knife, fought back even quicker than any of them had anticipated. He deflected the sword of the first one, pivoting as he used the attacker's momentum to slide under him, flipping him over and then bouncing back up just as fast to stop the second's sword from slashing down on him. Holding the blades in midair, the new man kicked the attacker in the knee, causing him to stumble, then slashed down with his knife, opening a cut down the man's chest. The man then did not hesitate to throw his knife into the first attacker's side just as he was getting up, sending him back down to the ground.

Only one was left now, and he had watched the man fight his friends while guarding the five captives, who stood in a terrified circle in the middle.

The new man approached the last attacker, knife back in hand, and jabbed toward his upper right shoulder. The man deflected the first strike and had barely deflected the second to the right hip when the man spun faster than light, impaling the knife into the man's left shoulder before the attacker could even process what had happened.

The last captor fell with a cry, and the new man looked at the five. "Follow me and you'll live," he said.

"Wha—" Elise managed before he cut her off.

"Just follow me!"

CHAPTER SEVEN

Birthrights

The man led them back to the very room they had started in, the small, dark, empty space that now had singed carpets and black streaks on the wall. "There are three hundred and eighty-seven passages in this facility, all of them the same," he said as he hurried them through the hall. "But only *one* we are able to access."

"Who is *we?*" Gerald asked from behind.

"The people trying to keep you safe," he answered. "Take a right here." He turned, ushering them through the door.

"And who exactly are they?" Gerald was pressing on.

"The good guys."

He revealed a white rod from his pocket that was exactly like the kind that had first brought them there.

"What are those things?" exclaimed Gerald once again.

The man gritted his teeth and replied, "Kid, you're killing me with the questions."

He tossed the rod and, with a *snap,* another portal opened. "Go through and wait for me," he said.

The small Russian boy didn't hesitate and immediately dove through, followed by Lee, then Darren, then Elise, and Gerald last. The man had his back turned, looking out for any intruders. When they had all passed through, he turned to follow, closing the portal behind him.

The atmosphere of this new place was still and quiet. The dark sky loomed over them. A grass field stretched in what seemed like all directions, until Elise spotted a bright city in the distance. Chicago, undoubtedly. Elise stumbled when she passed through the portal, tripping over the curb of a street that lay in front of her. The road extended toward the distant city and appeared to be well traveled but now empty. A few feet away, a gray van was parked at the side of the street. The man's van, probably.

"We need somewhere to hide," the man told them once they were all through and the portal was closed. "Somewhere secret and hidden."

"Where are we?" Darren demanded. "Why'd you take us here?"

"The transportation rod opens to here. Used to be a safe house; now it's nothing," the man answered. "But that doesn't matter. We need somewhere to hide. We *had* a safehouse but the transportation rod for it was destroyed by the same people who kidnapped you. And I can't take you back to the Arc City right now. They're not ready for you yet."

"What are you talking about?" Darren nearly yelled, just as freaked out and confused as before.

"We need somewhere to hide," the man snapped. "You're not safe here; it's too exposed. *I* won't even be able to protect you if they come, since that Second Reighba broke my gun." He opened the trunk of the van, removing a bag and digging through it furiously. "We didn't plan for this. There's no rendezvous, no backup safehouse, no contingency." Removing a small device from the bag, he pressed the large button at the top before tossing it back into the trunk. *Perhaps a panic button.* "Do any of you know a place? Somewhere secluded? Safe?"

The five stared at him blankly.

"Nobody?"

"I know a place," Elise blurted, vocalizing the first idea that popped into her mind. "9551 West, it's private property. I think there is a building there, but nobody knows for sure. Nobody ever goes there."

Laleitha stared at her.

"That will work," he responded almost automatically, walking past them to the van. "Everybody, get in the van."

They followed, Gerald taking the passenger side while the rest of them tucked themselves into the back, where no seats remained.

When Elise had set herself down, she took a moment to survey the situation, perhaps in an attempt to calm down and get a general idea—at least—of what was happening. She looked around at the others. Sweat and grime coated their skin, making it rather uncomfortable to sit within such close proximity to each other. All of them, save the man, were breathing hard and had pink flooding their cheeks. Their eyes held dazed expressions, as if they had seen a ghost. As the man situated himself and started the van, the only sounds that came from the five were the heavy pants of their hard breathing.

Elise's heart was still racing, providing no reason to believe it would stop anytime soon.

"Why did you bring us here?" the smallest boy asked, finally breaking the silence, as he looked up from his hands to the man in the driver's seat.

"The Lumerians once had a safe house here. It was torn down, but I didn't learn that until I was sent to retrieve you," he answered. "This protocol is severely outdated."

"Are you ever going to explain what that means?" Elise followed up with what was on everyone's mind.

"*I* will not, but your transitioner will."

"Okay, I'm done with this jibberish," Darren snapped. "I don't want anything to do with you or whoever your work for. I'm not going wherever you plan to take us. I want to go home."

"Home isn't an option anymore!" the man replied fiercely, silencing them all. "You are being *hunted,* so unless you want your families to die with you, then we are going someplace safe."

Everyone grew quiet and still. The man pulled the car onto the road.

The weight of what just happened suddenly crashed down on Elise. How long would it be before she could go home? If what this man was saying was true, she just had her life ripped away from her in a matter of seconds. *I can't see my family? What about Percy? What about Mom? They'll be worried sick. They'll have lost Marty, my dad, and me in a matter of a week!* Elise bit her lip to fight the tears that were beginning to pool in her eyes. *Mom will be angry. She'll think I ran away or went looking for Dad. She'll think I left without a goodbye.*

She'll think I left without a goodbye. It will break her heart.

Then she realized she *did* leave without a goodbye. Maybe it wasn't her choice, but the possibility remained that she wouldn't see her mother or Percy again. Suddenly, a wave of panic filled Elise's chest. Images of Percy driving her to school, Wellington park, sitting cross-legged in the basement as she tampered with her projects, sitting in church next to her brother, and everything she enjoyed about her life flooded her mind. She had always regarded her life as an unexciting if not crappy one, but now that she faced the threat of it being taken away, she desperately wanted it back. She despised her captors, she despised this man driving them away, she despised Marty. She wasn't ready to move on to a new chapter of her life.

"Do you know why they are hunting us?" Gerald quietly asked.

"Your blood is special," the man replied. "There are only seven people in the world with blood like yours, and that blood runs back all the way to the first Seven Majors."

"What the hell is that supposed to mean?" Darren asked, sounding exhausted and resigned, his head resting in his hands.

The man took a deep breath. "The Seven Majors were seven people who were elected to be the patrons of the seven capital cities in this place called Lumeria," he began. "They were given this thing called Lumire to help them protect their assigned region. Now this thing, the Lumire, it was injected into their bloodstream . . . and it allowed them to do things—strange things—like start fires with their mind, or change the material of their skin but, most notably, it makes them invulnerable to metals."

"That's why we could deflect the bullets," said Lee.

The man nodded. "The Lumire is passed down like genes, except once it is passed down, the parent no longer has it."

"How is that supposed to work?" Elise cut in. "There is no—"

"Just shut up and listen! Don't try to make sense of this stuff with your prior knowledge; it won't work. Anyway, it can only be passed down to a child of the same gender and only appears in the firstborn child of that particular gender. So, for centuries these Majors would protect the cities then pass down the Lumire so the line of Majors would never end."

"Wait," Elise interjected. "You're saying my mom had it?"

"Yeah," he said with a nod.

"But my older brother doesn't because he's a guy?" she continued.

He exhaled through his nose. "Are you asking me or trying to work this out in your mind?" he demanded irritably.

Elise paused then turned her gaze to the window. "Continue."

"They each had their own tower," he went on, "each of which only they could get into. But then, in 1968, this civil war broke out and the Majors fought for the separatists. They lost and the Majors were sent into a five-year exile to the

Other Society. When their sentence had ended, though, nobody could find them again and the lines were lost. Their towers haven't been opened since. And up until this point, Lumeria's been living without the Majors."

They sat in silence when he had finished, letting his last words linger for a few more moments, until Gerald spoke again. "So, you're saying that we are next in line to become these . . . Majors . . ."

The man nodded. "It's your birthright."

"But why are there people hunting us?" Elise inquired on. "Is it because they want to make sure the Majors never return? Or something else?"

He stiffly shook his head, his eyes fixed intently on the road. "I don't know," he said quietly.

The was a pause before Laleitha gave a frustrated sigh and asked, "So what do you want with us?"

"For you to reclaim your birthright," he replied. "I'm bringing you to the Lumerian Council so you can begin transitioning."

"But what if we don't *want* to be Majors?" Darren fired at him. "What if we never *wanted* to be pulled into this freak show?"

"Well, as of right now, you have no choice," he replied. "You stay here, or go home, or go *anywhere* outside of Lumeria, you will kill yourself, and whoever is with you, therefore ending the line of Majors. And it is my job not to allow that. If you come to Lumeria at all, you have to start training to become a Major. It's either death or this, kid, so take your pick."

Darren went quiet again, radiating bitterness.

"I don't want to die," Gerald began, "but I'm not prepared to be whatever it is you're talking about. Why can't we just go to this Lumeria place and be put under some sort of protection?"

"Because there are rules," the man responded.

"*What* rules?" Darren challenged, his voice scathing.

"*Big* rules, kid," he snapped. "Called the Ancient Convention. I'm talking about the rules everyone has to follow, and there are serious consequences if you don't. This is a hell of a lot bigger than just you and me. So if you decide you'd rather do the rational thing and come to Lumeria so you *don't die*, you are going to be a Major whether you think you're cut out for it or not. I'm not letting the line of Majors end today."

Silence followed his words.

A tear finally escaped Elise's eye, one that she wiped away just as quickly. Who was this guy and what gave him the right to take her away from her family?

She took a shaking swallow before asking, "Who are you?"

"My name is Joseph Talious," he said. "And you all?"

"Elise Montason."

"Darren Nosia."

"Laleitha Ataliarma," her sister said.

"Anton Hystar," the Russian boy answered.

"Gerald Rodum," Gerald said. "My friends call me 'King.'"

☓

Elise directed Joseph through town and right to the gates of 9551 West, which remained closed and locked. Talious parked the car directly in front of the gate, leaving the headlights on as they shined against the fence.

The gate was tall and obviously electric, just as Lee had described to her, but Talious had no problem grabbing a bolt cutter from the back and snapping the lock right off.

"What kind of maniac carries a bolt cutter in their car?" Gerald muttered to the others.

"There's a ton of stuff back here," Laleitha said. "He's got a lockpick set, something that looks like a saw, a case full of some strange liquid and syringes, some weird machinery . . . and, oh, look at that." She opened a large black container. "A rifle, ammunition, and two empty knife covers. Almost like he was planning to break into something."

"Or break us out of something," Darren suggested with a shrug.

The metal creaked as it slid open, the chains rattling as if they had not been touched in years. Only Elise and Laleitha understood how mysterious this place really was beyond its unwelcoming look. They sat in anticipation, waiting silently to see what secrets their friend had been hiding. Behind the gate was a gravel road flanked by a dense forest, leading over a curving hill, and plunging into the darkness beyond.

Talious stepped back into the car and began driving down the gravel road. "There's a place back here, you say?"

"I think so," Elise replied rather distantly, staring out the window as she watched the unfamiliar forest go by. "Laleitha and I saw it, but it shouldn't exist, and we've never really gotten around to visiting it since I only inherited it yesterday."

"Wait, wait, wait, slow down, say that again, but explain it in a way that reasonable people would understand," Darren said.

Elise sighed. "The property belonged to a close family friend, but he hadn't visited it in years and he said there isn't supposed to be a building here. Then he died and left the entire place to me." She did not wish to elaborate on the death part.

"Who was this 'family friend'?" the driver asked.

"His name was Hank Martinez," Elise answered.

The man went silent immediately, growing deathly stiff in his seat before slowly pulling the van to the side of the road and putting it in park. Rigidly, almost carefully, he turned around. "This belonged to Hank Martinez?"

Confused, Elise studied his face, trying to make sense of his distress. "Does that mean something to you?"

"What did he look like?" Tailous pressed.

"Um, tall, slim, straight black hair, brown eyes, pointy nose . . ."

"How long has he lived in this area?"

"I don't know—fifteen years or so? Why? Why are you asking me this?"

Talious turned back around, grasping the wheel with white knuckles and resuming his drive. "Hank Martinez is an alias used by a Lumerian fugitive. What his real name is, we don't know, but what we do know is he is the only person on earth who knows the whereabouts of a missing person who has been of interest to the Lumerian Council for decades. He killed some of us when we came looking for answers."

Elise stared at him uncomprehendingly then looked back at Laleitha, who reflected her incredulousness, then looked back at the man. *"What?"* she spat. "Hank? There is no way—he wouldn't—th-that's not like him at all!"

Gerald looked between Talious and Elise in confusion. "Do you think he came here because two of the Majors lived in the area?"

"It's possible Martinez is associated with the very people who abducted you," Talious said through gritted teeth. "Which is not good for either of our causes."

Elise could hardly take it. "You're wrong," she said conclusively. "There is no way. He was my friend. No, scratch that—he was the closest thing I had to a father! Besides, he died a week before we were abducted, so there was no way he could have been involved."

"He could have given them your locations."

"The locations of Lee and me, maybe, but what about the other three? And he had no reason to give them information like that anyway." Elise continued to fight back.

"*All* of his motives for *everything* he did is a mystery to us. We don't know what went through his goddamn head. All we know is he was hiding something and killed to keep it hidden, so just shut up and let me do my job!" Talious snapped at her.

Elise sat back in her seat angrily, refusing to believe a word he said.

The road wound on until finally, as they drove down a steep slope, the trees parted and a wide clearing opened up. At the end of the road in the middle of the clearing was a slim, plain building of gray bricks and no windows. It was a perfect cylinder, rising about two stories from the ground, Elise guessed. Facing the road was a dark brown door.

Elise and Laleitha were too astonished to react. Until she saw the building, there had always been skepticism in the back of her mind that anything actually was here. When the car finally parked, they stepped out only to stare up at it.

Whatever was in that building, it must have been important to Marty.

"Turns out there *is* something here," Talious said, closing the car door. "Just hope the door isn't locked."

Fortunately, the door was not locked and Talious opened it with no need to get any questionable tools from the van.

The room they entered was nothing like Elise expected. The staircase protruded directly from the center of the circular floor, and a small desk area was set up in the back of the room. There was a television set and a few cushioned chairs in the front of the room, though they were dusty and appeared to have never been used. The walls were an olive green, and the floor was pale wooden tiles. It almost looked as if someone had been living here, and it then occurred to Elise that she'd never been to Marty's apartment in the city. It may be jumping to conclusions to guess that he lived here, but perhaps he spent a night or two. Or maybe it was for someone else.

Talious flipped on the light, which made a low buzz as it turned on. "This is perfect," he said. "Here's my phone." He slipped a small phone from his pocket and offered it to Darren. "You guys can contact your families while we wait for my supervisor to arrive."

"Your supervisor?" Darren repeated.

"He should be here soon."

"He'll find this place?" Gerald asked.

Talious nodded.

"He won't be coming through those . . . portal things, will he?" Darren asked.

Talious snorted. "No. The transportation rods have to be programmed to a location, and to do that, you have to have been to the place before."

"How do those things work, anyway?" Laleitha asked.

"You'll learn about this kind of technology later," he answered simply.

"Mmm," Darren murmured unenthusiastically, beginning to dial a number on the phone.

Elise drifted toward the desk. Something else had caught her attention. A leather-bound notebook sat on the desk. Elise picked it up and ran her finger along the spine before opening it and flipping through the pages. The first page only had two sentences written at the top, one in English and the other in the same familiar code in the letter Hank had written to her. The first sentence read "the Diary of Hank Martinez."

"No way," she breathed. Elise looked up to notice the Russian boy named Anton next to her, examining the page with interest.

He looked up and met her eyes. "Do you know what that says?" He pointed at the strange characters underneath the first sentence.

She looked back down at it. "This"—she pointed to the first four words—"says 'the way is closed.' I know because I've seen it before."

"Where?"

"In his house. He also wrote me a letter in this same language," she answered.

This caught the attention of Talious. "Let me see that," he said.

Elise handed the book over.

"This is written in Old Lat. The dialect has been dead for centuries."

"Old Lat?" Elise repeated. "Is that like Latin?"

"Not at all," he responded. "My advisor will explain it to you. The point is, I can't read this and I don't *know* anyone who can. The only person I can think of that could is Orphia. And maybe Ms. Kilodrist. You'll meet her soon."

He handed the book back to Elise and turned around. "No more questions until my supervisor gets here."

Darren was still on the phone, looking exasperated. "That's what I said! No, Mom, do *not* put Dad on the phone . . . I don't care. I don't want to hear his explanation," he said. "The only reason I'm calling at all is so you wouldn't lose your shit when you realize I'm gone . . . No, Mom, I don't want to talk to Dad!" He threw up his hands and rolled his eyes.

His dad was obviously on the other end now.

"Yeah, hey, Dad, I have a bone to pick with you. Did you know that you just passed on some freak gene to me and now I'm being dragged into a parade of other freaks? . . . And you didn't feel obliged to share? A little heads-up would have been nice . . . No, I'm not going to be coming home for a while because now I'm kinda being hunted . . . You can't say that. You were the freak first!"

"Stop that," Talious commanded. "Don't call the Majors freaks."

Darren snorted. "Yeah, okay, so, see ya, Dad. I gotta go now. I'll accept your apology later." He hung up and offered the phone to Anton.

After a brief, hushed conversation with his parents, Anton handed the phone to Elise, who dialed her mother's number and set the phone against her ear, carefully preparing her words. How would she start? How would her mother react? Her contemplating got cut short when her mother answered the phone.

"Hello?"

Elise took a deep breath. "Hey, Mom, it's me."

"Elise? Where are you? Why aren't you home? I just about had a heart attack when I couldn't find you! Wha—"

"Yeah, Mom, I was abducted and then shot in the head," Elise said, coming out with it and praying for a good reaction.

There was silence on the other end.

"Mom? You know how this was possible?"

When her mom spoke again, Elise could tell she was on the verge of tears. "I do. My mother explained it to me when I was eighteen, just as I was going to do for you."

The words gripped Elise uncomfortably. "Well, it's kinda late for that. There are these people after me. They also got four people like me. Luckily, Lee is one of them, and—"

"Laleitha has it too?" Eleanor repeated.

"Um, yes, any—"

"*Oh, that man!*" her mother shouted in fury. "There is *no way* it is a coincidence that he had kids with *two different Lumerians!* Ugh! If I ever see him again—"

"Hey, Mom. Mom. Mom, just listen. I don't have much time. I won't be able to come home for a while. There is this guy—he is going to take us to the Lumerian Council, and we're going to begin training. I wish there was a way out of it, but if I come home, the people who are hunting me will kill both you and Percy," Elise said, firing out as much information as she could.

There was a beat of silence as her mother collected herself. "Okay," she said finally, her voice balancing on the edge of steady. "Somehow I always knew you'd be dragged into this." Her mother was crying now. "I'm so sorry, Elise. I'm sorry I didn't tell you sooner. I'm sorry about a lot of things."

Elise's eyes stung. "It's okay, Mom," she managed.

"Do you want to talk to Percy?"

"No, I don't want to know how he'll react. Just make sure he understands, okay?"

"Okay."

"I love you, Mom." The words felt disjointed to Elise.

"I love you too, Elise," Eleanor replied between sniffles.

"Bye." Elise hung up, heart heavy with confusion and anger. She wordlessly handed the phone off to her sister and stiffly sat down on the armchair. Distantly, she wondered if things would ever go back to the way they were.

CHAPTER EIGHT

The Ambassador of the Arc

All of them jumped when the door opened. A tall, broad-shouldered man with a square face and golden hair walking in the door, grinning. *Talious's supervisor.*

"Hello, Joseph. How on *earth* did you come across this place?" he greeted as he entered.

Talious grunted. "It was the kid's idea." He nodded to Elise. "My transportation rod to the safe house broke and the backup safe house was torn down years ago. Now let's get through with this."

The new man laughed at Talious's hastiness. "All right, I see it's been a long night for you." He turned to the five, who studied him with curious yet grim stares. "Take a chair, kids. I have a *lot* to explain."

Elise and Laleitha remained in their armchairs while Darren took the last one, leaving Gerald and Anton to plop down on the floor.

"My name is Stanford Ellington," he began. "I'm not going to go much into who I am just yet because even that will require an extensive explanation. You surely have a lot of questions about what happened and why you are here, but the best thing you can do right now is stay calm and think very carefully about what I'm about to tell you. You've been through a lot, but once I explain, it will begin to make sense. Now, I don't know what Talious told you, but I'm fairly certain you are all unaware of the existence of the Lat empires."

"Lat?" Gerald repeated. "You mean Latin?"

"No," Ellington replied. "Lat society is older than the Romans and still exists today, though hidden from the world as you know it."

Elise stared at the man, feeling as if she had not comprehended a word that flew from his mouth.

Darren squinted suspiciously at the man. "I'm not buying it."

"You're saying you come from a secret society?" Gerald said incredulously.

Elise tilted her head, her eyes still locked on the man as she listened closely to the others' remarks. Her head began to ache as she attempted to fit the puzzle pieces together. Or maybe she was just tired; it had been a long night.

"He said there were empires," Laleitha said. "I don't think that's possible. Definitely not if they still exist today."

Ellington opened his mouth, beginning to say, "No, they—"

"Yeah, how could an entire *empire* go unnoticed?" Darren demanded.

They all turned their attention back to the man, who let out a laugh. "Ha! To be quite honest, I'm not sure," he said. "We have concealed ourselves using Lumerian technology, but I'm surprised we have been able to stay separate for as long as we have. So, anyhow, this—*these*—societies are very different from the ones you are familiar with. Some of our technology—which, as you have observed with the transportation, seems strange to you—we have been able to develop due to a few natural differences in our environment. This may be the biggest snag between societies, so I wanted to get that out of the way first and foremost."

Yes, the transportation rods were indeed a snag. Elise's first assumption of how they worked was simply *magic*, as the idea that such a phenomenon could be explained seemed even more farfetched. It hardly computed for her.

"So, anyway, these people split into three main groups," Ellington went on. "And three separate empires arose, each with a different way of living. They were known as the Lumerians, the Juperds and the Inseanans. The Lumerians followed the traditional Lat practices while the Juperd empire took to more liberal ways. Inseanans, on the other hand, focused on stability and order. To keep the peace and stability between the three, there formed what was called the Ancient Convention and the Trials of Orphia. Orphia, the supreme and eternal judge, is from none of the empires, nor does he have any allegiance to them. He stands alone and so do the other members of Orphia's Council and retinue, as well as citizens of the Orphian City, centered in the middle, between all three empires. The Ancient Convention is mainly just the document that outlines inter-empire practices. It is very important, but you need not know much about it just yet. Regardless, by the Ancient Convention, in any of the empires, if there were any traitors, terrorists, war prisoners, or other such wrongdoers between the empires, they would be tried in front of Orphia to have their punishment decided. The court also oversees treaties and trade negotiations and determines whether an outsider is to become a citizen and of what empire, or whether the citizen should be deported."

Elise bit in a breath. This man was compelling, but words were mechanisms of manipulation and had nothing against real, undebatable evidence. If these empires, this "Orphia," and this *convention* existed, there was no way it could do so without giving them some sort of evidence. Then again, she did just jump through two different portals.

Regardless, she crossed her arms and said, "This is ridiculous. How do you expect us to believe you?"

"From your point of view, I see how you can think this ridiculous," he said calmly, "but if you have seen what I've seen, and experienced what I've experienced, you would know that what I am telling you is true."

Gerald shook his head, his eyebrows creased. "What are you talking about, man?"

"I am," he said, "among the Lumerian Ambassadors of the Arc. I am Lumerian, and I was sent here by the Lumerian Council to retrieve you five."

Elise shook her head, squeezing her eyes shut as if she believed he would be gone when they reopened. *He's crazy,* she repeated to herself. *They both are. They're crazy.*

"Where was I?" Mr. Ellington thought aloud. "Oh, yes. When the empires arose, the Lumerians were the most dominant and largest but struggled the most with their security. This led to the coming of the Seven Majors, who were each a patron of the seven largest and most important Lumerian cities. These seven saints, known as 'Majors,' each have a tower in their patron city that can be opened only by themselves or their fellow Majors. These towers have stood for centuries without relocation or renovation. Majors themselves carry in their blood a substance called the Lumire that enables them to get into the tower, as well as giving them abilities no others possess. It is passed from parent to oldest child of the same gender. Talious told you how it works, correct?"

They nodded.

"You each have the Lumire. Therefore, you are next in line to take up the post that has been lost for years after they never returned from their exile."

Elise stared at the ground. The idea still refused to materialize in her head. She had just learned about these empires. How on earth could she be expected to protect one? In the midst of this confusion, a strange excitement to finally be part of something bigger and much more important than herself tugged at Elise. Then, she realized how dangerous it would be, how unlikely it would be for her to be up to it, and how much she would have to leave behind in order to do this. The ache in her chest returned when she thought about the life behind her. Maybe her new one wasn't as tattered as she had thought, but she couldn't bring herself to walk away from King Avenue.

It seemed she wasn't the only one who had been bombarded with conflicting thoughts, considering the others moved uncomfortably in their seats. Anton would not stop fidgeting, while Gerald had leaned back, looking dumbfounded with the idea of being such an important part of such a mysterious world. Darren studied Mr. Ellington skeptically, and Laleitha's eyes were dark, fixed on the man. Elise knew that look. This was her look of concealing a storm inside of her, of rejecting something inevitable that she just couldn't accept.

"Hold on," Gerald said. "You said there were seven cities; there are only five of us."

"Five is all we need, the other two cities crumbled long ago. There are two more with the Lumire out there, I'm sure, unless one died with it. But there are only five remaining cities, so only five Majors are required."

Laleitha raised an eyebrow. "That's it? How did the cities crumble?"

Ellington swallowed. "Well, uh, in one of them, the War of the Three Empires resulted in a large loss of territory in the north, that which included the first city, Sappol Storm. We never reclaimed that city, but what it is now is a whole other world of things that you don't have to understand just yet. As for the other one . . . the tower was destroyed after an . . . *unfortunate* event that took place before the Redrawing of 1864. That was when it was decided that the city with the destroyed tower would act as a new central capital of the empire instead of the city of a Major. It was originally called Sappol Central, but now it is the Arc City."

There was suddenly a deep heaviness in Elise's chest when he spoke of such things. War . . . iconic towers being destroyed . . . he threw around the notion of such events as if it carried no weight. His descriptions were also rather vague, bringing a sense of ominousness to recollection. She would have to ask him later just what exactly destroyed the first tower and what the war was about, once she managed to wrap her head around the existence of such a place and her thoughts became settled.

He paused to look around at them and must have interpreted their silence as a cue to continue. "As you can expect, the Lat empires have modernized over time, just like the societies you know. They have a long written history—"

"Just," Darren interrupted, "cut to the chase."

Ellington did not seem to be the slightest bit irritated by their impatience, so he moved on without delay. "Okay, so you five are going to start training shortly. Becoming a Major would involve moving into the Major's tower, leaving your family, though you will be able to visit frequently. It also involves years of training. That will be handled by Mr. Talious here," he said, gesturing to Talious. "You will be training in combat but also enhancing the mind, as well as learning to use the Lumire. You will be expected at Lumerian Council meetings once you are inducted as a Major fully . . . and that should be it." He turned to Talious. "Did I forget anything?"

Talious shook his head. "I think you covered it."

Ellington clapped his hands. "Good then, you should all rest up. Tomorrow, I'll take you to the Arc City."

CHAPTER NINE

Welcome to Life

The staircase in the center of the room was just about as dusty as the rest of it, but at least it didn't creak. Before they could find themselves comfortable enough in this mysterious building to fall asleep, a thorough exploration of the place seemed to be in order. So, the five clambered up the stairs to peer into the second floor.

When Gerald finally found the light switch and flipped it on, the image of a room in disarray filled their previously pitch-black view. This room had a black tiled floor and tables of all shapes and sizes scattered across it. Shelves often sat next to these tables, mostly of odd fashion and set at an angle. Atop the tables and shelves, as well as spilling off of them, were various items and knickknacks. A sheet of dust covered all of them, making the floor hardly visible among the odd items and powdery flakes.

Elise drew in a sharp breath of the musty air as she took it all in. Gerald and Laleitha had already begun to stroll across the narrow aisles made by the tables, looking over the items.

"This place belonged to your friend?" Gerald asked, looking back at her.

"Who apparently is a Lumerian criminal," Darren added.

Elise glared at Darren, who looked at neither of them. "Yeah," she answered flatly.

"Well," Laleitha said. "It's yours now. So I guess all of this stuff is too."

Elise drew herself to the closest table and began examining it. An hourglass sat in the middle, sand spilling through it as if it had been recently turned over, but moving incredibly slowly. Elise didn't even realize the sand was moving until she kneeled to view it at eye level. Perhaps it had been turned over, but days ago. Next to the hourglass was a small metal cat with a ruby collar and black crystal eyes, a case that contained the smallest knives she had ever seen, and a few remarkably strange necklaces. Each of these sat atop scattered and worn sheets of paper. Elise slowly brushed aside the trinkets to inspect the pages. Diagrams of buildings and machines on faded grids were scrawled across the sheets, each one fascinating Elise more than the next. They were labeled in the strange language, what Talious called *Old Lat*.

"I found some blankets," Anton said from the other side of the room, tearing Elise's attention from the drawings. "I don't know what they're doing here, but I won't complain."

"Okay," Gerald said, "let's take those back downstairs and get to sleep. There's nothing here that'll hurt us."

They gladly agreed and retreated back to the less eerie and more reasonably set-up floor.

Gerald and Laleitha slept in armchairs, Laleitha pulling two to face each other so she could rest her feet on one, while Gerald just sprawled out on the cushions, disregarding where his limbs went. The rest curled up on the floor, trying their hardest to relax, their bodies eventually giving in.

When Elise awoke the next morning, she found only she and Anton were awake, while Talious and Ellington stood in the corner discussing something quietly.

Elise stirred, her body sore from last night's fright. Sitting up, she realized Hank's notebook was next to her. She picked it up once more and flipped through it. It was all written in Old Lat, but she came across a few sketches that looked like machines and one of a strange mummy-like creature.

She set the book aside and stood, stretching her arms above her head.

"You," Talious called, turning to her.

"Elise," she said.

"Elise, wake up your friends. We have to get going."

She rubbed her eyes drowsily. "What's the hurry?"

"Just do as I say."

"Mmph, okay." She turned and nudged Darren awake with her foot. He rolled over, pulling his blanket over his shoulder. "Get up. We have to go," she said, moving on to her sister, who would be a challenge. "Hey"—she gently slapped her hand against her sister's cheek a few times, as sisters did—"get up, you lazy pudge."

"Ugh, Mont, go away!" Lee moaned.

"I will drag you out of this chair," Elise threatened.

Her sister only groaned.

Gerald shifted in his chair.

Elise grasped her sister's ankles and began mock pulling.

"All right! I'm getting up!" Lee cried, kicking her sister away. Elise had used this tactic before, usually in the mornings after Lalietha somehow ended up at Elise's house in some nonsensical hour of the night, when her sister's combined laziness and stubbornness had threatened to make them late to school.

"*Sisters,*" Gerald remarked, shaking his head, leaning forward so he was sitting up.

Lee rolled off the chair, thudding to the floor and not bothering to move. "You have siblings, *King*?" she asked from the floor.

"Seven," Gerald replied.

"*Seven?*" Lee repeated. "I'll bet you anything Mont is higher maintenance than all of them combined."

Elise scoffed. "Please, I pretty much babysit you. If anyone is high maintenance—"

"Stop talking," Talious interrupted. "We're leaving." He kicked Darren lightly. "Get your fat ass out of bed or we go without you."

"Go right a-fucking-head," Darren replied, rolling over lazily.

"Grab your stuff," he told the rest of them, which was a pointless command since none of them had anything except for Hank's notebook. "We'll stop for breakfast on the way."

⋊

"Where exactly are we going?" Gerald asked after Ellington treated them to pancakes at IHOP.

"See what I mean?" Talious said to Ellington. "The kid will never stop with the questions."

Ellington shifted the van into gear and took off. "We," he said, "are headed to a Lumerian transportation center that we fondly refer to as 'the Port.' It was originally called 'terminal zero,' but that became too commonly used among Inseanans for transportation units that transverse Lat and Other Soci—"

"Okay, so where is the Port?" Gerald continued.

"Not far from here," he replied. "The passage to it is in a small bank in downtown Chicago. I'm fairly certain that ninety percent of the people who use that bank are Lat."

"We're going *back* to Chicago?" Darren exclaimed. "How many Lat places are in that city?"

"The port's been here for decades; that Silver Industries site is recent," Talious responded. "I'm pretty sure the only reason Silver Industries was built here at all is because of the Port."

Elise couldn't tell if he was accusing Marty of anything with this remark, but she decidedly ignored it.

⋊⋉

After half an hour of trying to find a parking spot near the Port, Ellington eventually decided the "No Parking, Fire Lane" sign didn't have to be taken seriously. They would never use the van again, he told them.

The bank he led them to was tiny and disorderly, with stained gray carpet and desks set up in no particular pattern with no common direction. Only one man, who nodded at them politely, stood at the several stations set up against the back wall.

"Good morning, sir," Ellington said to him before leading the kids across the bank to a hallway—that Elise hadn't even noticed was there until she was ushered into it—with a small "Employees Only" sign next to it.

The hall was short and the door at the end was unlocked, but what was behind it caused Elise's breath to catch.

She stood, hardly breathing, as she stared down from the platform she had just walked onto into a vast space. Platforms above her had small jet planes parked on individual pads. They were lined up in a row that protruded from the main cylinder-shaped hub, with a blue railing separating one parking pad from another. From there, a staircase ran along the curving wall to platforms similar to the one Elise stood on, with doors similar to the one Elise had just come through. Then, the steps continued on to several stations below her, where open portals sat, never to be closed, with a small sign in front of them that told their location. The Port bustled with people coming in and out, stopping to chat before hopping through the holes in the air, and occasionally a jet would start, and the wall in front of the parking pad would roll back, revealing a long runway that exited to a place impossible to tell.

"Well, what do you know," Gerald breathed. "These guys aren't crazy."

"Or maybe we all are," Elise offered, unable to take her eyes away from the open portals.

Ellington chuckled. "It is a sight, isn't it? Okay, I believe our destination is this way." He led them down the steps to a portal labeled:

Fort Kingshold
Arc City, Pallain, Lumeria

"How hasn't this place been discovered?" Laleitha asked.

"The Port has a top-notch security system," Ellington said. "The hall and doorway leading to this place through the bank can be closed off such that it doesn't appear to exist. And there has never been a need to investigate the bank. The owner knows to keep out of trouble, and there's never been any robberies, being that most people don't know about it, at least to my knowledge. Nobody knows to look, so nobody does."

Elise peered through the portal. The other side showed a wide concrete walk lined with berry bushes and an evening sky above.

"Ladies first," Ellington urged Elise on.

Elise took a deep breath then leapt through the wide hole. On the other side, she turned in circles, gazing at the city around her.

At dusk, the city took on a red glare. The architecture was nothing like anything Elise had ever seen; some buildings were shaped like giant detailed and jagged arrowheads while others looked like large, geometrical pillars, with layer after layer stretching into the sky, not one layer identical to the previous. A monorail train ran through the city, weaving between buildings and stopping at elevated stations. The portal she came through was situated in a large courtyard, forming a sanctuary from the looming buildings and busy city streets. Just beyond, Elise could see the moving crowds of people across the sidewalks and the parades of cars that strung through the streets. Aside from the bizarre architecture and the red haze that seemed to have swept over the city from the setting sun, it almost reminded Elise of Chicago. It almost reminded her of home. But this wasn't home. The passerby she watched were Lumerians and the cars she noticed looked much different than what she was used to, thinner in frame and slightly chunkier in style. She had just walked onto what felt like the surface of a different planet.

She hadn't even realized the others had come through after her, for they were just as silent from the breathtaking city.

"Holy shit," were the only words Darren could find.

"Come on," Talious said. "Let's get inside. You have people to meet."

He led the way to a complex of tied-together buildings, ones of boxy but otherwise ordinary architecture. The courtyard the portal had led them to was situated at the entrance of this building, Elise realized.

Elise glanced back the way she came. The portal remained open, but around it black-painted wood was set up like a booth, with the portal at the middle. There were three more like it that were placed next to it, each leading to different places.

She turned back and focused on what was ahead of her. The building Ellington and Talious were leading them to had a wide, arched entrance decorated with paintings of stars and crowns. A number of symbols had been painted across the very top of the black arch in gold.

"What does that say?" Elise asked, nudging Ellington and pointing to the symbols.

"That, Miss Montason, is the only Old Lat I know. It says, 'Across all worlds, the just will stand.' The famous phrase of one of the early Lumerian emperors when he negotiated our first treaty with the Inseanans."

Talious pushed open the tall door, revealing a grand hall. They stepped into the large circular room with a domed roof that opened to the sky above. The floor shone a turquoise blue in the moonlight, and the walls were covered with mirrors and mosaics.

"This," Ellington said, "is Fort Kingshold. The center of the Arc City and the primary institute of the Lumerian Council. The lifts are down this hall." He led them across the room where an arched hall opened up.

There, golden elevators awaited them. The doors slid open, revealing a small glass box with wooden floors. They stepped inside, tentatively waiting for doors to close and the elevator to lift.

Elise bit her lip. She so far enjoyed this strange new place immensely, but she knew Percy would, too, and wanted more than anything for him to be here.

Finally, the elevator opened again, revealing a narrower hallway with black carpeting and blank walls. Ellington steered them through a few bends and turns then instructed them to turn right into a new room where a secretary sat guarding the various halls and rooms behind her.

"I'd like to see Ms. Kilodrist," Ellington told the secretary. "My name is Stanford Ellington, and it is *imperative* that I see her tonight."

"She is teaching now, sir," the secretary replied, giving him a stubbornly defiant look. "She refuses to be pulled out of a session. I can schedule you an appointment if you'd—"

"I am here on business regarding the council. She has made an agreement to partake in the training of the *Seven Majors*."

The secretary's eyebrows flinched slightly, as if they wanted to shoot straight up, but she did not allow them. She glanced over his shoulder, eyeing the kids who stood behind awkwardly in pajamas, sweatshirts, or T-shirts. "*These* are the remaining Majors?"

"Yes, ma'am," Ellington replied slightly overconfidently.

"How can you know for sure?"

"The Prime Devise got to them first," Talious pitched in. "They were all put through the test by Second Reighba himself."

Elise and Laleitha exchanged confused glances. "Did you get any of that?" Elise asked.

Her sister shook her head. "What the hell is the 'Prime Devise'?"

Elise shrugged and they turned their attention back to the secretary.

The secretary had given in. Sighing, she took her phone and dialed, shooting another look at the five as she pressed the phone to her ear. "Ms. Kilodrist, I'm so sorry to interrupt but Stanford Ellington is here, and he insists that you see him now. He mentioned the training of the Seven Majors." There was a long pause as the secretary, becoming more and more defeated, listened to the woman at the other end. "Yes, yes, ma'am," she said, nodding as she did so. The secretary placed the phone back on the receiver. Then, she stood. "Follow me," she said with a hint of sternness in her voice.

They quietly trailed behind the brisk woman as she marched down another hall, stopping at a glass wall with a wooden door in the exact middle. She unlocked the door and held it open for them as they entered one by one.

"Take a seat," she instructed. "Ms. Kilodrist and her associates will be with you when she arrives." She turned and left the room, closing the door behind her.

They each took a chair, Laleitha and Elise sticking together at the end of the row, Gerald in the middle, Darren next to him, and Anton between him and Talious, while Ellington took head of the table. Gerald drummed his fingers on the table, obviously uncomfortable with the silence.

Elise, however, enjoyed the quiet stillness, finally giving her mind a break to let everything sink in. She glanced at Laleitha, who was staring over her shoulder at the exotic city outside. Elise knew exactly what Lee was thinking and, in all honesty, she thought the same thing. As frightening as this place was, it was nothing short of amazing.

Her thoughts were interrupted when the door opened again. A small, Asian-looking woman stepped in, with coarse black hair tied back in a bun, a thin face, and lots of precisely applied makeup. Following her was a tall man wearing a black and blue uniform with many badges and pins on the chest and hat; on his arm was a gold, white, and black flag. Behind them were two others; one was a young girl who looked about their age, like she could almost be the daughter of the first woman, with bright, large brown eyes and long black hair. The last to enter was a thin young man with curly brown hair, a pointed chin, and glasses so thick they made his blue eyes look twice their size.

They sat down on the opposite side of the table, across from the Majors. The girl went down to the very end and sat at the tail, laying down her notepad in front of her and clicking her pen.

The woman cleared her throat and grinned. "I'm so sorry to have kept you waiting. My name is Yugie Kilodrist." She stuck her hand across the table for each of the five to shake one by one. "I have studied the Lumire for years, so it is such an honor to finally meet the five remaining Majors," she said cheerfully as she shook their hands. "This is Captain Ferris Westbecker." She gestured to the uniformed man next to her, who nodded politely. "And this is—"

"Simon Arlington." The young man interrupted, introducing himself, shaking their hands. "I am Emperor Evanstin's personal representative."

Ms. Kilodrist cleared her throat. "And this"—she gestured at the girl down the table—"is my assistant, Lillian Lureman."

The girl gave a small smile.

"So," Kilodrist began, "let's get down to business. In order to become a Major, you must first be a Lumerian citizen, and in order to become a citizen, you must be inducted by Orphia and listed in Orphia's book."

"What's Orphia's book?" Darren asked, exchanging confused looks with the other four.

Ellington leaned forward in his chair. "It is his official registration for all Lat citizens, and it also lists which empire they belong to," he explained.

"Ah," Darren said.

"We'll send an ambassador to discuss trial dates first thing tomorrow. On a different note, you will be training here until you are officially named Majors. The minimum age for induction is sixteen years. How old are each of you?"

"Eighteen," Darren replied.

"Sixteen," said Elise.

"Fifteen," said Laleitha.

"Seventeen," answered Gerald.

"Fifteen," peeped Anton, shy as a mouse.

She pursed her lips. "Hmm, okay. Traditionally, those are very old ages to start training, but that is something we'll just have to work with."

Elise bit her inner lip. She didn't get the sense these people were very optimistic about working with them.

"Mr. Talious will handle your combat training, and Mr. Ellington has volunteered to be your sponsor on the Lumerian Council until you are officially Majors. When will training begin, Mr. Talious?"

"Tomorrow morning. You can begin transitioning with them in the afternoon."

"Good. The sooner the better." She turned to Lillian at the end of the table. "Cancel all meetings, classes, and consultations from twelve thirty to seven on weekdays and reserve them for transitioning."

"Yes, ma'am," the girl replied. "For which months?"

"The next three as of right now." She turned back to them. "Captain Westbecker will assign someone to supply you with our military protocols when Mr. Talious deems you ready for strategy training. A space has been reserved for you in a suite not far from here. As per custom, the Majors will be staying at the central location of the Lumerian Council until officially inducted. Lillian will lead you there. Mr. Arlington, is everything in order?"

"Yes, ma'am," the young man replied. "Though I would like to double-check the material that is being supplied by Captain Westbecker to make sure he is familiar as to which files are appropriate."

The man sighed. "That won't be necessary. I am perfectly familiar with our system of compartmentalization."

"And I would also like to look into the credentials and authorization of Mr. Talious—"

"That won't be necessary either, Simon. I am qualified to train the Majors," Talious interrupted through gritted teeth.

"But given your service record . . ."

"Just"—Ellington put up a hand—"let it go. He was elected for the job by the council."

"Though he is not a council member, and the emperor took no part in this election," the young man persisted, "so it would be in my best interest to look into his credentials on the emperor's behalf."

Ms. Kilodrist sighed. "All right. Lillian, you may escort the Majors to their training site. It shouldn't take much longer to clear up this issue. They don't need to hear it."

Lillian stood. "Yes, ma'am." She walked around the edge of the table. "Follow me," she said as the others argued behind them.

She led them back to the elevator and down to the first floor, then out of the building entirely, through the courtyard, onto an overpass to cross the street, and into the lobby of the nearest building, which, Elise soon realized, was a hotel. She'd been so busy taking in her surroundings during the walk she hadn't paid attention to where she was going.

The girl led them past the desk, to a small staircase, and then up, taking them to a small empty room with a single door on each wall. She stepped aside and let them tentatively enter the room, before retreating back to the staircase. "Talious will be joining you soon to unlock your rooms," she said. "Hopefully." Then left.

)(

"This is where you'll be living until you're inducted," Talious told them when he finally arrived. "But you'll be spending most of your time at Fort Kingshold. If you have half a brain, you've realized by now that Fort Kingshold isn't a literal *fort*. It's called that because it's home to the League of Lumeria, the emperor's personally selected team tasked with the protection of Arc City and the Lumerian Council." He began fumbling with his keys, trying to find the right one as he began to open the door across from the one they had entered. "It's also where the council meets, obviously, and one of the places where the emperor and the Arc Leaders work."

The door popped open, but before he allowed them in, he turned back to them and continued talking. "Fort Kingshold has a good number of purposes, but the most important, as far as I'm concerned, is that it's where the League of Lumeria trains. When the Majors first started being raised and trained here, too, a specific section of League equipment was reserved for them. For us, that means it has all that we need to train you like the previous Majors were trained."

He then pointed to the doors on either side of them. "Those are the offices, which are for your supervisors and instructors. For now, that means me, Ellington, and Ms. Kilodrist. Once you're properly transitioned, Captain Westbecker will replace Kilodrist." Then, he tapped the door he had just opened. "This door leads to your living quarters. There should be a room for each of you, and Ellington will bring you clothes and toiletries in the morning. Go there now and rest up. I know it was morning when we left the Other Society, but if you haven't noticed, there's a good nine-hour time difference here. You have a big day tomorrow and didn't get a lot of sleep last night, so some rest should help. Be ready to train by *eight* tomorrow."

The five agreed, and with that, Talious opened the door for them, bidding them goodnight and making his way back to the stairwell.

Elise found herself suddenly apprehensive in the absence of Talious and wasn't entirely eager to see the new space she'd be living in just yet. Settling into a new life meant letting go of her old one. Regardless, she followed the others as they filed through the door. It opened into a large living room with a kitchen connected on the far end, a few bedrooms on one side, and a staircase leading to the other bedrooms on the opposite side. It resembled an almost-luxury hotel suite, with the north wall made entirely of glass looking out at the city, dark wood floor polished and clean, and curtains reaching all the way up to the tall ceiling.

Elise grabbed the first bedroom she reached, opening it to reveal a small, plain room with bed, lamp, mirror, and nightstand.

That was enough for her. She tossed the notebook onto the nightstand then flopped on the bed, letting her body sink into the chilly, smooth comforter, burying her face in the fluff.

If she was home, it would be about ten o'clock in the morning. She would be sitting in English class reading about people she didn't care about and writing about their problems that she could hardly relate to. Nope. She was here, preparing to learn about Lumerian culture, and various forms of combat, and how to use whatever exotic substance had apparently been in her blood for a good sixteen years. Elise couldn't settle her mixed feelings on the matter.

Elise strained her muscles as she pushed herself up off the bed. There was a clock above it that she hadn't noticed before, and it read 9:00 p.m. It felt like several hours since she had arrived in the Arc City, but it hadn't even been one. She resisted the urge to collapse back down onto the bed.

She reemerged from the room to find Anton in the kitchen, gazing out the glass wall. The rest were either showering or sleeping.

"Knock knock," a voice from behind sounded.

Both Elise and Anton turned to see Ellington entering from the hallway, a stack of clothes in his hands.

"I brought some clothes—wasn't sure on the sizes. They should suffice until you get a chance to go out and buy your own." He set the stack on the couch, and the kids were immediately drawn to it. "I was supposed to bring them tomorrow morning, but I thought you'd appreciate them now. I *would* take you back to your houses so you could've packed, but the Prime Devise has resources everywhere and I don't want to risk your family's safety."

"The Prime Devise?" Elise repeated, looking up from sifting through the clothes.

"The people searching for you. The man who tested you is called Second Reighba, the son of Alfred Reighba, who is the chancellor of the Prime Devise. They are Inseanans. Ms. Kilodrist will explain them to you."

"Hmm. Okay," Elise said, not even bothering to pry on.

My supervisor will explain, Talious had said. *Ms. Kilodrist will explain,* Ellington said. Elise was beginning to sense a pattern.

"Thanks for the clothes," she told him.

He nodded. "Yup. Anytime. Tomorrow night, you guys can go out and get your own. I can pay."

Elise grinned. "Thanks!"

He nodded again and turned to leave, before Elise called for him. "Mr. Ellington?"

The man turned back to her, eyebrows raised. "Yes?"

"I have a question," she began, shifting in her stance as she attempted to word it properly.

"Well, I imagine you have many," Ellington said. "Ask away!"

"Um," she stammered, still trying to find her words. "How do you . . . *tell* if someone is Lumerian?"

Ellington raised an eyebrow.

"I mean, where I come from, you can usually tell where someone's family or ancestors are from based on their features like skin color or name or accent . . . but I'm seeing a bit of everything here."

The man smiled. "Ah, I can see how you are confused. Well, I cannot give you any explanation that you would like. The Lumerians and the people of the Other Society are often very similar when compared side by side. They are both human, after all. However, within the Lat empires, there *are* some general differences in respect to region. For example, people farther south tend to be of darker complexion and people of far east Inseana usually have a distinct accent. Furthermore, it is not uncommon for people of the Other Society to move here upon discovering it, but this usually happens when they marry a Lumerian or Inseanan. Lumeria has diversified quite a bit since its beginning, especially recently."

Elise thought about this. "So, there is no way to tell if somebody in the Other Society is actually Lumerian?"

"Honestly," Ellington said, "the best indication is the name. Lumerian names are different from that of America's. Some aren't very different, but some are. It is a tricky business."

She nodded, figuring this was the best answer she would get. "Okay," she said. "Thank you, Mr. Ellington."

He nodded. "Always welcome, Miss Montason."

With that, he turned away and left the room, leaving Elise alone with the persistent feeling that she did not yet belong here.

CHAPTER TEN

Catching Up

"Where on earth are we, do you think?" Elise asked the others after two hours of trying and failing to fall asleep. They sat around the kitchen island, except for Anton, who sat by the large windows, staring out at the city. "Should I ask someone? Do you think I'd get an answer?"

"Some island?" guessed Gerald, looking up from the newspaper spread out in front of him, which Ellington had left under the pile of clothes. "I really don't know how they've managed to keep all this from the rest of the world."

"Some shared fever dream, probably," muttered Darren.

"Well, I don't really care right now," Laleitha replied. "What I care about is finding out who is after us, why, and when are they going to leave us be."

"Ellington mentioned that the people who are after us are part of this thing called the Prime Devise, and they are probably after us *because* we're Majors," Elise explained, sharing what little knowledge she had on the subject.

"The Prime Devise? What is that supposed to mean?" Lee said.

"I don't know," Elise answered, shaking her head. "But apparently we're a big deal."

"Are they like terrorists? A political party? What?"

"A political party? Do you think they're Lumerian Nazis?" Elise laughed. "No. He said they're Inseanans, so I guess that means they aren't exactly in favor of Lumerian protection."

Lee snorted. "Us? Protection? Right. And that seems like pretty aggressive foreign policy. "

Elise shrugged. "I'm just telling you what he told me."

"Hey, look at this," Gerald said, pointing to a story in the newspaper. "That guy Orphia that Ellington was telling us about—he has a son. And this son is missing."

"Orphia's the guy with the court, right?" Lee said. "And he's . . . immortal? That can't be right."

"What did Ellington say?" Elise asked, looking around. "Immortal, right? Eternal judge?"

"I don't know," Darren said, shaking his head.

"Well, he has a kid, and this kid had been missing for decades," Gerald said. "And your Hank friend is the number-one suspect. They have a story in here about his death."

Elise frowned. "What does it say?"

Gerald scanned the article. "Well, they're saying this guy has been using the alias Hank Martinez for years, and they didn't realize it until they tied him to the search for Orphia's missing son. Apparently when they came asking questions, he tried to sabotage the investigation to protect some secret about the missing son, and when the Lumerian Security Enforcement closed in on him, he started killing."

Not possible. Marty would never murder anyone.

Gerald read on. "They say he's responsible for the death of eleven LSE officers. Ten have been confirmed, but the body of number eleven was never found . . . After number eleven went missing, the trail went cold and they were never able to find him again . . . But now they know he was living in the suburbs of 'the Other Society,' with a capital O and S, for fifteen years."

"Right across the street from me," Elise said solemnly, unable to hide her growing distress at what Gerald was reading.

"Then," he continued, "an LSE officer in the Other Society reported Hank to have died on the nineteenth of April with 'mysterious burn marks on his chest forming the Old Lat symbol for *stones.*"

That's what the burn was. What does 'stones' mean?

"The same officer reported that she'd discovered why the Council of Orphia wasn't able to find him—because he was building something called a *vortex harnesser,* which blocks their vision. I don't know what any of that means."

He looked up to scan the faces of the others, which were just as blank as his, before looking back down at the article. "And it looks like the rest of the article is just a long pondering of whether or not his death means the story is over or there's some greater conspiracy in the works," Gerald finished, looking back up at Elise.

They were all looking at her now; even Anton had slunk over from his place at the window to give Elise an inquisitive look.

She swallowed the lump forming in her throat and took a breath. "I refuse to believe it," she declared. "He wouldn't hurt a fly."

"Well, apparently, he did a little more than that," Darren said.

Elise looked back down at the picture of Hank in the paper. It *was* him and Elise resented it. She resented *him. If* any of this were true—and none of it was—it meant he had built up a lie to live under, foolishly thinking his old life wouldn't come back to bite him. He came to care about people and brought them to care about him too. It made her sick.

She bit back her spite and let out a sigh. "This still doesn't explain his death. And the burn marks—what do you suppose they mean by *stones*?"

"Maybe he was killed with a rock," Darren said with a snicker.

"I think it could be part of a serial element," Elise suggested. "Serial killers usually leave a signature, or a clue to their next killing, or something along those lines."

"Mont, stop. You read too many murder mystery books," Lee said.

"Yeah, the killing may not have even been related to . . . all this," Gerald said, gesturing around him. "But it most likely is, given that he was building a, what did they call it, a vortex harnesser? What does that do?"

"I think that was the machine we saw at Silver Industries," Elise said. "That could be what the article was referring to. I could ask Ellington if he knows."

She hoped it was the machine she saw at Silver Industries. Then maybe she could go back and examine it, perhaps try to build one herself. Elise didn't know what it did, but she desperately wanted to find out and could probably do so while assembling it. If she did figure it out, it could hint at what her friend had been up to.

"Whatever it was, it used the same energy source as the transportation rods," Anton pointed out.

"So far, that's been the common denominator of Lumerian technology," Laleitha said.

"He was probably living a double life," Anton added.

"I guess, technically, so are we at the moment," Gerald added. He tossed the paper aside. "I'm hungry. Is there any food around here?"

"Nope," Darren said. "Ellington is brining us breakfast soon. I did find a ten-year-old box of instant rice, though, if that interests you."

"I'll have to pass."

✕

By eight o'clock, they were changed into workout clothes and down in the training gym in Fort Kingshold, which Ellington had led them to, awaiting Talious. Ellington arrived early in the morning to offer them breakfast, which ended up being some Lumerian ham-based dish called *falitan,* before showing them the way to the gym. After a few moments of silence, Talious burst through the doors and strode into the middle of the room.

"Good, you're here on time," was the only preamble he gave. "Training starts now. How many of you know how to punch?"

They looked at him blankly.

"Uh, I've thrown a few punches before," Darren said.

"Fight club or schoolyard brawl? Because neither of those will suffice," Talious responded, silencing him. "We have a lot of work to do, so let's start simple."

He led them to the punching bags and demonstrated the punching technique, talking them through it as he went. He spent little time on strikes, however, before moving on to blocking and dodging. Talious's style was strict and hardened, and Elise had to try very hard not to resent it. A slow response or slight slipup in technique meant "personal physical improvement" of Talious's choosing, which usually meant running laps, push-ups, or sit-ups. He taught them proper kicking techniques, testing their flexibility constantly. He showed them takedown techniques, strategic positioning, and how to use the opponent's momentum to their advantage. The emphasis mainly rested in defensive strategies. "You're not skilled yet," Talious said. "Not nearly at the level of anyone you'd be unfortunate enough to face. But if you can defend yourself for long enough, opportunities will open up."

By the end of the hour and a half of tedious repetition and strenuous practicing, the five were exhausted. Talious, however, refused to cease fire and, after their combat session, gave them cardio and strength-training exercises.

"In the future, we'll have a rotation," Talious informed them. "Half combat, half strength training; the next day, half combat half cardio training; then a full day of combat training; repeat."

At the end of the third hour, Talious instructed them on stretching then sent them off to wash up.

Transitioning started at twelve thirty. Feeling tired but somewhat refreshed, Elise waited in the living room of the living quarters for Ellington to retrieve them.

"Any idea what transitioning is?" Gerald asked from the armchair.

Elise shook her head. "Your guess is as good as mine."

At twelve twenty, Ellington and Talious arrived with a cheerful greeting and a short "hello," respectively, and led them through the building to a skyway that took them to an indoor train station. They waited awkwardly in the crowd, surprised they weren't catching any strange looks from the others who waited with them, all of whom were well into adulthood and dressed in suits.

When the monorail train arrived, Ellington and Talious led them inside and placed them in a seat across from none other than Yugie Kilodrist, sitting with perfect posture, pursed lips, and hands folded in her lap. The seats were wide enough for all five of them to squish together on one side, while Ellington and Talious took their seats beside Ms. Kilodrist.

"Hello again," she greeted. "This is where our transitioning will begin. Now we are going to start by explaining the norms of Lumerian culture to you, as well as our connection with the other empires, and catching you up on the basic important events in our history. Sound good?"

Everyone nodded somewhat hesitantly.

"Good. Now, if you haven't already been told, you are in Arc City, the official capital of Lumeria," she said as she removed an odd-looking tablet from her bag beside her. On the tablet, she opened a presentation then turned it so they could see. "Originally there were seven different capitals, one for each country in the empire, guarded by each Major, but Arc City became the center of all the nations' activities in what is called the Redrawing of 1864. This was a very significant event in Lumerian history because it restructured our system of government to the one we have today. The first Major's city, Sappol Storm, was lost to the Juperds—we'll cover how this happened later—and the Major who was initially assigned to Sappol Storm would float around, traveling to the places she was needed in. Soon after, the second Major's city, Sappol Central, was destroyed by a separate attack, another thing that we will cover later. Each of the Major's cities stood as capitals of the Lumeria's countries at the time, and because there were then only five capitals to seven states, some reconstruction was necessary. At the same time, though the states were united under an emperor, they were all mainly autonomous and strikingly different in both ethnicity and governmental structure. Lumeria wasn't so much an empire at that time as it was a confederation. Then, in response to the destruction of Sappol Central, the Conference of 1864 was held. There, it was decided that the countries' lines should be redrawn so that Lumeria consisted of only five countries rather than seven, putting the Arc City as the center of all Lumerian activities. This conference also led to structural changes in the government such that Lumerian power was more centralized under the emperor."

She pushed a map in front of them. "The five countries that make up Lumeria are Staris in the far north, Pallian in the west, Lestin in the east, Elevis in the southwest and Ikollis in the southeast. The capital of each of these is one of the five remaining Major's cities, meaning that the city was built with the Major's tower at the center. When you are officially inducted as Majors, this will be where you reside."

They studied the map in front of them.

Lumeria and its five countries sat at the eastern side of the map, with Inseana next to it at the west. Above these two, a triangle cut dented the northern borders of both empires, comprised of several smaller states of unfamiliar names.

"What are these?" Elise asked, tracing her fingers along the names.

"Those are the countries that arose as a result of the Juperd Empire collapsing," Ms. Kilodrist answered.

"Wait, when did that happen?" Laleitha cut in.

"Oh, I'm sorry. I thought Stanford told you," she said. "The Juperds and the Inseanans were allies in the War of the Three Empires. We, the Lumerians, were victorious, and the Juperds were left in ruins, as their territory was the main battlefeild. The Inseanans failed to provide sufficient aid to the Juperds, instead focusing all their efforts on their own recovery, which led to a chain of events that resulted in Juperd dying and becoming several small, usually peaceful territories." Kilodrist explained. "This one—" She pointed to one next to Staris, Lumeria. It was among the largest of the Juperdian countries, with bold, red letters spelling out "Trimeterous" within it. Near its border was its capital city titled *Stormy City.*

"This one sits on a lot of territory that was once part of Lumeria before being taken by the Juperds in the War of the Three Empires. When the Juperds collapsed soon after that, Trimeterous was the first country to establish itself. Its capital, the Stormy City, was built on what once was Sappol Storm, the Major's city. Trimeterous is currently the richest territory in all of the Lat Empires. I feel that you will learn much more about the Stormy City the longer you stay here . . ."

She exchanged glances with Ellington, who tapped her tablet as if to tell her to continue.

"You are probably right, Ms. Kilodrist, but the Stormy City isn't of much significance to them at the moment."

"Why didn't we try to get that territory back?" Laleitha asked.

Kilodrist waved a hand. "Many reasons. For one, we thought it was useless. The flat plains and constant storming made it hard to harvest crops, there was no valuable minerals, only one major river. We also were left weak, even in our state of victory, and the Juperds—what was left of them—refused to diplomatically give up that land."

Ignoring the confused looks of her students, she continued on with her presentation. The words "Lumerian Civil War" crossed the screen. "This," Kilodrist said, "is the most recent and relevant historical event you will learn about today."

Elise tilted her head as she listened to the woman explain.

"During the emperorship of Trace Orbeck, there occurred a series of events that left a large percentage of the population in poverty, as well as exposing a certain level of corruption in the council. As controversy arose within the capital about how to combat the corruption, the people, whose dire needs were being brushed aside, grew angry at the emperor's form of governing. They called the Majors to act, and a separatist state formed under the Major's protection. Thus, the civil war began in 1968. It lasted for five and a half years before Lumeria prevailed. The Majors were held accountable for the rebellion and given a five-year exile to the Other Society."

"And that's when you lost them," Gerald finished.

She nodded. "The council lost contact seven months into their sentence."

"Until you found us," Darren added. "And that still doesn't really make sense to me. How did you find us?"

Kilodrist sighed. "That entire situation is strange and difficult to explain. We have been preparing for a few years now, ever since the critical need for you has begun growing more . . . well, critical. We were investigating the machine that Martinez was working on when we realized that the Prime Devise had already found you. We then took you from there."

"You were investigating the machine?" Elise repeated. "Why? How did you know about it?"

"Our discovery of the machine was the byproduct of a different investigation in the area. I'm not at liberty to discuss it."

"Then why didn't Talious seem to know about it back there at Silver Industries?" Laleitha asked.

"Talious's job was simply to retrieve you five and nothing else. He didn't need to know about it," Kilodrist explained. "We didn't expect to need to send him in. The plan was to approach you each individually and explain the situation gently. It was our people who investigated the machine who noticed the presence of Prime Devise officers in the same area, but we didn't realize the Prime Devise was planning an abduction until it was too late."

"Hold on," Laleitha said. "What the *hell* is the Prime Devise?"

"That is what I was getting to next," Kilodrist said. "The original Inseanan order has lost sovereignty over many of its territories, and the power is being taken by a state known as the Prime Devise. They are currently governed by a man named Alfred Reighba, who is probably one of the most brilliant but most dangerous people alive. The Prime Devise is basically his way of overthrowing the Inseanan Order, without a war and without the country falling apart. Prime Devise power has been rising since the 1930s, replacing the reign of the order with one of their own."

"Why doesn't the order stop them?" Laleitha asked. "How is the Prime Devise taking over without anybody else putting up a fight?"

Ellington shook his head. "Inseana was collapsing in on itself when the Prime Devise was created. In fact, that was the main reason it was created. The Prime Devise started as a coup in Insen"—he tapped the map before them, which showed Insen to be the easternmost territory in Inseana—"which went remarkably well, seeing as very little violence followed. Anyway, by the time the order figured out how to respond, they found themselves lacking the resources they needed. They had an incredibly weak army and incredible poverty and dependence rates. While the original order sank, the Prime Devise began to thrive under their new leadership. They just couldn't afford to put up a fight against a rising power that had double the resources they lacked."

Ms. Kilodrist nodded. "In fact, it was the falling of Inseana that allowed the Prime Devise such power in the first place. The people wanted change, a new order, and the Prime Devise gave it to them. Under them, they saw quick improvement, so power quickly spread."

Gerald lowered his eyebrows. "It almost sounds like the Prime Devise *saved* Inseana."

Ellington shrugged. "One may view it that way. But a powerful Inseana makes for a paranoid Lumeria. With good reason, of course. Relations between the two empires have never been friendly. Not since their creation."

"This line"—Kilodrist traced her finger across a blue line that encircled a large portion of Inseana—"marks the edge of their power."

Elise studied Inseana. It was broken into three countries: Insen, which was completely swallowed by the Prime Devise; Tensinire, below Insen, which still belonged to the original order; and Wilph in the west, which was split in two by the blue line.

The cold fear that had been stirring in Elise's chest since the night before was beginning to seep into her skin again. She forced herself to keep a neutral expression as she listened to the woman speak on.

"We believe their intentions to be sinister, as they have been spying on both us and their neighboring nations. Our intelligence suggests they are building an army. They . . . they have also dedicated a curious amount of resources, so we understand, to the search for the Lost Son of Orphia."

"That is why you need us now, isn't it?" Anton said. "You said there was a 'critical need' and the Prime Devise is it."

Kilodrist nodded grimly. "We believe they pose a threat to Lumerian society. When they sent a bounty hunter out for you, that was a sure sign that they are planning against us."

Elise's heart sank as the cold tingle under her skin began to intensify. She was supposed to protect a nation, *an empire,* against a growing, organized army that could attack at any minute, when she had just learned how to punch this morning. She was supposed to reach the bar that her great-great-grandmother who had been born, raised, and trained here since birth had set. There was too much here to process. There was way too much to achieve in such little time.

"Okay," Gerald said slowly. "So what does this son of Orphia have to do with anything? Why is the Prime Devise looking for him?"

Kilodrist pursed her lips. "Well, we have no idea. Orphia's son dropped off the grid in 1967. Orphia asked Lumeria, Inseana, and the Juperd countries to search for him, promising reward. The search was given up until we discovered the Martinez lead. Since then, the Prime Devise has picked up the search as well and has maintained an intense focus on the matter. We think this is an indication that one of their plans involves him or the reward offered for him. If this is true, it could mean a lot of trouble for us."

"Another theory," Ellington said, "is that they want access to Orphia's Tower, which is the most secure place on earth. Only his son and his Omenescents were ever given access to it. The mysteries of what it holds passed into rumors centuries ago, so it's impossible to determine which rumors are true, but the only thing we can confirm is that it is where all the information collected by his Omenescents is stored."

"His Omenesecents," Kilodrist began before somebody could ask, "are also referred to as the Council of Orphia. Like him, they do not age, and possess a variation of the Lumire that gives them irreplaceable gifts."

"There are four of them," Talious added, the first time he had said anything since they began their lesson. "Two can see anything anywhere, one can read minds, and the last can catch glimpses of the future."

Ellington nodded. "Mr. Talious is correct. And they are named in respect to their gifts. Antedal, Avisil, Thentis, and Clair."

"And only Thentis, the mind reader, attends the trials; the others stay in the tower beside his courtroom, directly above his locker," Kilodrist added. "Nobody knows what the other three look like."

"So the Omenesecents have the Lumire too," Laleitha said. "I thought we were the only ones."

Kilodrist shook her head. "The Seven Majors weren't the only ones with the Lumire. It was first given to Orphia when the empires were established, then he gave some to his Omenescents. This original Lumire that they have makes them ageless, and they wouldn't lose it if they were to pass it down to their children. Then, Orphia gave a modified version to the Seven Majors and one Juperd who reigned as queen—she was later killed—and then he offered to give an Inseanan some to balance the scales, but the Inseanans saw such a power as a threat to their order and turned it down. The remaining Lumire was destroyed."

"So now it's only us and Orphia's council people," Darren concluded.

"It is *supposed* to be," Kilodrist responded. "But a phenomenon that has been occurring is what we call 'mistakes.' In a rare case, the Lumire will be passed down to somebody of a different sex, or it will occur in both the first and second child. These people have the Lumire, but their Lumire is harder to control and less powerful."

"So how do we know one of us isn't a mistake?" Elise inquired, one eyebrow raised.

"We don't. But as long as you have the Lumire, you are eligible to be a Major. The point is, there *are* more people out there with the Lumire, but very few." She paused to let that sink in.

Elise was uncomfortably stiff. She had to go through with this, but she wasn't sure she was brave enough to.

Ellington seemed to sense her distress and added, "What is fortunate about mistakes is that their power is usually so weak, they can lead an entire life without even realizing they have it. They pose no threat to you. Not to worry."

Darren cleared his throat. "Where is this train headed?"

A small smile crept onto Kilodrist's face. "We'll start in Sappol West."

"I'm sorry, where?"

"Sappol West means 'west tower' and is the name of a city in Pallain," Ellington explained. "At its heart is a Major's tower."

Kilodrist nodded. "Over the course of your transitioning, we will go to the other standing towers—Sappol North, South, East, and Sunust. These trips will be rather rare, however, since their significant distance makes it inconvenient to be constantly traveling."

"What does 'Sunust' mean?" Gerald asked.

"In Old Lat, it means 'twilight,'" Ellington said in reply.

"But nowadays people just call it Sappol Sun," Talious added with a shrug.

Ms. Kilodrist cleared her throat. "Any other questions?"

The five were silent.

"Okay, this is good. Now today, once we get to Sappol West, we are going to start training you with the Lumire. Tomorrow, I'll begin teaching you the key Lat scientific concepts, which will probably take around a week or two. The next few weeks, I'll be teaching you Old Lat, which is tradition for the Majors to be at least somewhat well versed in, and throughout this entire session, you will be working with the Lumire and training in combat."

The five hardly knew how to react.

"Uh," Gerald grunted. "Ah, okay. Lots to do,"

"Little time, yes, I know, but you have to understand," Kilodrist finished. "Times are growing wilder and . . ." She took a deep breath. "We need the Majors now more than ever."

CHAPTER ELEVEN

The West Tower

Elise had expected a tower similar to the one Hank had given her: plain, simple, small. Never before in her life had she been so incredibly wrong. It wasn't gray but silver and maroon. It loomed above them with the most elaborate and intricate detail Elise had ever seen in a building. The tower was shaped in the most eccentric way a fortress could be but, as Elise's eyes traced the edges, she found each peculiarity had its purpose—secure balconies, windows to look through, windows to fire through, places to mount oneself for whatever reason, and other features that Elise couldn't work out the function of.

Ellington led them to a small doorway. Above the door, several red panels with black symbols were stacked in a vertical line that reached quite far up the tower. Her guide noticed her eyeing them and jumped into an explanation. "Each Major of the tower has their tile added to the column. You will be added to the top once you make yours."

"What do the symbols mean?" Anton wondered.

"Old Lat," Elise said, recognizing the style. "Their name?"

Ms. Kilodrist nodded. "This first one," she said, "says Areinite Rodum."

All eyes turned to Gerald, who sat staring at the panel in stunned silence.

"King's got quite a granddad," Darren remarked with a smirk. "How many generations of Majors are there?"

"You'll be the fiftieth generation," Ms. Kilodrist replied.

"The *fiftieth*?" Gerald exclaimed.

"Milestone," Darren remarked.

"Not all of whom have been accounted for," she went on. "Some chose not to become Majors before Orphia and the emperor agreed that all those with the Lumire must be Majors. And another few have had children and passed down the Lumire before they officially became Majors. Not to mention the generation that has been lost since the civil war. Rodum is the only name that has carried all the way until now. The females are especially harder to keep track of."

Gerald looked back at the door. "So this is my tower?"

"I believe so." She gestured to the door, which, in the direct center, had a black square rimmed with metal and a small, metal circle in the center.

"What is that?" Gerald asked, inspecting it.

"Pierce your thumb," she instructed, producing a small blue needle from a case in her pocket and extending it to him.

"What?"

"Pierce your thumb," she repeated the order. "Draw blood. The needle's plastic; it can cut your skin, but it won't hurt."

Gerald tentatively took the needle from her and poked his thumb, trying not to wince as he pricked himself. A small bulb of scarlet blood began to well, and it wasn't long before it began trailing down across his skin, outlining every ridge and crevice in his fingerprint with the runny red it left in its narrow path.

"Now place your finger on the panel," Kilodrist said, though he had already begun moving forward, figuring that was what he needed to do.

He pressed his thumb against the metal circle in the middle and waited in anticipation.

The others watched the door expectantly from behind. Nothing was happening.

"Now will the door to open," she went on.

"Excuse me?"

"Open the door," she said, "except do it with your mind."

"How do you expect me to do that?" he questioned, turning his head to look at her.

"You're using the Lumire. It should be very simple."

"Oh, really?" Darren said. "It's simple? Have a lot of experience opening doors with your mind?"

Ms. Kilodrist didn't respond to Darren's sarcasm, but a displeased look crossed her face. Instead, she turned her attention back to Gerald.

He looked skeptically back at his thumb. He took a deep breath and then concentrated on the door. To all of their surprise, there was a small *whir* followed by a *click* and the door popped open.

A smile spread across Miss Kilodrist's face upon seeing this, and she said, "Well done."

Elise, Anton, and Gerald alike were all stiff with anticipation. *These towers haven't been opened in years.* Darren and Laleitha, however, didn't hesitate. Darren crowded next to Gerald, pushing the door open even more.

Light poured into the dark area where the door opened, with the three at the door silhouetted in darkness on the wooden floor. Darren's hand groped for a light switch until he finally found it and a small light at the top flickered on.

The room they found themselves in felt straight out of a medieval castle—if medieval castles had light fixtures and electricity. Walls of stone surrounded them, a staircase against the wall going up and other against the left wall going down. An old untouched fireplace sat against the right wall before a long, antique-looking table, lined with chairs of the same style. On the wall hung a large map of the Lat Empires, but it looked to be quite old and had a few notes scribbled on it. Besides these few things, the room was completely empty.

"Whoa," Gerald remarked as he slowly wandered toward the table. "This is where the last Major lived."

"I would offer you a tour," said Ms. Kilodrist, "but I've never been inside a Major's tower before."

"The living quarters are below," Talious said, nodding to the staircase going down. "All the floors above are functional."

"Can we check them out?" Elise asked.

Ms. Kilodrist exchanged glances with Ellington. "I suppose you can explore the second floor, but I think we should limit it to that for now. We have lots to get done."

Excitedly, the five made for the staircase, racing up to see what the second floor was like. This one was divided into four rooms, Elise soon discovered: two rooms of empty shelves and boxes, a study, and a very old, very gross-looking bathroom. Naturally, Elise found herself most interested in the study. Across the walls of this quaint room were maps upon maps, many with lines and directions scribbled on them in black pen. A desk sat near the center of the room, though it appeared to be empty, and a bookshelf was set up against the far wall.

Gerald and Darren walked over to the desk and began rummaging through the drawers as Laleitha inspected books on the bookshelf and Elise and Anton surveyed the maps.

"What do you suppose this is?" Gerald called, taking out a few papers from the bottom drawer.

Elise and the rest clustered around him to see what he held. The first sheet listed several names, none of which Elise recognized, with notes written next to some in red pen; a few were crossed out and a few were circled. The next sheet was a map of a building that Elise was unfamiliar with, but again, there were notes made in red. The last page was too chaotic to make out anything; it had diagrams and notations everywhere, and in the very center, circled, was "*ORPHIA.*"

Elise carefully looked over the papers, interest growing with each one.

"What is that?" Anton asked quietly, pointing back into the drawer at a small black and brown rope.

Darren reached down to pick it up. He lifted it out, and Elise realized it wasn't a rope at all but a scaly dead snake with ruby-colored eyes, dangling limply in front of them by its tail. The minute Darren spotted the head and realized he was holding a snake, he let out a revolted yelp and dropped it onto the desk.

"A snake?" Gerald said, sounding somewhere between disgusted and incredulous.

"Your granddad is messed up, man," Darren told him, wiping his hand on his shirt.

Laleitha bent into inspect it. "It's not real, dummies," she said, picking it up between two fingers. "Look, it's metal." With her other hand, she pried its mouth open, revealing that the unpainted interior was, in fact, metal.

They huddled around it curiously, now comfortable with the fact that they hadn't just found a dead animal in the desk.

"What did Ms. Kilodrist say the Majors were banished for?" Anton asked, eyeing the snake suspiciously.

"They led a rebellion," Laleitha replied, looking back down at paper with the scribbled mess that lay on the desk in front of her.

"It looks like they had a lot more up their sleeve than that," Gerald remarked. "What do you think this means?"

Elise picked up the snake and began inspecting it. She poked her thumbnail into the slit that was supposed to be its mouth and propped it open, peering down its throat. Inside, a network of rods and wires were plastered to the shell of the machine. Small devices that Elise couldn't figure out the purpose of were set up in a pattern across it. Two wires ran from the eyes to a small box in the snake's stomach.

"Looks like it's a camera or recorder of some sort," Elise observed. "It must store the data here." She leaned toward Gerald so he could see, pointing at the small box.

"It's a little spybot," Gerald concluded. "Like, it records what the eyes see."

"That's not suspicious," Laleitha said.

"Why a snake, of all animals?" Darren said. "I mean, they could at least be creative and make it, like, a bug or something since it's a *bug*."

"A bug records audio, dumbass," Lee told him. "Why would a robotic snake record audio with its eyes?"

"Back off, it was a joke!"

"It looks like it has a microphone too," Elise interjected, peering back into the serpent's mouth.

Darren gave Laleitha a smug grin. "There. See? Microphone."

Lee shook her head. "Still not a bug."

"Piss off. That wasn't my point."

"You had a point?"

"My point *was*, why a snake? A snake seems really, I don't know, *sinister*," Darren remarked.

Elise looked back down at the snake in her hand. She thought it looked rather beautiful, but Darren was right, snakes were often seen as a bad omen or symbol of evil in literature and myth. She gave a shrug and set it back on the table.

"What I want to know," Gerald said, "is *why?*"

Anton nodded and opened his mouth to speak, but Ellington suddenly appeared in the doorway. "We should begin training," he said. "You can explore the tower some other time. Now, if you please, let's return to the first floor so we can begin."

All five obeyed, following Ellington back to the first floor, where Ms. Kilodrist had taken five chairs from the table and turned them toward the middle of the room. They each took one.

"Okay," Miss Kilodrist began, stepping into the middle of the room, "from what I have studied about the Lumire, there are two main ways you can use it: to convert and manipulate energy or to change your form."

"Or both," Ellington added.

"Manipulating energy is by far the easier concept to learn, since changing form requires much more concentration and energy and is a multistep process. We probably won't get to that until your second year of training, at the earliest. So, let's start with the basics."

She reached into her bag and removed five small, corked glass bottles, no more than five inches tall, and placed them on the floor a few feet in front of each of them. "One by one, I'm going to have you move the bottle in front of you. What you have to do is concentrate on the bottle as hard as you can. You should feel like you sense it. Once you reach that point, you should be able to control it just by thinking about what you want it to do, just like controlling your limbs."

Darren grimaced at that comparison.

"Who would like to go first?"

"I will," Gerald said.

Elise, and everyone else, turned to watch Gerald, who sat forward in his chair and focused his dark brown eyes on the bottle on the floor.

The room was silent, all eyes on their friend, who had so much intensity in his gaze that Elise was almost certain the bottle would burst into flames. He was beginning to tremble now, unconsciously holding his breath, before relaxing his muscles and sitting back in his chair. He was probably about to say something along the lines of "I can't do it," but at the very moment he relaxed, the glass bottle shot up to the ceiling. Ms. Kilodrist jumped back and Ellington let out a startled cry, as Elise and the other three flinched when the bottle hit the floor and shattered.

Everyone stared at it in astonishment.

Elise looked from the shards on the ground to Gerald, then back to the shards. "How did you do that?"

He put a hand to his forehead, looking ecstatic. "I don't know. I, I felt *something*. I tried to control it but I, I don't know—I couldn't."

Ellington beamed. "Well done! Well done, Mr. Rodum. We didn't expect you to even move it at all, yet you threw it at the ceiling!"

Ms. Kilodrist was giving him a slightly exasperated look as he spoke. She then straightened her blouce and cleared her throat. "You next, Laleitha?"

Laleitha, who was sitting closest to Gerald, didn't say anything. Her stare started as a glare, but slowly her eyes lit up, and a look of intensity began to turn to a look of interest.

Elise glanced at the bottle, which didn't move. Her sister was feeling something, Elise could tell, but the bottle didn't seem to be doing anything. Then, Elise smelled it before she saw it. *Something is burning.* Then, the cork began to smolder. Elise almost laughed for her sister, delighted at her success.

Her sister let out a breath, and her eyes grew unfocused. Laleitha carried a look of mixed excitement and shock on her face when she looked at Elise, who only smiled back.

Ms. Kilodrist then gave Darren a nod, and his face turned slightly pinker. "Me? No, I don't think so." He eyed the bottle nervously, almost afraid of what it would do.

"Go on," Ellington encouraged. "Do you want to be a Major or not?"

"Not really," he muttered under his breath, but neither Ellington nor Ms. Kilodrist heard him.

He reluctantly leaned forward and focused on the bottle. Minutes passed as nothing happened, and Darren began to grow frustrated. "Nothing," he growled.

"You can try again later," Ms. Kilodrist assured him. "We will come back to you. Anton?"

Anton shrugged and turned to the bottle. After a few minutes of staring, he merely achieved a wobble, the bottle tilting slightly one way, then rocking back the other. Ellington and Kilodrist seemed pleased with that, meaning it was Elise's turn next.

"You're up, *Mont*," Gerald said with a snicker, using Laleitha's nickname for Elise.

Elise looked at the bottle. It was so still, lifeless, and distant. How could she possibly make it move? She concentrated on it, imagining what it would feel like, willing it to fall to its side and roll along the ground in front of her. Then, she felt the familiar pulse in her forehead and it was as if the world collapsed in on her. She could feel everything in the room, the body heat of her friends, the chill of the smooth, cold floor, the glass of the bottle, stable and solid. She could even feel the slight tingle of dust particles in the air.

It was overwhelming. Everything around her stirred and she felt it all at once, as if it were all connected to her. It all built up inside her like a fire in a corked bottle. She had to focus this energy on something, and she directed all of her senses toward her target. She felt it in much more detail now, with everything else out of focus. This state was incredibly difficult to maintain, as every time she thought about how she could no longer sense the walls of the room, they would come back into focus. *All I have to do was move it a few inches. This shouldn't be so hard.* It was if her imaginary hand closed around it, but as she tried to hoist it in any direction, it seemed to resist. Her attempts to move it with her mind were as useless as using a plastic spoon to lift a concrete block.

Finally, the tension within her rose to her head, and her skull felt like it was compressing both ends of her brain. Elise let herself grow unfocused, and the pulsing in her forehead slowed, and then stopped. Her senses seemed to contract until they fit back into her body, and all of the energy she felt was now memory.

She didn't bother looking at her friends, but her disappointed gaze remained on the small bottle.

Gerald went again, this time, moving one shard of glass a few centimeters forward. Anton tried next. He didn't move the bottle, but the map on the wall ended up falling from its suspensions and shooting toward him, causing everyone to start. Darren went again, and Elise could've sworn the cork loosened a bit. Then, she tried once more.

The pulsing began and the room grew more familiar around her. Her senses reached outside of her once more, stroking the walls and embracing the warm bodies of her friends. At first, the sensation was overwhelming; once again, information flowed to her brain like a waterfall, filling it with chaos. She winced as this happened, still not used to this kind of discomfort, but quickly targeted her senses on the bottle. Again, the bottle refused to move, even when she began pushing herself to the point of pain. The pulsing in her forehead grew deafening. Every heartbeat seemed to rattle her ribcage more than the next. Her skin felt as if it were tightening around her as she focused every fiber of her being on the bottle on the floor. Nothing happened.

The pain was overpowering.

Finally, she gave up, sighing and running a hand through her hair, not surprised to feel sweat there. How was it that she could push herself to the point of nearly excruciating pain and make no progress whatsoever? Gerald moved the bottle, Anton moved the bottle, Laleitha nearly set the bottle on fire, and even Darren got at least a hint of something. Shame began to burn in her cheeks. She was on the *verge* of progress; she could feel the Lumire working, but still nothing happened. The Lumire was having physical effects on her by the time she gave up: sweating, trembling, heartrate spiking. How was it possible to exude so much effort and not even have a glimmer of success to show for it? It maddened her.

"I can't." She let her body slump miserably, her fingers curling into white-knuckled fists. "I can *feel* the bottle there, but it won't budge," she gritted out, drawing in a shaky breath to calm herself. "It *hurts*."

She didn't look at her friends but kept her glare on Ellington as he approached. He knelt in front of her seat. "This isn't about moving a bottle," he told her softly.

"Isn't it?"

"The fact that you felt it there means that you initiated the Lumire on command, which means progress."

Elise sat forward, hands trembling in front of her, the burn of frustration beneath her skin refusing to cease. "It's not amounting to anything! What will I be able to do against the Prime Devise if they come for me, and my sister, and all I can do is *feel* them there?"

"Look inside of yourself, Elise," he said, his gentle tone unwavering. "You'll find that you're so much more than you could've ever imagined. Here, you are faced with two choices. The first is to stop now and leave that part of yourself undiscovered, let your potential stay just that and become your shackles, or you can endure the pain and let it be your liberation. You were meant for so much more than this, but if you cannot take the pain, then this is who you will be. Your work won't amount to anything unless you put yourself through a great deal of pain to complete it."

Elise considered these words before reaching up to tuck a strand of loose hair behind her ear and nodding. "Okay," she said.

"Don't get frustrated yet. That comes later."

"Great."

Ellington grinned. "Good then, but now it is your sister's turn. Hopefully she doesn't fry her bottle before you get a chance to try again."

Laleitha was the last to go a second time.

Come on, Lee. Elise watched her sister begin to focus herself on the bottle. Again, the orange glow of heat began to sizzle from the cork. Then, suddenly, to everyone's fright, the cork burst into a storm of uncontrollable fire, reaching all the way up to the ceiling, filling the room with a flickering orange light.

All except Anton and Laleitha jumped to their feet. Ms. Kilodrist let out a shriek as she stumbled away from the column of fire in front of her. Elise watched with wide eyes as clouds of black smoke rolled to the ceiling and spread across it to the walls. Gerald had exclaimed something to which Darren had replied—likely sarcastically—but Elise couldn't hear over Ms. Kilodrist's cries.

The bedlam was brought to an abrupt end when Ellington threw his coat onto the burning bottle and began patting it furiously.

When Ellington sat back on his heels, Elise and the others finally calmed.

Anton was laughing in his seat.

When Ellington removed his jacket, the half-melted bottle and burned-to-a-crisp cork sat there motionlessly, the fire fully extinguished.

"Okay, I think that is enough with the bottles today," Ms. Kilodrist said hastily.

"Moving on," Ellington agreed, standing up. "Time for activity two."

※

Since Laleitha had a knack for setting things on fire, Ms. Kilodrist decided next to teach them to channel their body energy into a manipulatable form. She placed a little piece of paper in their hands and told them to use their body heat to set it on fire. It took Elise a while, but she eventually got it smoldering from the base before burning her hand and dropping it quickly while Gerald and her sister laughed.

What astounded all of them was Anton's progress. Though he wasn't able to set it on fire, he had folded it in half, which Ms. Kilodrist and Ellington found most phenomenal.

Slowly, they began to grow more enthusiastic about their training.

"It's addictive," Elise remarked, concentrating on the paper to spark another flame. "I could do this all day . . . never mind, I'm getting a headache."

Meanwhile, Darren pestered Anton for tips on how he was able to fold the paper so easily. "Come on, I *know* you know," he said. "Just tell me, like, what you were thinking about."

"I was thinking about moving the paper," Anton answered flatly.

"Yeah, but *how* were you thinking about it?"

Gerald glanced between them. "How many different ways are there to think about moving paper?"

"I'm going to make an origami bird," Anton decided, picking up another slip of paper.

※

Their next exercise was Elise's least favorite. Their instructors ordered them to run eight laps around the nearby block, until they were sweating through their skin, then told them to transfer the energy from the grass beneath their bare feet to themselves until they were no longer tired.

The block was probably a half mile, and Elise had finished her laps panting, with excruciating pain in her side and blurred vision. When she stepped onto the cold wet grass, she didn't have the focus or patience to suck the energy out of plants. Her skin was on fire, and it wasn't long before she collapsed. She sank into the dew-covered grass, feeling the chilly touch of its bristly fingers. Then, her forehead pulsed again, and suddenly, the grass around her stiffened, making a strange, crackling sound. The burning within Elise began to die, as if the fire had run out of oxygen, and her legs, which felt like lead, began to lighten. She opened her eyes to find that the grass on which she lay was now crusted with ice.

Ellington and Kilodrist were smiling down at her as she rolled over.

"Well done, Miss Montason," Ellington said.

Elise groaned as another energy surge worked its way into her veins, this time being almost painful as her body adjusted to this new state so quickly. She sat up and put her head in her hands.

Laleitha had just finished her laps and Anton had nearly finished. It almost hurt to look at Anton, skinnier than a broomstick, his ribs were visible through his sweat-plastered shirt, which now stuck to his skin. The older boys, however, had finished before both of them, neither able to get the same results as Elise.

"Save some energy for tonight, kids," Ellington said. "You still have training with Talious."

Everyone groaned.

𝕏

"What do you think the snake was about?" Darren asked that night after long hours of training with Talious. Ellington had stopped by, offering to do some shopping for them and pick up anything they needed, additionally promising them each a toothbrush and hygiene products, more clothing, their own small wallets of Lumerian money, and, for the girls, lady products, just in case. Now, they sat around the coffee table in their living quarters, exhausted, as they waited for his return.

"I mean, what possible use is there for a small metal snake with camera eyes besides spying?" Darren added.

"I don't know—maybe checking to see if the bathroom is occupied?" Gerald offered.

"I'd still classify that as spying," Elise said.

"I wouldn't," Gerald argued. "On what planet is that considered spying?"

"You're telling me that if you were in the bathroom and you saw a little snake with video cameras for eyes come in and look at you, you wouldn't think someone's trying to spy on you while you did your business?"

"Why would *anyone* want to see me take a shit?"

"I don't know, but it's still spying."

"Wow, okay, so spying includes a lot of things," he said. "My point is, just because they were spying doesn't mean they were up to something."

"Then how do you explain the papers?" Anton asked. "Looked like they were planning something."

"Maybe they were up to something," Laleitha said. "But *something* doesn't mean something bad. I'm with King on this one."

"Exactly," Gerald agreed.

"No, you're not with King. You're just against me," Elise responded. "You wouldn't agree with me if the world depended on it." Elise had discovered long ago her sister's favorite pastime was arguing. She figured it was because Laleitha took pride in the fact that only she could annoy Elise as easily as she did.

Darren shook his head. "Sisters. Don't live with them, nor do I want to."

"Technically, we're half-sisters," Laleitha pointed out. "And we don't live together."

"You're at my house all the time," Elise said.

"Hmm," Gerald said, sitting back. "Same mom or same dad? If you two had the same mom, that means one of you is a mistake."

"Same dad," Elise replied.

"Mont was a different kind of mistake," Lalietha added.

"Damn," Darren remarked. "What's the word for gold digger but with powerful Lumerians? I mean, no way that's a coincidence."

"That's exactly how my mom reacted," Elise told Darren. "Except she screamed it."

"Yeah," he replied, "my family hardly took well to the fact that I was being dragged into this."

"Neither did you," Gerald said with a chuckle.

"Must get it from them," Laleitha added.

Darren snorted. "Well, at least *I'll* have the decency to tell my kid that he might get abducted for his freak-gene. Maybe I won't be a jerk to him, not to his mom either, or have a jerky wife. Wouldn't make him memorize a bunch of rule-breaking rules—"

"What?" Gerald exclaimed, stifling a laugh.

"Or get on his case whenever he wanted to go out with friends. There's a lot of things I would do different than my dad."

Elise and Laleitha exchanged glances.

"What about you, *King*?" Darren said, jokingly using Gerald's nickname, just as the girls had been doing. "You're having a hoot over there. You get along with your parents?"

Gerald shrugged. "I don't know. My mom's all right. She works from home. Kinda has a lot to take care of, eight kids and all that. Being the oldest that's home, I have to help."

"You're the oldest?" Lee asked.

"Oldest at home," he answered, nodding. "I have two half sisters in college from my dad's last marriage. Then there's me, my little sister, Maria, who's fifteen, my little brother, Carlos, he's twelve, the twins, Marco and Hugo, who are nine, and little Stephanie, who's five. I'm close with Maria and Stephanie but not so much the others."

"And your dad?" Elise asked. "How's he?"

He shrugged. "He's all right. We're not very close." Then, he turned to Anton. "Your turn, man. You haven't said anything yet."

Anton shrugged. "My parents are pretty cool. Dad used to take me to concerts every month, and Mom taught me how to whittle and carve wood. I mean, things used to be pretty good before my dad got laid off. Now things are kinda going downhill, but they're probably glad they don't have to worry about taking care of me anymore."

Elise wasn't sure what to say to that. She wanted to assure him that his parents certainly never wanted him gone, nor did they enjoy having him gone, but she didn't want to make him feel like he should be worried for them either. Given how uncomfortable he looked having just said that, she began to wonder if it were her place to say anything at all on the matter.

"That sucks," Darren offered.

Anton shrugged. "Um, Laleitha?" he said, looking desperate to get the spotlight off himself.

Lee's humorous smile returned. "Ha. Our dad's a fucking lunatic."

That earned her several confused and slightly alarmed looks.

"He cheated on my mom with hers and then walked out on both of us," Elise explained. "He's made a number of questionable decisions."

"And apparently he had a thing for powerful Lumerian chicks," King added.

"Yeah, he's pretty much crazy," Elise said. "You wouldn't be able to tell just by talking to him, because he seems pretty normal, but whenever I talk about him with people and I hear myself say the things that he's done, I realize that he's . . ." She hesitated, searching for the right word.

"A wacko, completely bonkers, clinically insane," Laleitha suggested. "Take your pick, Mont."

Darren laughed quietly. "Yeah, okay that's enough about that. I thought mine was screwed up enough."

Elise couldn't help but grin. It was a wistful yet peaceful, sad yet accepting, conflicted yet comfortable grin. She couldn't really explain how she felt about her father.

"So," Darren said, ripping Elise from her thoughts, "*King*, where'd that nickname come from?"

Gerald smiled. "I don't know. When I was younger, old enough to start taking care of my siblings, I'd go on power trips, I guess. So I've been told, anyway." He paused to chuckle. "My parents would make fun of me for it; they'd call me 'Your Highness' sarcastically, and apparently, I would eat it up. Some of my friends caught on later and somehow the joking just turned into a regular name. I kinda like it, if I'm being honest."

"I guess it's better than narcissist," Anton remarked flatly.

"Hey," King protested.

※

She found King standing by the wall, watching a painting as if to make sure it didn't move. Most had showered and gone to bed by then, and Elise had just changed into the pajamas Ellington brought back for them.

Elise walked up next to him. The painting was strange. It showed a small device in the left corner with swirling black clouds bursting from it. Two girls were shown, one with long, tightly wound black hair that was flying behind her as if a great wind filled the hall they stood in. The other girl had bright blonde hair, like Elise, and had fallen backward, facing the mass of swirling black air.

"What do you think it's supposed to mean?" Gerald asked.

Elise looked at him. "Hmm?"

"Aren't paintings supposed to mean something? Usually I can BS at least some sort of symbolism, but I've been staring at this one for a while and I can't work anything out."

Elise looked back at the painting. "Maybe the painter is like Lee. She just paints weird things because they make her happy."

Gerald considered her explanation. "I don't like it."

Elise shrugged. "It might have meant something to the painter."

"Lillian Lureman," he said, putting his finger on the signature. "The girl from the day we came here. She was Ms. Kilodrist's intern or something, right? She was pretty."

"And an artist as well, apparently," Elise replied. "I'm going to bed. Have fun staring at the painting."

"You bet."

CHAPTER TWELVE

To Orphia

Ellington brought them breakfast the next morning, promising their cupboards would be filled by that night so they could make their own food. He ate with them, first serving them *something*—Elise promptly forgot what he called them—that had wavy designs imprinted into them and tasted somewhat like waffles.

"Are you enjoying Lumeria so far?" he asked.

"It's a lot to get used to," Gerald remarked.

Laleitha and Anton nodded.

"That's an understatement," Darren huffed. "It feels like we're on another planet."

Ellington looked as if he were about to respond, but Darren muttered on.

Darren gave a small snort of laughter then said, "Here you are telling us we're supposed to protect it." He shook his head. "We can't even protect ourselves. And if I could, I sure as hell wouldn't be *here*." Slowly, the bitterness in his voice began to turn to anger. "This place is a nightmare. I've been trying to wake up since the moment we stepped through that portal. This place isn't home; it never will be!" He abruptly rose from his seat. "I don't care about you Lumerians and your problems. I'm only here because apparently I have to be. I thought I could do it, that I could maybe go through with this and *do* something with my life, but yesterday it clicked—I don't belong here. None of us do!"

"What, you'd rather go back?" Gerald snapped in response. "Then what?"

Ellington, Elise, and the others sat in stunned silence as Darren glared at Gerald, seeming to consider his point. "There were things I wasn't ready to leave behind," he said. With that, he turned his back and stormed into his room.

"Wonder what his deal is," Laleitha muttered. "He seemed fine with everything yesterday."

Elise nodded in agreement. Darren had seemed grumpy ever since he woke up that morning, and she couldn't help but wonder if something happened.

Ellington cleared his throat. "This actually brings me to my next topic. I dearly hope that you don't share Mr. Nosia's views. Emperor Evanstin inquires . . . do you *want* to become a Major?"

"Well, we aren't exactly being given a choice," Elise pointed out flatly.

"I understand that. But if you were, what would be your views?" he pressed.

Elise hesitated, waiting for the others to speak.

Gerald was the first to do so. "I want to," he said. "I want to become a Major. I mean, it's . . . a lot . . . but I think I like what it involves."

Lalietha nodded, pushing around the food on her plate with her fork. "I'm not afraid," she said. "I want to be a Major too."

Ellington smiled. "Good. This is good." He raised an eyebrow at Anton. "And you, sir?"

He shrugged, his expression neutral.

Then, the man's attention swung to Elise. Suddenly, feeling the pressure to answer, she pondered the words to describe how she felt. Lumeria was fascinating, thrilling. It gave her a set path to follow. It made her somebody, a part of something. But she didn't think she'd ever be able to let go of the world she knew.

She looked over her shoulder at the city behind glass walls. "It's not home," she said.

Ellington's face softened. "It will be," he promised gently. "In time."

※

Transitioning that afternoon took place in the room in which they had first met Ms. Kilodrist. They had no tower to see that day. When they entered, their transitioner sat waiting for them. A broad smile crossed her face when the door opened.

"Good news," she said. "The date of your hearing has been set."

"Hearing?" Gerald repeated, his face twisting in confusion.

"In front of Orphia," she clarified. "Seeing as it was a high-priority inquiry, it was set as early as possible. Having a persistent emperor can get you such benefits. Several things were moved around, which Orphia apparently wasn't very happy about, but the sooner we get it over with, the better."

A sudden nerve knotted in Elise's stomach as she took her seat. From what she had heard about Orphia, his trials sounded earthshaking.

"So, when is it?" Darren asked.

"Next Thursday, May tenth, at eleven in the morning."

Elise flinched. Orphia, the immortal judge who had seen so many Majors before her and would basically determine her fate, was going to be inspecting her up and down next week. What if he had her deported? What if he questioned her relationship with Hank Martinez, the man who had information on his son?

Yes, Marty—Orphia would question Marty. It was Hank Martinez who made her relationship with Orphia terrifyingly personal. A reasonable grudge could be held against the friend of his enemy. The thought chilled her very bones.

What did he look like? Probably large and intimidating, his years shown on his skin and in his eyes. He probably sat at the head, looking down at people with a cold, damning expression, acting like a god because he is the only person on earth who can tell people who they are. She shuddered at these thoughts.

"Anyway," Ms. Kilodrist said, "let's get started with today's lesson."

"You should enjoy this one," Ellington said. "You all seem like smart ones," he added with a wink.

"Except maybe Darren," Gerald muttered teasingly.

Darren rolled his eyes.

The lesson this day was on the important pieces of Lumerian technology that, being from 'the Other Society,' they would not understand. Ms. Kilodrist placed a number of photographs on the table, some of devices, some of stones, some of strange plants or animals.

"The main difference," she said, "that you must understand in order to get the general idea of how this technology was invented is that there are certain natural elements in the Lat empires that the Other Society simply does not have." She tapped the image of an odd silver fish, then of a curly plant. "Certain species of plants or animals," she said, "can alter the environment. For example, this fish you see is called a Setsino, and they shed parts of their scales in small particles at a time, which are compacted over hundreds of years to form a stone called a palsalt, which has a chemical structure unique to any other stone, allowing us to use it to power certain types of machinery. Other natural minerals can be used in much the same way and were incorporated into many machines."

And on she went, describing inventions beyond Elise's imagination. Microscopic devices that are connected in colonies, called "imitators" because of their use in analyzing body functions by imitating neurons; transportation rods; genus chambers; rod conductors; vortex harnessers—which the newspaper claimed Marty was building—that can alter the weather.

"There are only fifteen in existence, and they are all located in the Stormy City in Trimeterous," Ellington told her. "These fifteen were all built by a man named Henry Heddison, who was particularly paranoid about his ideas and secretive with his notes. Only he knew how to build them, and this was a secret he died with."

Elise frowned. "Has anyone figured out how to build one since then?"

Ms. Kilodrist shook her head.

Elise's frown deepened. "Is anyone trying?"

She thought about this. "I don't know, exactly. We have no real need for any at the moment. Not like the Stormy City did. As you can imagine, they experience several extreme storms, hence the name. They also require an extreme amount of energy to power, so any research into them would be an enormously spendy affair."

Elise's mind flicked back to Marty. "They said Hank Martinez built a vortex harnesser. Why did he do that?"

Ms. Kilodrist exchanged glances with Ellington, who slowly leaned forward and folded his hands in front of him. "A strange property of the vortex harnesser," he said, "is that it blocks the view of Antedal and Avisil, the two Omenescents who can see any place on earth. We expect Martinez did this in an attempt to keep Orphia from finding him."

Elise wanted to ask more, but Ms. Kilodrist stopped her, insisting they return to the lesson.

"Lastly is the Inseanan mind stone," Ms. Kilodrist continued, addressing the group, "which is not so much a machine as it is a procedure that involves several machines. The principle purpose of the mind stone was to give one the ability to trap their mind within an object, usually a brick or block of metal. This was so one could continue a legacy past their own death. In Lumerian culture, it is seen as unethical and morally wrong for one to do that, and several people lack the money or resources to. In fact, it is legal only in one Lumerian country, so it is very uncommon."

"How does it work?" Gerald implored.

"Only a few Lumerians know," she replied. "I can understand how it is a puzzling concept."

"This is an inconceivable concept," Darren huffed.

"The mind itself isn't some entity that can be trapped like a butterfly," Ellington explained calmly. "In order for the mind to be recreated, imitators have to map one's very brain. Their data is then somehow imprinted into the stone. That is step one of the process and what to do from there is yet unclear to all but specialists in a very specific branch of neuroscience. The brain's structure is literally mapped on the stone. Every cell, every neuron. Sometimes those who attempt to make one are killed in the process by the imitators swarming their head. Therefore, it is technology that Lumeria is far better off without. The lure of escaping death prompts far more sinister things than you'd expect."

Elise's eyes trailed away from Ellington as she thought about this. Darren looked as if he had completely zoned out, but Gerald looked deeply disturbed at Ellington's final statement.

She thought about the idea of the mind stone for a moment, wondering how many people had died prematurely in an attempt to preserve themselves. No, not themselves—their legacy, whether it was a significant one or not. Perhaps that was one of the most haunting things about death: knowing one would die without a name, without a purpose.

Then the thought hit her. *This is what I will die for.*

This would be her purpose, the thing she devoted her life to. This would be how she spent her days, with the constant assurance she was doing good and building a legacy. That was a blessing that not many people lived with.

She was ripped from her thoughts when Laleitha asked, "So, then, what happens if they are successful?"

"Then their mind is preserved in the stone," Ms. Kilodrist replied.

"And people can communicate with it?" Elise asked.

The woman shook her head. "Not yet. That requires a mind stone interpreter, a whole other machine. A working interpreter has not been successfully built yet. Unless the Inseanans have discovered it by now . . ."

"Naturally, the only way to make use of an invention that people *die* trying to make is with another machine that hasn't been conceived yet," Gerald remarked.

"Yes, that's a very Inseanan characteristic of the matter," Ellington responded.

"Anyway," Ms. Kilodrist went on, "the transitioning curriculum mandates that you have a basic understanding of these topics, but it also requires that you read these." She removed a few books from her bag and pushed them in front of the five.

Elise looked down at hers. It was brightly colored and titled *Basic Lumerian Scientific Principles for Transitioners.*

"Read a chapter a day, and the lesson will be over in a week or two. We can discuss the concepts in further depth when you are finished reading each chapter. Meanwhile, we are going to begin learning Old Lat."

Excitement stirred up inside Elise. *I'll be able to read Marty's diary.*

"While teaching the entire language of Old Lat isn't usually in the transitioning curriculum, most Majors have traditionally learned enough of it to get the general idea of some old passages," Ms. Kilodrist informed them. "Mr. Ellington recommended you learn it entirely. Apparently some of you expressed interest in it."

Elise's gaze shot to Ellington. He sat with a broad smile on his face, glancing at Elise as Ms. Kilodrist said this. Gratitude toward the man began to fill her, and she made a mental note to thank him later.

The lesson began and rolled on through the rest of the session. By the time the day of transitioning had concluded, they had learned a few Old Lat prefixes and suffixes.

From that point forward in the day, it was almost identical to the previous day. They trained with the Lumire, making slow progress—Elise briefly levitated a book, made the paper ball explode in her face, and was again able to use the moisture and energy in the air and grass to restore her own energy—followed by training with Talious, which ended with a promise that he'd get them all permits to carry firearms so they could start gun training. That night, however, they had no time for chats on the couch and went straight to the showers and beds. Elise, however, was again wide-awake.

She hardly bothered touching her covers; she would just grow uncomfortable and sweaty in her sheets as she tossed and turned. Her soft bare feet made hushed footsteps as they brushed across the floor, headed to the window-wall, where she sat cross-legged right in front of the window. Resting her chin on her fist, she looked out at the city in front of her. The sight still astonished her. She had noticed earlier that a thin silver fog sat over the city almost always, forming a transparent sheet only a few buildings could pierce. Now, at night, it formed a reddish haze with the refracted light from the buildings. It was strange but beautiful.

And she could still see the stars.

As the thought crossed her mind, her eyes immediately began searching for familiar constellations. Ursa Major, Orion, and Cassiopeia, probably the easiest to spot, were located instantly. At that moment, she was back home.

It seemed strange to her that Lumeria was under the same sky as home, but she liked the idea of it. *Maybe this can be home. Eventually.*

)(

"Orphia's courtroom is incredibly large and very intimidating," Ellington told them the next morning as they sat across from him, Talious, and Ms. Kilodrist on the train to the Orphian City. "There will be several people there spectating, but they sit above Orphia's retinue. You will know Orphia when you see him— he is the one in the large throne-like chair."

Elise nodded. This was nothing less than what she expected.

"What you are going to do," Ms. Kilodrist went on, "is take a right when you walk in, find the door labeled *Citizenship Hearing Subjects*, and go down that hallway. There should be a room designated for the Majors. It will probably be the first one you come to. There, you will each be addressed by a man named Horace Zembisuly. Swear your oath of truth to him and then await instruction. At the front of the room, there will be an open hallway that leads to the courtroom. When you hear Orphia invite you to enter, walk through that doorway into the lowest part of the courtroom, called the basin, and take a seat in the chairs set up for you."

"Do not speak unless asked a question, do not answer for each other, and, for the love of God, tell the truth," Ellington stressed.

Elise felt a little pale. Their instructors seemed more worried for them than they were for themselves. They must be missing something. Perhaps, in their case, ignorance was bliss. Maybe it was better that they didn't fully understand the weight of Orphia's power.

"What kind of questions will they be asking us?" Darren asked tentatively, looking as sick as Elise felt.

"Nothing that you won't know," Ellington replied. "You'll do fine."

"Ha," Talious said. "Grown men have wet their pants up there. I suggest you brace yourself. Be ready to think about every question he asks and why it's significant. There will be people who don't want you to be Majors, and if you allow them to make any good points, that could tip the rest of his retinue in that direction . . . which means you should also be prepared for a screwup."

"Why exactly do you have doubts, Mr. Talious?" Ms. Kilodrist challenged, sounding annoyed at his remarks.

"Well, they didn't necessarily have the previous Majors to pass the baton to them."

"They'll do fine," Ellington said. "His retinue should have no reason to be skeptical of anything. Not enough to keep them from becoming Majors, anyway. They're making progress, and Thentis will be able to see it. It doesn't matter who's training them."

Talious said nothing but didn't seem convinced at all. He shifted his glance back to the five. "Think through what you say before you answer," he repeated. "The thick, blond jackass with the bifocals who sits at Orphia's left—he's gonna try to trip you up."

"Talious—" Ms. Kilodrist began.

"I'm just warning them," he said, putting up his hands. "They say Orphia beats the bias out of them, but that man is still as Inseanan as he was when he was born. I think it would be helpful if they were aware of that."

"They have to go in with an open mind," she said. "That is essential."

Gerald lowered his eyebrows. "Why is that?"

Ms. Kilodrist took another deep, nervous breath, but before she could speak, Gerald went on. "Is the mind reader going to be in our heads? Are they interrogating us? What's even the point of this hearing?"

"One at a time, kid," Talious grunted.

"Thentis will look into your mind only if there is anything that can't be explained," Ms. Kilodrist said. "He doesn't have to engage his power to sense if somebody is lying or hiding something, so *please* don't even try it. As for the purpose of this trial, your official induction criteria will be decided, the debate on whether or not you should be Majors at all will convene, and if it is decided you shouldn't, Orphia will have to determine what to do with you."

"They *will* try to get to you," Ellington said. "Many of Orphia's retinue are going to test you. Keep your emotions in check and your morals straight."

"It is not as difficult as it sounds," Ms. Kilodrist assured them. "And once the trial is over, we are presenting you to the people of Lumeria," she added, an excited grin spreading across her face.

"What?" Laleitha exclaimed.

"Presented?" Darren repeated. "You mean like—"

"Your arrival is all over the news. The people will be assembling outside of Fort Kingshold. Stanford will lead you there when your trial is over. There will be celebrations!" Ms. Kilodrist went on, sounding more delighted with herself with every word.

"All over the news?" Darren repeated. "I haven't seen anything."

Ellington coughed.

When Elise's eyes flicked to him, she noticed a rather nervous expression on his face. Then, she thought back to the newspaper he had brought them just the other day, and it occurred to her that perhaps he took out a page in which they were featured. *If that's true, why?* The illness in Elise's stomach was becoming more violent by the minute.

"Why weren't we told sooner?" Anton questioned.

"Well, we have been busy, have we not? We didn't want you to stress."

"I'm fine with it," Gerald said with a shrug.

"It will be brief," Ellington assured the skeptical ones. "There will be no pressure on you to say or do anything."

"Yeah, okay," Darren said. "I just don't get *why* we are being celebrated."

"The Majors are the Lumerian's symbol for peace and security," Ms. Kilodrsit said. "Now that you have returned, citizens believe that their safety has been restored. It is a festival-worthy cause."

Elise sighed, letting her body sink into the cushions of her seat. She had never grown used to the overwhelming storm of crowds, and being put in front of one intensified the discomfort by a hundred times. But she had already decided this was what she wanted to do, and if it entailed being put in front of a crowd for a few minutes, Elise could tolerate it. Hopefully.

Laleitha opened her mouth, but Elise's fingers closed around her arm. It seemed Anton had also given Darren a sharp elbow to the side to shut him up as well.

"Just," Elise muttered to her sister, "go with it."

None of the five liked the idea of the trial, only one liked the idea of the celebration, and not many of them had any faith in themselves to live up to the people's expectations, but in a silent agreement, they decided to keep that to themselves. Fighting this was getting old.

"Prepare yourselves," Ms. Kilodrist said. "We are almost there."

⚡

"What do you think's going to happen," Anton said quietly to them as they stepped off the train, "if we actually do become Majors? What do we do then?"

"Whatever they need us to do, I guess," Gerald replied with a shrug. Ellington, Talious, and Ms. Kilodrist all walked ahead of them, guiding them through the busy station.

"But do you ever wonder"—Anton hesitated—"why the Majors didn't destroy those papers? Or even hide them?"

Darren raised an eyebrow, looking down at him quizzically.

"The papers in the tower?" Gerald asked and was answered with a nod.

Elise leaned toward him. "You think," she said, "they want us to finish their work?"

The small boy nodded again.

Gerald looked at each of them, intrigued, as if he were studying them. "There were maps, lists, charts, and lines connecting them," he began. "There was a name on that list, circled in red, a line drawn from him to 'Orphia.' It caught my attention because it's who we've been talking about a lot. The name was *Hank Martinez.*"

Elise lowered her eyebrows, her mind beginning to spin all over again. "He should have been a *kid* at that time."

"I know," he replied. "Which got me thinking, how long ago did Orphia's son go missing?"

"1967," Laleitha said.

"And when did the civil war that got the Majors exiled start?"

"1968," Elise said. "The next year."

"They had to have been looking for the Lost Son of Orphia," Anton concluded. "That might have something to do with why they were exiled. And if we have a man who killed a ton of Lumerians to protect this conspiracy," he continued, gesturing to Elise for her connection to Hank Martinez, "and a group of Majors who might have started a civil war after looking into this conspiracy, what does that mean for us?"

Darren looked from Anton to the rest. "You still wanna try and finish their work?"

"*Yes,*" Elise exclaimed. "If this is why Marty died, I want to find out what he had been hiding."

"Marty?" Darren repeated.

"What? Oh, Hank Martinez. I mean Hank Martinez. I'd always call him Marty as a kid because, you know, *Mr. Martinez, Marty . . .*" Elise explained in a hurry. "But my point is, he devoted his life to keep this secret, and if we can get to the answer first, then we can keep it out of the wrong hands."

"But who decides whose hands are the wrong hands?" Gerald asked. "Lumeria? This pertains to all the empires. Doesn't it?"

Elise paused, thinking. "Orphia," she said after a moment. "We'll find this guy and return him home. We'll prove ourselves to the very master of everything Lat."

※

The courtroom was a large brownstone building with endless stone patterns stacked on top of each other. It was capped with a dome of stained glass with three sides that showed three different pictures on each side. The first picture had a white tree in the center of a white archway with a navy blue sky behind it. At the end of each branch, a smaller scene was shown, of people doing noble acts of both peace and war.

"That is Orphia's depiction of the Inseanans," Ellington told her.

The second had a green background and showed two gray towers with a bridge in between toward the bottom. Across the entire picture, people were shown doing acts of generosity and kindness, but the window upon which this picture had been shown was on the verge of shattering, with a network of cracks bursting from a weblike epicenter. It almost looked as if somebody had struck the mural with a massive fist.

"That," Ellington said, "is the fallen empire of the Juperds."

The last one was a strip of yellow, with a single crowned man standing in the middle and a halo of fifteen faces. At the edges of the sea of yellow, seven warriors were shown, each holding a weapon and a single flower. The picture showed a tiny city shaped into an arch across the yellow, intersecting the waist of the king. Under the arch, beneath the king, was a bouquet of flowers.

"That is the Lumerian mural."

Beside the courtroom, a large tower stood tall and proud, reaching high into the sky.

"And that's the tower of the Omenescents," Ellington said. "At the top, Antedal and Avisil are perched. They're the ones who can see anything, anywhere, watching everything that happened across the empires."

Elise's throat seemed to close and she struggled to swallow as she stared up at this magnificent structure.

Ellington led the five to the large archway that was the door and opened it for them, revealing a wide, dark hall. The hall didn't stretch on, but only a short distance away was another set of large doors. To either side, smaller blank, black doors were hidden in the shadows of the glowing corridor.

Their instructors directed them to the hall on the right, while they continued on through the larger doors. Elise looked over her shoulder at them as they walked away. The large doors opened into a massive staircase, and Elise desperately wished she was with her guides again, going up that same bright staircase rather than this dark hall.

King led the way, while Elise and her sister hung in the back. Anton would sometimes look back at them, his eyes glinting in the darkness.

The narrow hall eventually led them into a small, low-ceilinged room with amber-colored walls and five cushioned chairs. A slim old man stood in the corner, awaiting them.

"Welcome Gerald Rodum III, Darren Nosia, Anton Hystar, Elise Montason, and Laleitha Ataliarma," he said each of their names as they walked through the door. "Come here, please."

They did so, a nervous and uncomfortable tension filling the space as his sunken gaze traced their faces.

He extended a small paper to Gerald. "Read this aloud, please. Do your best with the pronunciation."

Gerald took the paper and held it in front of him, his face scrunching when he glimpsed the content. "Um, *boso vid quepul ats quopsus lea . . .*" He glanced back up at the man with his eyebrows raised.

The man nodded him on.

"*Sa idoupi us bib simul queposal, us likumi bib desobos.*"

"Pass it along," the man instructed.

Gerald passed it to Anton, who mumbled it quietly before handing it to Laleitha. Darren read it last, after Elise, whose relentless questions were corroding her mind as she spoke.

"What do you suppose that meant?" Gerald whispered to her.

"That's what I'm wondering too," she responded. "Maybe Old Lat for 'Tell the truth, full truth, and nothing but the truth.'"

"So help us God," Gerald added, taking a deep breath.

"You are now under oath," the elderly man told them. "From this point forward, if you tell a lie, withhold information, add to the truth with false testimony, or exaggerate the truth for a different result, it will be held against you in a later trial."

One by one, they all nodded.

"You cannot speak unless in reply to Orphia or another member of his retinue or unless you are invited to speak freely," he continued. "You are to follow Orphia's exact instructions and do nothing without instruction unless invited to act freely. You are to conduct yourselves in the acceptable manner in his courtroom, and you will not leave the basin until Orphia dismisses you."

A booming voice sounded in the distance. It was powerful and deep, like a trombone, and Elise knew right away it was Orphia speaking. He droned through a long introduction that mainly consisted of listing names and topics and redundantly bringing up the purpose—determine the Majors' place in Lumerian society.

"You enter when he calls you," the man said to them.

They each nodded again.

After a few more minutes of Orphia's extensive introduction, he then said, "The Majors may now enter."

Then, there was utter silence.

CHAPTER THIRTEEN

The Trial of Orphia

Gerald was the first to duck through the small doorway, his eyes gazing curiously upward. Elise tentatively followed, but the moment she realized what she was stepping into, chills ran through her every limb, lingering in her shoulders and down her spine. Her breath caught in her throat as her heart thumped so hard the veins in her temples bounced.

What she walked into was nothing short of an arena. The massive circular room had a marble floor, with marble of the same type making up the walls surrounding them, which stood at least twelve feet high. That was only the mixing bowl in a large kitchen, however, and when the marble wall had ended, the room opened further into a stadium of spectators. Balconies protruded from the wall above the stands and spiraled on until the wall reached the domed roof with backward murals casting colorful spectrums of light down into the tiny marble basin so far below.

In front of the stands, still above the five's marble containment, was the bench. It curved around the lower room in a semicircle. At the highest desk sat a large, pale man draped in purple robes. He was broad but aged, looking about sixty, except his snow-white hair was much paler than it should be and had hardly receded. His nose was crooked and his green eyes seemed to glow. His cheeks were sunken, sagging down to where his face sloped to his pointy chin. His mouth was locked into a small frown, the corners of his lips digging into his cheeks.

This man was Orphia, and he was not at all who Elise expected him to be.

At Orphia's right was a frail man who seemed to have no life left in him except in his eyes, which glowed a bright diamond blue. He gazed upon the five intently, as if he were looking into their very souls. This must be the mind reader.

At Orphia's left was the man whom Talious had described. He was plump, with his blond hair combed and greased back. His bifocals sat on his nose, barely reaching around his chubby cheeks.

There were several others on the bench, but Elise hardly had time to take notice of them before Orphia, in his booming, mesmerizing voice, said, "Sit."

Five identical chairs were set up toward the middle of the circle behind a simple table that had five microphones mounted on it and a small water bottle at each spot. They each took one. Elise moved slowly, gazing at the faces of the benchmen as she did so.

"These are the descendants of five of the lost Majors," Orphia began. "Laleitha Ataliarma, Anton Hystar, Elise Montason, Darren Nosia, and Gerald Rodum III. By request of their emperor, they wish to retake the post of Major using the revised induction criteria. Given the circumstances, exceptions will have to be made, but we will limit those to as few as possible. It is up to us"—he gestured to his benchmen—"to determine which exceptions should and should not be made, what taking up this position entails, and the legal means by which it should be done." He set down his papers. "To begin, Mr. Quingimont, please read aloud section one of the revised Major induction criteria."

A man at the end of the bench stood, opening a black binder in his arms as he did so. His mouth was set in a constant frown, causing him to resemble a frog when he spoke. "The Official Induction Criteria of the Seven Majors, section one. First and foremost, the Majors must have the Lumire. The Majors must be trained with the Lumire until they are fit to use it under any and all circumstances. The Majors must be trained in combat at least to an acceptable level of fourth-rank Lumerian Security Enforcement officers and in military and legal procedures to at least a first-rank military officer level. Before taking up their posts, the Majors must have completed this training. Their completion is subject to the judgment of their instructor, ideally the Major before them or somebody with a background in the Major's department."

"Good. Thank you, Mr. Quingimont," Orphia said, turning to stare down at the Majors. "Laleitha Ataliarma, I speak directly to you. Do you have the Lumire?"

Laleitha swallowed. "Yes." She stifled the quiver in her voice with a hard tone.

"And you inherited it from your mother?"

"I think so," Laleitha answered. "She never told me, but it couldn't have been my father because he had two children before me."

"Good. You are not a mistake. Have you begun training? If yes, then under whom?"

Lee nodded. "We have. Ms. Yugie Kilodrist is training us with the Lumire and Joseph Talious is training us in combat."

Orphia turned over a page. "Anton Hystar, I now speak directly to you. Do you have the Lumire?"

"Yes," Anton said, his voice near silent.

Orphia craned his neck in an attempt to move his ear closer to the boy.

Anton seemed to sigh inwardly before repeating himself more loudly.

"And you inherited it from your father?" he went on.

Anton nodded.

"I presume that you began training with Miss Ataliarma under the same instructors?"

He nodded again, grateful that Orphia seemed to accept his silence.

"Elise Montason." Orphia turned his mesmerizing green gaze onto her. "I speak directly to you now."

Elise swallowed.

"Do you have the Lumire?"

"Yes," she answered stiffly.

"You inherited it from your mother?"

"Yes."

"You have begun training under the same instructors as your fellow Majors?"

"Yes," Elise answered, relaxing a bit as she expected him to move on.

"Before you were brought to Lumeria, have you had any encounters with Lumerians or Inseanans?"

This question struck her. Why hadn't he asked Laleitha or Anton this question? Elise wasn't particularly sure how to answer. It was impossible to tell whether anyone back home was Lumerian, as apparently there were no physical indicators and most Lumerians presumably took precautions to blend into the Other Society. As for Inseanans, she'd never met one besides the masked man. There was Marty, of course, who Talious told her was Lumerian, but she still doubted whether to believe it, and was not particularly inclined to tell Orphia about him if she didn't have to.

"I . . ." The words caught in her throat. "I'm not sure. I could have, but I didn't, or, I mean, but if I did, they didn't tell—I didn't know they were. I suppose anyone could have been—"

Orphia spared her by interrupting. "Did anyone, for example, expose you to any aspect of Lumerian culture, language, or technology?" For as stony and stiff as this man was, he seemed to be trying to be patient with her. Elise distantly wondered if he felt sympathy for them.

"Um, yes," she said slowly. "I saw the transportation rods."

Orphia pursed his lips. "When was this?"

"The night before I came here," Elise answered.

"And according to the report submitted to the Lumerian Council by Mr. Joseph Talious, this was April twenty-ninth of this year?"

That sounds right. "Yes."

Orphia looked at the mind reader to his left, who shook his head. Elise's heart sank. The mind reader had seen something in Elise's head that she must have missed, but how could *he* have a better grip on her memories than she? Panic began to swell within her at the thought that they might think her a liar and proceed to treat her as one. She had no idea what punishment that would entail, but she forced herself from thinking about it.

Orphia turned back to her, something new flaring in his eyes. "Describe that night, if you please."

Elise shifted uncomfortably. Where should she start? "I woke up in the middle of the night when I thought I heard something downstairs," she began at a sluggish pace as she sorted her thoughts. "And I went out to the hall . . . and there were two men there. One grabbed me and the other opened a transportation rod. I was thrown in, then I was in a dark room with a masked man sitting in the corner. Then, the two men went and brought five other people to the same room. The men called each other Sar Prague and Dawson." Several eyes grew wide at the mention of this, a few people turning to murmur to the people next to them. "The masked man forced us to line up and then . . . then he shot each of us in the head . . ." She hesitated, recalling the awful memory. "One girl didn't make it. She must have been taken by mistake . . ." She paused, trying to figure out how to go on. "Then, the two men caught fire.

I don't know how. It was out of nowhere—one of us must have been using the Lumire. But that was how we escaped. A lot of other people in masks came and began pursuing us through the building, then Joseph Talious came and brought us out of danger."

"Where did the two men take you?" one of the benchmen asked.

"Silver Industries," Elise answered.

"Why did they take you there?" the man to Orphia's left whom Talious had described inquired on.

Elise thought for a moment. "The masked man, he said something about it being out of sight from the Council of Orphia."

"You saw something there," Orphia said. "Something that caught your attention."

Elise swallowed again. She knew exactly what he was referring to but was bothered by the fact he somehow knew. "I saw a piece of technology that looked strange. It had the same glow that I noticed in the transportation rods, but its structure resembled a reactor or something of the sorts. That's what—" Elise stopped. She was about to mention Marty, which likely would be opening a can of worms, seeing as he was the man who apparently had information on Orphia's lost son. "That's . . . I . . . I'm not sure what it was."

Orphia sat back in his chair. "Interesting. Darren Nosia, I speak directly to you now. Do you have the Lumire?"

Elise felt like deflating. She had hoped he would be able to provide some clarity on any one of the vague and confusing aspects of her story that he had asked about. Instead, he had dragged her through a series of painstakingly difficult questions that led to nowhere.

"Yeah," Darren said softly, as if he were a student being lectured by a principle.

"You inherited it from your father?"

"Yeah."

"Isaac Nosia?" one who sat toward the end of the bench asked. She had tightly coiled hair that extended wildly in all directions. This, combined with her long, pale neck, gave her a striking resemblance to a peacock.

Darren looked confused and turned to the man. "Um, yeah . . " He looked like he was about to ask how the man knew, but another went on.

"The Lumerian hero? He was a Major this entire time?"

"Was he aware that he had the Lumire?" another asked, who had craned himself so far over the bench he looked as if he would fall with the simplest slip of the hand.

Darren opened his mouth to respond before Orphia waved his hand.

"Isaac Nosia's affiliation with the Majors is an irrelevant matter. Mr. Nosia, I assume you train with your fellow Majors-to-be?"

Darren nodded.

Orphia turned another page over. "Gerald Rodum III, I speak directly to you now. Do you have the Lumire?"

Gerald sat a little straighter now that the attention was on him. "Yes."

"You inherited it from your father?"

"Yes."

"And you've begun training alongside the others here today?"

"Yes."

Orphia looked at the mind reader, who nodded, his eyes ever grim. The large man cleared his throat. "I'm sure you all have similar stories of how you came here? You were all abducted by the same men?"

They nodded.

"I was told they were members of the Prime Devise," Gerald said.

Eyebrows everywhere shot up. A few people gasped and murmurs began to break out among the spectators.

"That is a serious accusation. A proofless one, for that matter," a benchman remarked. "I say—"

"The girl mentioned a masked man," another benchmen said, and he looked at Elise, who suddenly jolted upright when the attention shifted to her. "What did he look like?"

Elise opened her mouth but another person spoke.

"You think she was referring to Second Reighba?"

"It would only make sense . . ."

"It would make no sense!" the man to Orphia's left interrupted. "The Prime Devise is a peaceful association and they have no business with the Majors—"

"Which is exactly what is concerning about this matter," another said. "If the Prime Devise is directly involved, they would have committed an act of war against Lumeria."

"Which they have no reason for, unless it is a part of a grander scheme," another added.

"This conclusion is based off of proofless accusations," a different benchman said.

"Order," Orphia commanded, slamming his gavel against the sound block on his desk. "It is no concern of this court whether or not the circumstances of the Majors' arrival warrant further action. We've already discussed the purpose of this hearing. If everything regarding section one is in order, Mr. Quingimont, will you please read section two?"

Mr. Quingimont stood again, turning the page in the binder. "Section two. Before given the authority of a Major, they must work in a task force under the Lumerian military to provide experience in the field. They must have committed at least one act of the patriot's labor. They must face the penalties of any crime or act of terrorism they have committed against Lumeria or the Lumerian Council. The minimum induction age is sixteen years of age. The ideal age to begin training is seven years of age."

Elise's face slowly paled as the man read on. By the time he finished and sat once more, she could have collapsed onto the floor. *A military task force? A patriot's labor?* It nearly sounded like she was signing up for death.

"They will finish their training much too late if they have only begun training two days ago," the peacock lady remarked.

"There's no 'too late' in this context," one on the other side of the bench said. "The induction criteria state no deadline."

Another spoke. "The usual time it takes a Major to complete training is nine years; that is why they have the ideal training age listed."

"So by the time they are Majors, they will most likely be in their twenties!" the peacock lady exclaimed.

"Not to mention the claim that they are too old to even begin training," the man to Orphia's left said.

"Wha—" Gerald said before his voice was drowned out by another benchman.

"The children that are referred to in this script are children who knew from birth who they were and what they were born to do," he said. "These *teenagers* have already developed lives outside of Lumeria. Their concept of the Lat empires is already confused, their priorities lie with their families and friends at home, and they have an unclear idea of their task here. They are not fit to be Majors and, even if they did complete the training, their place is not really *here*. This is not their home."

Elise could agree with that.

"So what would you have them do?" another pressed.

"Grow up here," he said, "and pass the Lumire on to their children so that they can grow up correctly."

Correctly?

"But if the threat on their lives is as dire as they suggest, both the Majors and Lumeria are being threatened at this very moment," an elderly man said from the edge of the bench.

"He is right," Orphia said. "By the Ancient Convention, the Majors must return and it must be as soon as they are capable. Laleitha Ataliarma, you have a family and friends and a life back in your previous home. Since the life of a Major prompts only a dangerous future, why are you here?"

Elise shot a worried look at her sister, who stared at a distant speck on the floor. "I . . ." she began after a tense moment.

Orphia stared at her expectantly.

"I can't go back," she said finally. "There is nothing but this in my future. I can't go home. I won't be able to live knowing that . . . *this* is out there . . ."

"She's simply confused, then," a bitter-sounding benchman concluded. "She has no idea where her home is, so making a commitment will be especially difficult."

Orphia waved his hand. "If her words were deceiving, we would know," he said sternly, nodding at the mind reader. "Don't try to take meaning from a feeling you do not understand, Mr. Arolson."

Mr. Arolson nodded, a simultaneously shamed and spiteful look on his face.

"And you, Anton Hystar?" Orphia turned to him. "Why are you here?"

Anton didn't say anything.

"Well?" the man to Orphia's left said after a moment.

He still didn't speak. Several long, uncomfortable moments passed, in which Elise could no longer look at him without trembling with anxiety on his behalf. He simply stared at the table in front of him, head down, eyes wide, looking as if he willed it all to go away.

"Elise Montason," Orphia said, giving up. "Why are you here?"

That's a good question. She had already decided that she wanted to stay, she wanted to be a Major, but the question of why still was incredibly difficult for her to explain, even to herself. Because it was her only option? That wouldn't fly.

Because the Prime Devise would come after her regardless of who she was and where she was? That wouldn't appeal. She was thinking too selfishly. Because she'd be putting lives in danger if she wasn't there? The Lumerian people hardly seemed real to her. She had been cooped up in a tower, fort, or train this entire time. As ashamed as she felt to admit it, she didn't see the Lumerian people as her concern yet. They seemed to be getting along fine in these years without the Majors. Because she wouldn't be able to live knowing she could torch men and levitate herself without a purpose to put that to? *There it is.*

"I'm here because . . . I guess I'm supposed to be," Elise said, her voice soft and not quite sure sounding.

Eyebrows raised.

"I've always been confused about who I was and who I was supposed to be," she went on. "I always thought I was meant for something more. I just never found it. Until I came here. Now I have something to fight for. I wanted a purpose, and it was handed right to me."

Orphia seemed content with that answer, and Elise internally patted herself on the back.

"Darren Nosia, why are you here?"

Darren was pale, paler than his hair. "There are people I need to protect," he answered. "I won't go home."

He refused to say anything more, even when Orphia and his retinue pushed on. Several long and tense minutes passed as curious benchmen attempted to pry an explanation out of Darren, but he continued to stare at the floor. He looked ghostly, as if he were staring into the face of death itself. Elise had never seen Darren like this. In fact, she had never seen anybody like this. Whatever Darren wasn't telling Orphia, he hadn't told *them* either. Whatever it was, it seemed like his life depended on it. The thought was beginning to frighten Elise.

Orphia continued with several frustrating attempts to get Darren to specify then moved on, giving up. "And you, Gerald Rodum?"

"Like Elise said," he stated. "Purpose. I'm here because it's my duty now."

Orphia nodded and looked down at his desk, opening his mouth as he prepared to read aloud, before a different voice quelled him.

"Is that so?" a grim tone challenged.

The entire room jumped at hearing that voice. There were gasps, and a million heads turned toward the chair at Orphia's right. It was the voice of the mind reader. His diamond-blue eyes were locked onto Gerald, staring into him. Something within this frail man burned like fire.

"Is that *really* the only thing that pushes you, Gerald Rodum?" the mind reader—Thentis, Ellington had called him—spat.

Just the sound of his voice made Elise's heart sink. Judging by the spectators' reaction, whatever was happening was not good at all.

"Is this your pride or your ambition speaking?" Thentis went on, his words cutting sharper than knives. "Should we ask your siblings why you are so possessive of them? Only your sister has seen who you *were*—before your father lost himself, before the obsessions came into play. Who is to say that you would not do the same as he? You? Because you resent him now? Does that make you any different?"

Gerald's face turned red. His fists were clenched so tightly his knuckles turned white. "You may know me," he said through gritted teeth, "but you do *not* know my father."

Thentis's chilling gaze turned to the rest of them. "Your ideals, your virtues, your *code*, they'll all fail you when the times turn. They always do. So many Majors before you, much brighter, stronger, and more dedicated have fallen to themselves. I don't see anything different in you than I saw in any of the others."

These words seemed to empty of Elise of all her remaining faith. She was beginning to feel hopeful about this new course in the future, proud of the progress she'd been making, but Thentis made it sound like she stood no chance. It seemed the only path she could walk led to nothing but pain. The insistent feeling of helplessness—hopelessness—that had prodded at the back of her mind since she arrived in Lumeria suddenly became a sharp sting.

Thentis sat back in his chair, his eyes locked on none but Anton, who stared back, terrified. The entire hall was silent.

"You are suggesting they are unprepared emotionally?" a timid benchman asked slowly, trying to keep the hearing moving.

"I think he meant they possess a quality that brought about the fall of the other Majors," another said.

"What fall?" the one to Orphia's left said. "How many Majors have been struck down?"

"None," the peacock lady said, rummaging through her papers. "All seven bloodlines remain unbroken, as far as we know. But certain events have triggered a change in an individual Major's incentives in the past. Some have been emotionally compromised beyond the point of returning to their post, some have been crippled, some have grown reluctant to do their sworn duty, becoming less involved with their role. In a few situations, the Majors have committed high treason against the Arc Leaders!"

"A few situations?" an appalled benchman repeated. "How many?"

"Three have been recorded," she replied.

"One conclusion that can be reached," the man to Orphia's left said, "is that whatever qualities these Majors possess, it makes them no better than the average Major of the past, in a time that demands they be better than the average Major. With these children's late training, personal distractions, and little understanding of Lumerian culture and history, these five are not fit to become Majors and will not serve the purpose they are here for."

"Perhaps they will not live up to the Major's standards, but Lumeria will do better with them than without them. They will even be able to pass the Lumire on to the next generation who will be raised with the proper treatment that Majors should grow up with," another pointed out.

"That is assuming they will even make it long enough to pass it on," one said, prompting Elise to nearly faint on the spot. "If they are needed now because of the danger they will potentially face, who is to say they won't be struck down? Who's to say that they won't end the line of Majors, losing the Lumire while they are at it?"

"They will indeed have to proceed with caution, but that was a risk every single Major before them took," Orphia said.

"Laleitha Ataliarma," the man to Orphia's left said suddenly.

Laleitha looked up, suddenly sitting attentively.

"Significant challenges will arise that will test you physically, but more importantly, mentally. What challenges have you faced in life that have tested your emotional or mental limitations?"

Laleitha hesitated. Elise knew what her sister was thinking but wondered whether she'd have the courage to explain it.

Lee opened her mouth. "I've never had the support of parental figures. My father has issues with . . . commitment, I guess . . . so screw him. And my mom's been trying her best, but she's always working . . ."

Elise mentally applauded her sister for mustering up the courage to talk about that part of her life to so many people, hoping she would somehow telepathically get that message across to her.

"And you responded to this how?" the man pressed on.

Lee shifted in her spot. "I removed myself from certain places that made me think about it. I found a thinking place. I spent my time there."

"With company?"

"Not usually. Sometimes a few close friends or Elise," Laleitha answered, looking at her sister, who looked back with the same nervousness in her eyes.

The man adjusted his glasses. "So, you drove yourself inward."

A few benchmen nodded or raised their eyebrows, and some looked at Thentis.

Elise immediately thought back to the peacock lady's words. *Some have been emotionally compromised beyond the point of returning to their post, some have grown reluctant to do their sworn duty, becoming less involved with their role.* That was the point this man was trying to make, that their methods of overcoming emotional challenges would tear them apart. Elise felt like shouting at this man. In spite of herself, her face grew heated at the realization.

"How about you, Mr. Hystar? What was your greatest hardship in life?"

Anton's face was angled downward, but as he spoke, his large, dark, terrified eyes drifted upward. "Kinda the same. Things changed with my family, and I can't really rely on them anymore."

"Oh, I'll bet that was difficult," the man replied, though no sympathy shone is his voice.

Elise's hatred for him expanded in her chest like a balloon, making it harder and harder for her to breathe.

"And how did you deal with this pain?"

This time, Anton didn't even bother making eye contact and his voice was only a mumble. "I got past it."

"What?"

Anton shrugged. "I got past it. Became who it made me. Life went on."

"Interesting," the man replied. "How about you, Elise Montason?"

Where should she start? Not including Marty's death—which would not sit well with Orphia since he was a fugitive with information on his son—there had been no events in her life that made her suddenly devastated, no challenges that suddenly sprang up, nothing that threatened her. All of the pain her life developed gradually—her mother's detachment, her father's expulsion, her confusion in her life, the isolation, purposelessness, and meaninglessness she felt. It was unexplainable, and if she even attempted to explain it, she would sound melodramatic. This was a corner she couldn't work her way out of.

"I . . ." she said, "I guess I've never had anything happen to me that really . . . was a huge challenge." She went on slowly, trying to gather her words. *That's not right.* "I mean, my dad was gone just like Lalietha's, but he was always gone, so it wasn't like anything changed to make that happen. I just tried to teach myself to not let things bother me if I knew I was walking into something that would." She cringed inwardly at her own answer.

The man didn't say anything but turned to Darren, who shrugged. "My life has been fine."

Given his reaction to Orphia's last question, that's a blatant lie.

Thentis shook his head, catching the man's and Orphia's attention, but the man disregarded this, murmuring something to himself then moving on to Gerald. "Mr. Rodum?"

"Thentis knows," Gerald said through gritted teeth, staring at the grim, frail man with fire in his eyes.

"Yes, we've heard about your father," the man responded. "Tell me about him."

Elise scanned the audience, looking for her instructors. Talious probably winced at the man's every word.

"He was erratic," Gerald said. "Always angry. He was vile, sometimes cruel . . . it goes on and on."

Elise closed her eyes. *Watch your words, King. He is trying to make you angry.*

"He didn't have any respect for any of us," Gerald finished.

"I see," the man said. "Thentis implied there's a story there."

Gerald set his jaw, clearly not wanting to talk about it.

"Do you have nothing to say?"

He looked up toward the audience, searching, before looking back at the man, then staring at his hands. "He hit my mom a few years ago."

"Just the once?"

"*Yes*, just the once." Gerald sounded like he was prepared to murder this man. "But there were a million times I thought he was about to do it again. Not just with her, with my siblings too."

"Did you have any fears of this before the incident occurred?"

"I thought he was better than that."

Stop it, stop it, stop it, Elise thought desperately, horribly afraid for her friend.

The man opened his mouth, prepared to ask another question, before he suddenly closed it and looked over at Thentis, who stared at him with his cold blue eyes. The moment lasted only a fleeting second before he turned back to the Majors. "So *this,* ladies and gentlemen," began his conclusion, "is how frail the Majors are. How *easily* they will be torn down, if not physically then emotionally. One will isolate herself, one will attempt to brush it off as nothing, one tries not to feel at all, one can't see beyond what he wants to see, and the last becomes hateful and paranoid."

This isn't fair. It was an echo of a thought at this point. It meant nothing. It did nothing.

"I agree," another concurred. "These five are not in any way prepared for this role."

"Is that not why we are gathered?" another woman said. "To figure out which exceptions should be implemented in order for them to be inducted? To keep them in Lumeria for the sole purpose that they may pass on the Lumire is absurd, even a violation of the Ancient Convention!"

"The induction hardly seems possible at this point," the man who read from the scroll said.

"But it must be done, regardless," the same woman replied. "One way or another, these five will become Majors. That is not up for debate."

Eyes turned to Orphia, who nodded. "She is correct. It must be done."

"We give them eleven years to fulfill these requirements," the man to Orphia's left proposed. "And due to the late start, we will push the minimum induction age back to twenty."

"The minimum induction age cannot be changed," Orphia told him. "It was set there because that is what the first Arc Leaders believed was the proper age. When the Majors were still young and learning, gaining experience, but old enough to make wise decisions."

"And what do you propose would be done with the Majors if they do not fulfill these requirements within your eleven-year time frame?" one from the end of the bench asked.

"Sit as council chairmen but not Majors," the man replied. "Perhaps even military leaders until they pass the Lumire on. If this is to be done, they will be able to use the Lumire in emergency situations."

"The induction criteria said nothing about a time frame in which the training must be completed," one pointed out.

"Yet if they do not complete their training in eleven years, that will suggest they are not fit for the role and will not provide sufficient protection even if they do reach the requirements," he replied.

Orphia cleared his throat. "We can agree that section two is a point of concern, correct?"

The bench agreed.

"Mr. Quingimont, will you please read section three?"

Mr. Quingimont stood once more and read aloud. "The official induction ceremony must take place before a Major is given authority, in which they swear the oath that binds them to their assigned region. Once given the authority of a Major, the Majors must uphold their seat in the Lumerian Council with the manner and responsibilities of all other chair holders. Once a Major is given full authority, their own task force will be given to assist them. These people are known as minors and take orders only from the current Majors. After obtaining at least fifteen years of experience as an inducted Major, the military decisions of a Major can be overruled by the Lumerian Council, but the decisions of all the Majors can be overruled by the Arc Leaders only if the opposition is unanimous." He looked at Orphia briefly before closing the binder and sitting down.

"Well, there is nothing that is in need of discussion," Orphia said. "We are now open to plan proposals."

"The eleven-year time frame sounds reasonable," a benchman said.

"No exception should be made to the training or the patriot's labor," one suggested.

"Agreed," several said together.

"In fact," Orphia said, "it seems only logical, since most Majors begin training at a young age, and since these five need to *prove* their dedication, they should have to complete more than one patriot's labor."

"Perhaps three," the man to Orphia's left said.

Orphia looked around his bench. "Three patriot's labors?"

"Agreed," several said again.

Elise turned to Anton beside her to whisper, "What is a patriot's labor?"

"I don't know," he whispered back. "Hercules had twelve labors, maybe it is something like that."

"Those seem so specific though," Elise said. "There aren't any hydras here, are there?"

Anton shrugged.

"Are there any other aspects that need addressing?" Orphia asked, looking around at his bench once more.

No voice rose.

Orphia closed his files. "So we have come to a conclusion then." He looked down at the Majors. "Within eleven years, you must complete your training and perform three patriot's labors, then you may be inducted if you are sixteen or older. The rest of the guidelines, though they follow more general and less relevant conditions, can be found in the revised criteria for Major induction. As of tonight, you will be officially registered in my book along with the information the Lumerian Council supplied to us. Now, we'll break for lunch, and the assigned instructors of the Majors will give their testimony. The Majors are dismissed."

CHAPTER FOURTEEN

"Your Five Majors!"

Talious was the only one who sat with them on the way home. "Well, I'd almost think you're beginning to enjoy the fame," he said to them.

"What makes you say that?" Elise asked.

"You kids got Thentis to *talk*," he said. "He hasn't spoken in years. Centuries. Maybe ever, I don't know."

"Well, he sure didn't seem too happy." Darren snorted. "Probably would have been better if he kept his mouth shut."

Talious shook his head. "He's never pleasant. Usually all he does is shake his head and stare people down."

"Talious, what is a patriot's labor?" Elise asked, changing the topic.

He shrugged. "An act of bravery that somehow benefits Lumeria. People usually get medals for them," he briefly explained. "When we get back to the Arc City, it's going to be my job to get you to the stage on time for you to be presented, so stick with me through the station."

"Stage?" Laleitha repeated.

"Yeah. Did you think you were being presented in the street? People from all over Lumeria are coming to see you."

Elise knew better than to ask why. She would get the same answer as before. She simply turned and stared out the window.

People from all over an *empire* were traveling to see her. She hadn't done anything celebration worthy. She didn't even know if she could. Thentis sure didn't think she could, and there was a good chance Thentis knew her better than she knew herself. She shuddered at this thought. Thentis had looked right into her, watched her temper flicker, read her very nature like a book, saw each and every one of her qualities, her glaring flaws, her strange quirks, her weird, twisted sense of self that allowed her to be confident sometimes but left her extremely insecure other times. He knew her inside and out, just like he had with so many other people. He'd seen braver people, smarter people, more determined and strong-willed people, or maybe people who at least knew what they were doing.

Elise didn't deserve a crowd. Elise didn't *want* a crowd. They'd look at her expecting some great icon, and if they didn't see how she betrayed this expectation when she was presented, they would eventually when she failed to uphold the legacy.

Evening had fallen, the sky streaked with gold and indigo, by the time they finally arrived. They stepped out of the silver train, which gleamed in the fading sunlight, and onto a crowded platform. From the moment the door opened, people began crowding around, cheering and shouting questions. A few journalists pushed their way to the front of the crowd; one even had a cameraman stumbling behind her.

Elise was immediately overwhelmed. Talious led the way, shouting right back at the crowd. She followed close behind, slipping between bodies and stepping over people's feet. She sent a glance back at Laleitha, who stared at people's shoes as she scrambled after her friends. Gerald seemed to be trying his best to be polite as he walked between the small splits in the densely packed area, nodding a greeting to some and uttering an apology to those in his way. Darren looked like a ticking time bomb that would blow any moment, and sooner or later a rude remark would leave his lips, most likely to one of the journalists. Anton was nowhere to be found.

"Get out of the way," Talious said. "Move it or you're gonna suffocate the poor kids. Get out of the way. Put the microphones away; they aren't answering questions."

Security guards stood at the door, in black and yellow uniform.

"When did they have this arranged?" Elise thought aloud. Then she remembered that this great "presentation of the Majors" was not nearly as last minute as it seemed to them, as their transitioners had neglected to tell them about it until before their hearing. The Majors had been the top news since their arrival, but Ellington in particular had guarded them from this. Elise wasn't sure if she should be resentful or appreciative of that.

Talious pushed open the glass doors and Elise dashed through, followed by Darren, then her sister, then Gerald. Anton emerged from nowhere and Elise found him right beside her in the room. The crowd tried to funnel through after them but the security guards closed the door behind them and tried to calm the raging mass of people.

Talious briskly took them along the hall to a skyway that opened into a completely empty and locked-down building Elise had never been in before. It was not as grand as Fort Kingshold but it was laid out identically, with white walls replacing the dark blue.

"Where are we?" she asked Talious, trying to keep up with his pace.

"Fort Rookshield. The twin of Fort Kingshold. These two are part of a three-building system with the Cylinder, which is where the Arc Leaders meet."

"The Arc Leaders are . . ." Laleitha said.

"The leaders of the Lumerian Council," he answered. "Kind of. It's hard to explain. No more questions for today. You got that?"

He led them through a few halls until they reached the front entrance, with doors the same style as Fort Kingshold's except these were milk-white. When Talious opened the door a crack, instead of seeing an exit to the beautiful Lumerian city, a blue curtain hung above, shielding them from the outsiders.

The moment the door opened, the buzz of a ginormous crowd radiated throughout the empty hall.

After a moment's hesitation, Talious opened both doors wide. Only the curtain separated the Majors from the crowd now. A lump formed in Elise's throat.

"Come on, then," Talious said, ushering them through the doors, where they were forced to step up on a slightly raised stage just outside, enveloped by the safety of the curtain.

Then, Ellington appeared from the other side of the curtain, poking his head through and beaming when he saw them. "Good, you are here on time. The people are anxious. The emperor himself came and will be addressing the people after we present you. It will be quite the speech, I imagine. Emperor Evanstin is an excellent speaker, I personally think. He would like to speak to you after the presentation, by the way. Just a meet and greet—low pressure."

With the emperor? That hardly sounded low pressure.

Ellington clapped his hands together, looking incredibly pleased with himself. "Okay, here is what we are going to do. You five will stand in a row, and when the curtains lift, stand here and await my instruction. I will answer questions for you. You just stand and look dignified. You are basically celebrities. Then, the emperor will speak. Okay? It's very simple; you don't have to do or say anything."

"All right," Gerald replied as a few others murmured.

"Sure," Elise said, clipped.

Her bones were tingling with apprehension and, at the moment, a great deal of spite toward Ellington's enthusiasm welled within her.

He turned around. A deep breath filled his lungs, followed by a swift exhale. "Okay," he said without turning around, "let's get started."

Elise pushed down her rising anxiety. *Get it together. Just need to get through this. Just a few minutes. Just a few minutes.*

"Oh, and by the way," Ellington added, turning back around. "You will see some men carrying guns and pacing across the rooftops. Don't be alarmed. They are there to protect you."

"What?" Lee exclaimed.

"Here we go," Ellington breathed to himself before walking around to the other side of the curtain. There must have been a microphone set up, because within seconds, his voice boomed out over the exhilarated crowd. "Ladies and gentlemen, may I have your attention, please?"

The million voices began to settle. He had to repeat the request a few times before the crowd finally quieted.

After a few opening remarks, they heard Ellington hand the microphone off to some representative of the emperor, who apparently had prepared a speech for the occasion. It drew out for hours in Elise's mind as she snapped in and out of focus from horrible anxiety and hurried reassurances. She adjusted her outfit—which Ellington had helped her pick out for the occasion, being that she needed to dress formally for her hearing in front of Orphia—a white blouse with simple floral patterns and a plain black skirt that reached her knees.

The speaker was honoring those who lost their lives in the Lumerian civil war now. Elise played with her hair restlessly.

Now he was talking about the Majors as a symbol of peace and prosperity. Elise picked at her sleeve.

I just want to get this over with.

Elise didn't hear what the speaker said, but suddenly the crowd roared, clapping and cheering. It must almost be time. "Of course, now seven has turned to five," he said, "and these five come here from the Other Society, an outside world. But as our first emperor said, 'Across all worlds, the just will stand.'"

The cheering grew louder. Elise's stomach twisted in knots. In a few seconds, her face would be front and center and these people would be cheering for her. Elise Montason. Elise Montason, who had done nothing for them.

"And these five will stand with the just, as they exist only for you, the Lumerian people. So, I present to you," he exclaimed, "Your! Five! Majors!"

The curtain swung upward, reeling around a large pole overhead, revealing a million bouncing, cheering people and thousands of flashing cameras. The crowd filled up the entire block, spilling up the stairs where fences were set up on the third step, extending through the streets ahead. They covered the field that flanked the fort like bees on honey chambers. There were millions of them, all cheering for her because they expected her to protect them. All of them. Cameras began flashing the minute the curtain had started upward, and Elise's heart nearly stopped when she finally saw what it hid from her. Her eyes went wide and her mouth fell open. Her body stiffened and her veins went cold. These were the Lumerian people.

Until a day ago, the "Lumerian people" was a concept Elise couldn't grasp. It was like reading a book about a civilization on the other side of the world. It was obvious they existed, but they hardly seemed real. Now, as Elise looked over them, her last remaining spirits were crushed by the weight of the Lumerian people's hope. Making it through today would be a minor challenge, seeing as every day from that moment forward would be the same battle as today's. She would face the judgment of Lat leaders, the expectations of the crowd, laborious hours of physical pain, and the constant threat of the Prime Devise looming over her day after day.

She stood, just as Ellington instructed, only because she had to. Her eyes were glazed with moisture, her chest was moving too much. She was petrified.

Even Gerald's pride faltered here. The five stood, solemnly looking out at the huge body of people. Elise stiffly turned her head to meet her sister's eye. Laleitha had a single teardrop rolling down her cheek. Anton was pale as a ghost. Gerald mirrored Elise's horrified expression. Only Darren stood with his mouth closed and his eyes fixed solemnly ahead, but he looked as comfortable as a brick wall, sucking his cheeks in and pursing his thin lips.

Ellington had taken a few steps down the stairs to speak to the reporters who were nearly toppling over the barrier, microphones outstretched.

The streets where people crowded were lined with various stands and food trucks, and Elise was again struck by how many people had been long prepared for this event that she had only just been informed of.

Atop a few buildings, which Elise had to strain her eyes to see, were the silhouettes of heavily armored men carrying large long guns. If her heart could have sunk any further, it would have upon seeing them. Some paced across the very edge of the rooftops, while several others could be spotted stationed on balconies, all of them with guns at the ready.

The thought of somebody attacking them was the last thing she needed, so she decidedly tore her gaze away. Instead, she scanned the crowd until her sight fell upon a single area blocked off from the crowd. Among them stood a well-dressed, dark-skinned man surrounded by security guards. He stood tall and proud, and on his head was a simple silver crown. He wore a sleek black suit with a few golden traditional Lumerian designs by the collar and the bottoms of the sleeves. Beside him was a young girl who wore a yellow and white dress, with a white flower in her hair. The man smiled at them, pride in his eyes, looking more dignified and composed than Elise had ever felt.

The man began coming toward them, the guards falling into a two-man line, with two flanking this man—whom Elise assumed to be the emperor—and the girl beside him.

The fence by the stairs opened to let him through. The security guards and the girl stayed behind. The man stepped up to the entryway where the five stood, watching him.

He headed toward Elise, closest at the end of the row. He was taller than Elise had anticipated.

"Welcome at last, Five Majors. My name is Sowl Evanstin," he said, shaking her hand with a firm grip. "I'm the emperor of Lumeria."

Elise cleared her throat, her mind completely blanking. "Uh, Elise Montason." She finally found her words. "Nice to meet you."

He nodded and grinned. "You, as well."

He moved on, greeting Anton, Laleitha, Gerald, and Darren. He began talking with Gerald, who seemed to be the only one on the cusp of functioning at the moment. Elise's gaze went back to the crowd.

Suddenly, something caught her eye. On the building across from the fort, behind the crowd, on one of the ledges sat the lumpy silhouette of an odd figure. Elise squinted, straining her eyes for more detail. He was holding something—something long. Then, in the middle of the black shape, a red light began to beam.

Suddenly, a window in a nearby building shattered and all of the rooftop guards' guns snapped in that direction and fired. Loud cracks rapidly sounded, echoing throughout the streets. Gasps and screams erupted from the crowd as the attention turned to the shattered window in the distance. If there was any attacker there, he would have been killed.

Elise's eyes flicked back to the red light, which still remained, that she had been looking at before the window shattered. What the light meant clicked too late and before she knew it, there was another loud crack.

"Get down!" somebody shouted, and she dived to the cement.

Something whizzed over her head and impaled the ground a few feet behind her. Elise looked up, blood pumping in her ears. People continued to shriek and panic, this time louder as they rushed in a mass of chaos. The dark figure that shot had stood and was headed toward the edge of the building's ridge. To the right, on another building, two more figures dove from their ledges. A black cord burst from one of the attacker's dark shape, latching onto the adjacent tower. The man swung and landed on the rooftop of another building, speeding away. The man who fired at her dropped out of sight while the last used a similar cord to swing into a different position.

Elise scrambled to her feet, looking at her sister.

"There are six!" Talious shouted from behind. "Armed and moving. You five, get to safety!" he yelled at them.

Elise, bewildered, looked toward the emperor, who had taken Gerald by the arm and was pulling him in her direction. Her view was obstructed when people began rushing by, headed toward the fort, toppling over whatever was in front of them. Then, suddenly, she was lost in a sea of panicking civilians.

Elise weaved her way between frightened bodies, her sense of direction completely disoriented. She couldn't see beyond the swarm of people running back and forth in front of her. Desperately, she shoved her way through, eyes latched to the building that the two gunmen had swung from. Finally, she broke from the crowd, finding herself in the street far from where she had started. There was nowhere to hide, no better place to run. *Think!* She rushed along the road. *The best way to keep from being caught by surprise is to always keep your attacker in sight.* Talious had said that. She stopped, facing the building the man had been perched on. She felt something within her, her purpose, bubbling like boiling water, compelling her to follow this man. Standing in front of the Lumerian people was far too much for her, but here, on the ground, she could focus. Here, she knew what she had to do and that she could do it.

She dived into the alley beside the building, trying to picture where he had gone from there. *What do I do when I find him?*

Make sure he doesn't see you, obviously. She answered her own question.

Elise emerged to find another street, this one slightly narrower. This time, however, she spotted another dark figure leaping along the rooftops.

She pursued from the ground, eyes not leaving him.

I am not ready for this! Elise had felt her purpose inside of her, a sense of duty that would have relentlessly prodded at her mind if she had hesitated, but now that she faced the moment, she was beginning to doubt herself.

Internally, she panicked but she kept running. The cold hand of fear squeezed her heart, making it hard to breathe. She suddenly flashed back to the night Sar Prague captured her. If she had known about the Lumire then, before she had accidentally used it to save her life, would she have tried to use it to fight back? She had killed a man with it, set him on fire. That was a part of the story she had forgotten about. Elise Montason was a *murderer.* How had she not thought about that until then? Unless, of course, she had unconsciously blocked out those horrible details of that night. The thought of what she had done seemed distant and almost unreal, so Elise elected to process that night later and turn her attention to the present issue. *If I can get through that, I can get through this.*

She pushed on.

The man ahead of her gained speed and, suddenly, he leapt, another black cord extending from his outstretched arm. The man curved in the air, making a wide turn across Elise's path until he hit the ground running on the other side. There was one building between them now, and Elise took off in that direction, the man flashing in and out of view as they passed buildings. This man was faster than she and began to pull away.

Desperate to catch up, Elise strained to quicken her pace, before suddenly, the man stopped reappearing. Elise skidded to a halt.

He had turned and Elise had lost him. She took a deep breath, now realizing her forehead was lined with sweat. A humming shadow passed over her and she looked up to see an oddly shaped helicopter flying overhead, a spotlight angled from its bottom, scanning the ground.

Taking another deep breath, Elise plunged back into her chase, diving between the two buildings the shooter had disappeared behind. Out of sheer luck, she glanced into an alley and spotted the man climbing the fire escape.

The man then noticed her and paused. In the middle of the street, Elise froze, feeling the dark figure's stare on her. In one swift movement, he took the gun from its harness on his back and pointed it at her.

In fright, Elise jerked herself sideways as another *crack* echoed through the air. She tumbled, rolling back into a crouched position as her eyes frantically scanned the scene to locate the man. An aircraft's light suddenly turned in the direction of the sound, but the man was concealed in the shadow of the building.

Before she could even process what happened, the pulsing in Elise's forehead returned, and her senses exploded. Dazed by her suddenly hyperactive awareness, Elise staggered to a wall for balance. She had not yet gotten used to the sudden sensory overload. The hum of the Lumerian Security Enforcement helicopter was amplified, and she could feel the pressure of its engines in an area a few feet away. The man's movements were clear now, too, and Elise sensed the heat of the gun's barrel.

Focus on that. All of the other feelings began to dissolve as her focus converged on the man.

She could see him much more clearly now, perched on the fire escape, angling the gun at her. Within it was some sort of dart. A sudden sharp pain made Elise flinch. The man's gun exploded in his hands.

The man's surprise paralleled her own and his wide eyes, the only part of his face showing, fixed on the shards that remained suspended in the air.

Elise approached, eyes intent on him. He began to scramble up the fire escape. The shards of the gun were still in her control. It was as if they were attached to her and she could move them like she could move a hand.

Her senses traced a dart; it was smooth and metallic, and there was some sort of poison embedded into its tip. In a chance move, she willed the dart toward the man, but moving it was more difficult than she had anticipated.

I just need to threaten him with it, move it in front of him to stop him in his path.

The pulsing intensified, but the dart only dangled in the air. Her vision blurred. She was pushing too hard, but nothing was happening.

Then, to Elise's surprise, the dart shot forward, straight past the man. The man had reached the roof by now and suddenly ducked in a frantic attempt to avoid the dart.

Before Elise knew what happened, the aircraft's light turned onto the man and gunshots began rapidly sounding in the air.

The man's body jerked as something hit him, and he fell from his perch at the building's edge, landing with a sickening thud in the alleyway. Elise involuntarily let out a cry of alarm at the sight, both hands shooting up to cover her mouth.

There was a long moment in which Elise just stared at the body, her mouth hanging open, her body trembling. With immense relief, she realized they hadn't killed him, merely stunned him, and he lay half-conscious on the ground. Soon, LSE officers would likely come to take him into custody. She stood then, alone in the street but for him, hearing nothing but the sound of her breathing, feeling nothing but a bead of sweat slowly roll down her forehead.

A distant crack split the air and her head snapped up. Another dart had been fired, most likely at one of her friends. She dashed toward the noise, running as fast as her legs could move.

It was growing darker by the minute and Elise could hardly see, but it wasn't long before she heard familiar voices in the distance.

"Is he okay?" Gerald's voice asked.

"He's fine!" Darren yelled.

"I'm okay!" Anton exclaimed. "Where did the shooter go?"

"I don't know!" Gerald cried.

Elise slowed her pace as she exited the alley. "Are you guys okay? Did you see him? Where did he go?" Her words spilled out between breaths.

"Elise!" Gerald beamed.

Anton was on the ground. Gerald knelt next to him as Darren stood to the side.

"I think he went back the way he came," Anton said, pointing at a rooftop.

"Where is Lee?" Darren asked.

"I don't know," Elise responded. "I haven't seen her. We need to follow him."

"Follow him? Isn't he the one we're trying to get away from?" Darren almost shouted.

"Calm down," Gerald ordered, standing up.

"We have to know where he is," Elise said. "Then he won't be able to surprise us and kill us. We have to do something, Darren. We can't just cower down and hope they won't find us."

"She has a point," Gerald agreed, remarkably calm.

"And what will we do when we find him?" Darren questioned with a raised eyebrow.

Gerald helped Anton to his feet "We use the Lumire."

"We're barely trained!" Darren protested. "And I'm just gonna take a wild guess here and say that those men—the people who are trying to kill us—they're *very* trained. And, the people who are after them, the LSE or whatever, they've had years of training too."

Elise bit her lip, looking between Darren and the alley she'd just come from. He was right, she knew, but she had survived an encounter with one assassin, right? Or maybe that thinking was dangerous. After all, Talious did tell them to find safety, and if Talious thought they were still out here, he might send people after them, putting more people in danger.

"He's right," Elise said. "We should go back to Fort Kingshold."

Before any of them could reply, another gunshot sounded, deafeningly close, and Elise let out an involuntary shriek.

She barely had the time to look up and see the man standing on the rooftop of the building beside them before Darren shouted, *"Run!"* and she took off, sprinting for her life.

Paying no attention to where she was going, Elise weaved through the streets at a hundred miles an hour, running until her sides ached. She didn't even realize that Gerald, Anton, and Darren weren't with her until she chanced a look back over her shoulder to see if she could catch a glimpse of her attacker. She didn't have time to fear for them though. She needed to get back to Fort Kingshold.

When she arrived back at the fort, the crowd had scattered. A few people still ran around, mothers looking for their children or people asking around for news. More officers had spread out through the dispersed crowd, urging people to get to safety. Elise ducked and swam through the chaos until she found a familiar face at the entrance.

"Elise! Where are the others?" Ellington gasped upon seeing her.

"Which way did Lee go?" Elise sputtered, breathing hard now after all the excitement. "I haven't seen her anywhere. Do you know where she is?"

Ellington gave her a worried expression. "You are the first I've seen. Are any others okay? What happened? There was a firefight?"

"The boys are fine, at least the last time I saw them," Elise explained at lightning speed. *"Where is Lee?"*

"I'm okay," a voice that sounded like Laleitha's said.

Elise turned. Her sister was in tears and had a cut across her cheek, but Elise embraced her sister anyway. Laleitha nearly collapsed onto her, her entire body weight crashing down, except for her vice-like grip around her sister's shoulders.

"I killed him, Mont," her sister whispered in a shaking voice.

Elise pulled free of her sister's grip to scan her face with concerned eyes. "What happened?"

"He attacked me and I killed him," she said, trying to hold back a sob. "I stabbed him with his own knife."

"How many are left?" Elise asked, turning to Ellington, a hand remaining on her sister's shoulder. Her mind refused to process the fact that her sister had just killed somebody. "The boys are okay," she added, looking back Laleitha.

"We need to keep you two safe," Ellington said, gesturing toward the doors to Fort Rookshield. "The skyway to Kingshold is on the second floor, right side. Go and wait in your rooms."

After a few fruitless protests, Elise and Laleitha followed his orders, eventually finding their way back to the magnificent blue hall. This time, the hall was busy, and people were running from room to room calling reports on various topics to each other.

"We have six response teams still out there."

"I need Westbecker on the line *now.*"

"Get this man to the hospital."

"Captain Westbecker is being updated now on the pursuit of the shooters."

"The protection of the Majors are top priority. Where are they?"

Elise raised her voice to call to the person who asked this. "We're okay. The other three are alive and should be here soon."

The lady who had asked for them turned in surprise. "Thank God, you're alive." She almost laughed. "You just made my job about ten times easier."

Elise exchanged glances with her sister. This woman was young, only slightly older than them. This seemed to be the case quite often in Lumeria.

The woman straightened up, her smile gone and her formality returning. "Uh, come with me, please." She led them left, down a busy hall and into a room titled *L.L. Command* and below *Authorized Personnel Only*. Ellington's instructions would have to wait.

The room they entered was dimly lit and relatively small. A large table sat in the middle, around which a decorated man and a few others stood facing the far wall. A large screen covered the middle of the wall, while six others lined either side of the central screen. The middle board showed a bird's-eye view of the city and several moving icons that Elise guessed to be the planes—or perhaps troops on the ground. The other, smaller screens showed videos being recorded from cameras on the vests of the officers or cameras mounted on the planes.

"Captain Westbecker," the lady said, calling his attention from the screens.

He turned, looking at the two.

The young woman cleared her throat and adjusted her glasses. "These are two of the Majors. The others should be here shortly."

The man nodded. "Thank you. They'll remain here until the situation is under control."

Captain Westbecker, whom Elise recognized from the first night she arrived, turned to them. "Wait," he instructed them. "Don't touch or do anything." He turned back to his work. "Officer Garvis, update on the pursuit?"

A muffled voice sounded from a speaker. "We found the body of the fifth."

"And the last one?"

"We lost track of him on the Seventh Avenue loop."

"Good God, you *lost* him?" Westbecker said. "Red team, take Fifth Avenue, try to follow their tracks. Black team, I need you on Westing Street cutting off the exit. Converge at the capital skyscraper; he seems to be headed there."

"They tried to take out our academy headquarters. If they have another explosive set up in the capital skyscraper, the damage would be catastrophic," said another who stood to the Captain's right.

Explosive?

"These are trained killers," Westbecker told him. "They aren't hired assassins. Their mission is to take out a target while they are in the open, and if it doesn't go according to plan, they take as many as they can with them to their deaths. *Garvis, where is our man?*"

"We've located him and are in pursuit," the speaker-voice replied. "Stand by."

Elise's eyes scanned the screens until she found the small one on the bottom left that showed, from above, a man running along the buildings.

Suddenly, the man was struck backward by an unseen force. A smaller pair of arms protruded from the edge of the roof and up climbed a familiar friend.

"Oh, no," Lee groaned, her tone dreadful.

"What is he thinking?" Elise gasped.

The man, still on his back, angled his gun and fired. Gerald's hand shot out and the dart paused in midair, hanging in place as if suspended by string.

Confused and panicked, the man threw himself at Gerald, tackling him off the edge. The dart dropped to the ground as the two fell.

Elise gasped, her heart thudding in her chest like a deadly metronome. Gerald would be mauled; he was going against an assassin who had years of training while falling off a building. Elise could almost picture his bloody and broken body lying on the cement below.

"What the hell was that?" Westbecker exclaimed. "Garvis?"

"Target is down," the voice in the speakers said.

"And the kid?"

"He's okay, somehow."

Elise allowed herself to breathe again. She cast a glance to Lee, whose tenseness had passed as well.

Captain Westbecker straightened, looking somewhat proud and very relieved, as if four tons of stress had been lifted from his shoulders. "Well done. Clean up teams will be arriving on scene shortly."

The door opened again and Anton scampered in.

"Anton, thank God," Laleitha said.

"How is it out there? Are King and Darren alright?" Elise asked.

He nodded. "They're coming."

Captain Westbecker turned to them. He had a hard, stony face, clean shaven and fighting wrinkles. His black hair hardly peeked out from under his hat, which was decorated with badges and pins that Elise couldn't tell the meaning of. He was tall and built, had brown skin, and wore a blue and black uniform with badges and pins that matched his hat.

"Well," he said, "you three are worth quite a riot. As you might remember, I'm Captain Ferris Westbecker. We've met before."

Elise nodded. "I remember."

He folded his hands behind his back. "The other two?"

"They'll get here soon," Laleitha responded.

"Good. Our highest-ranking LSE investigators will get to the bottom of this . . . incident. You shouldn't have to worry about your safety going forward."

Elise wasn't so sure.

"I will be personally instructing you once you're transitioned. Alongside Mr. Talious, of course." He turned back to the table and addressed the others. "You're dismissed."

They nodded and exited the room. As they were exiting, Gerald and Darren slipped inside. Elise caught Gerald's gaze and gave him a silent greeting. The five followed Captain Westbecker to the table in the center.

"I meant to catch you after your presentation, but obviously that was derailed rather quickly," Westbecker said. "While I don't have any business for you today, I'll be taking over your training for the next two months."

Elise exchanged confused looks with her sister.

Sensing the confusion among them, Westbecker explained. "You're wondering why. Well, this may come as a shock to you, and I completely understand that, but it's extremely important. Keep in mind that what I'm about to tell you is completely confidential and you cannot tell anyone what you will be doing, not Ellington, not Talious, and especially not Ms. Kilodrist. Do you understand?"

Elise nodded slowly, growing increasingly anxious.

"I'm going to be giving you your first assignment," he said, "and it will go down in the capital of the Prime Devise."

CHAPTER FIFTEEN

The Hidden Passage

The entire next day, the five were a jittery mess of nervous energy, dreading the moment Captain Westbecker would walk in and give them their assignment. Darren had been especially irritable, snapping at people whenever he got the opportunity and making snide remarks constantly. Anton, on the other hand, spoke even less than usual, wordlessly drifting though the day like a ghost. Laleitha shut herself away at every opportunity she was given. Even Elise felt the tightening coils of stress in her muscles. Her stomach churned at even the mention of what Westbecker had told them. Gerald perhaps had been able to compose himself best, but even he was slightly jumpier than usual.

That moment came in the evening, when their usual training was scheduled. Instead of going to the gym with Talious, they met Westbecker in a dark conference room.

He placed a large map of Inseana before them before plopping down at the head of the table and skipping the preamble. "We know that the Prime Devise is behind these attacks," he said, "but we can't let them know that we know, or our access to the information will be cut off. We have a man on the inside. Keep in mind that this is highly classified information, so what I share with you now is never to be repeated. I don't believe in keeping my operators in the dark unless I have to and, given your positions, I doubt the Prime Devise will think you're particularly aware of what's going on in the LSE. The point is, as long as the Prime Devise is oblivious to our man, he will keep feeding us information."

"But we have to act eventually, don't we?" Gerald said.

"If your training goes according to schedule, you will be the ones that will carry out my developing plan."

"A plan for war?" Gerald pressed, sounding slightly mortified.

"A plan to prevent a war. All-out war with the Prime Devise would be catastrophic. Our plan won't be put into effect for certain, but I have been pushing for it. The details are still sketchy as of now, but I'm certain that having the Lumire involved will make it much safer," he explained. "Their military revolves around a system of schemes that lay out a plan for any given military scenario, with a backup plan and a backup backup plan, all ready to be set into motion the minute their initiating variable is altered. As long as they have that, they are unbeatable. It is the most effective system in Lat history, and since the Prime Devise took power, it hasn't ever failed them. Ever. It is all held in a highly classified hard drive in the central command station in Litrite, the capital of Inseana. I believe if we take out that drive, they have nothing."

"And you think that will prevent war?" Gerald said, raising his eyebrows.

He raised his hands. "Let me rephrase that: we will win the war before they start it."

Elise and the others exchanged skeptical glances.

"Why does there have to be war in the first place?" Darren said, his voice flat and somewhat sheepish.

"You think the threat against your lives is the only offence the Prime Devise has committed against Lumeria? They're planning something, our man knows that, but he can't figure out what. And Lumeria can't afford to wait to find out."

"What about the guy in the mask?" Laleitha said. "What if he is there?"

The captain looked slightly surprised by this. "Oh, yes, Second Reighba. He will be there, you can count on that, but you should hardly have to worry about him. It's his father, Alfred Reighba, who is the real problem. He is the chancellor of the Prime Devise, codeveloper of their master drive and arguably the most dangerous person alive."

Elise shared another look with the others. They were all nothing short of unsettled by these words.

"And we'll eventually have to face him?" Gerald said.

Westbecker nodded.

"And you think that his drive is his main source of power?" Elise said, her eyes unfocused as she put on her thinking face.

"The Prime Devise uses what it called the Domino Tactic. It's not dependent on strength, ability, or the Lumire. What somebody does is set up everything in a way where if he tips the scales just a little bit, everything will go his way. Like pushing one domino and watching the rest fall. First, he sets up the dominos, then when the time is right, he pushes them down. They already have all of their dominos in place, but none have fallen yet. The Prime Devise has become especially skilled at making these dominos undetectable and misleading. That is what the drive is responsible for, and that is why they will be greatly weakened if it is taken out."

Elise nodded, catching on.

"Now, the entire reason the Prime Devise is so desperate to take you out is because, so our information suggests, you will get in the way of one of their plans. Every one of your actions must be kept secret, because our spy has also informed us that the Inseanans have an inside man within our order who has been leaking our movements."

"The Prime Devise has an inside man too?" Gerald repeated.

Westbecker nodded grimly.

"So any of the people we talk to here could be the spy," Elise said, her calm voice betraying the nervousness that chilled her bones.

The captain sighed. "The Arc Leaders are doing everything they can to identify the spy. We are taking as many precautions as possible. Especially with you five."

"So we're going to be doing what?" Darren asked.

The captain put his finger over the red dot in the center of the map. "You are going to destroy their master drive."

✕

Transitioning. Lumire training. Sparring. Strength training. Cardio. Lumire training. Sparring. Planning. This was every day for the next two months.

Ms. Kilodrist could tell something had changed, as Elise and the others always came to their lessons tired and sore, but she said nothing. Ellington expressed mild concern, but they all assured him it was nothing.

Despite the terrible strain, Elise felt she was truly making progress, as she could now move small objects pretty masterfully with the Lumire and sparred decently against her fellow Majors.

The sparring was, surprisingly, the most brutal part. After forcing them to face each other, Westbecker would force them to fight *him,* insisting that anyone who would attack them in the Prime Devise would be around his size and strength. Westbecker would lunge at them, punch them, while shouting instructions to block, dodge, and counter. He sent them tumbling away time after time. After several rounds, Elise would remain on the ground, trying to catch her breath, until Westbecker yelled at her to stand. Even then, it was nearly impossible. After each terrible defeat, they left frustrated and humiliated.

And so this became routine. Though Elise's body was straining through nearly every second of it, by the end of the two months, she felt leaner, quicker, and stronger. Most importantly, however, she felt like she knew what she was doing for once in her life. She could think much more strategically than before, and she could apply these skills to the reality in front of her. Her reflexes were quicker, her instincts were more refined, and she no longer found herself terrified at the idea of sparring.

But every time she reminded herself that she would soon sneak into the heart of the Prime Devise to destroy their most vital master drive, she still felt years away from ever being ready.

Ж

"Memorize this layout," Westbecker told them, placing three blueprints before them in the same conference room they started in. "Our inside man managed to provide this for us: the layout for the Prime Devise base in Litrite. This"—he tapped a red line drawn with a marker—"is your route. Memorize all of this."

Ж

July 3rd was the day it happened.

"Be ready," Westbecker told them the night before. "I want you in the conference room by seven o'clock tomorrow night. It is imperative that nobody knows about this. Do you understand? Not even council members because that is where the leak is."

"Nobody knows about this?" Anton asked.

The captain shook his head. "Nobody can until it's done. We don't have time for a council meeting; we hardly had enough time to prep. This has to work, and it will."

"And if not?" Elise asked.

"Then we'll have to answer to both the council and the Prime Devise."

⚔

That night, Elise woke from her nap at 6:20. Westbecker's words had itched at her mind all day. After an extended day of transitioning, in which she tried her hardest to behave as normally as possible, her few hours of downtime were spent sleeping or tinkering with whatever materials she could find.

She pushed herself from the couch on which she fell asleep and wearily made her way over to the kitchen.

"She lives," Gerald remarked, leaning on the island with an energy drink in his hand. Only he and Darren were in the kitchen, while Laleitha and Anton were nowhere to be found.

Elise picked up a glass from the counter and poured herself some water. "You guys ready to fuck up the Prime Devise?" she muttered, still half asleep.

Darren snorted. "Hell, no. This all seems very wrong."

"Well, he is technically one of our instructors," Gerald pointed out.

"But carrying out an attack on the Prime Devise without consulting the council?" Elise said. "Darren's right—this feels wrong."

"Would you prefer we just sit here?" Gerald responded. "I feel so useless right now. We have the Lumire, and we're potentially the most powerful people in this entire city, this entire *empire*. I want to be able to put that to some use. I'm not just going to sit here and wait until some council thinks I'm ready when there are people out there trying to kill us."

"Orphia said we respond to the needs of the council and the emperor," Elise said, her voice cold. "Not the needs of ourselves. Westbecker is sending us in without an okay from the council *or* the emperor."

Darren shrugged. "Yeah. Then again, with all that stuff that Orphia was throwing in our face, I kinda feel like we have to. You know, to prove ourselves."

King nodded in agreement.

"To who?" Elise scoffed. She looked at Gerald. "Thentis?"

He shrugged. "Ourselves, I guess. We're going to be protecting an empire; may as well start us off with something that is simple and important."

"There's nothing about this that's simple," she remarked.

Gerald shot her a look, one that said, *You're not making things better.*

Elise sighed. "Let's just not screw up," she said, setting down her glass and walking from the kitchen. "We'll call that plan A."

When they arrived at the room, Captain Westbecker was waiting for them. He laid out the map for them one last time to go over the plan. "That is where we will enter," he said, tracing his finger along the outline. "You know the floor layout; the entrance you want will be on the west side. You get in, plant the changes in the room with the drive, and get out, nothing else. Be ready to fight if you run into any guards, but only fight with the objective to get away, not to kill. The electrical networking you want is here." He pointed to a circle drawn at the east end of the facility. "Disable that to put out the power and get in. From there, taking more than fifteen minutes to get in and out is dangerous. Got it?"

They nodded.

"Good. Gear up," he said. "We're leaving."

Moments later, Elise found herself in a gray and black task force uniform with two daggers she hardly knew how to use strapped to her back. Westbecker considered giving them handguns, but none of them had any firearm training, except for Laleitha, but she had fired only rifles before. The five crammed into the back seat of a van, not unlike the one Talious retrieved them with before bringing them to Lumeria, while Westbecker drove.

"You know I did my homework on this guy," Gerald whispered to his friends. "A lot of people have their doubts about him."

"Why is that?" Elise whispered back.

"Mostly because they don't think someone who wasn't born in Lumeria should have the authority that he does."

"He isn't Lumerian?"

"Not by birth," he answered.

The five watched from the windows as the vehicle turned from the road into a forest. "I'm taking you to a hidden place," Westbecker told them from the front seat. "A little shack in the woods. I have a transportation rod there that will take you to a small hideout just outside of the Litrite base. It's against the laws of the Ancient Convention for transportation rods to cross borders among the empires, so I have to keep it out here."

They drove on. The forest seemed to stretch on forever, and by nine thirty, Elise was beginning to grow anxious.

I can't believe I'm doing this. What if I fail? What if I die? What if Lee dies? She took a deep breath, trying to shove those thoughts away. *You are a Major. You can do this.*

Finally, Westbecker pulled up to a tiny wooden shack that looked to be on the verge of falling apart, and stopped the engine. "Take these." He held out comms to each of them. "I'll be listening in the whole time. If I tell you to abort, get the hell out of there no matter what. Do you understand?"

"We understand," Gerald said, hooking the comm into his ear. "We got this."

"Don't get cocky. You haven't done anything yet."

Westbecker led them into the shack, which contained nothing but a small stool, on which a glowing green transportation rod sat. "This is it," he said, taking it in his hands and tossing it out in front of him. It opened with a *snap*, and a green-banded portal extended before them, revealing a window to a small tunnel of jagged rocks. Near the ceiling of the tunnel, the rocks split, and moonlight poured through into the darkness.

Swallowing their fear, the five crept to the hole. It was difficult to squeeze between the jagged edges that made up the narrow passage, which Darren, the first to attempt it, learned.

Elise cocked her head to try to peer through the cracks and catch a glimpse of what lay ahead. All she could see over her friend's shoulders were the stars. Polaris, at the top of the Ursa Minor, to be more specific. It was still the same sky in Inseana.

When Darren, Laleitha, and Gerald had made it through, Elise slipped between the rocks, twisting her body as she did so. Anton followed through last. The small space was hard to maneuver, but when she emerged, she found herself on a sloped landscape in what appeared to be a forest.

"Good luck," Westbecker said through the comms in their ear. "Be careful. Be quick."

"It's this way," Gerald said, kneeling behind a shrub and nodding toward the west. In the distance, gleaming walls could be spotted behind several staggered trees. They were in a reserve of some sort, because city surrounded their cover of the trees. It looked to be only evening in Inseana by this time. The other four crouched behind a bush, facing the facility, as Elise ran in circles to catch a glimpse of every angle. A slow understanding built within her. The small forest reserve flanked the Prime Devise command base, which sat in the middle of the Litrite, the capital of Inseana. They were about to enter the heart of the Prime Devise.

They approached the base until they reached the edge of the trees, ducking behind another large shrub. In front of them was a large lot in which several cars were parked and loading crates were stacked.

From that position, Elise finally saw the base and its landscape. The facility was on a steep hill. Far below it, the city began and stretched on into the horizon. On the other side of the facility, curving around toward the back side, a river ran over a hydroelectric energy wheel before spilling down the steep slope into the sparkling lake below. Several different buildings were strung together, winding around each other in a tangle of halls. Most were boxy, but there was one tower at the far west end and one that protruded toward them, shaped like a short but wide cylinder. The walls were a dull but sleek silver or black, with wide, clean windows that shone with the light within. It was nothing short of beautiful. At first, this bothered Elise, but as she stared at this base, the home of the masked man, the beauty almost seemed sinister.

"What does it look like out there?" Gerald asked.

"We are surrounded by city," she said. "Meaning we can only escape through the passage we came."

"Well, did you think Westbecker was kidding when he said we were in the center of Inseana?" Darren scoffed.

"Quiet!" Gerald snapped.

"Look," Anton whispered, pointing toward the lot in front of them. A line of trucks was driving into a large garage as loading containers upon loading containers were being lifted and brought inside by large forklifts, trucks, and even a small crane.

"We'll catch a ride in one of those crates," Gerald said, which was far better than their last plan: momentarily disabling the security system in order to get in.

"Okay, but that means we're going to have to run across that empty lot with no cover and a shitload of eyes on us," Darren said.

"We're going to have to be fast," Gerald said.

"We need cover," Elise responded.

"We don't have cover."

"We *need* cover," she hissed again.

"We can't run out in the open, Gerald," Laleitha agreed.

"Well, unless you have any ideas on how to get some, we're going to have to do without," he spat back.

"This is sure jolly and grand," Darren muttered. His friends ignored him.

Gerald was right. As much as they needed to hide themselves, there was no way they were going to do so.

"Then we need a diversion," she decided.

"I have an idea," Anton said, standing up.

"Anton, you can't go alone," Laleitha protested.

"Chill your tits, I'm going with him," Darren said as he stood up next to Anton. "Lead the way."

The two scampered off, headed left, away from the trucks.

Elise surveyed that direction. In the distance, a circular room protruded from the main building, overlooking the lake, with blue-tinted windows. She strained her eyes to catch a glimpse of what was happening inside.

"I need glasses," she muttered to herself.

Moments passed. *What are they doing?* Suddenly, one of the windows of the circular room shattered. Fire rose both inside and outside the cylinder, and shrill alarms began to scream.

Gerald almost jumped to his feet. "Where are they?"

"I can't see them," Elise said.

"There's our diversion," Laleitha remarked. "We have to go."

Elise took a deep breath, trying desperately to soothe her anxiety. *You think too much,* Talious had told her on her first day of training. *Don't think. Just do it.*

Laleitha stood, taking form as a dark figure in the bushes. "Now." She took off, at first in a slow crouch. Gerald sprang from his cover as well. Elise pushed up from the dirt, silencing the nervous thoughts that buzzed in her mind.

She charged on, into the open lot. The cement sped under her as she strained to keep her footsteps light. Any minute, somebody could glance in their direction and see them, and any second, the security alarms could start to ring instead of the fire alarms. This was taking too long; she had to move faster. Wind howled in her ears and her heartbeat thudded in her temples. *Go!* she internally screamed, frantically pushing her legs faster. Cold, fear-ridden sweat speckled her forehead. She was getting close now.

The crate was growing larger. It was long, blue, and made of crinkled metal.

Laleitha and Gerald had slid into cover. Elise followed, diving behind the crate and rolling back into a crouch. The three hung there for a moment, listening to their steady breathing as footsteps and vehicles passed by.

"You good?" she asked Laleitha.

Her sister nodded. "I'm good."

Gerald stepped around to the edge of the loading container. After pulling on the lever for a few seconds, he figured out how to unlock it. He pushed one metal flap open just enough for them to slip in.

The container was dark and loaded with smaller boxes, each shut and sealed tightly. A few small holes lined the side near the door, and two vents opened at the top of the walls.

Gerald quietly pulled the door shut, wincing at every slight creak. Elise took to the holes, peeking out at the crates beside her.

Finally, voices sounded outside of their hiding place. Elise held her breath as she strained her ears to catch their words.

"He said keep working," one was saying.

"I'll just be gone for five minutes," the other complained. "I want to find out what that was. I'll fill you in on the details when I get back."

"No, you won't, because you'll be *here*, working. We have a job to do. Now, hop to it. We gotta finish this load before the night crew arrives."

The sound of footsteps faded, and Elise spotted a body pass by through her narrow looking space. This was followed by the sound of a machine firing up. Elise exchanged glances with Laleitha and Gerald.

"Brace yourself," Gerald mouthed.

The crate lurched. Elise stumbled and fell against one of the boxes, biting her tongue to keep from yelping. The crate shifted sideways, sending a few boxes sliding. The three braced themselves on the boxes, peering through the holes to see the shadow-lined cement moving under them. A few seconds of moving later, there was a bump in the road and the light from the stars was suddenly cut off. Elise pulled herself to one of the larger holes to peek through. They had entered an industrial garage and were being placed among several identical loading containers.

There was another rumble that sent the three staggering and then a beeping sound of a vehicle backing up. A shrill hum followed and, through her hole, Elise watched her crate pulling away from the floor. This garage was taller than she had realized, and they seemed to be rising higher than Elise previously thought the roof permitted.

Finally, the hum stopped, and the container rattled backward as it was pushed into the stack. The crate stopped moving and everything was dark. It was then the three allowed themselves to breathe again.

Gerald went to the front of the container. "How high are we?"

Laleitha climbed onto one of the boxes to look from the wider slots in the walls. "I can't tell."

"How long is it until they'll be back?"

"We'd have to wait to detect the pattern," Elise told him.

"We don't have time for that."

"Why not?" Elise asked. "The longer we go undetected, the better."

"Yes, but what about Anton and Darren? They'll have to find their own way in and we can't guarantee they won't go undetected. The quicker we get this done, the less time they'll have to figure out we are here," Gerald explained in one breath.

"But if we act rashly, we'll be detected before Anton and Darren can even get in," Elise pointed out.

"Will you two shut up?" Lee snapped from her perch on the boxes. "We were part of the last load. They're closing the door."

"We have to go," Gerald said.

He leaned against the door, pushing one side open ever so slightly.

"Keep going," Lee said. "They aren't looking."

"How exactly do you plan to get down?" Elise whispered to him from over his shoulder, gazing at the downward drop.

"I'll figure something out," Gerald replied, irritably.

"Well, you might want to do it sooner rather than later because if you don't, you'll die."

"I said I'll figure something out. I didn't say when," Gerald snapped.

Elise sighed, unwisely looking back down at the floor so far below. "Why did Westbecker pick us for this?"

"Because you have the Lumire." Westbecker's voice rang in her ear.

Elise jumped. She'd forgotten she had her comm in.

"So it may be a good idea to use it."

"Lumire, right," Elise said. "Why didn't I think of that?"

"Because you're dumb," Lee replied without taking her eyes from the vents.

"The lift," Elise said to Gerald, pointing to the rising platform that had hoisted their container into position.

"I see it," Gerald murmured, focusing on it. Moments passed with no progress. "Everyone stop moving. You're distracting me," he snapped.

"We're not moving, King," Elise said.

"Right . . ."

Suddenly, the lift shot upward.

"Stop!" Lee cried. "People are looking this way. It grabs too much attention."

"You know what?" Elise opened the door a little more. *If I can move objects through the air with the Lumire, I should be able to keep myself from falling.* She grabbed onto the outer lever that connected to the lock, pulling one foot up to it as well, awkwardly tuning her body from the inside of the container to the outside.

"Elise, what—" Gerald reached for her.

"Hold the door," she said. "Don't move it." She pulled her other leg up, forcing herself to let go of the lever to make room for her foot. There she balanced, refraining from making the fatal mistake of looking down again. "I have an idea," she said as she did so, "that is somewhat logical but has a better chance of working than our other ideas."

Elise groped for a hold until her fingertips ran across the slots Lee had been looking through. Jamming her fingers into the narrow openings, she gave herself something to hang on to, letting her extend her legs wearily until she was standing, a foot on either end of the lever. She reached her other hand to the top of the crate, where she scratched for something to grasp once again. Her fingers caught hold of the end of the door. Taking a deep breath, she jumped, almost groaning as the pain filled her muscles. Forcing her arms to bend, she fought through the excruciating sting until she was able to hoist a leg over the edge and pull herself onto the container's roof.

She stood there, breathing heavily, finally allowing herself to look down. "Yup," she said. "This should work."

Gerald and Lee followed while Elise walked to the long end of the container. The stack next to theirs was at least twenty feet lower.

Gerald had reached the top now and was crouching on the roof, eyes intently darting among the passersby below.

Laleitha had almost made it and was rolling herself on when Elise looked back. "We're going to have to jump."

"That will make too much noise," Gerald protested.

"Guys," Laleitha said, pointing upward. A few feet above them, a jungle of roof support beams and air conditioning tubes ran across the ceiling.

Before they knew it, they had climbed up into the network of narrow walkways and balance beams. It was darker up here, shielded from the light that poured from the fixtures suspended on the very rods they walked on.

Elise ventured ahead, following the path of a large tube with air flowing through it. She traced a hand along the tube to keep her balance on the beam, her gaze wandering below, locking onto any person who still lingered. The distance between her and the floor made her stomach clench, but she found it imperative to keep an eye on the enemy.

Where did she need to go? It was almost a maze up there, extremely disorienting. The tube Elise followed curved downward and came to a stop, blowing cold air to the ground so far below. She continued on, walking steadily but at a brisk pace. It wasn't long before she leaned down and supported herself with her hands as she went on.

She reached a wall and, looking below, noticed a large door opening into the room behind the wall.

From so many hours of staring at the layout Westbecker provided, Elise knew this was the entrance to one of the halls. Scanning the beams for Laleitha or Gerald, she found Laleitha perched on a beam across from her and Gerald skimming across one ahead of her.

Now, there was no choice but to drop. Elise warily looked downward at the descent, instantly thinking back to the time she fell on the night she was captured. She had saved herself using the Lumire before she even knew she had it. If she could do it then, she could do it again.

Laleitha met her eyes and Elise pointed downward. She looked down then back up at Elise skeptically then shot a glance to Gerald.

Elise took a deep breath and closed her eyes. If she failed this, she would die. It wasn't long before the pulsing in her forehead ignited again and her senses exploded.

Inward. She immediately had control over herself. She looked at Lee, whose eyes glowed like a cat's. *Down we go.* With that, Elise slipped off the bar.

CHAPTER SIXTEEN

Inside the Prime Devise

Elise immediately regretted her decision. The earth rose to meet her at a ridiculous speed, and not only did she struggle to control her body, she fought to keep the panic from engulfing her like a spider's dinner.

Her heart rate spiked as the earth flew by her. *Stop!* Frantically, she extended an arm, becoming more and more desperate by the second, then abruptly, she paused. Her body jerked from the inertia as she caught herself, still suspended in the air only a foot off the ground. Carefully, she lowered her feet to the ground, one at a time.

There was a crash from behind, and Elise whipped around to realize she had been noticed. One of the workers had dropped the boxes he was carrying and stared at her.

"Hey!" another shouted.

Elise ran. She darted through the doors and into a white hallway. It curved and split into junctions, and Elise racked her brain for the directions she needed to go to. First, she went right and found herself in an empty hangar, likely for airplanes. It was long and dark and opened in the middle where a long, navy blue, raised platform spread across almost the entire length of the hall.

She took to the walls, weaving between the columns that supported the overlook above her. *Stealth.* Westbecker had taught her. She jumped, catching hold of one of the beams and hoisting herself up. She would not have been able to do that a week ago. Clambering to her feet, she tiptoed to the edge of the beam, taking hold of the edge of the overlook and pulling herself up onto the higher platform.

Alarms began to blare all around her and lights began to flash.

"Shit!" Westbecker shouted in her ear. "Where are you?"

"Too far in. There is no exit," Elise whispered into her comm and continued on.

Of course, there were the hangar doors, but by the time she figured out how to open them, she would most likely be caught. Using the Lumire on such a large structure was out of the question. She turned into an empty hallway and took off down it. She was still relatively close to the building's perimeter, but she needed to get to the main control center, which was near the middle.

She took the first right she found and dove into a narrow room with nothing but machinery lining the sides. A startled woman looked up from her work and reached for the phone. In panic, Elise threw herself at her, wrestling her to the floor. The woman, who was larger than Elise, kicked and thrashed and threw Elise off as the she attempted to scramble to her feet. Rushing to be rid of her, Elise slammed the woman's head against the wall, a strategy Talious told her to do when given the opportunity, and the woman went limp, dropping to the floor.

There was a door at the other end of the room, but Elise stared at the wall of buttons, compartments, wires, and levers, taking a moment to catch her breath. She then realized what she was looking at. Elise stood at the heart of the facility's mechanical network. If she could just figure out what did what, she could cut the power. *Never mind figuring things out. Just disable everything.*

She reached for the knife strapped to her back. Tugging the blade from its harness, she cut every wire she could find, opening compartments to find more. Sparks flew as she did so, and she made well sure to keep her face clear of the popping and sizzling flames. Finally, she cut the right wire and the alarms were abruptly cut off. Machines everywhere powered down and the lights flickered to black.

She looked around, admiring her work, before taking off once more through the door at the other end of the room. This one led into a narrow hallway with railings instead of walls, ending in an open network of rooms and platforms below her. People were scrambling everywhere, but luckily, there were not many on her floor.

So much for stealth.

Guards would be on her any minute. If she was ever going to make it to the master drive, she needed to get out of the open.

Elise didn't know this part of the base, meaning she would have to improvise. Their plan had gone sideways and she was now flying blind. She tried with every fiber of her body not to panic as she ran through unfamiliar halls, fearing at every turn that she'd come face to face with a guard. Voices sounded ahead of her, coming around the bend a few feet away. Looking right, she spotted another corridor breaking off the main hall. She ducked into the passage, pressing her back against the wall and praying they didn't see her.

Four men, large, muscular, and angry, were running from one hall to the other, all wielding guns. Luckily, they didn't pass her but opened a large door on the left wall before coming to the area where Elise hid.

"Get to central command. Its protection is top priority," one man commanded.

Peeking around the corner, she noticed their uniform. They were the guards she had to avoid, and they had guessed where she was going. Waiting for them to pass through, she stepped from her hiding place, making her steps as quiet as she could.

This was both fortunate and unfortunate because it meant they would lead her straight to where she needed to be, but also it would be under guard.

As quietly as she could, she followed them through the door. She entered a staircase winding downward. It was chilly black metal and took wide curves that circled the entire hall. She glanced over the railing and saw no end to the staircase, as if it spiral on forever.

Glancing over her shoulder every other moment, she continued down the steps. Finally, she came to a dark hall. She heard beeping in the distance, but otherwise it was silent. Elise cautiously made her way through the darkness until she came across the guards again, only to find them scattered on the floor, half-conscious. Bullet holes seeped with red, most of them digging into the stomach or shoulder. Against the wall crouched the last guard, slightly smaller than the rest, with his hand on his head. He looked up when he noticed her and sprang to his feet.

Elise's veins tightened and she put a hand out for no apparent purpose except to signal him to stay away.

"Elise!" he exclaimed as he jumped to his feet.

She stood frozen, staring at him with wide eyes.

"It's me," he explained.

He held his hand in front of him and his skin seemed to move over him as his entire body transformed, until she was staring into the face of Anton.

Elise was speechless. "How—"

"I don't know," he said. "I was with them. Then I . . . shot them. I . . ." He ran a hand through his hair, looking painfully at the bodies. "I don't know. I can . . . I can *shape-shift.*"

Elise let her gaze slip from him to the bodies. "I don't understand."

"I turned into one of them," Anton said, still breathing hard. "And then I shot them. I . . . I . . . How do I make sure they don't die?" he cried.

"You shape-shifted using the Lumire?"

He nodded, sniffling.

Elise's mind began spinning before she realized she was getting distracted. "We have to finish the job," she said.

He nodded and turned. "The drive should be around here somewhere."

"Where are the others? Where is Darren?" Elise asked, following him.

"I don't know. I lost him somewhere in the main hall," Anton answered.

The hall curved, seeming to go in a circle until a doorway opened to their left. Inside, they caught the attention of four more guards, who looked up from their work. Instantly, hostility flared in their eyes and they raised their guns, firing.

Elise's arms instinctively went up to protect her face, but the bullets bounced off her harmlessly. *They don't know we're the Majors!*

She reached for her knives, sliding them from their sheath on her back. The pulsing in her forehead resumed, and she immediately felt her unstable power weaving around the handle of one of the knives.

The confused guards had stopped firing and briefly looked at her as if she were an alien. One flew at her but she threw her knife at him. It impaled him in the stomach and flew right back into her hand on her command. She paused, suddenly impressed with herself, but before she knew it, another had knocked her backward so hard she was slammed out of the room and into the wall. Stumbling, she tried to regain her balance, but the man flew at her again, thrusting her head into the wall and putting a hand around her throat.

Her head rang and a cough fought its way up her throat as the man choked her. With all of her desperate strength, she jammed the knife into him. The stress on her neck instantly went limp and the man fell, sliding his body off her blade.

Lunging herself back into the room, she sloppily kicked a man off Anton. The man's head flew backward when her foot smashed into it. The last man grabbed her from behind, one muscular arm squeezing her throat while the other lifted her from the ground.

Anton had sat forward and bared his knives to the man, but Elise's vision was blurring too much to watch. Her head began to burn as she was unable to breathe in. She fought and kicked furiously, but her energy drained too quickly to put up a longer fight.

Suddenly, there was a crash and something burst through the ceiling. Debris and dust showered, one brick hitting Elise's strangler in the head and stunning him, giving Elise enough wiggle room to break herself free.

The thing that had smashed through the floor lay in the middle of debris, stirring and groaning in pain. The body rolled over and there sat Darren, covered in white dust.

Elise hardly had time to react; the other two men had broken from their stunned trance and had lunged for her again. She threw a knife at the one who had tried to strangle her; he knocked it aside, flying straight toward her. She swung her other knife but his arm shot out, stopping her swing with the knife inches from his face. His other arm jabbed at her face, hitting her square in the cheek. Pain flared through her, and she cried out in agonized anger. Another blow was fired before she could react, knocking her backward once again. The man pounded, sending her stumbling backward. Elise let out a furious grunt before finally ducking his next punch and slashing her knife across his stomach. He yelled and punched her again, this time forcing her to the ground, where she jabbed at his feet with her own in one hard kick. The man staggered away and Elise advanced. She lunged at his chest, knife ready, but he countered her strike again and threw her away from him. She landed on both feet and immediately pushed herself back. Suddenly, Darren flew at the guard, slamming his head against the wall at full impact and knocking him to the ground. He stayed down.

Elise glanced in Anton's direction. He lay on the floor, blood running from his nose and his eye beginning to swell. His attacker lay on the floor on the other side of the room. They sat there for a moment, breathing heavily.

Elise's face burned where she had been punched over and over again. Her vision was still slightly blurry, but luckily her mind was still sharp. That must be the Lumire at work.

"Well," Darren said between breaths, "that went well."

Anton groaned, sitting up. "King has the charges. Where is he?"

"I don't know," Elise said. "This is it?" She walked to the large computer against the wall; buttons and levers covered the panel in front of it.

"I think so," Darren replied.

They'd be damned if they were wrong.

Elise's fingers hovered over the keys, hesitating before she hit the return button. The screen flickered to life. Apparently, this drive was connected to a different energy source than the rest of the building. The screen opened to the last page it was on before it went to sleep. *Attack on Master Drive. Retrieval of Backup System,* she read aloud.

"They have a backup?" Darren repeated.

Elise opened the plan's details. "It's a hard drive. It's hidden in . . ." She scrolled through the information. "The Way?"

"What's that?" Darren asked blankly.

"I don't know."

"Where is it?"

"Doesn't say."

Suddenly, Gerald and Laleitha ran into the room from the hall, pausing when they spotted their friends.

"You missed the fun," Darren told them.

Gerald tilted his head. He was breathing hard and had a bleeding cut along the side of his face. "Oh, trust me. We've had plenty of our own."

"All right, let's blow this place," Laleitha said, unhooking the charges from Gerald's belt.

"Guys, they have a second drive," Elise told them.

"What?" Gerald exclaimed.

"You heard that, Captain?" Laleitha said into her comms.

It wasn't until then Elise realized she lost hers in the fight. "It says they have another set of plans in a drive in a place called 'The Way.'"

"It doesn't matter. We're still blowing this one." Lee placed the first small explosive on the computer screen, the second and third on the machinery surrounding it, and the fourth in the middle of the room.

"Detonator," Gerald narrated, pulling out a small trigger. "You ready?" He looked around at his friends, who nodded. "We have five minutes to get out the moment I activate them. Let's try to stick together and exit through the industrial garage."

They nodded again and he pressed the button.

The explosives lit up, a high-pitched beeping suddenly beginning. The five took off, dashing back to the staircase. Elise darted up, taking two steps at a time until her legs grew painfully tired. Finally, the stairs ended and they were back into the bleak white hall.

"This way," Gerald said, taking a right.

Suddenly, their escape route was cut off by armed guards who were racing down the hall toward them. Elise skidded to a halt and dived in the other direction, sprinting as fast as her legs could carry her.

They charged down another passage, this one opening into the hangar. More guards came rushing, firing at them with bullets that had no effect. In a panic, they rushed into the nearest escape that wasn't blocked by guards. Suddenly, the door snapped shut behind them and they found themselves in a dark room.

Darren slammed himself back against the door. "No!" he shouted.

The lights flickered on, revealing a white, blank space with a window across the far wall. On the other side of the window stood the masked man.

"Welcome back," he greeted them.

"King?" Elise said, directing her attention to Gerald. "How much time is left?"

"My father has been looking forward to meeting you," the masked man said. "Though we expected it to be under different circumstances."

Another man approached and stood next to him. He was leaner and shorter than the masked man, but there was something sturdy and solid about him. His face was slightly wrinkled and his eyes were strangely soft, despite his stern, carefully guarded expression. He folded his hands behind his back as he surveyed the five, showing particular interest in Gerald's threatening look.

"These are the Five Majors," he murmured. "I shouldn't be surprised. I don't know what I expected, but now I'm not sure what my colleagues were so afraid of."

Suddenly, there was a muffled *boom* in the distance and several computers behind them began to buzz. The power had apparently been restored.

The man winced and kept his eyes closed for a moment before saying, "There it is."

There goes the drive, Elise thought grimly.

"I'm sure Captain Westbecker was excited to have a new set of toy soldiers," the man went on. "What is he trying to achieve this time? Is he trying to prove himself? Prove you? Or maybe he just can't live without a war to fight."

"Sounds like you've been searching for one yourself," Darren pointed out.

"Makes for a good story, doesn't it?"

Elise's gears began to spin. What *did* Westbecker want with them? They had hardly any knowledge of the Prime Devise besides what they had been told and he had sent them to blow up their most crucial strategy component. He had turned the Five Majors into pawns on a chessboard.

"Who can be a war hero when there is nothing but peace?" the man continued.

"You think he sent us here so he could be a hero?" Gerald snorted.

"I think that there is more to this story than he's letting on," the man said. "And you should come to wonder what that may be. But that is not why you are still here."

"Our borders are closed, all underground passages have been obstructed and the skies are being monitored," the masked man told them. "Yet you've managed to get past all of that and we want to know how."

"So let's start the easy way—the straightforward way," the older man said. "How did you get in here?"

Elise looked from Gerald to Anton, who exchanged looks with Darren and Laleitha. In a silent agreement, they all kept their mouths shut.

"Why are you here?" he questioned on.

The Majors said nothing.

"Why were you sent? Was it a council decision?"

"We were looking for vacation spots," Darren answered in full seriousness.

The man shook his head, a tinge of frustration working its way into his face. "Here is how we are going to play. Peter will interrogate you each individually and if you continue to remain quiet, we will kill one of you to demonstrate our resolve."

The masked man reached up and took off his mask, revealing the face of a boy no older than Darren, but his face was hard and tough. He had black, messy hair, emerald green eyes, and a small, white scar along his chin. He was not at all who Elise thought he would be.

"If you continue to hold your tongue, we will strangle all but one of you and return your cold corpses back to Lumeria in a routine shipment of rice," the elder man went on. "Now, who would like to go first?"

"I will," Elise said, refusing to look at her teammates.

CHAPTER SEVENTEEN

Second Reighba

The room they led her to was as blank as their first one, except this one had a cement floor and dark walls with a few suspicious stains splattered on them.

Elise had met the eyes of each of her friends, except for Lee, before being escorted out. In the corner of her eye, Elise had noticed Laleitha's expression, pale, unmoving and not breathing, a mortified look. Elise would reveal too much if she met her sister's eyes, so she continued forward. It was her silent plan to stall their captor's attention as long as possible so that the other four could develop an escape strategy.

Her escorts had put a dagger to her neck and warned, "If you try anything, you die." Somehow, since she had reached the drive, she didn't feel afraid. She wasn't sure if it was the work of the Lumire, adrenaline, or if fear had become such a standard feeling by then her body stopped reacting to it. Either way, all she felt was focused.

Elise sat completely still, occasionally glancing up at the camera in the top corner of the room.

When the man under the mask entered the room, Elise didn't move. Her gaze followed him as he walked across the area and sat in front of her, placing his mask next to him on the table.

"How did Westbecker convince you to do this?" he asked, his voice carefully neutral.

She didn't speak, her face remaining blank. *Think, Lee, think. Get us out of here.*

Elise had her moves carefully planned out in her head. Though improvisation definitely was not an area in which the thrived, when she was prepared, she was at her best.

"He ordered you. You're his attack dogs now, apparently. How long has your council been conspiring against Inseana? Did Westbecker think he had a foolproof plan?" Second Reighba asked on.

I'm sure you know all about those. Elise still said nothing.

"How long did the journey take?"

Elise shrugged.

The man—boy—whom Reighba had called Peter, and Captain Westbecker called Second Reighba exhaled, moving on. "Why did Westbecker send you?"

Elise gave no answer, but let her gaze trail to the table, where it remained.

He tilted his head. "Why now?"

These were questions Elise didn't know the answers to. She remained silent.

"Why *you*?" was his next question. "Was this a practice run? To see if you could ever serve any purpose here? Were you trying to prove you're worth something? That you even belong in Lumeria? Or is this just the council's way of getting rid of you in a way that they could pin on us?"

"We were trying to stop the attacks," Elise answered, her voice quiet.

She wanted him to stop; he was picking at a wound Elise would rather let close. These had been questions she murmured to herself at night, too disturbed to search for the answers to. She feared if she found the answer, she'd lose all sense of purpose for being in Lumeria. The very thought of never belonging in Lumeria nor the Other Society—being outcast from every possible home, shut out from every identity—it was almost too crushing to consider.

"Which attacks?"

"You know which attacks."

"Which. Attacks?"

"The one at Fort Rookshield," she answered. "And the one that landed us here. Before we knew about Lumeria."

His intrigue visibly deepened. "Hmm. And how were you able to confirm that the attack on Fort Rookshield was issued by us?"

"It doesn't take a genius."

"Is that what they told you? That we're the enemy?"

Elise bit her inner lip. "I think I came to that conclusion myself when you sent a guy to abduct me and my sister."

He studied her, pausing. Sitting up a little straighter, raising his chin slightly, he said, in his same, meticulously neutral voice, "It's been months since Sar

Prague brought you to me, months since you discovered the Lumire. You've obviously been training with it. Why, then, does Lumeria feel threatened by us when their symbol for protection has returned?"

"I remember Sar Prague." Elise responded, ignoring his question. "Didn't you kill him after you killed that little girl?"

"Like you did today with the Prime Devise officers who were trying to do their job?" He fired back.

Elise was struck silent, her feeble illusion of being somewhat poised stifled. She hadn't even realized what she had done. She was so caught up in securing her own safety, in the intensity of the moment she didn't think about who these men were, didn't comprehend they had names, faces, voices, maybe even families. Who would have to tell their spouses or children they weren't coming home? Elise had created demons in a split second and didn't realize it until somebody brought it to her attention. *Oh no.*

Oh no. She could not live with this.

"Sar Prague's death was in his deal." Second Reighba—Peter—said. "If he brought me the wrong person and an innocent died, he would die too. The girl's death was his fault so he paid for it."

"You were the one who pulled the trigger." Elise said, sounding much more upset than she had hoped. Tears were beginning to well in her eyes, blurring her vision, but she pushed every ounce of energy left in her to fighting them down.

"I pulled the trigger while the gun was against your forehead too," he said. "And look where you are now."

"Lumerian or dead," Elise replied, her voice breaking slightly, thinking back to that night. "That's what you said to my sister."

"Too bad 'neither' wasn't an option," he replied. "Because now, you'll either talk or die. It will be reported to the public that you were caught in the explosion that you initiated. It will be very tragic, but it can only be expected from an othslic."

"A what?"

Second Reighba looked at her with raised eyebrows. She couldn't tell whether he was amused or exasperated at her unfamiliarity with Inseanan slang.

Elise closed her eyes and took in a shaky breath. "You're going to kill me regardless. That was the gamble last time. The only thing that's dependent on my choice is the method of *how* you kill me."

Second Reighba smiled, seeming genuinely entertained. "You're getting the hang of this." He then leaned forward, his voice growing dark. "But Talious isn't here to save you this time so it looks like you aren't getting out of it. *How did you cross our secure borders?*"

Now was the time to play the card she had up her sleeve, the reason Westbecker sent her. "I still have one thing you don't."

He jumped to his feet, throwing one of the knives from his belt to the camera. The knife impaled the unit right in the middle of the lens. Elise sprang to her feet as well, tipping her chair backward and stumbling over it as she backed away.

He turned to her, reaching for a small device on his left arm with his right. It appeared to be a black cylinder he wore like an armored bracelet, but in it were tiny rods of differing material. He turned it with a small click and suddenly, his skin began to change. Like Anton had done with his appearance, Peter's skin morphed into a dull-colored but magnificent metal.

Elise had put her hands up as she backed away, praying for the pulsing to begin. "H-how?"

"You're not the only one with tricks up your sleeve," he said as he advanced, taking up his mask and slipping it over his suddenly featureless metal face. "And you are one of few to have seen this. Not even my father knows." He lunged for her, his steel hand clenching her throat and slamming her against the wall before she could put her hands up in defense.

She choked, gasping for breath, but his uncompromising metallic fingers only tightened. Her face grew red as panic began to rise inside her. She tried to thrash but her body didn't respond. Both hands had shot up to the cold arm that grasped her and tried to push him away, but her efforts had no effect. The pulsing had begun in her forehead, but the world was already growing hazy around her as the life struggled to remain within her. She felt as frail as a flame that had run out of oxygen and grew smaller and smaller until it was nothing but a trail of smoke in the air. Desperately, she pushed herself harder than ever, then something within her snapped.

⚔

Everything was tinted red. She walked through a busy city, sidestepping cars and weaving between faceless people. The only thing in full, vibrant color was a pair that walked along the sidewalk: a mother and her son. The mother was beautiful, but there was something about her that made Elise feel wistful. She didn't understand why. The young boy, who was about five or six, would occasionally get distracted by the images in the windows as they passed by and have to hurry to catch up with his mother.

Then, something else caught Elise's attention. Among the red, another man, whose face was just as blurry and blank as the others, was walking toward them, but each part of him, the clothes he wore, his skin, his fingernails, was entirely black. The young boy looked at the man with interest, and then, abruptly, there was a bright flash that blinded Elise.

Suddenly, she was looking through the eyes of the little boy, and the man who was black as smoke was now white as a ghost and lying on the sidewalk, a flame eating away at his lifeless body. Elise—the young boy—had tears running down her—his—face. The terrified mother tugged on the boy's hand, urging him away.

The faceless people suddenly had eyes, yellow eyes all staring at him, and even though they didn't have mouths, they were whispering, some even shouting at the mother.

Then, the scene changed. Elise was in her own body again and the little boy was perched on a stool in a tidy kitchen.

"You were born to be great, Peter," a man was saying.

The mother, who was fixing a meal, gave the man a look filled with pride and love.

Then the scene changed again and the boy—Peter—was standing on a ledge that hung over a sea far below. He was slightly older now, maybe in his early teens, and seemed solemn, but at the same time, angry. Everything was vivid and oversaturated, and the sun seemed far too bright and far too hot. Suddenly his father was behind him and the two were fighting, the father punching, Peter dodging before firing back.

The ground twisted beneath them and there sat Peter. The world was gray around him and he was cross-legged on a rock, looking down at the same sea. *Your mother,* a voice said. *She's gone.*

Splotches of red began to dot the surface of the water below, some lingering but others fading away. *How?* his voice said.

It was your father, the same voice answered, and immediately the scene became overwhelmingly red.

Reighba's face appeared in the haze, saying, *I swear to you, my boy. I would never do such a thing.* Peter believed him, but hearing the others whisper about it, calling his father a murderer . . . it hurt too much.

Everything began to fade back to gray. *I loved her . . .* his father's voice echoed. The scene faded to black.

When light appeared again, it was in the form of stars in the sky. Elise sat with a familiar man on wet grass as he pointed out stars and said something in Greek.

Elise scribbled what she saw into her notebook. She was young and had tiny fingers that were hard to control. Everything seemed to be lighthearted and comfortable, as if there really wasn't much to the world, as if nothing was so complex as to have to ponder it. *This is wrong.* A moment ago she was in Peter's memories, but now she was seeing her own. *This is very wrong.* She, a young, clumsy girl, sat up and looked behind her. A bewildered Peter stood at a distance, his eyes fixed on her and his mouth hanging slightly open. She suddenly felt exposed.

When the world shifted again, she was in a white and gray world. She was in the body of a fifteen-year-old Peter Reighba, and he had impaled a man on a knife. The dying body was falling toward Peter and he put up a hand to stop it. The life drained from the man, a single tear of red ink falling from his face and blotching the gray floor. When his body finally fell to the floor, more red began to seep into the gray. Tears were streaming down Peter's cheeks. He looked down at the bloody knife, squeezing the handle so hard in his hand that it broke.

Your father loves you, Peter, his mother's voice said from behind. Peter whipped around and suddenly everything was tinted yellow, and he was now Elise.

Elise stood where Peter was a second ago, finding herself face-to-face with her brother. They were in some sort of hall, and a blinding light was behind him. "Why did you leave, Elise?" he asked. "I wake up one morning and you're gone."

Tears hit her cheeks and she couldn't tell if they were hers or Peter's. "I would've stayed if I could've," she whispered.

"Why don't you come back?" he said.

He sounded almost heartbroken, which made Elise want to fall to her knees. Elise opened her mouth but couldn't answer.

Then, Elise heard the footsteps before she saw them, and from the light emerged the ranks, carrying guns and wearing uniforms, their steps exactly together. Among them was Peter Reighba, looking grimly at the future. *Your father loves you, Peter,* his mother's voice said again.

Suddenly, Peter was in a small, dark room. His skin was changing. He was becoming wooden and stiff. His heart was beating quickly. *What is going on?* He wanted to cry. *Father can't know about this. He can't know about this.*

The mirror in front of him shattered, and Elise was instantly stumbling off a small ledge that hung from the thick branches of a willow tree. Percy and Laleitha's terrified faces were shrinking out of view. When she should have hit the ground, she found herself in the dark room of Silver Industries, standing next to Peter, in his mask, looking at five in front of her. Though she should have been, Elise was not among them on the floor. Peter pulled the trigger on the small girl, and with a bang, everything turned a bright orange, the other four trembling in icy blue.

Peter swallowed back the cold feeling in his chest. *It's not my fault,* was the only distinguishable thought running through his chaotic head. *I didn't kill an innocent girl. I couldn't have. It's not my fault—it's his.* Two bullets fired from his gun at Sar Prague. As if a bomb went off, a million images exploded across Elise's eyes. A million memories and feelings running by her before she could interpret them. Excruciating pain overwhelmed her, and she fell to her knees.

Then Elise came back to reality and the metal hand released her throat. She sank to the floor, trembling, the pain not yet fading from her head.

Peter shivered as well, backing away slowly. "What did you do to me?" he whispered, his voice quivering as much as Elise's body. "What did you do?"

"I don't know." Elise sobbed, shaking her head.

She had just been in his head, seen his memories, felt his pain, and he had seen parts of her she had been trying to bury ever since she came to Lumeria. He still stood in front of her. Never in her life had she felt more vulnerable. The fear she had been swallowing the entire night finally took hold of her, threatening to make her implode.

Suddenly, the wall exploded next to her. She cried out, scrambling away. Dust lingered in the air, curling in strange clouds of pale yellow and stretching far into the room. A gaping hole had been blown in the wall just inches away from where she trembled. A million questions stormed through her head before her sister emerged from the dust. Peter had stumbled backward when the explosion blew, but he had by then braced himself against the wall. He flew at Laleitha and she shrieked, diving to the side. He swung at her with his metal fist, but it smashed into the wall when she ducked.

It was all happening in another world to Elise. She shook uncontrollably as she tried to stagger to her feet. Everything around her was blurry, and the images still lingered in her mind, sometimes flashing before her eyes.

"Elise!" Laleitha screamed.

She stared at her sister and then she ran. The two of them darted away, Second Reighba pursuing them like a dog on a rabbit; they had not much time.

Elise should have found herself running into a hall, but she had entered into a chasm of burning debris. Above her, floors with singed edges were exposed through the gaping hole that had blown through every level of the building. Debris fell like rain and piled up along the side of the fissure. Terrified faces gathered at the edges of the chasm, peering down at the commotion below.

On the floor above them, a wide, jagged window was torn through the wall. Moonlight and fresh, crisp air from the outside poured in through this hole. *There* was the escape. To the left, a portion of the above floor had crashed to their level, hanging by a thread to the piece of hall that it initially connected to. Gerald was scrambling up this, half carrying half dragging an unconscious Darren behind him. Anton was halfway up and had quickened his pace when he spotted Second Reighba—Peter—charging after them.

Laleitha leapt up onto the pile, Elise stumbling at her heels. They scrambled up at full speed, finally making it to the second floor, where the gaping hole tore through the wall. From behind, a force suddenly slammed the breath out of her, sending her toppling over herself. An aching pain rippled through her muscles. When she finally regained control of her tumbling body, she looked up to see Second Reighba had caught up to them. Gerald had dropped Darren and was engaging their enemy.

Suddenly, Anton appeared at her side. "We have to jump."

Her unfocused eyes finally fixed on him. "What?"

He nodded toward Elise's left and she followed his gesture. Through the hole that would be their escape, she peered and found herself looking down not at a two-story drop like she had anticipated but a cliff that the building was built on. Far, far below was the sparkling lake.

"Jump," Anton said again, this time more urgently. He looked over his shoulder at the tussle between King and Second Reighba behind him before turning back to her.

She hesitated at the drop.

"Jump, Elise!"

Then, she was free-falling through the air. Where the ground should have been was only a steep hill, leading all the way down to a field of water at least one hundred meters below. Elise shrieked, falling once again, plunging through the whipping wind that deafened her so she couldn't even hear herself scream. All she had to do was put her hand out. Why was that so difficult? Her heart was beating at a deadly rate; something was very wrong with her. Fear gripped her as the water neared, growing closer and larger each millisecond. Her arm flung out, reaching toward the water. Then, her body jerked, suddenly swallowing the momentum, but her control slipped and not a moment after she put her hand out, she fell into the icy water.

Her body went numb as she sank, the cold stinging her every muscle. Millions of white bubbles spiraled around her, making it impossible to see. A distant boom rippled through the water as another body slammed through the surface. Elise pushed upward, propelling herself back to the glittery surface. When her face broke back into the warm air above, she gasped for breath, bobbing as she turned in a confused flurry. She could do nothing except turn in place, trying to determine which direction led to shore.

"Anton!" Gerald's voice yelled. "Elise!"

They must have jumped not long after her.

"I'm here!" she gasped.

Forcing her aching muscles onward, she slowly made her way through the water toward the voice.

"Anton, *where are you?*" Gerald shouted.

Elise could see him now; his head bobbed in and out of the water as he hoisted an unconscious Darren out by the collar.

"Where is Lee?" Elise sputtered, water spilling into her mouth each time it opened.

"Elise," he grunted in surprise, only taking notice of her now. "I just saw her. Take Darren." He thrust the limp body onto her, sending her briefly sinking under again. "Get him to shore. I'll look for the others."

She grunted in response. Darren was far heavier than she was. She slung an arm around his neck and tucked her hand under his arm, dragging him along with her, swimming with one hand. It felt as if she was going nowhere as she swam, but eventually her feet touched the ground and she staggered into shallow water. When her torso finally lifted from the wetness, her hold on Darren loosened and he flopped into a watery mess. She took a handful of his shirt and pulled him along until he was safely suspended in the rocks.

※

Laleitha forced her eyes open in the murky water, watching Anton's body sink out of sight. She broke the surface, breathing frantically, before diving back under, straight down. The water pushed against her, tugging her upward, but she flapped her hands over her head, trying to push herself further in Anton's direction. Her lungs screamed for air, and it wasn't long before she would pass out as well. Finally, she gave in to the tug and drifted up to the surface again, taking a few more giant breaths before submerging herself again. She kicked furiously, her hands outstretched. Finally, the boy's limp fingers brushed her palm and she grasped him tightly. Shifting her body, she kicked upward. Air in her lungs was running out; the water pressed against her hard enough to suffocate her. Only a little further—the surface wasn't far.

At last, she tore from her watery restraints, lifting Anton's limp body up with her. She gave a loud gasp and forced herself on.

"Laleitha!" her sister shouted in the distance.

Laleitha turned in circles, not enough air in her lungs to cry out. The only thing she could see were waves on all sides of her.

"Laleitha!" her sister called again.

Suddenly, a body hit her from behind, gently tugging at Anton. "This way," Gerald's voice said.

The two of them pushed on, dragging Anton behind them. When they finally reached the rocky shore and pulled Anton to safety, Elise ran toward them, leaving Darren's body in the distance.

"What happened to him?" Elise shouted.

Laleitha looked down at the limp body and realized Anton had a long cut that stretched diagonally along his torso, soaking his shirt with thick scarlet blood.

CHAPTER EIGHTEEN

A Narrow Escape

Elise stepped around Anton's bloody body as Gerald gently set him down. "What happened to him? Why isn't he moving?"

"He passed out in the water," Laleitha explained, breathing hard.

Gerald pressed his fingers to Anton's throat, searching for a pulse. "His heart's still beating and . . ." He listened. "He's still breathing."

"We need to stop the bleeding," Elise said, trying to press on the cut with her hands but only succeeding in covering them with hot, sticky blood.

"Agreed," Gerald concurred. "But how?"

"I have an idea but it's not a good one," Laleitha exclaimed.

"Well, it's our only one," Elise said.

"Wait—" Gerald began but Laleitha had already ignited a fire in her hand.

Elise jumped back, startled. Laleitha put the flame to Anton's skin, pressing the cut together as the skin fused. She worked along his body slowly and carefully, her actions eliciting the sickening sound of simmering flesh. Finally, once the entire cut had been cauterized back together, Laleitha stood.

"W-when did you learn to do that?" Elise asked as she stared at her sister in frightened disbelief.

Laleitha look down at her hand as the flame faded. "While you were in interrogation," she murmured.

"What?" Elise sputtered.

"I don't know," Lee said. "A lot of things happened. I got angry and I accidentally did this to myself." She rubbed an awful burn mark on her left arm, shaped like her fingers. "And I thought if I could be more deliberate with it, I may be able to put it to use. So I did this." She showed her sister a wound on her leg that now was merely an odd clump of raw, pink, melted skin.

"Lee, that's . . ." Elise examined Anton's body. "That's actually amazing."

Laleitha didn't say anything.

Suddenly, as Elise was standing up, Anton jerked to life, coughing up water. He coughed for minutes before the only thing that dripped from his mouth were a few green drops.

Gerald sighed with relief and put a hand on Anton's shoulder. "Don't do that again," he said.

Anton shook his head. "I don't think I want to."

"Can you stand?" Gerald asked, slowly getting to his feet.

The smaller boy nodded and clambered to his feet. The four made their way back to Darren, trying to catch their breath. Anton limped slightly when he walked, sometimes having to grab King's arm, but each time he looked around to see whether his friends noticed. Elise did, but the problem of Anton would be addressed when it had to be.

"What happened to him?" Elise asked, looking down at limp form of Darren. He had bruises all over his body and forehead, and his skin was burned pink in a few splotched areas.

"He blew up," Anton said.

"We don't know, exactly," Laleitha said. "He caused that explosion. He's the reason we escaped, but whatever he did wiped him out."

Elise looked back down at Darren. He seemed almost peaceful when he was completely unconscious.

"They'll be coming any minute," Gerald said, looking back up at the building far above. "We need to go."

"We need to wake him up first. He'll slow us down if we have to carry him," Elise responded.

Laleitha kicked his foot, which only flopped in the other direction.

Gerald knelt by his head. "Maybe I can . . ." He hovered his hand above Darren's forehead.

Suddenly, Darren's head kicked forward, almost hitting Gerald's hand. "Gah," he exclaimed. "What happened?"

"Whoa," Laleitha remarked at Darren's sudden energy.

"And you learned to do that when?" Elise asked again.

"I don't know," he said, looking at his hands.

"You don't—"

"I don't know, Elise," he assured her, gravely. He looked back down at Darren. "You ready to go?"

"Go where?"

Gerald stood. "Out of here."

"I've been ready since several hours ago," Darren muttered.

Gerald offered him a hand and pulled him to his feet. Darren blinked several times once he was upright again, rubbing his face with his hands. Elise then noticed bruises on his nose and cheek.

"Reighba really did a number on me, man," he grunted. "That son of a bitch."

"Wait, what? What happened while I was in interrogation?" Elise demanded, looking around at her friends.

"We'll tell you later," Gerald said.

The five crept along the side of the hill, slowly working their way around to the other end of the lot. Search teams had been sent down to the lake and arrived soon after they left. They were looking for them or their bodies, and when they didn't find anything, they'd know the five had escaped.

When Elise and her friends made it back to the lot they began in, facing the forest reserve, they crouched behind an empty vehicle.

"We just have to make it back to the portal," Gerald whispered.

"Do any of you remember where the portal is? Because I sure don't," Darren said.

Anton, who looked painfully pale, spoke. "I do."

"Getting there will be the hard part," Gerald continued. "We can't attract any attention because then they'll discover it."

"Anton . . ." Elise turned to him. "You were able to disguise yourself as a guard before."

He nodded. He even remained in the guard's uniform, which was too big for him and sagged off his frail body from their lovely swim in the lake. It had a gash across the middle of it, stained with fresh blood.

"Do you think you can do it again?"

He was silent.

"I don't think that's a good idea," Gerald said.

"The kid's lost a lotta blood. It's hard enough for him to walk as it is," Darren added.

"We're going to have to run," Laleitha said. "We have no cover, no time for a diversion, and no disguise, and it worked before."

"They didn't know we were here before," Elise pointed out.

"Let's just be quick," Gerald said conclusively.

Elise took a deep breath, focusing herself, ready to take off once again.

Laleitha was the first one to spring from cover, running with graceful but frantic strides. Darren shot after her, then Elise followed. The familiar howl of the wind screamed in her ear as she charged on. Her steps were heavier now and her lungs felt painfully strained.

Suddenly, a fiery force hit her from behind, bouncing off her, painlessly. Instinctively, she whipped around to see two gunmen standing atop a ledge from the base, as well as seven people running after them. *Shit!* She pushed herself to a new speed, despite her exhaustion.

The ground began to slope upward slightly when they ran into the trees. They couldn't lead them straight to the tunnels! Laleitha stopped in her tracks, letting Elise, Gerald, Darren, and Anton fly by her. Elise tugged on her arm to urge her on, but Laleitha shook her off. Anton led them to the small crack under a bush that was their entrance to the cavity where the portal hid, but they turned to wait for Laleitha.

Elise shouted for her frantically. "Lee! What are you doing? We have to go!"

Laleitha snapped a hand out and the ground between them and the pursuing guards burst into flames at least ten feet high. The girl turned and fled, diving over the bush and through the gap into the tunnel as her friends followed hastily.

Darkness swallowed them but for the green glow of the portal. They all dived through immediately, Darren closing it behind him as he did so.

In a split second, Elise found herself on the floor of the old shed they began in, her skin flushed, her chest heaving, the others on the floor beside her, sharing in her exhaustion.

Darren groaned, letting the green rod roll from his fingers.

"Hey!" came a cry from above. *Westbecker.* "Are you okay? What happened?"

Elise struggled to lift her head, spotting him rushing toward them through the doorway.

"We did it," Gerald said weakly. "Not exactly how we planned, but we did it."

⋊

"What happened? I lost contact with you. They have a backup? Where? How did you escape?" It was Westbecker's turn to be nervous. He sat in the front seat of the van, driving them back through the forest from which they came, as the rest of them piled in the back, heads resting limply against the walls of the van or each other's shoulders.

"They have a backup," Elise said, too exhausted to keep her voice from reflecting it. All of the panic, frustration, and fear she felt in the last hour had crashed down on her by then.

"Shit," Westbecker muttered. "Why don't we start from the beginning."

There were a few moments of wordless, heavy breathing before Gerald spoke. "Anton and Darren went to create a diversion so we could get into loading containers."

"We busted a window by launching flaming logs through it," Darren added, bluntly.

"Then, when we were inside, we were spotted in the industrial garage," Gerald went on.

"I was," Elise corrected, her voice hoarse and her thoughts scattered. "I had to run, so I got separated from them."

"Then Anton somehow changed into a guard . . ." Darren added. "He went with the group that were assigned to protect the master drive. I had no idea where I was going, so I tried to make my way around as best I could. Got into a fight with a guy that thought I looked suspicious, and what happened after that is blurry."

"He ended up through the floor," Anton said, still out of breath and wincing in pain when he spoke.

"There were guards there," Elise went on, quietly, her voice still wavering. "In the central command room." *I killed them.* A mournful, cold hand wrenched her heart. "We didn't even move them before we blew it up," she whispered.

Gerald took over again. "They caught us on our escape, forced us into a room by cutting off all our options. They took Elise into interrogation to figure out how we crossed their borders and why. He told us his son would kill her if none of us talked. Then Reighba surveyed the damage on one of the computers. When he found out that we had blown up their master drive . . ." He shook his head, squeezing his eyes shut. "He seemed angry but he didn't act out or *anything*—he just . . . he calmly took Darren out of the room, right in front of the window where we could see him . . ."

"This is still fuzzy," Darren remarked, rubbing his hand across his forehead.

"That's when he went full-on psycho," Laleitha said.

"He beat him," Gerald said. "Yelling at him to stand up and fight back, taunting him about the Lumire. Toward the end, he grabbed Darren by the collar, turned to us, and threatened to kill him in front of us."

"He's a monster," Laleitha whispered. "When Reighba didn't react at first, I wondered if he was mad, but then he turned around and we saw his eyes. When he was fighting Darren, he just—" She squeezed her eyes shut. "He was so *angry*."

"I'm not even sure what happened after that. Darren started flipping. Reighba was gonna kill him," Gerald continued. "I busted the window and we jumped through. I flew at him and he knocked me aside. We bolted out. Darren was still crazy, then there was an explosion."

"The explosion came from Darren," Anton said. "He was convulsing and his fists kept clenching and unclenching. His veins were popping everywhere. Then he fell to his knees and a really bright light flew from him. I don't know what happened but I think he kinda snapped."

"I think I did too," Darren murmured, rubbing his head again.

"I went to look for Elise and found her in one of the rooms Darren blew through," Laleitha continued. "His son was there, too, but there was something wrong with him and Elise was curled up on the ground."

Elise didn't say anything; she bit the inside of her lip as she stared out the window. She felt her sister looking at her.

"It was like you were in a trance," Laleitha continued, now speaking directly to Elise. "What did he do to you?"

Elise shook her head. "I don't know." This one she was keeping to herself.

The memory was still too disturbing, and the connection she built in that moment with Peter was still too confusing. *Second Reighba, not Peter.*

Her sister narrowed her eyes, suspecting Elise hid something, but then turned away, moving on. This, Elise was grateful for.

"Anton was the first up the slope," Gerald said. "I dragged Darren up and then the girls came running with Second Reighba on their tail. Elise and Lee jumped first while Anton and I delayed Second Reighba. We tried to fight him off but he fought like a demon. He threw us off—Darren too—and we fell into the lake."

"He gave me this," Anton rasped, shifting his weight, closing his eyes in pain. He traced his finger along the burns where his cut had been.

"He lost a lot of blood in the lake but Laleitha cauterized the wound somehow," Gerald explained. "Then we woke up Darren and made a break for the exit."

"So, when did you find out about the backup drive?" Westbecker asked.

"Before we blew up the drive," Laleitha answered. "We were all there, and Elise got into the plan that they last opened."

"They have a backup hard drive that they hid in this place called *The Way*," Elise said, still refusing to make eye contact with anyone.

All of the stress of the last few hours began to strangle her. The initial shock had passed, but now she was left with a weight in her chest she could hardly bear. Something was beginning to sting in her eyes. She shouldn't speak, she needed to lock herself down, she needed to be alone, she needed to keep herself in check or she would act out, which was the last thing she needed. The agony sat on her spine like burning coals.

"What the hell is *The Way?*" Westbecker remarked.

"We don't know," Gerald replied, shaking his head.

Then, a deadly, sickening realization hit Elise. "The way is closed," she said. "The Way is closed."

The color drained from her sister's face. "The Way is closed."

The others looked between the two as Elise choked back a sob. "I need Marty's diary," she declared once she swallowed her shock. "I think he knew where it was."

CHAPTER NINETEEN

Westbecker's Penalty

Elise had never seen Ellington angry before and, frankly, it was more terrifying than the entirety of the night before.

While they meant to begin translating Marty's diary once they arrived back at their living quarters, exhaustion grabbed them in a choke hold and they all fell into a fast slumber on the couch and floor. They were roused when Ellington stormed in.

"Get up," he snapped, slapping a file down onto Gerald, who lay face down on the couch.

Gerald instantly sat up, pulling the file off of his back. *July 3rd. Prime Devise Central Command, Litrite, Inseana. Captain Ferris Westbecker.*

"What did Westbecker do?" he demanded, towering over the wakening teenagers. "You haven't been here half a year, and you're already carrying out secret attacks on Lumeria's biggest threat *without the council knowing*, let alone granting approval! What were you thinking?"

"We were just following his orders," Gerald protested.

"Well, the Lumerian Council has been called together in an emergency session to discuss his actions, and you five are expected to attend. So I suggest you make yourselves decent because we are leaving"—he checked his watch—"in thirty seconds."

The five were too worn down to do anything but follow Ellington to Fort Kingshold, where he led them into a tall, dimly lit cylindrical room lined with narrow steps to white ledges of varying height, on which long tables and chairs were lined up. The table in the center, marking the exact middle of the chamber's height, curved in a perfect circle that traced the circumference of the room, and each seat had a golden nameplate in front of it.

Ellington, who usually would explain everything to them as they went along, said nothing but stiffly led them to one of the ledges above the circular center table. Their table was long, with seven chairs set up. Two plaques read "Yugie Kilodrist" and "Stanford Ellington," but the other five seats had no plaque. Ellington sat them down in between his chair and Ms. Kilodrist's empty one, as though he expected them to escape if they weren't secured between two supervisors.

As Elise looked around, she began to make sense of the room's format. A few tables sat only one, while others sat several; some of them had their profession engraved beneath their name on the golden plate in front of them. "Representatives of Staris" sat just above the central ring, beside the "Representatives of Pallain," and the representatives from the other Lumerian countries as well. She also made out "Chamber of Order," "Budget Office," "Arc Conditionary," and various other positions and titles.

As Elise examined her surroundings, she realized the room wasn't shaped in a cylinder but rather an inverted cone, with the stations at the top curving further outward from the ring of the Arc Leaders and the stations at the bottom curving further inward, so all eyes could see the Arc Leaders at all times.

Then Elise's eyes landed on the "Defense and Protection" table, where a tense Ferris Westbecker sat with his hands folded, shoulders hunched, and lips pressed together so tightly they turned white.

Then, sixteen formally dressed people filed in, taking their places around the center round table, sitting down all together. The emperor, whom Elise had met the day an assassination attempt was made, was among them, and it was he who spoke first.

"The Arc Leaders are in place; the session may begin. We have been called together this morning to discuss the recent events that unfolded in Inseana last night under Captain Ferris Westbecker's command. Westbecker sent the five Majors-in-training to infiltrate the Prime Devise's central command base and destroy the database that controls all of their current and future military procedures. As emperor, I declare that Captain Westbecker abused his power and, in doing so, endangered the lives of our five Majors-in-training, whom it is his responsibility to protect."

"Your Highness—" Westbecker began.

"He writes in his report," Emperor Evanstin went on, ignoring him, "'The Majors successfully entered the base and planted the explosives but were soon captured by Alfred Reighba, and Montason was taken into interrogation. Engaging the Lumire, the Majors were able to escape into the lake beside the base. They then made it back to the rendezvous point and proceeded back to Lumeria.' He also mentions"—the Emperor set down his papers—"that the Prime Devise does indeed have a backup drive hidden in an unknown location."

"We know its location," Gerald blurted.

All eyes turned to him, causing him to shift in his seat, regretting his words.

"Well, not exactly, but we know it is in a place called The Way."

"How do we know this?" one of the Arc Leaders at the circular table asked.

Gerald looked to Elise, who took a deep breath, praying her voice didn't fail her now. "I looked at one of their plans before we blew them up. It described a hard drive containing all the plans that we had just destroyed, hidden in a place called The Way."

"So last night's attack was pointless," said a man who was sitting back in his chair.

"There was no way of knowing," a sympathetic-sounding woman pointed out.

"The only thing achieved by last night's events was taking another step toward war with the Prime Devise," an Arc Leader said firmly. "We sent the potentially most powerful people we have right into their home base, where they killed Inseanan guards, critically damaged the integrity of their base, and took out a major key to their inner workings. We cannot expect the Prime Devise to wave this off and accept our apologies."

"There has to be a diplomatic solution," an elderly woman, also an Arc Leader, remarked.

"First things first," the emperor interjected. "Westbecker's actions cannot go unpunished. Lumerian Council protocol mandates that in the event of a rogue action that is made without the approval of council, they be removed from authority and suspended from the council until the conflict is resolved." He looked up at Westbecker, who nodded solemnly.

"What were your intentions when you sent these five kids to do your bidding?" one Arc Leader pressed on, leaning forward.

"Mr. Reiliet, that is an unnecessary question," one scoffed.

"Let him answer," the emperor said. "His actions classify as rogue, so we must be sure he himself is not a rogue to this order."

Westbecker shifted uncomfortably. "The Prime Devise intended to attack us. They've been targeting our Majors. I didn't want to let that happen."

"Whoever said they meant to attack us?" one questioned.

"If they don't want the safety of Lumeria to be ensured . . ." one began before being interrupted by another.

"The safety of Lumeria is and has been ensured with or without these *children*."

"What I was getting at," the first said, "was the Prime Devise is afraid of them, afraid of what they could do. They wouldn't be afraid of them if they didn't think they could spoil one of their plans."

"They're not Majors yet," one pointed out. "They are still children, meaning as of right now, the council is liable for each and every action they commit for the benefit of this empire or otherwise."

"All due respect, sir," Westbecker interjected, "but if the Prime Devise didn't have a backup, this mission would have been a success."

Many council members sat up in their chairs, intrigued and ready to retaliate.

"They took out a highly secure database and escaped Prime Devise custody," he went on. "I haven't seen LSE officers with over four years' worth of training do that. They may be children, but the Lumire is perhaps the most valuable asset to our protection we could ask for, so why wouldn't we use it? This task may have been just a stepping stone to even larger missions."

"Larger missions?" one challenged.

"This is a good point," an old man with tiny circular glasses said. "The success of this operation, though perhaps not exactly how Westbecker intended, is the result of the Lumire functioning as it is supposed to. Contrary to popular belief, it goes beyond just giving them inhuman abilities. It also engages when they are put to a certain level of mental stress. Studies performed on the Majors in the 1960s concluded that, when they experience fear and basic survival instincts usually kick in, the Lumire interacts with the brain to quell the physiological processes associated with fear and direct more focus toward decision-making and awareness. It also protects them from harm and allows them to heal quickly, meaning the threat the Prime

Devise poses to the Majors cannot be appraised as the same threat to any LSE officer."

"Regardless," one of the Arc Leaders agreed, "they've only been training with the Lumire for two months. They will be of much more use to this empire when they've fully developed their skills, which cannot happen when they are recklessly thrown into enemy territory. They are to continue training as planned."

The emperor cleared his throat. "Back to the topic at hand, please. Captain Westbecker's justice."

Gerald, looking sick, abruptly stood, pushing his chair back. Luckily, no attention was drawn to him. He slipped past Ellington, murmuring something about the bathroom before disappearing out the door.

"I believe a conference with the Prime Devise is in order," the emperor said. "War is not an option. We will have to fund the repairs in the base and assure them Westbecker's actions were rogue and he is being punished. They'll likely want to put him in front of Orphia, and if that's the case, it will have to be done. If this is still not enough, perhaps we'll even have to go so far as to propose a permanent partnership between us."

"An alliance with the Prime Devise?"

"In order to prevent war."

Elise sat back in her chair, no longer listening but thinking about what Westbecker had said. *The Lumire is perhaps the most valuable asset to our protection we could ask for.* While she knew the Lumire made her special, she hadn't fully understood until then just how powerful it meant they were. If this was what she could do with two months of training, what could she do with ten years? By the time she was inducted, maybe she wouldn't have to be afraid anymore.

"Where would this meeting take place?" one asked. "It would not be prudent to enter a Prime Devise facility after this incident."

Elise stood, slipping behind her chair. "Gerald's been gone for a while. I'm going to go see if he's okay," she whispered to Ellington.

He nodded reluctantly. She crept out the door and, for no reason in particular, tried to make her steps silent. Maybe it was because she didn't want to be noticed by these sophisticated, authoritative, and extremely intimidating people. It didn't take her long to reach the men's room.

When she reached the bathroom, Elise gently knocked on the door. "You in there, Gerald?"

A grunt came from the other side of the door, followed by Gerald's voice. "Yeah. I'm fine."

Elise lowered her eyebrows. "Uh, you sure?"

"Spectacular."

"You've been in there forever. Can I come in?" she asked, turning the knob.

She entered to find Gerald standing at the sink with a few drops of water still falling from his chin. Something was obviously wrong, judging by the dark look in his eyes and the sweat on his forehead. Elise pondered her next move. After a few moments of silence, Elise asked, "What's bothering you?"

He shook his head. "I couldn't breathe there for a moment."

Elise pulled herself up onto the counter with a stony expression.

"Listening to people talk about us, decide our future." He shook his head. "I hate it. I've never felt so . . . helpless." He jumped up onto the counter next to Elise. "I've been pushing it aside for a while now. That's what I've always done. I've always been the oldest of the kids at home, the leader, the one who has to support everyone without being supported."

Elise nodded. "So you thought you couldn't rely on anyone."

"I've been fine with it all my life, up until . . . *this* . . . when everything got complicated. I thought I could handle it."

"I don't think anybody can," Elise said, shaking her head. "It's a lot."

"Oh, yeah, a *lot*," he agreed. They were silent a moment before he spoke again. "I have meds at home for this. Don't know where I'd be able to get any here."

"You could ask Ellington," she suggested.

He shook his head. "I don't want to ask Ellington."

She looked at him sideways. "Why not?"

"I don't want him to know," he answered stiffly, sounding like his throat was beginning to close up a bit.

Elise frowned. "You can trust Ellington," she said. "I think he'd understand. He wouldn't tell anyone, if that's what you're worried about. And trust me, you're not going through this alone. All of us are scared, and we all miss home."

He nodded. They were silent again.

"Have you ever been in Anton's room?" he asked out of the blue.

She shook her head.

"He carves," Gerald explained, a small smile working its way onto his face. "Apparently he asked Ellington for a knife and has been using it to carve up little pictures all over the walls of this room. He carved that place up from top to bottom, just little scenes and patterns. Things that mean something to him."

"You've been in there?"

"Yeah. Sometimes I sit in there with him and we talk about family. He isn't the sort of person I usually talk to, but the kid's like a little brother to me now."

Elise almost smiled. "I guess he kinda is. I mean, you're stuck with us now, so I guess that makes us family."

He looked at her and smiled, comforted by this idea. "I can live with that," he said.

So could Elise.

※

Elise couldn't sleep that night. It was one thing to comfort a friend, but comforting herself was another story. She had killed people, people who devoted themselves to a cause because they believed it was right. What gave her the right to take their lives just because she didn't share their point of view? Worse, she hadn't given a second thought to her actions as she had done so. She had hardly cared until it was brought to her attention. At that moment, Elise hated herself. *I should have never been in Litrite in the first place.* Bitter tears began to roll down her cheeks. *Look what Westbecker made me do. What was he thinking? What was I thinking?*

Biting her lip, she resented herself even more. She was too ashamed to even take the blame, take responsibility for her actions. Instead, she pushed the responsibility on Westbecker. Maybe there had been a way around killing those men, but thinking about that made Elise's heart feel heavy as stone. There was no excuse for what she had done, and she was going unpunished for it. Even the masked man was like them, fighting for what he believed was just. Being in his memories disturbed Elise, solely because she realized he was the same as her, just slightly more driven.

And trained.

Elise sobbed, fighting relentlessly to get herself back under control. "Fight back," she whispered. These feelings were overwhelming her. *Fight back!* She had to maintain her focus; there was no future left for her if she let her emotions consume her. *Is this how the Majors before me felt?*

After hours of sitting against the wall, biting her lip until it bled as her chest heaved while tears slowly dried on her cheeks, Elise finally slowed her breathing and suppressed the dark, heart-wrenching thoughts. Gently laying her head on the pillow, Elise took a deep breath as her thoughts settled, but tears still leaked from the corners of her eyes until she lay still and asleep.

)(

"A meeting between the Prime Devise High Order and the Lumerian Council has been arranged and will take place on the twenty-sixth of July in Hiseroth, Inseana. Until then, the Majors are to operate under probation from here on in until this conflict has been resolved. Their training progress will be monitored until it is completed and the Majors are eligible for induction."

This was one of many conclusions the council had come to, and the five collectively resented it. Ellington had been assigned to remain with them at all times unless they were in their living quarters. After a long day of training and lessons, the five hastily fled back into privacy so they could speak freely without taking caution in their words.

"This is stupid," Darren complained as they sat in the kitchen of their living quarters.

Elise had perched cross-legged on the counter while Anton and Gerald sat on the stools. Darren paced across the room angrily, and Laleitha stood at the stove, heating up some chicken and wild rice soup. "We can't do anything now without a committee debate."

"I'm pretty sure that's the whole point of the system," Elise pointed out. "They don't trust us *or* our instructors anymore."

"I mean *us*," he said. "How are we expected to live a life while the council has us under a microscope?"

"None of us have lives here, Darren," Laleitha said. "It's just learn, train, do what people tell us, then more learning and training."

"More important," Gerald said, "how are we going to carry out our plan to find the son of Orphia?"

"Am I the only one bothered by the fact that we might go to war?" Anton interrupted. "We attacked their headquarters and they still have their plans, so our attack didn't even weaken them."

"Not necessarily," Elise said, the gears beginning to spin in her head again. "They have to retrieve the hard drive manually. What if we found it first?"

"And took it before they could get to it," Laleitha added, her eyes lighting up. "Then leave without a trace and they'll never know it was us."

"And if the council doesn't know about it either, if the Prime Devise accuses them, they'd be telling the truth when they say they know nothing about it," Gerald concluded.

Darren threw up his hands. "So do exactly what Westbecker did? Go behind the council's back? Look where that got him."

"And to do so, we'd have to escape unnoticed, find out where The Way is and then get there before the Prime Devise, who knows exactly where it is," Anton added.

Gerald nodded, silently, pondering a solution.

"Speaking of which," Darren said. "What was that 'The Way is closed' crap you two were yammering about?"

Elise exchanged glances with her sister before silently leaving the kitchen as Laleitha began to explain the ominous warning Hank Martinez gave in his death. After retrieving the notebook from her room, Elise took it back to her perch and began flipping through it.

"You think it's the same Way?" Gerald asked when Laleitha had finished.

"It's all connected," Elise said, refusing to lift her eyes from the pages. "A Lumerian fugitive, a reference to The Way in his house along with the same thing repeated in Old Lat, a strange tower, his ties to Orphia's kid, the Prime Devise plans hidden in The Way . . . it's like one big puzzle." She paused. "I found something."

Her friends gathered around, looking over her shoulder at the strange writing.

"Is that the tower?" Darren wondered aloud, his eyes on a drawing on the page.

In the top right quadrant of the page, a tower was sketched, with the Old Lat symbols wrapped around it.

Elise nodded. "I think so. I don't know what this says though."

"Something about an indicator," said Anton, who had learned the most Old Lat the quickest.

Gerald shook his head, stepping back. "This is too weird. I think this time it would be better to leave it up to the council. Their plan is to make reparations. I think that's the easiest way out of this."

"That we can agree on," Darren said.

"However, I don't think we should leave everything up to the council," Gerald went on.

"You're talking about our other project, Orphia's kid?" Elise asked.

"I want to go back to Sappol West," Gerald said. "I want to take a better look at those papers we found, maybe bring them back here."

"You think we should tell Ellington about it?"

"There'd be no harm," Anton answered with a shrug.

"But he is under an obligation to consult the council," Gerald pointed out.

"Why don't we want the council to know?" Laleitha asked.

"They wouldn't want us investigating it. If we have any leads, they'd just hand them over to the investigators," Gerald explained. "If we want to do this ourselves, prove ourselves, find out what your friend Martinez was hiding, the council can't know."

"Now you sound like Westbecker," Darren remarked.

"*We're* not starting a war though," Laleitha pointed out.

Elise agreed. "We just want closure and a bit of freedom."

"I should go," Anton said, out of the blue. "I can disguise myself; if anyone sees me, they won't know it is me."

"All right, so how do you plan to get to Sappol West without Ellington riding your tail?" Darren asked Anton.

"I'm going out," Elise said. "And Ellington will come with me. Just to buy a few things I can tinker with, and maybe an Old Lat dictionary, but I'm likely going to need some money. All I have was the small pouch that Ellington gave me."

"You can take mine," Anton offered. "I won't be using it."

Elise beamed at him. "Thanks, Anton."

Darren grunted. "Take mine too. I don't see any use I'll have with it."

"Thanks."

"Okay," Lalitha said. "Ellington'll go with Elise, and Anton will slip out and catch the late train."

"And the rest of us will relax with some soup," Darren added.

"So is it agreed then?" Gerald asked. "We're going to The Way? *Not* to look for the backup drive but for Orphia's son?"

Elise nodded.

Anton shrugged.

"Yeah," Laleitha agreed.

"Looks like it," Darren grunted.

Gerald finally smiled.

After Darren and Anton gave Elise the money from their pouches and she had safely tucked it away in her own, she left the room, leaving Anton taking deep breaths as he attempted to change his form once again.

CHAPTER TWENTY

A Late Night Excursion

The sky was dark but the city was bright. Ellington followed closely behind Elise as she tried to develop a sense of direction.

She wandered along the city sidewalks, Ellington pestering her with pointless questions as she walked along.

"Do you know where you're going?"

"No."

"Is this really necessary?"

"No, but I'm doing it anyway."

She wandered through every hardware store and craft store she could find, buying tools, wires of various sizes and materials, paints, fabrics, screws, nails, nuts, bolts, springs, gears, wooden dowels, small pieces of sheet metal, a roll of chain, and a small desk lamp.

Their last destination was a bookstore, where Elise intended to spend what little remained of her money. She scanned the shelves until she found an Old Lat dictionary, but then another book caught her attention. It had a thick spine and thousands of words squeezed on every page, alongside sketches and diagrams. It was titled *The Amateur Engineer's Manual: a Guide to the Most Commonly Used Lumerian Devices.*

Elise traced her hand along the spine. This was exactly what she needed. As she walked to the cashier to purchase the two books with the last of her money, the television in the corner caught her eye.

The only sound in the entire room echoed her deepest regret. "In a stunning turn of events two nights ago, a rogue Lumerian captain took Lumeria's strained relationship with the Prime Devise into his own hands . . ." a female reporter said.

At the bottom, a red banner ran across the screen with the words "Lumerian attack on Inseana?" in bold white.

"Allegedly, this captain sent the five Majors, who returned to Lumeria two months ago, to attack the Prime Devise central command station in Litrite, Inseana," the reporter went on. "The Arc Leaders refused to disclose any details on the event, but reports of at least two explosions in the base were confirmed. The Prime Devise states three were killed and fifteen were injured either in the explosions or by the Majors."

Her heart sank.

Three people.

"According to the Lumerian Council, these actions were not approved by the council, nor were they even proposed. They also note the Majors are not to blame for following this captain's orders and they are currently under the probation of the Lumerian Council."

"Can I help you?" the cashier at the desk asked, pulling Elise back to reality.

Elise had paused in the middle of the room and was staring at the television. She turned away and set the books on the desk, the sound still ringing in her ears.

"Will that be everything?"

Elise nodded. "Yes." She collected her books and hurried out of the store, where Ellington was waiting for her.

"The event raises concerns everywhere in Lumeria . . ." The reporter's fading voice continued to say.

They also noted the Majors were not to blame, the reporter had said. She was wrong. The council was wrong. Elise should have thought ahead; she should have realized this wasn't right. She should have found a way around killing just to carry out orders. Her hands were as dirty as Westbecker's. The entire way back, Elise maintained a stony silence.

When she finally arrived back at the suite, lugging her bags of goods behind her, all of her purchases piled up within them, she was greeted by her sister.

"Ellington went to his office. Is Anton back?" Elise asked before Laleitha could say anything.

"Yeah, Anton's back. What is all this?"

"Things I can build with."

"A lamp?" her sister asked, picking up the box.

"To see what I'm doing," Elise explained.

"You have eyes, don't you?" She set it back in the bag before leading her into the kitchen where the boys gathered around the island.

Papers were spread out all across the surface, and Gerald held a black marker in his hand.

"Elise, we found something," he exclaimed when he spotted her.

"Regarding . . ."

"The Way," all three said together.

Elise joined the circle, listening intently as Gerald took off into an explanation. "It's mentioned everywhere, but we have a full explanation around here somewhere." He rummaged around then pulled out a sheet covered in writing and began to read aloud. "The Way to Orphia's Tower was built in 1572 by Orphia himself. As his Omenescents have never left his tower, a series of hidden passages were built with a few exits to the outside world so the Omenescents may entertain themselves with long excursions while still never straying from home."

"Wait, wait, wait." Elise stopped him. "Did you even figure out what these papers are? Why the Majors had them?"

"This one looks like it was torn out of a book," Laleitha remarked, running her fingers across the frayed edge of the paper Gerald held.

"They're notes of some sort," Anton said. "The Majors were looking for something. We just found what they were examining to find it."

Gerald nodded. "Right. It seems like they were looking for Orphia's son. There's a lot of stuff about Orphia and his Omenescents."

"His Omenescents are his council, right?" Lee asked. "The mind reader, future seer, and people who can see anywhere?"

"Thentis," Gerald muttered to himself. The only Omenescent he knew was but a bitter name to him.

Elise rested her chin on her elbow. "Yeah. Ellington said all of them except Thentis stay in his tower so nobody has ever seen them."

"And apparently in this 'Way' place too," Gerald remarked.

"Keep reading," Darren told him.

Gerald obliged. "'Many have led quests to find these entrances and the names of the people successful have never been recorded. In 1812, a group of conspirators used The Way to sneak into Orphia's tower in an attempt to compromise the information collected by the Omenescents. They are the only outsiders to have ever been in Orphia's tower and they did not make it out alive. As a result of this, to ensure that the tower is never entered again, The Way was moved out of existence'—that can't be right—'and closed. The Way opens during random periods of time, usually decades apart, and stays open for a matter of months. It is rumored that the opening and closing of The Way is controlled by Orphia himself, but that has never been confirmed. It has been the topic of interest for many scientists and conspirators just how the closing of The Way apparently wipes it from existence, but so little is known about The Way that a conclusion cannot be found. What is known about the opening and closing of The Way is as follows: when The Way opens, it comes with a flash of green and the appearance of a stone tower. The contents of the tower conform to the wishes of the person or persons who opened The Way . . .'"

Elise's heart skipped a beat.

"9551 West," Anton said with a small grin.

"So The Way is open," Darren added. "And as long as the tower is there, we'll be able to get in."

"I thought you didn't want to go there," Laleitha interjected.

"Not to get the drive, but to find out what Martinez was hiding. Who wouldn't want to go?" Darren replied.

Elise looked among her friends. "Then we need a plan. It will take time."

"We don't know how long The Way will be open, though," Laleitha pointed out.

"But we have to go unnoticed," Gerald added.

"All right, screw this, just plan and go," Darren scoffed. "No more debates, please. You people are killing me."

"What will we need?" asked Anton.

"The schedule of all of our supervisor's activities," Elise said.

"A method of transportation," Gerald added.

"And an alibi," Laleitha said.

Darren gave a small grunt. "Where do we start?"

※

The next morning, Elise had been slowly waking up, until the thought of the plans they had fallen asleep working on crossed her mind. She woke fully with a jolt. She was in her bed with her shoes removed.

She sat up, confused and tired, rubbing her head with the cool side of her hand. *I have to hide the previous Majors' notes before Ellington enters.* When she emerged from her room, everything had been sorted away neatly, and the notes had been tucked in the desk drawer. The desk sat in the far left corner with a computer and several stacks of unused paper. It was often ignored by the five.

Anton and Laleitha were the only other two awake, and they sat in the kitchen nibbling on bagels.

Elise trudged in, still half asleep. "Hi," she murmured quietly.

"Morning," Anton greeted.

"You look like shit," Laleitha said.

"I feel like shit." Elise took a piece of bread from the cupboard and slipped it in the toaster. "Who was the last to fall asleep last night?"

"I was," Anton answered.

"And I assume you were the first to wake?"

"Yeah."

"Do you ever sleep?"

"No," he replied.

Darren entered the room, looking as zombie-like as Elise, not bothering to greet his friends. "Phase one is a go," he muttered. "I'm awake."

"You don't look like it," Elise pointed out, her eyes as droopy as his.

"You should talk," he scoffed. "Did you guys hear Gerald flip out last night?"

"What?" Elise and Laleitha said.

"Yes," Anton answered.

"Yeah, he was sweating out of his skin, breathing like he just ran a marathon," Darren remarked.

"Panic attack?" Laleitha speculated.

"He had one of those two days ago at the council meeting," Elise said. "I'm worried about him."

"He's been having them for a while," Anton said.

Suddenly, a voice behind them said, "I'm fine, you morons. And I didn't know our kitchen discussions took place this early."

They went silent when they heard him speak, all turning to look at him as he entered the kitchen. He paused when nobody said anything, obviously wishing to let the topic slip out of memory.

The silence was broken when Elise's toast popped from the toaster, causing her to jump and let out a small yelp.

"Your toast is ready," Darren said as she turned to spread butter on it.

"Yeah," she muttered.

The plan was the only thing on her mind through breakfast. More than anything else in the world, she wanted to enter The Way. She wanted to find *anything* that could give her a clue as to how Marty died or at least what he was up to at the time. She might even find the answers he was trying to hide: the whereabouts of Orphia's son.

After a sullen breakfast, Gerald was the first to rise. "Are we all clear on the plan?"

Everyone nodded.

"Are we all clear on the consequences if we are caught?"

They nodded again.

"All right," he said, "let's hop to it then."

CHAPTER TWENTY-ONE

Into the Mind of Joseph Talious

"Are you feeling all right, Elise?" Ms. Kilodrist asked when she caught Elise staring down at the table, her gaze unfocused.

It was three days before the Lumerian representatives were to leave to meet with the Prime Devise—therefore the day they would execute phase one of the plan—and too many thoughts were clouding Elise's mind. Days had passed since they made the plan, and she had spent almost every night rereading and revising it. Now, it was time to execute it.

Elise looked up at Ms. Kilodrist, startled. "Um, yeah. Can I talk to you?" *She is suspicious.*

The others looked at her. Gerald's eyes were wide, as if to say, *"Don't you dare tell her."* Darren's look was pure confusion, and Anton had lowered his eyebrows. Laleitha didn't question her sister but couldn't help looking at her, trying to grasp some sort of information.

"Oh. Yes, okay." Ms. Kilodrist looked at Ellington, who picked up on her cue and took over the lesson.

Elise led Ms. Kilodrist to an empty room in one of the smaller of Fort Kingshold's halls, closing the door behind them and turning to face her. Her expression wasn't as suspicious as Elise had thought but instead turned only to concern.

Elise took a deep breath. She didn't want to talk about this, but for the sake of the plan, it appeared she had to, as it offered an explanation to why she'd been acting strange. "When Westbecker sent us to Litrite, and Pe—Second Reighba tried to kill me, something strange happened."

Ms. Kilodrist didn't give Elise a shard of a reaction beyond the lowering of her eyebrows.

"We both went into this dream, but it only lasted for a split second, and in it, I saw his memories." Elise grew agitated as the memories began to flood back to her. She had felt his pain, as well as her own. It reached too deep within her to forget, and that was a stake she'd rather not try to pull out of the ground.

"And then mine started showing up too," she went on, just to break the agonizing silence. "Not just random memories, but the kind that stays with us. It was . . . a lot of pain."

Ms. Kilodrist was stiff. "This," she said slowly, her eyes distant as she tried to put her words together, "is not unheard of for a Major, and we do have a plan for this, in case one of you were to display these abilities. If you'll excuse me, I'm going to get Mr. Talious. If this means what I think it means, we're going to have to develop this skill as quickly as we can." With that, she turned and left the room.

Moments later she returned with Talious following her. Ms. Kilodrist gave him a quick nod then closed the door behind her so it was only the two of them in the room.

Silence.

"So," Talious said after a moment, "you got in his head."

"Is there something wrong with me?" Elise asked quietly.

"Yes," Talious answered, bluntly. "But it's not necessarily bad per se. This has been the case with a few Majors before you. It means you're different."

Elise winced. "You aren't exactly helping."

He threw up his hands. "I tried to put it lightly."

"By saying I'm *different*," Elise said, her words beginning to speed up, "that either means something really great or really shitty. Considering I have terrible memories of my worst enemy imprinted into my brain, I'm going to assume it's really, *really* shitty."

"What I meant was," Talious began, "there is something you can do that the others can't, and it's that you could potentially penetrate the mind using the Lumire. Those are Yugie's words, not mine."

Elise rubbed her forehead with the ball of her hand. "So like . . . telepathy?"

"Yes. Lumerians call it the practice of semerisee, but telepathy is pretty much the same thing."

"Okay, so what are you here for?" Elise asked.

"To help you learn to use it," he replied simply.

Elise frowned. "How?"

He pulled up a chair and sat down facing her while she remained standing. "Get into my mind."

She was taken aback by this. "What? Just like that? On command?"

"No questions. I really can't answer them."

"Right, sorry," Elise said, trying to focus her scattered mind. What if he began seeing her thoughts, too, like Peter did, and saw their plan? His dark eyes seemed to be scorching her skin as she grew uncomfortable under his expectant gaze.

She shook her head. "I don't know how I did it."

Talious sighed. "What I expected. I didn't want to have to follow through with the original plan but . . ." He held out his hand to her.

Slowly, Elise reached out her hand as well, laying it in his. He took her wrist gently before removing something from his pocket she couldn't see. Suddenly, he was stabbing a long, cold pin through the tip of her middle finger.

She yelped in surprise and pain, trying to yank her hand away from his, but his grip on her wrist tightened. A horrible stinging throbbed in her hand, making her entire arm grow tingly and numb. Crying out in alarm, she thrashed her entire body in an attempt to get away from him, but he didn't budge.

"What am I thinking, Elise?" he repeated calmly.

"What's that for?" she cried.

"The Lumire engages under stress. I really didn't want to do this but you have to learn how to use it," he said. "What am I thinking?"

Elise closed her eyes, fighting to forget the stinging in her hand, letting the pulsing in her forehead reengage. She sensed Talious in front of her but didn't know how to get into his head. The stinging in her hand was unbearable, making it nearly impossible to focus all her energy on the Lumire.

Talious inserted a second pin into her pointer finger, doubling the sensation. "Get into my head. You can do it, Elise," he said.

Elise's breath quivered as she tried desperately to stay focused. Images of the first guard she killed flashed through her mind, causing her to shake her head furiously.

"You can do it, Elise," he told her again. "Read my mind."

Elise pushed on, her head beginning to ache as random images flashed before her eyes. A terrible feeling of overwhelming distress had flooded through her. She began to tremble while trying to hold herself in one place. Talious inserted another pin into her ring finger, and she let out a strangled shout. Suddenly, something green flashed before her eyes and she was looking through the eyes of a man in a suit as he walked along a quiet hall. Everything was moving in fast motion as the man opened a door, looking around for any passersby before he entered. The images flipped out of her vision with an excruciatingly painful snap somewhere in Elise's forehead. She cried out in pain before sinking to the floor, her wrist released but the pins still protruding from her fingers, her face buried in her hands.

"You got a glimpse," Talious told her. "Now try to maintain the connection."

"It hurts!" Elise cried, removing her hands and looking up at him, panicked, pleading. A few tears had escaped her and slid down her cheeks as the pain became overwhelming.

"This is essential, Elise," he told her, grabbing her by arms and pulling her back to her feet.

She stumbled back against the wall, her sweaty palms pressed on the cool surface as she tried to ground herself.

"If you are who we think you are, you need to master this."

Elise braced herself, letting the Lumire take hold once more. The pain blew through her body again and she cried out, slamming herself back against the wall, tears streaming down her face.

"You can do this," Talious told her, his voice calm.

Her chest heaved, her hands trembling from the strain. Panic took over. She couldn't do this. She couldn't get into somebody's mind. She didn't *want* to get into somebody's mind. Now, a sob was climbing up her throat as the pain, anger, and helplessness all drove her over the edge.

"You can do it, Elise," he said calmly as she tried to focus herself again.

"It hurts!" she screamed once more, the agonizing pain fueling her tears.

"You can do it," he told her again.

"No, I can't!" she yelled in complete distress, collapsing against the wall.

"Elise!" he roared, quelling her protests strikingly quick.

Terrified, she looked up at him and his expression softened.

"I don't want to hurt you again," he told her steadily. "Please, try to do this."

A long silence drew on between them as Elise tried to catch her breath. The room filled with the sounds of her shaky inhales and exhales. Finally, she looked back up at him to find him pleading silently with her, then she looked down at her hand, with three pins protruding from her fingertips, which had gone numb and tingly by then. Slowly, she nodded, and Talious exhaled audibly.

With her eyes closed, she tried once more, slowing her breathing until she was as close to calm as she could get. Talious looked at her expectantly—she knew this without opening up her eyes. She could feel his thoughts now, buzzing around his head like bees. His mind was cloudy, too many memories and ideas. She felt just as helpless as she had the first time she tried to move the bottle; she could feel the bottle, but she couldn't control it.

Then, quicker than lightning, the world changed around her, causing her to choke on her own breath. Talious sat on the couch with a woman in his arms, the fireplace had just died, and they were enjoying the comfortable silence.

"You can't leave," the woman whispered. "Not tonight. Not while everything is perfect."

At first Talious said nothing, then rested his head on hers and murmured, "Everything will be perfect again."

"How do I know you'll come back?" she asked, looking at him with wide, worried eyes.

"I will," he assured her. "I promise."

The scene evaporated and Elise found herself once again walking down an empty hall. Talious wore a suit and tie, absentmindedly adjusting his cufflinks as he walked, attempting to look as innocent as possible . . .

Suddenly the hall turned into a dark underground passage that Talious trudged through, among several others. They turned and boarded a silver elevator with bright yellow lights, causing him to have to strain his eyes before they adjusted. The door closed in front of him and the elevator began to move upward. Sweat beaded his forehead, and he gripped his daggers in the slots of his belt. Ninth level, eighth level, seventh level.

The elevator paused and three men walked off into another cavern before the door shut and the capsule resumed its journey upward. Sixth level, fifth level. If he was going to do it, he had to do it now.

Suddenly, Talious whipped out his daggers, slashing the necks of the two people next to him before they could even process what had happened. Alarm filled the other men, but they were quick to fight back. One struck his left arm as Talious whirled around and plunged the knife into another. A man kicked his legs from behind and another grabbed Talious's neck in his arms and began to squeeze. Talious attempted to stab his choker, but the knife was knocked from his hand. He threw the other knife straight down, impaling the bigger man's toe. The man yelped in agony, giving Talious the wiggle room he needed to break from his grip.

One of the other men punched him, sending him bustling backward, then punched again and again, his fist becoming bloodier and bloodier each time he wound up. Finally, Talious countered the man's blow, at the same time kicking away another attacker. He twisted the man's arm backward, hearing him yell in pain. Talious landed a side kick to the man's ribs, sending him stumbling. Ripping his knife from the toe of the choker, he dug it into the one he had kicked away. His choker slammed Talious's head against the wall, holding his neck there as the last man repeatedly struck his ribs.

Talious, his vision blurring and his head pounding, reached desperately below, willing his fingers to feel the hard hilt of his knife. Finally, in one last burst of desperate energy, he found his knife and took hold of it, wasting no time to swing at the man punching him. The man jerked backward, a long cut opening on his cheek. Talious's attacker jumped away from the knife, giving Talious just enough time to throw the dagger straight into the first man, who let out a terrible cry when it stuck through his gut. Talious dove, scooping up the other dagger as the last man lunged for him. They wrestled furiously on the floor until Talious's hand finally reached the knife and he stabbed it into the man's throat. Hot, sticky blood spewed all over Talious as he lay there in exhaustion, before the elevator doors rolled open again.

The scene flipped back to the first hallway as the man stopped before the door labeled *Vault 3* and turned the knob. He looked around for anyone as he opened the door, preparing a cover story for any inquiring minds . . .

Elise tumbled back into reality, the most pain she had ever felt in her life burning inside her chest. She sobbed on the floor, trying to catch her breath. Talious knelt beside her, gingerly picking up her hand and removing the pins from her fingertips. She barely felt it.

"I think that's enough for today," he said quietly, standing up, once her sobs became slow, heavy breaths.

Elise's voice quivered as she forced the words out of her. "Talious?"

"Yes?"

"What was in that room? Why did you kill those men? Who was that woman?" The words rushed out as she tried to fit them all in between her gasping breaths.

He shook his head. "For future reference, what you see in my head stays in my head," he told her, his voice stern.

"Okay, okay." She conceded quickly, pushing herself from the floor with trembling arms. "But can I please get a complete explanation for once?"

He sighed, turning away from the door and sitting back down in his chair. He leaned forward and folded his fingers together. "What do you want me to explain?"

Elise braced her back against the ice-cold wall again, still trying to stop the heaving in her chest. Her left leg remained flat on the floor, but her right one bent at the knee. "Ms. Kilodrist said," she began, stopping to take a few more breaths before continuing, "before she went to get you . . . that she thought she knew what was happening."

"Yes?"

"And you called those pins 'the original plan.'" Her eyes lifted from the floor to study him.

He said nothing.

"You knew I was like this before I told you," she said, less a question than an accusation.

Her breathing had not yet slowed.

"No," Talious said, "we didn't. But we suspected one of you would be."

Elise shook her head. "I always get the feeling that you're not telling us something. You, Ms. Kilodrist, and Ellington. I want a full explanation."

He paused for a moment, possibly contemplating whether or not to tell her. "We were tracking you for a long time before you came here," he explained softly. "We wanted to prepare for every scenario, including that one of you would be a semeric. A telepath."

"We?"

"The Lumerian Council," he said. "We had a meeting to discuss you a few weeks before Sar Prague abducted you. That's when I was sent to follow you guys. Well, your sister because she was the first we planned to retrieve. The initial plan was to bring you here one by one and by your own choice. The Prime Devise forced our hand."

Elise didn't say anything. She just rested her head against the wall as she felt a particularly large drop of sweat roll down her left temple. Her entire body felt like it was overheating.

"And about Kilodrist," Talious said, "you guys will feel like she's been keeping things from you for a long time. She's probably the most informed person in the building besides the Arc Leaders. Once you start to understand Lat society, you'll feel like you have more pieces to the puzzle. That only comes with time. There are things that she actually can't teach and that she's not even allowed to teach."

"Such as?"

"The Stormy City's situation, Lumeria's constant feud with Inseana that nobody knows when started, the political minefield of the Lumerian Council. That's just the few of them," he explained. "Just be patient."

"Okay." Elise sighed.

"And about Ellington, give him time too. He knows how you are feeling because he isn't Lumerian by birth either."

"He's not?"

"He said he was born in a town in a place called *England*, from the Other Society," Talious said. "He came to Lumeria when he was very young."

Elise was struck for a moment, briefly wondering how she hadn't figured Ellington was from the Other Society. It would explain how understanding and patient he was with their transitioning, having gone through it himself. Simply knowing that he had been transitioned, even if he was born oceans away from Elise in the Other Society, made Elise feel a certain tie to him.

"And you?" Elise asked. "Where are you from?"

"My home is in Elevis," he said. "A city called Valehessuir. That's where my wife is. Don't mention her ever, okay?"

"Okay," Elise obeyed.

"I'm going back there when you guys are inducted," he went on. "And Kilodrist is going home once you guys are done transitioning, which will be by the end of the year, hopefully. She lives in the Arc City, so you'll still see her around Fort Kingshold. Ellington will stay with you though. He's your sponsor and that doesn't change, even when you are inducted," he said.

Elise nodded.

"And, between the two of us," Talious added, "he'll tell you anything if you press him hard enough—doesn't matter how sensitive. Just go to him with your questions."

"Okay," she said again, her voice beginning to come back. "I'm assuming the opposite goes for you?"

He raised an eyebrow.

"Am I going to have to read your mind to figure out why you killed those men? Or what was in that room?" Elise had her suspicions for a few of them, and she figured the woman she'd seen with him was his wife, but she didn't want to jump to any conclusions. If Talious willingly told her now, perhaps her trust in him would be secured.

His rare softness immediately vanished as he abruptly stood. "Yes." He turned to leave the room. "I'll be with the others. Stay here until you're ready to come out," he said. "And as long as you don't tell a soul what you saw, I won't tell Ms. Kilodrist you are hiding something."

CHAPTER TWENTY-TWO

Phase One

Elise didn't tell anyone about her semerisee. All they needed to know was that their instructors still didn't know about the plan, which commenced when they returned from transitioning and Lumire training.

Ellington's office sat right next to their living quarters, so it was impossible to leave the building without him noticing. He looked up when he heard Elise pass by.

"Hello, Miss Montason," he greeted. "Going somewhere?"

"To the bathroom," she said. "The guys are showering in the ones in the rooms."

"Very well." He sighed, standing up. "Let's be quick."

When Elise and Ellington reached the bathrooms, Ellington stood outside the door as Elise entered.

Now, I wait. She looked in the mirror. Staring back at her was the face of a girl who quite likely killed someone. *Stop that.* Elise turned her back to the image of herself, nervously clenching and unclenching her fists. She couldn't afford to think like that, not now. She had resolved long before to just go with it during the day and save trying to make sense of things for the night, regardless of emotional struggles.

Soon, she heard a tap on the bathroom window, which was short and wide, positioned high on the wall toward the ceiling. Elise opened it quickly.

In climbed a girl with wavy, shoulder-length blonde hair falling in front of her deep brown eyes as she struggled to climb down from her entrance, and an oval face of fair skin and acne scars.

Elise looked into the face of herself.

"How do I look?" Anton said in his best imitation of her voice.

"Exceptionally terrifying," Elise replied. "I think he'll buy it."

Anton nodded. "Hide yourself."

Elise slipped into a stall as Anton, disguised as Elise, exited the bathroom, leading Ellington away so Elise could escape.

⋊

Meanwhile, Laleitha snuck out of the living quarters, making her way into Fort Kingshold. The particular wing of the building she found herself wandering through looked strikingly similar to any office building in the Other Society, with walls of soft gray, dividers sectioning off desks in groups of four, and the occasional plant. The budget offices.

The five had carefully chosen this place, as it was far enough away from Ms. Kilodrist's office that attention wouldn't be drawn to Lee when she snuck in, but central enough for the entire building to be evacuated.

Now all she needed was to get past the secretary unnoticed so she could make it to the back office where she could safely set her fire. The only problem was, this secretary was a particularly attentive one.

They had found a way around this, however, as Gerald was dialing the secretary's number back in the living quarters at this very second, about to ask her to find someone to take the most recent report on the decided-upon funding for Lumire training over to Ellington's office at the Major's suite. Ellington, of course would not receive this file because he was waiting for Elise at the bathrooms. Darren would retrieve the file from his desk the moment Ms. Secretary—as they called her in the plan—left the hall, so Ellington wouldn't find out.

Looking around to ensure nobody was approaching, Laleitha pressed her ear to the door to listen. The secretary was on the phone, speaking in an exasperated and forceful yet respectful tone. "Can this not wait?" There was a short pause. "Yes, sir. I'll get that to you right away," she responded, giving in as Gerald chattered on, posing as the LSE lieutenant Aro Sherlock.

Laleitha backed away from the door, turning the corner and putting her back against the wall. It wasn't long before the door opened and the *click-click-click* of the woman's high heels grew louder. The woman passed by without noticing Laleitha, as planned.

Scanning the room to ensure nobody was looking, she crossed the space quickly. She followed the walls to avoid drawing attention to herself and walked as fast as she could while still managing to look like she was walking at a normal pace. Everyone at their desks kept working or chatting with the people beside them. Nobody noticed her as she made it to the back office.

Here she would have to start a fire. It was the logical place to set ablaze because the fire would be noticed but not right away, giving her enough time to escape. An investigation on what started the fire would occur, but they had been "in their rooms the whole time."

Laleitha pressed her hands to the table, feeling the Lumire sweep through her veins. An orange glow began to light up the small channels under her skin as a crackling began to commence at her fingertips. The wood beneath her hands began to sizzle and pop as the heat flowed through it. At last, a small flame ignited between her thumbs. A smile creased her cheeks. Fire came quite easily to her. She turned, slipping from the room and making her escape.

Within moments, alarms began to blare. By then, Laleitha had already escaped the wing and was making her way to the entrance hall, which she knew would soon be swarming with people as the evacuation began. Resting her back against the wall, she closed her eyes and counted the seconds until the sound of voices and footsteps approached from all directions, growing progressively louder as the people made their way from the building in multitudes. Deciding it was safely crowded, she took this opportunity to escape from the building, crossing the street quickly to find Ellington, the others, and fake Elise standing out on the sidewalk where another crowd gathered to see what the fuss was about.

"Where is Laleitha?" Ellington asked, looking around.

"I'm here," she said.

He turned around quickly, spotting her, and a look of surprise crossed his face. "When did you get here?"

"She's been here all along," Gerald said, sounding as confused as Ellington. "Did you not notice her?"

"I was just trying to see where the fire started," she explained, lying through her teeth.

"And Anton?"

"He went with her," Darren said.

"He went further than I did," Laleitha added. "He's probably still mixed in with the crowd somewhere."

"Well, I suppose we should try to find him," Ellington concluded, still sounding utterly bewildered.

)(

A dense, mildly concerned crowd was perhaps the easiest thing to sneak through, so getting into Fort Kingshold while everyone else made their slow but steady escape proved no challenge. Now, Elise needed to find Ms. Kilodrist's office. She knew where she was going—at least, she thought she did. In preparation for their plan, Elise had memorized the map of Fort Kingshold and knew which turns to take. That was the Majors' thing now, she decided, memorizing maps and creeping around bases.

Soon, she found Ms. Kilodrist's office, which was large and perfectly organized, without a paper out of place. Quietly closing the door behind her, she approached the computer, hitting the return key so the light flashed on. The screen was completely blank except for a small box in the middle reading "Password."

Shit. She gritted her teeth. They had anticipated this, yes, but had no solution to it. She had assured King she would figure something out, so figure something out, she would.

Hurriedly, Elise rummaged through the stacks of paper, the filing cabinets, any piece of paper she could find that might have the password written on it. It had to be written down somewhere. Elise could easily imagine Ms. Kilodrist changing it on a regular basis, so perhaps there was some sort of log she could find.

Suddenly the knob twisted and light from the outside hall poured in. Elise froze, staring at the silhouette in the doorway.

A girl, no older than Elise, looked sideways at her. "You're a Major," she said. "What are you doing here?"

The girl had long, tightly knit black hair with exceptional poof framing her chocolate-colored face. Her eyes glowed intelligently, and she wore a short yellow dress and a silver necklace.

Elise stuttered, trying to find her words. "I, uh, I'm just . . . I could ask you the same question."

The girl smiled, amused by Elise's lack of composure. "I'm looking for my father. The firefighters have already arrived; they have the fire under control. I can't find my dad though. I'm afraid this might be another elaborate Prime Devise scheme meant to kill him."

"Okay," Elise replied, her eyes still wide and her body still frozen. *Damn it, she actually has an excuse. I need to stall until I think of one.* "Why . . . uh . . . who is your father? Why would they want to kill him?"

The girl smiled again, sticking out a hand. "Ella Evanstin," she said as Elise cautiously shook her hand. "Emperor Evanstin is my father."

Okay, that makes sense. "Elise Montason."

"So, um, why are you here?" Ella asked, tilting her head once more.

"I . . ." She turned around. *Am busted,* she thought. "I was looking for someone—anyone—who would have information regarding The Way."

She nodded. "Yes, Dad told me about that. This isn't the place to find information, Elise."

Elise looked back at Ella, who gave her a suspicious stare.

"What are you really up to?"

Elise swallowed. She had to lie. She had to think of something shameful or suspicious, something that would make her seem like she had a reason to lie about it. "I was looking for information on Captain Westbecker," she decided.

Ella raised her eyebrows. "Why?"

"I want to know why he sent us into that Prime Devise base."

She nodded. "That *was* a bit suspicious, but I'm sure my dad has people investigating it."

"I want to know for myself," Elise said firmly. "I doubt we'd be told when they do find out what was up."

The other girl shrugged. "Okay, so you're trying to get into Ms. Kilodrist's computer. Good luck with that."

"Do you know her password?" Elise asked, hopefully.

A smirk tugged at Ella's lips. "All passwords of government-administered computers go through my father. Of course I do. But what do you plan to look for when you get in?"

"I don't know. Some sort of communication between Ms. Kilodrist and him, a background record. I feel like this is one big game of chess that he's been setting up for a while," Elise explained, making up her plan as she went along.

The girl smiled, mischievous glow in her eyes. "Fine, I'll get you in. But Dad has been wanting to meet you and the other Majors for a while, so if I get you in, you need to agree to meet with him. Like an actual meeting. Not just shaking your hands and then almost dying like what happened last time. He wants to talk to you guys."

Elise nodded. "Deal."

Ella approached the computer, shooting a look at Elise, who turned away while Ella put in the passcode.

"Thanks," Elise said, turning back to her once she was in. "And can we agree that we aren't telling anyone about this?"

Ella snorted. "I'd get in so much trouble. Besides, I like snooping around in my dad's secrets."

"You do?" Elise asked, slightly taken aback by this strange comment.

"Yeah," she said. "His plans, his records. Not for any particular reason— just because I'm curious. It's fun to know when something is going to happen before it happens, especially when no one knows you know."

Elise nodded, turning back to the computer. "I get that."

Ella tittered. "I didn't think anyone would. I thought it would make people suspicious."

"You've never told anyone?" Elise asked.

She shrugged. "No one ever asks. I'm the daughter of the emperor; all I'm here for is to follow him around and look pretty. Nobody ever cares about what I'm up to."

Elise didn't know how to respond. Show sympathy? Change the subject? Ask her what she *was* up to in order to establish a bond? A bond with the emperor's daughter could be advantageous.

"What . . . *are* you up to?" Elise asked, trying to sound interested in anything other than sticking her nose in the information in front of her.

"Besides hiding the empire's secrets? Following my dad around and looking pretty."

Elise snickered and opened up the *Schedule Overview and Assignments* tab. In front of her was a detailed list of what was happening on which days and who would be responsible for what. Perfect. Her eyes scanned the page. Ellington was scheduled to meet with the Prime Devise while a man named James Yusef took responsibility for the Majors. Even more perfect. She opened up Ms.

Kilodrist's email and searched "James Yusef" in the address box. In the box below it, she began to type, trying to sound as formal as possible.

To James Yusef,

As you have been notified, the surveillance of the five Majors has been transferred to you, as their previous supervisor, Mr. Ellington, is to be in Hiseroth for a diplomatic meeting. However, Stanford Ellington has abruptly opted to remain in the Arc City, so you are no longer needed to supervise the five Majors and are free to resume your daily schedule. We thank you for your willingness to help.

Elise paused. Was it too brief? *No,* she decided. *It's fine.*

"What are you doing now?" Ella asked from behind, looking over her shoulder at the message.

"Getting us some free time," Elise answered honestly before she clicked the send button and stood. "Thanks for your help."

Ella still had a mischievous look in her eye. "Glad I found someone who shares my hobby."

Elise nodded. "I should probably get outside. Ellington's looking for me."

"Good idea."

When Elise arrived outside, joining the massive crowd of confused people, she sought out the others. They had planned to scatter, "accidentally" getting lost in the crowd so Ellington couldn't keep track of any of them, let alone notice one's absence.

She had only just begun wading through the people when she found herself face-to-face with her sister.

"How'd it go?" Laleitha asked.

"We're free the minute Ellington leaves," Elise said, excitement shining in her eyes.

"Yes!" Lee laughed. "Okay, we need to find Ellington. He's getting suspicious."

"Have you talked to Talious?" Elise asked, the excitement suddenly turning cold in her veins.

"No," her sister answered, sounding confused. "Why?"

"Because he knows we're up to something," she answered, her voice low.

"How?" Laleitha asked, her eyes suddenly turning hard, as they always did when she worried. "You didn't—"

"No, of course I didn't tell him," Elise said. "But he figured it out somehow. I'm not sure if he's going to tell Ellington."

Lee frowned. "I'm not sure we can do much about that except hope he doesn't."

When they finally found Ellington in the crowd, he seemed relieved to see them—Darren and Gerald as well, who stood at Ellington's side.

"Where's Anton?" Elise asked, looking around.

That was the signal to the others that it was the real Elise, not Anton disguised as Elise.

Ellington sighed. "It is impossible to keep track of anyone in this crowd. I haven't seen him since we came out here."

"I'm here," the muffled voice of Anton called quietly from behind.

Ellington turned. "Ah, good. Finally, I've found you all." He looked around. "It looks like people are heading back in now. We should hurry so you don't miss your combat training."

✕

It wasn't until late—after their training, after strenuous exercise, round after round of sparring, Talious yelling encouragement at them when they grew tired, and technique critiquing—that the five were gifted with well-earned alone time.

"So, she just . . . let you in?" Darren asked after Elise explained what had happened.

She nodded. "She thought I was curious about Westbecker and that I didn't mean any harm."

"We *don't* mean harm," Anton pointed out.

"And apparently she herself has been poking through the computers for years, just because she likes to know what's going on. I think we developed a strange acquaintanceship," Elise went on.

"A useful acquaintanceship," Gerald added. "I mean, she's the emperor's daughter. She has access to everything."

Their voices suddenly hushed when the door opened behind them. In walked Ellington, wearing a large, proud smile. "Your night has not come to an end yet," he told them after a brief greeting. "Emperor Evanstin himself has requested to meet you—officially, anyway, since your first meeting was cut short."

"Right now?" Darren asked.

Ellington shrugged. "It appears to be the most logical option, as the emperor is at a breaking point in his schedule and you are doing nothing in particular."

The Majors exchanged glances.

"Okay," Gerald said, standing up. "Let's go meet the emperor."

CHAPTER TWENTY-THREE

The Emperor's Suspicions

The emperor's keep was nothing short of luxurious, with long glass windows and a golden glow radiating from the fancy light fixtures above. Polished wood panels covered the walls that did not face outward to the city, and the entire room was carpeted. The left side had a large desk setup with a few chairs against the wall, while the right side had a circle of couches and lounge chairs surrounding a coffee table. It was the right side of the room that the Majors were invited to.

Emperor Evanstin sat back on one couch with his daughter—who shot a wink at Elise when she entered—next to him. The sisters sat next to each other on the adjacent couch while Darren and Anton took another and Gerald claimed a lounge chair.

Elise was especially uncomfortable now. She had given up objecting to the pointless respect she was given, but now she was sitting in front of the emperor, carrying a pressing secret on her back.

"I have been looking forward to meeting you," the emperor said. "You've stirred up quite a fuss here. Things we haven't seen in years."

"I'll say," Darren muttered.

"First of all," Evanstin said, a mildly amused look spreading on his face. "Your session in front of Orphia had people talking for weeks. Even without Thentis speaking, it was an incredibly nerve-racking affair to watch."

Gerald grunted. "Yeah, we were told Thentis doesn't speak much."

"Yes, he hasn't spoken since after the fall of the Juperds," the emperor said. "Not the most indignant or confusing people could get a word from him. I wonder why he spoke to you?"

"I almost wished he hadn't," Gerald admitted.

"I personally believe," the emperor said to him, "that his mind is growing shriveled from all of the years he's lived and all of the minds he's seen. He is a crazy old man lost in despair."

Elise swallowed. She was learning to read minds as well. Would she be driven the same way? Would she feel the pain and suffering of every mind she touched? Would she know all this hate and all this hopelessness piled up from one mind onto another? What if she had to kill again? What if she connected to someone's consciousness as they were dying at her hand?

"So, how has transitioning been going?" the emperor asked, the new topic bringing Elise back to reality. "Ms. Kilodrist is a very fine teacher, one of our best. She's been trained as a historian and a diplomat, she's studied the Lumire for years, and I'm sure she's been up to much more than I cannot recall. Choosing her to be your transitioner was probably the best thing we did in the whole messy ordeal of brining you back from the Other Society."

"You . . . chose her to be our transitioner?" Laleitha asked.

He nodded. "That's right."

"But when we arrived, we were taken straight to her without any instruction or notice. That was before the council even knew we were here. There was no way you had time to appoint her unless you had been planning this," she reasoned.

Elise recalled what Talious had told her before. The council had been tracking them long before their encounter with Sar Prague and Second Reighba. She hadn't yet told the others about this, nor anything she learned from Talious after their session.

Evanstin shifted in his spot. "Before we sent Mr. Talious and Mr. Ellington to retrieve you, we had been keeping tabs on you for a while. It was the conclusion to a long search for the missing Majors, and though we only informed a small portion of the council that we had found who we thought were the Majors, the Prime Devise's spy got their hands on your location. The Prime Devise got to you first, as things turned out."

Elise nodded; she had forgotten there was a spy within the borders. Westbecker had told them that.

"What's being done about the spy?" Gerald asked.

Ella let out a small laugh. "It's a nightmare. We tried putting all the Arc Leaders through the kiln, but they all came out clean. Now we have a group of three Arc Leaders and the LSE investigating it around the clock."

"I'm sorry, the *kiln*?" Darren repeated.

"It's a psychoanalytical devise that we use in situations like this," the emperor explained. "When we have to question people individually."

"So it's like a polygraph," Anton said.

He nodded. "Like one, yes, though far less error prone."

"And everyone came back clean?" Darren went on.

"Everyone," the emperor confirmed. "The investigation is continuing, but it is essential that we get to the bottom of this, solely because of the stakes set by Westbecker when he sent you to attack the Prime Devise. If this situation escalates . . . well, we might have to remove some power from the council to keep sensitive information from the spy."

"But don't we also have a spy within the Prime Devise?" Elise asked.

The room became silent as Emperor Evanstin and his daughter stared at her. The other four, confused by their sudden change in mood, looked from the emperor to Elise.

"How do you know that?" Emperor Evanstin asked, his voice grim and suspicious.

"Westbecker told us," Gerald explained, sounding alarmed by their seriousness.

The emperor's face grew flushed and he looked at his daughter, who stared back at him. "Nobody is supposed to know about that," he said. "That information was highly classified for fear that the Prime Devise would discover his presence through *their* spy. Do you know if he told anyone else?"

Elise looked around at her friends.

"We don't know," Gerald replied. "But he made it clear what would happen if *we* told anyone, so I don't think he would."

"Have you told anyone?" Emperor Evanstin pressed further.

"No," they all replied.

He relaxed ever so slightly. "Good," he said, his face muscles still tight.

Darren cleared his throat, desperate to change the topic. "So, Orphia and Westbecker said something about us being part of a task force before our induction."

"Yes," the emperor said, his mood lightening. "Your training will continue on a regular basis once that has been officially formed. We initially chose Captain Westbecker to run this task force, but as I'm sure you've guessed, we're now assigning someone else."

He paused, tilting his head sideways as he looked at the five. "You show a lot of promise given the circumstances you're transitioning under. I'm quite impressed with your work in Litrite, rogue as it was. When I heard he'd sent you, I thought for sure you'd gotten killed or captured and I'd have to fire Westbecker in disgrace before resigning my position. I couldn't have been more thankful when I read about your success in his report. I don't think any of the previous Majors were put to such an intense challenge so early in their training. There's something special about this group, I can tell."

They looked at each other bashfully, flushing under his praise.

"Which reminds me," he said as he arose from his seat.

He turned to one of the glass panels on the wall, reaching to the ceiling and pulling down on a string. A large painting unrolled like a scroll as he pulled the string downward. Elise recognized the painting; it was the same one that the stained glass above Orphia's courtroom depicted. It was all yellow with a crowned man in the center. Fifteen faces made up the halo above his head. This represented the Arc Leaders. Across the middle, a city rolled over the yellow sky. At the borders were the seven black silhouettes, each wielding a different weapon and a single flower, the original Seven Majors.

The emperor placed his finger over the Major at the top. "The weapon this Major holds," he said, "is called Axis, and is passed down from generation to generation."

The Majors watched as he crossed the room to a long wooden cabinet. "When the Majors were exiled, however," he went on, "Axis was turned in to emperor Trace Orbeck. Unfortunately, he was assassinated not long after the Majors' exile, and emperor Iowyn Barbestdale inherited it. Then, when he stepped down, he passed it on . . . to me." Inside the cabinet, he pushed a button, opening a small safe at the bottom. He took out a silver baton with a crease in the middle, holding it like a fragile piece of glass.

He walked over and handed it to Gerald, who examined it closely.

"You may want to step away from your friends," the Emperor warned.

Gerald stood, stepping behind the couch.

"Now hold it out in front of you," Emperor Evanstin instructed. "And twist each side in a different direction."

When Gerald did this, there was a snap and, in a startling flash, the rod extended, becoming long and skinny; at its end were two curved blades. The blades were stunning, each with a sharp edge winding over its silver surface, turning it into a short, curved ax. The two blades faced different directions, sitting at the end of the now thin and long rod holding them together. The five admired it as Gerald slowly spun it in his hand.

"This weapon hasn't been used by the Majors since the early 1800s," the Emperor said. "But tradition dictates that one of you wield it, if nothing but for the symbol it represents."

Gerald twisted the staff again and the rod folded back into itself, the blades collapsing inward as it became a small baton again.

"One of you will possess it when you become Majors officially," the Emperor explained to them. "If I remember correctly, the last Major who had it was Indrid Rodum."

Stunned eyes turned to Gerald, who looked curiously back down at the baton.

"Of course, it is rather fortunate that Rodum was the only one of the seven surnames that carried all the way down to you five." The Emperor chuckled. "You four, however," he went on, gesturing to the others, "are much harder to place. Many of the Majors changed their last names after they were exiled. We believe they did so in order to stay in hiding; what we don't know is why they wanted to hide in the first place."

"It does seem strange," Elise agreed. There was no apparent reason to stay in hiding. Why would they want to end the Majors, a tradition that Lumerian society depended on so greatly? There had to be a reason, and something told Elise it involved The Way.

"You don't know why they went into hiding?" Anton asked.

Emperor Evanstin shook his head. "Our investigators at the LSE believe they were being hunted by someone or something, but conspirators often throw around much bigger and much wilder theories. In reality, we simply don't know."

"Strange," Gerald agreed quietly, nodding along as if deep in thought.

"Another weapon that was passed down was a golden knife," Evanstin went on, relaxing back into his spot, putting an arm around his daughter. "Of course, it wasn't real gold. The rumor was that it was real gold and the gold was enchanted, but nobody would ever imagine how. It was called Bane, but it was stolen years ago right from the Major's hands."

"Why did people think it was enchanted?" Darren asked, frowning.

"One of the many secrets that the Lumerian Council holds," the emperor said, "pertains to a weakness of the Majors. Of course, I can disclose this information to you, because you can't possibly abuse this information. There are procedures that can be done to metal that makes the Majors vulnerable to it. Bane had undergone that procedure, but of course the public has no idea of this, so wild rumors had spurred."

Elise exchanged glances with her sister.

"Any chance that the Prime Devise's spy got their hands on that?" Laleitha asked.

"Well," the emperor said, "I'm afraid the only way to find out would be for them to attack you with it. I pray that doesn't happen."

"That makes six of us," Gerald agreed.

"So," the emperor said, "what have you been working on in transitioning?"

"Lots of practice with the Lumire," Darren replied.

"Lumerian scientific concepts, Lumerian history, Lumerian society," Gerald went on.

"Usually followed by more practice with the Lumire," Elise added. "Levitating books, lighting up light bulbs just by touching them . . ."

"Melting wax with our minds, building houses of cards without touching them . . ." Darren continued.

"Anything that could have been the cause of the fire in that area?" the emperor pressed, his eyebrows raising.

Elise grew colder. *He isn't suspicious. He is just understandably curious.* She hoped she wasn't as pale as she felt.

"We *have* been setting some papers on fire just by staring at them," Gerald answered, trying to suppress the nervousness in his voice. "But I don't think that'd be the cause of it."

Evanstin nodded, not looking convinced.

He is suspicious. No, he just isn't stupid. Anybody could have thought of that. No, he knows we're up to something, but he doesn't want to be overt about it.

Gerald shrugged. "We don't know, sir. Is it being looked into?"

The emperor nodded. "We just want to make sure there aren't any gas leaks or fire hazards. Though, our security footage also failed at around that time. Do you think there is a possibility they could be connected?"

Elise's heart dropped. *Security footage?* How was it that the footage had been deleted? She looked at Ella, who gave her a quick wink and a smile. *It was Ella.* Elise had a grateful twinge of affection toward the girl.

"The security footage failed?" Darren repeated. "How? Like a malfunction in the system or something?"

There came a meow from behind them and a silver cat strode into the room. It had a ruby collar and gleaming black eyes. It leapt up to the couch the sisters sat on and nestled itself next to Laleitha.

"Yes, it appears the cameras stopped transmitting at the time of the fire. Either that or the footage was deleted and the cameras deactivated, but that seems a little farfetched. We fear the Inseanan spy may have something to do with it," the Emperor said, his eyes lingering on Darren, who managed to keep his composure under the intense stare.

The cat purred as Laleitha stroked its silver fur.

"I see you've met Nattie," the emperor said with a chuckle. "She is quite the sweetheart. I bought her for Ella as a birthday present, but she's become more the cat of Fort Kingshold. She is social when she is in a good mood, but when she is tired she retreats back here. She seems to be quite comfortable with you."

"Are you going to the meeting with the Prime Devise?" Anton asked, changing the subject.

Emperor Evanstin shook his head. "I'm sending a few personal representatives, as I was advised. Given our track record with the Prime Devise, I figured it was the wisest course of action. I know Chancellor Reighba quite well, and he doesn't often concern himself with symbolic gestures, so I don't believe he'd take my absence as a slight as long as I'm sending my handpicked reps."

Darren nodded. "That makes sense."

"This meeting has spurred controversy, as you could probably tell from the council meeting. Many believe it shouldn't be convened at all, given the Prime Devise's patterns of aggression and retaliation in the past. But I'm afraid it is rather late for that since we've already coordinated with Chancellor Reighba."

Reighba. The name made Elise wince, as images of Second Reighba—Peter Reighba—flashed back through her head, his memories, his words, his pain, his *anger*. It made Elise sick. His father had been cruel to him, like he had to Darren, except Peter couldn't get away.

No. That doesn't justify what he's done.

"I have a question about that," King said, "Why do we keep trying to smooth things over with the Prime Devise when they keep attacking us? Shouldn't we be confronting them about it? Or at least address it in a conversation with *them* and not just the council?"

Emperor Evanstin shifted uncomfortably. "The Arc Leaders and I are and have been debating this. Given the Prime Devise's military and technological advantage over us, we don't want to risk any full-scale military incidents. Not to mention we don't want to jeopardize our trading interests in Inseana."

"You think they'd beat us if we went to war?" Lee said.

"Not necessarily, but even if they didn't, they'd inflict damage on a scale we simply cannot afford," he replied. "The Prime Devise has the strongest and most active military in all of the Lat nations. We can only hope that, if we're able to ease away the tensions between us, we'd be setting the basis for future partnerships. At the moment, their primary concern seems to be your arrival, for reasons we have yet to work out fully. Hopefully, we'll be able to clear that up at the meeting."

Elise pulled at her sleeve uncomfortably. She couldn't imagine why the Prime Devise would see *them* as such a threat. Then again, they did carry out an attack on their central command base within their first two months in the empire.

"There is one thing I ask of you," the emperor said, leaning forward, "and I presume you know what it is. I want you, my faithful Majors, the idols that people look to for hope, to refrain from giving yourself any skeletons. Imagine what would happen if the people who hold you in such great esteem were to learn that you're no different than the last Majors, who attempted to tear apart the empire. I hope to my heart and soul that you had nothing to do with that fire and the security camera malfunction, and I hope you are not scheming against the Lumerian Council. You do not know how much I hope that."

X

The emperor's last words echoed through Elise's head while the five trailed behind Ellington as he escorted them back to their living quarters. *He knows. And he's giving us a chance to back out of it. No. We are going to The Way. These questions will eat me alive if I don't find the answers.*

When they arrived back in the familiar set of rooms, with Ellington departing for his home, Elise sat at the couch and spread her supplies out in front of her. It was late, and with the curtains still open, she sat in front of a starry sky with so many constellations she recognized.

She had no chance of sleeping. If she were to lock herself away in a dark room again with nothing to stimulate her mind, she would just float back to the belly of the beast that had consumed her—*guilt*. She couldn't escape the monster forever. It was always looking at her through the windows of the rooms, but she had pushed it aside to focus at the task at hand. *During the day, just go with it. During the night, make sense of it.* That resolution to her confusion and regrets didn't seem to be working as well as she had predicted. The anger and remorse was always there, lingering under her skin, ready to spring out at the first sign of distress. Elise had to wrestle to restrain it every time. Eventually, she had to face the monster herself but until then, she wouldn't let herself feel it. She didn't want to know the same pain that drove her enemy; she didn't want to know pain at all.

"Elise?" a voice from behind asked.

She turned to see Darren standing in the doorway to his room. "Yeah?"

"Are you scared?" he asked. They'd go to The Way tomorrow.

There was something new in his voice, something she hadn't heard in it before. "I'm terrified," she admitted, because perhaps he just needed to know he wasn't alone.

"Me too," he said.

With that, he stepped into his room and closed the door behind him. Elise turned back to the layout in front of her. Pieces were spread out everywhere; she had no idea where to start or what to make. She focused her eyes on a sheet of metal and lifted a hand, feeling as the Lumire stroked it, engulfing it with Elise's tentative power. The sheet levitated ever so slightly and drifted toward Elise, who took it in her hand with a twinge of satisfaction. She was in touch with the Lumire now, like she had finally discovered how to control it after her horrible session with Talious.

Elise's other hand began to heat up, glowing with an orange haze. She placed two fingers on the sheet and bent the metal until a small lip came loose. Holding the tiny piece of metal in her hand, she knew exactly what she wanted to make, and her plan began to hatch in her head as she looked over her material.

The next morning, Gerald emerged from his room to find Elise still sitting on the couch. He approached her slowly, as if she were a wild animal who might be spooked by him. Her hand was held out in front of her, vertically, with a long object winding around her.

"Good morning," he said to get her attention.

She looked over at him, rather startled. "Oh, uh, hi."

"Were you up all night?" he asked.

She nodded. "I made this." She extended her arm to reveal that the long object she held was a mechanical snake. With scales painted black and olive green, it was shorter and slightly thinner than the one they had found in Sappol West. The scales seemed to rotate when it moved, in a vertical and horizontal motion, digging itself into any surface it touched in order to gain traction, clicking and whirring as it moved.

"How?" Gerald asked, taking the snake in his hand and examining it. "Elise, this is . . . really well done."

"The Lumire makes it much easier to shape," Elise said. "I based it off of the design from the snake at Sappol West, with the eyes recording what they see, except instead of storing data, they transmit to the computer here," she explained, gesturing to the desk in the corner.

"Elise, this is amazing," he exclaimed.

"Thanks," Elise replied. "Now, be gentle. Its scales are fragile."

He set it down and Elise poked her nails under the loose scale right below its head, searching for the hidden off switch. When she found it, the snake's eyes dimmed and the scales settled into a still, locked position. "Do you know who taught me how to do this?" Elise asked.

"How to build things? Your dad?" he guessed.

She shook her head. "Hank Martinez."

"Ah." He nodded, turning to make himself breakfast. "The criminal."

Elise bit her inner lip, beginning to stash her supplies away. "Criminal? Maybe. But he's not a bad person, King. I've known him since I was five."

"I never said he was," he replied. "I just think a man who kills just to keep a secret is a little . . . odd."

Elise paused, knowing what he said was reasonable. "Maybe it will make sense when we figure out what that secret is," she said. "And who knows, we may even find the son of Orphia."

CHAPTER TWENTY-FOUR

Phase Two

"Where is he?" Ellington asked as he threw on his coat. "He is supposed to be here by now."

The Majors stood silently outside his office, offering no responses to his angry questions. It was bright and early in the morning and their substitute supervisor wouldn't be coming, but Ellington didn't know that.

"We'll be fine," Gerald said. "I'm sure he'll be here soon. We won't leave our living quarters until he arrives."

"No, I have to be here when he arrives to give him your locations. Emperor Evanstin thought it would be productive if you were each given a place to be and a job to do for the day, and Mr. Yusef was only supposed to escort you to your assigned places, which I have a list of."

"What?" Gerald exclaimed. "Why?"

Ellington looked around for his case. "I'm sorry if this intrudes on any plans you had. We just saw this as an opportunity to familiarize you with Fort Kingshold and the people. These are the faces you will have to be well acquainted with by the time you are officially inducted." Finally, he located his case, which had fallen under his desk. "I suggest you get to know them."

"We can give him the list," Laleitha offered.

"You're going to be late. We'll take care of it," Gerald assured him.

They were too eager for him to leave. *He'll be suspicious.* She pushed these thoughts away, knowing there was no time to be suspicious of Ellington's suspicions. This would surely slow their plan—being placed in different assigned locations. They would have to improvise. They'd been having to do that often lately.

Ellington sighed. "Very well." He took a sheet from his desk and handed it to Gerald. "They are expecting you now, just as I am expected at the train station now. Hurry. I will leave a note for Mr. Yusef."

The five all nodded as he set off down the hall. When they were absolutely sure he was gone, Gerald eagerly turned to his friends. "Okay, this throws a wrench in the plan. We're all in different places, but we still need to get to the hub on time without anyone knowing we're missing. Ideas?"

"We each need to escape independently," Anton said.

"Without a noticeable gap," Elise added. "Nothing should be stalled due to our absence."

"How do you expect us to do that?" Darren exclaimed.

"We also need to be able to communicate somehow," Gerald went on, ignoring Darren's remark.

"Who is assigned where?" Laleitha asked. "One of us may be able to slip out and run messages between us—"

"And then slip back in before they're noticed," Elise finished. "Good thinking."

"Okay," Gerald said, looking down at the paper. "Lee, you're helping digitalize files in the archives to, quote, 'learn about the notable events the last Majors played a part in.'"

She groaned. "Why do I always get the boring jobs?"

"I'm in the transportation office to learn about the layout of the city and the empire. Mont is sitting in on the training of a League of Lumeria troop . . . and Darren and Anton are going to aid the interns in the basic daily operations of Fort Kingshold. Jesus, this all sounds terrible."

"I can be the runner," Anton offered. "It will be easy for me to slip out."

"Okay, that works," Gerald said. "As for escaping, that is a risk we'll have to take. Just get out unnoticed and hope that nobody realizes you're gone."

"We need a cover story," Elise said.

"We'll figure that out on our way back," he replied dismissively. "Until then, just worry about escaping. We need to get to the hub before one o'clock, agreed?"

"Agreed," they all responded. They departed from one another with a brief "See you."

Elise's location was easy to find, luckily. It was a large, outdoor, shaded semicircle with a short brick row acting as a railing. In the courtyard below, which took the shape of a large triangle formed by Fort Kingshold, Fort Rooksheild, and the Cylinder, about thirty men and women were doing push-ups, planks, curls, jumping jacks, and several other exercises in orderly rows, all under the instruction of their sergeant, who stood at the head of the group.

When Elise emerged from the hall inside, walking slowly as she looked around cautiously, feeling rather lost, a man who stood in the very center turned to greet her. "Ah, Miss Montason. I'm glad you could join us. Emperor Evanstin thought it would be beneficial if he gave you and the other Majors exposure to some of the fields you will have to look into in the future." He led her up to the brick railing.

Elise rested her hands on the cold stone, looking down at the soldiers below.

"This is the emperor's league of high-risk responders, nicknamed the League of Lumeria, the most elite, intelligent, and well-trained soldiers of all Lumeria. They are kept next to Fort Kingshold so they can respond almost instantly to any threat to the city or the emperor. These are the men and women who pursued the assassins at your presentation to the Lumerian people."

"Ah," Elise said, nodding. "I remember."

"Imagine yourself here in a few years," the man said, "when you are fully inducted as a Major. You will be asked to select a number of people to act as your minors. Looking at these soldiers now, who stands out to you?"

Elise scanned the rows, her eyes drifting across each body. "The man with the black hair and pointy nose," she said, pointing. "And the one with the prosthetic leg, the girl with the white hair, and the guy with the tattoo on his leg."

The commanders barked something, some of them waving a hand, and the soldiers hopped to their feet from their planks and began to fall into formation.

The man nodded. "Good choices. Why them?"

"Well," Elise said, "the first guy seemed bigger than the rest, the guy with the prosthetic leg obviously can overcome challenges, the girl with the white hair had the best technique of all of them, and I don't know why I chose the last guy."

"Is it because he strikes you as rebellious?"

Elise looked at him curiously.

"The tattoo, which he was forbidden to get, got him into much trouble. He is a troublemaker, that one," the man said, "which we often associate with leadership and courageousness. You don't realize that you do, but that assumption is always there. With good reason, of course. When somebody isn't afraid to do things their way, thereby defying the rules, they will find themselves challenging anything. That is why they stand out more so than the ones who are too afraid to try."

Elise shrugged. "I think he just reminded me of my brother."

She couldn't help but picture Percy among them and distantly wondered whether she'd be able to choose *him* as a minor so he could come to Lumeria and stay with her.

Her teeth dug into her inner lip. She couldn't think about her family right now; now was the time to focus on her escape. No matter what Darren said, or what they told Darren, she was going to The Way to get the backup drive, not just to investigate her old friend. Otherwise, the night that had caused her and so many others to experience so much pain would be for nothing.

※

Anyone who didn't stop to look at Anton for more than a few seconds contented themselves to ignore his existence. He liked it this way.

This way, freedom wasn't such a hard thing to attain.

It didn't take long for him to slip out, offering to bring some mundane file to some mundane council member's office with no intent at all to do so. He took his hands from his pockets, four sticky notes folded between his fingers that he had stolen from a desk he passed, and a pencil in his other hand. On the first note he wrote:

I can get one out, but not all

He'd take this one to King. He would know where to go from there. Anton only prayed he didn't fail now, not when it mattered.

Anton considered sneaking a talent of his, even without his newfound ability to change form. A certain confidence hid within him, a bit of wild glee that burned within him at the thrill of knowing something another did not, that he disguised in order to maintain. He didn't mind knowing things that perhaps nobody would ever discover, nor did he bother to tell somebody whcn he'd discovered something about them, because knowing was much more fun when everybody else was oblivious.

Elise cried at night, he knew, with the same guilt and confusion that haunted his own sleep. That night when they had all fallen asleep in the kitchen, exhausted from working relentlessly on the plan, he had dragged them each to bed, and Elise murmured in her sleep, *"Peter,"* the name of the man who attacked them. Laleitha didn't sleep most nights; she just sat by herself, singing quietly as she drew in her sketchbook, likely afraid of what her dreams would show her. Darren always spoke on the phone with a girl named Jenna when he was alone in his room, using a phone he'd spent nearly all of his money on not long after they arrived, and hid from the rest of them. He told her about everything, told her very sweet and heartfelt things Anton had never spoken before. And King . . . he was the only one who already knew Anton knew everything he did. They spoke a lot, like brothers.

Anton tiptoed into an elevator, praying nobody else would enter as the doors closed. The box began to move downward but, to his dismay, it stopped at the second floor and the doors rolled open once more. In stepped a beautiful girl with soft, chocolate skin and tightly curling hair that puffed out around her. *Ella Evanstin.* She smiled at him and gave him a kind greeting before she pressed the ground floor button and quietly stood next to him.

He shifted uncomfortably, hoping with all his heart she didn't ask what he was up to. When the elevator reached the ground floor, the girl stepped out and turned left. Anton followed quietly but turned right, watching her leave before he turned.

Anton shifted past a few hallways before finding himself in the circular entry hall. At this time of day, people were bustling through and from hall after hall, meaning more people who could potentially recognize him. Luckily for Anton, light poured in from the glass above, creating shadows from the pillars lining the room's circumference. He slipped into the nearest shadow, ducking his head low, feeling himself melt into the colors of the dark wall. The people continued hurrying by, minding their own business. Nobody would notice him here; nobody ever did.

The darkness subsided when the wall was interrupted by the looming doorway. Just as he slowly approached, the door opened and a large group of people entered. He stepped behind them, using their moving bodies as cover as he moved to the other side of the room, working his way over to the west hallway.

When he finally reached the transportation office, he searched along the rows of desks and offices, most of which were empty, in an attempt to spot Gerald. Anton found him looking bored in an office with a middle-aged woman who was showing him various transit maps.

After a few moments, Gerald happened to glance up toward the door and spotted Anton, who held up the note briefly to signal him then ducked out of view before the woman spotted him. Carefully, Anton tucked the note behind the trash can next to the door before maneuvering into an empty cubical in the corner.

He waited there for several moments, until Gerald and the woman exited the room, presumably so she could take him around to meet everyone in the department. Anton strained his ears to hear Gerald ask to go to the bathroom, then he swiftly exited the room, stopping by the trash can to pretend to tie his shoes. When Gerald reentered, he walked past the Anton's cubical, discretely letting a paper slip out of his hand as he did so.

Anton scooped up Gerald's response and hurried away, not reading the note until he was back within the safety of an empty elevator. The note read:

Get Darren or Lee.

X

Laleitha had been given a desk, which was the only perk to being given the most uneventful job of all of the five. She was told to go through old Major-related case files and type the information into a program. The thought of this job alone made her cringe. Why couldn't Mont have been assigned here? Knowing Elise, she would probably get even less done than Laleitha because she would begin reading through the cases. At least she would be interested; Lee didn't exactly want to know how great the Majors before her had been.

Laleitha had already begun thinking of excuses to get away when a familiar face arrived in her empty cubicle. He laid a small piece of paper on her desk and darted away before she could say anything, disappearing back into his domain—where no one could see him.

She reached over and turned over the note. It read:

I can get you or Darren out
I'll be back soon

Her or Darren, huh? It wouldn't be too hard to get out herself. All she needed was an excuse. Darren needed to remain unseen and unnoticed, which was an area he didn't excel in.

She turned the note to its blank side and wrote:

Take Darren—I can get out

Darren was stationed with Anton, and if Anton could remain gone this long, he could probably help Darren out as well. This thought provoked a much more gripping concern in Laleitha's mind. *Can he stay gone for this long? Has anyone noticed?*

What would Anton say if he were confronted about it? What if their absence was noticed after he and Darren escaped and left for The Way? *Then we're screwed.*

Underneath her first message, Lee wrote:

Do they suspect?

She did this so Anton would check, and, perhaps, to soothe her own nerves.

X

The exercises droned on, the man asking Elise strange questions about particular men or women from time to time, but he and the others on the overlook spent most of their time writing notes in large black portfolios.

Elise's thoughts kept jumping back to Percy. She needed something to stimulate her mind—a book, a puzzle, pieces to tinker with—otherwise, it would just bounce back to the same images she saw every night: the men she killed, Peter Reighba, what she saw in his mind, what she saw in Talious's mind, her family back home, her fear . . .

She shook her head, forcing the thoughts away.

The man who had talked to her first closed his folder. "Miss Montason?"

"Yeah?" Elise replied, standing upright and turning away from the wall she had been leaning over.

"Would you mind taking this folder down to Mr. Alvenice's office for me? He's in the Arc Leaders' wing. Hurry back though."

Elise nodded, taking the portfolio from him and heading back into the hall. Taking advantage of the opportunity, the minute she turned the corner, she opened the folder and slipped the pen from its socket. The pages held notes on each of the officers, but she had no time to read through them. She found an empty sheet in the back and tore it loose.

*At 12:20, I'll ask to read through basic protocols, meaning I'll have
to get them from you. That is my escape and yours.
See you at the hub.*

She folded the note and slipped it into her pocket, closing the portfolio once more. When she reached the elevator and it opened in front of her, she found herself face-to-face with Anton. He stepped out wordlessly, holding his hand out.

Elise pressed the note into his hand, telling him, "Lee."

He nodded and they continued on.

✕

Gerald tried not to die of boredom as the woman droned on and on about how the layout of the Arc City had changed over the years and how the invention of the transportation rods impacted yada yada. He'd stopped listening once she finished describing the Downtown Hub, their rendezvous, which was filled with chambers of open transportation rods leading all over the empire.

"Um, Mrs. Pate?" he interrupted as politely as he could. She looked up from the map she was showing him, her bug-eyes wide under her thick glasses. "I'm feeling a bit nauseous. Would it be okay if I went back to my room to lie down a bit?"

"Oh, honey." Mrs. Pate immediately raised a hand to his forehead. "You don't feel too warm, but you look like you're about to be sick. Will you be okay walking back alone?"

He nodded.

"You go lie down then," she said. "Feel better, honey."

That escape was much easier than he thought it'd be.

When he stepped off of Fort Kingshold property, he found himself once again facing the dense city that surrounded the complex. He slowed his pace to a casual walk, slipping his hands into his jacket pockets as he strolled over the crosswalk, accompanied by several others who paid no attention to him.

Going unnoticed was never something Gerald was used to. Eventually, he would cave and seek something—someone—an uncontrollable feeling to isolation would pile up, against all logic, if he allowed himself to be alone in the crowd. It was rooted deep within him.

In his pocket, he fingered the small bag of dollar bills Ellington had given him. As he sat down at the bench next to the bus stop, he removed the pouch from his pocket and busied himself with inspecting the strange slips of white paper. Hopefully nobody would recognize him with his head down. The bills were white with a blue stripe down the middle and a few holes punched along the side that indicated their value.

"This seat taken?" an elderly man asked, gesturing to the seat beside him.

Gerald looked up at the man. "No, go ahead," he said politely as the man sat down.

The man rested his arms on his cane between his legs as he got comfortable. "Where you headed?" he asked.

"Just to the hub," he responded. "I'm meeting someone there."

"A girl?" the man asked, raising an eyebrow, creating even more wrinkles on his forehead.

"Yeah," Gerald answered, deciding that was the simplest and most understandable story he could exhibit.

"Ah," the man said. "Be careful with them."

Gerald chuckled wryly. "Not a fan of the ladies?"

"I am, but you see," the man replied, "but you see, it's tricky when you're young. People are always telling you to go for this one or that, avoid the one type, chase the other. It's nonsense, all of it. They'll stick their fingers in and twist you around till you don't know which way is what."

Gerald nodded, not exactly following what he was talking about, but the man seemed to be getting into it.

"They'll tell you what she's supposed to look like and talk like, what she's supposed to let you do with her. They'll tell you, 'Go for the girl who makes you win her over' because that means she's worth something, or they'll tell you, 'Go for the girl who's afraid she's gonna lose you' because then you can do what you want with her. All of it's nonsense, the purest load of shit you'll ever smell, that. Let me tell you, I went for the girl like that. My folks loved her, my friends loved her, and I thought I did, too, but let me tell you. Twenty-five years later, she took both my kids and left me in an empty house. Got herself a new husband who showed her around to his folks and his friends and they all loved her too. That one lasted ten years."

Gerald frowned. What was his point?

"Went for the other type," he continued. "I loved this one true, but she didn't want a family."

"Did you find someone it worked with?" Gerald asked, trying to get him to the end of his story.

The man barked a laugh. "Let me tell you, son, let me tell you straight. I found the one and she was a good one, but I didn't find her quick enough. Breast cancer took her three years after our wedding. You know how I found her? I took all the advice my folks and my friends ever gave me and said fuck it all. The types to avoid, the types to chase—it's all bullshit. There's no types; there's only the ones who value love and the ones who'd rather run around chasing something, whatever that may be. You pick the one who's the same as you, and you love her good, then you won't end up sitting on city benches telling the stories of your failed marriages to boys who don't want to hear about it."

That was enough of the old man and his rambling. Gerald decided to walk.

)(

Laleitha's eyes trailed up to the dark-haired boy just as he walked past her. He dropped two sheets of paper on her desk before disappearing once more.

She unfolded the first paper, the same note as before, except this time with Anton's handwriting underneath hers.

Do they suspect?

No.

She held the paper in her palm and the Lumire flowed into her veins. The paper burst into flames, searing it until it was nothing but a pile of ashes in her hand, which she then brushed into the garbage.

The next note was from Mont.

*At 12:20, I'll ask to read through basic protocols, meaning I'll have
to get them from you. That is my escape and yours.
See you at the hub.*

There it is. She smiled. Her good old sister with a plan tucked up her sleeve.

Lee glanced at the clock, reading 12:18. *Close enough.* She stood and pushed in her chair, tucking the note into her pocket.

Now she had to find the woman who had loaded the paper into Lee's arms and set her to work. It didn't take her long. "I was asked to bring up the military protocols documents to the overlook," she said.

The woman pursed her lips. "Asked by whom?"

"Elise Montason," Laleitha answered. "She's up there and her supervisors wanted her to read it over."

"And they called your desk specifically?" the woman continued with eyebrows raised.

"Yes."

"Hmm," the woman said. "I suppose. You know the way?"

"Yes," Laleitha answered, nodding.

The woman waved her hand, turning away. "Go."

CHAPTER TWENTY-FIVE

Captain Westbecker

"Follow me," Anton told Darren as he hurried him through the halls of Fort Kingshold. He took them through the back entrance, a smaller, more tucked away door that exited across the street from a large hospital. Darren couldn't begin to guess the route Anton was taking them through, but the little man seemed to know what he was doing.

"Where's the hub again?" Darren asked, following Anton as they sped along the sidewalk by the windows of the hospital.

Suddenly, Anton stopped in his tracks.

"What is it now?" Darren sighed, nudging the smaller boy onwards.

"Captain Westbecker," Anton said.

"What?"

Anton stared through the window. Inside lay Captain Westbecker, indeed, and he had bandages over his forehead, as well as a number of tubes and wires Darren didn't understand hooked up to him.

"What is Westbecker doing here?" Darren murmured.

Anton looked up at him. "Let's find out."

"Anton, it's almost one. We're supposed to be at the hub," Darren began, but Anton was already starting toward the doors of the hospital.

"They probably won't even let us see him," Darren continued to protest.

All it took was telling the man behind the desk that they wanted to see Captain Westbecker because they were the Majors and they could. This man seemed to be well aware that he was breaking protocol by letting them see him, but something about being Majors seemed to make people listen to them. And break the rules for them. Perhaps this man thought he was doing some sort of justice unto Westbecker for endangering the Majors' lives, or perhaps he simply wanted to please two public icons. This was a power Darren could get used to.

The nurse discretely led them to his room, opened the door for them, and closed it behind them, leaving them to their business. Westbecker's eyes rested on them as they entered, but he did not stir.

The two approached his bedside, staring down at the bandaged face.

"I understand you have a lot to say to me," Westbecker rasped. "After what I had you do."

Darren opened his mouth, but Anton spoke before he could. "What happened to you?"

Westbecker spoke in slow, confused, cracking sentences. "I didn't send you into that base in Litrite. I'm not that rash. I . . . remember it all . . . as if it was a dream. Images but nothing solid, nothing with real . . . fear. I could see what was happening but I wasn't able to control it. It hardly seemed real . . . like reading a book. It all hit me after the council meeting . . . reality, but I still wasn't . . . in control. Something had swayed me, like something was in my head. So I took a frying pan and tried to get it out."

Darren looked at Anton, his face saying what he didn't dare to. *This man is crazy.*

"I don't understand." Anton said, looking back down at the bruised, beaten man.

Westbecker closed his eyes. "I . . . couldn't feel anything. Nothing felt real." He shook his head as much as his neck apparently allowed. "Nothing felt real. I, I couldn't control what I was doing . . ."

Darren looked up once more at Anton to see if he was buying it. The boy narrowed his eyes. Westbecker sounded like a murderer who was pleading insanity. There was no explanation for what he was saying, but he seemed to be under control. Other than his anomalous story, he was acting perfectly regular, but if there was one thing Darren learned from his time here, it was not to make any assumptions.

"I know it sounds crazy," Westbecker admitted on seeing Darren's look, still speaking in soft whispers. "I know you have no reason to believe me, but I would never put you in harm's way. Not while you are only kids."

"Do you at least know *when* you lost your mind?" Darren asked.

Both Westbecker and Anton glared at him.

He put up his hands. "Sorry. How long have you not been in control of yourself?"

Westbecker's glare remained a few moments, but he soon blinked and moved on. "The last thing I remember is when I went to your trial," he answered. "I haven't seen my daughter since. I had said goodbye to her, went to Orphia's courtroom . . . sat in a booth next to Emperor Evanstin and Harold Alvenice— he's an Arc Leader. When I came back, the emperor's cat started hissing at me. I felt strange, but I had some sort of sense of . . . initiative. As time went on . . . I don't know—my memory gets fuzzier and fuzzier. I started taking walks at night, started hearing voices. All I could think about was the Prime Devise, how I hated them. I was overwhelmed with . . . *something* . . . but none of it seemed real."

"You said that a couple times," Darren remarked. "And, all due respect, sir, but that sounded like a descent into madness."

"The frying pan worked," Westbecker pointed out, presumably unangered by Darren's words. "It hurt, but nothing's hazy anymore. I think if I was going mad, the solution would require a bit more than a good hit on the head."

"Do you think someone did this to you?" Anton asked.

"I don't see how," Westbecker said, almost laughing nervously. "Unless mind manipulation is in that arsenal of things you can do with the Lumire."

"We didn't do this to you," Darren said, defensively. "We wouldn't know how."

"You aren't the only ones with the Lumire," Westbecker pointed out. "There are the Omenescents—but their Lumire is different than yours—and the Vortex Queen."

"The Vortex Queen?" Darren repeated, frowning.

"The queen of the Juperds before the empire fell," Westbecker said.

Darren remembered Kilodrist mentioning something about her.

Apparently so did Anton, who asked, "Wasn't she killed?"

"Her granddaughter was."

Darren shrugged. "Well, then, she is definitely out of the picture."

"There are still the other two Majors," Westbecker pointed out. "There were seven."

This caught Darren's gravest attention. He folded his arms in front of him, shifting his weight. Maybe there was somebody out there with the Lumire who had trained with it on their own until they knew how to use it for anything imaginable. It didn't seem likely, but it was a possibility. And if there *were* somebody out there, they could be Inseanan, or from one of the shards of the Juperds, or a part of the world Darren once knew—which prompted the question "Are they Lumerian?"

"If we knew who they were, they'd be here," Westbecker said flatly.

"But they could just be anybody?" Darren said. He was slightly mortified by this thought.

Westbecker nodded. "And the council hasn't expressed any interest in finding them. We just assume that they are living among the Other Society, oblivious to our existence or their power."

The Other Society, the Lumerians called it. The term never failed to catch Darren off guard. The normal society? The one that had no idea there were empires living on the same globe as theirs? The one that didn't concern itself with the disputes between a confused council and a sinister, power-hungry organization? The one that didn't have a mad judge who lived forever inspecting them up and down, perhaps hiding a secret corridor that Darren and his friends planned to sneak into? Darren was beginning to miss that society.

"Can Inseanans enter the courtroom when a Lumerian is on trial?" Darren asked.

"You think one may be living among Inseanans?" Westbecker raised an eyebrow.

Anton shrugged. "It's possible."

The older man closed his eyes. "Anybody can enter the courtroom as a spectator, no matter where they are from."

Darren and Anton exchanged glances. "Do you think Reighba was at ours?" Anton whispered to his friend as the thought crossed Darren's mind.

"I hope he wasn't," Darren whispered back, shuddering at the remembrance of that man's terrifying eyes, so filled with rage as he beat Darren over and over again.

Darren remembered the fear that moved up and down his spine when Reighba pulled him from the chamber. He remembered his confusion as Reighba left him standing there, pacing away, *daring* Darren to try something. He remembered when Reighba threw his first strike. Darren had tried to block it, to duck away, to flee, and even to fight back, but blow after blow to his cheek, his throat, his ribs landed. He remembered stumbling and falling, praying Reighba would be satisfied. He remembered Reighba screaming, "Get up!" and "Fight back!" and every time obliging wholeheartedly. He remembered the frustration that boiled in him, the furnace overheating. Every time Darren grew angrier and angrier, more determined and more dependent on his *need* to see Reighba bleed, but every time he grew weaker and weaker. Time after time after relentless time he would end up on the floor, his own blood trickling from a new wound.

Then, he remembered breaking. That was where his memory ended.

"What else could it be?" Westbecker said, snapping Darren back into the present. "I've tried explaining this to the doctors, to the other council members. They don't listen. They think I'm crazy. But, of course, they wouldn't believe me; they haven't seen what we have—the Lumire."

Anton said to Darren, "We need to leave."

Darren looked at the clock, which now read 12:54, and nodded.

They gazed back down at Westbecker, who was looking between them with both curiosity and a hint of pleading in his eyes, as if he didn't want them to leave like everybody else had when he tried to talk to them.

"Sorry, old man," Darren told Westbecker. "We've got bigger fish to fry."

CHAPTER TWENTY-SIX

Number Eleven Found

Elise's heart raced as she marched through the doors of Fort Kingshold. The realness of the situation was beginning to sink in, as she was only hours away from standing at the doorstep of The Way.

What if The Way was closed by the time they got there? What if they found the entrance but couldn't get in? What if they got in but it was filled with a multitude of dangers that ended up killing them all? What if Marty was trying to warn her about those things in his diary?

Shoot, his diary. Something told her his diary would be important. It might contain an explanation of how to get in, or navigate it, or open and close it. If she were to find any important instructions regarding The Way, it would be in his diary. She had little time to get back to the living quarters, but the more she thought about it, the more she felt she needed it.

She stopped in her tracks on the sidewalk. The building the suite was in was right there, but the more time she spent near Fort Kingshold, the more likely it became that somebody would catch her. Elise turned back in the direction she was initially walking, but still found herself at a halt. She stood there for a few moments, paralyzed by indecision.

I need his diary. She finally decided and headed for the building of their living quarters.

She hurried through the lobby and into the stairwell, sprinting up the minute the doors opened. Voices suddenly echoed from above, and Elise slowed to the best casual walk she could muster in her anxious state. *I have to hurry.*

A group of three people, engaged in what appeared to be a gripping conversation, rounded the corner, coming straight down toward her. Elise's heart caught in her throat. *Don't look at me. Don't look at me.* The mantra repeated over and over again in her head as they approached. After their presentation to the public, anybody could recognize her if they focused on her. She hoped her face wasn't flushed.

Time had been rushing by a moment ago; now it seemed it couldn't move any slower. Finally, *finally*, they passed her, opening the door to their floor and disappearing behind it. She let out a long exhale, her muscles relaxing slightly.

The rest of the way back to the living quarters was quick, with a few more encounters going much like the first one.

At last, she shut the door to her living quarters behind her. She stood there for a moment, taking a few breaths as she tried to slow her racing heart. *We're going to The Way. We are finally, stupidly going to The Way.*

Soon, she would reach a point of no return, and half of her considered turning back while she could. The council was not going to like this, but it was for the sake of learning how Marty died and putting a purpose to the death of three Inseanans.

She hurried into her room, found her bag, and took Marty's diary from her nightstand. She rummaged around for a few moments before finding the Old Lat dictionary on the floor under a dirty pair of jeans, next to her engineer's guide.

Upon seeing the book, she paused, considering taking it too. *I might need it. It's not likely, but it's possible.* She picked it up and examined it.

"Yeah, sure, why not?" she muttered to herself and shoved it into the bag. *Time to make a hasty escape.*

⚹

When she arrived at the hub, she dropped her bag at her feet, finding that only Laleitha was there, sitting on a bench at its entrance. Elise walked over and sat beside her sister, wordlessly accompanying her.

"Ready?" her sister asked, her voice softer than usual.

It was strange for Elise to hear her sister speak like this. She knew enough about Laleitha to tell this meant she was afraid. Very, undeniably afraid.

"Yeah," Elise said. "I hope so."

Laleitha didn't meet her sister's eyes. "But you're afraid of what you'll find."

"Is that a question or a conclusion?"

"I'm your sister, Mont," Laleitha said, turning to face her. "I know you're afraid."

Elise said nothing but simply faced forward, watching the citygoers come and go. "Lee," she said after a moment, an idea hatching in her mind. "Watch this."

Focusing on a man who had just come through the doors of the hub and was headed for the street, Elise felt the familiar pulsing in her head return. Within moments, the man yelped in surprise as his pants were yanked down by an unknown force, stumbling to pull them back up again, baring his white underwear to all the alarmed onlookers.

Laleitha stared back at Elise, her eyes wide, looking as if she was trying so hard to contain a laugh it was causing her physical pain. "How do you do that?"

"Do what?"

"Control it so easily?"

Elise shrugged. "I don't know. After the incident with Talious the other day . . . I don't know. Something just clicked, I guess."

Lee furrowed her brow. "What incident with Talious?"

Right. Elise hadn't told them about her semerisee. Suppressing a sigh, she figured it couldn't hurt to tell Laleitha. "When we were in the base in Litrite . . ."

"Talious wasn't in the base in Litrite," Lee said blankly.

"I know that, dummy. Just shut up and listen," Elise snapped in response. "When we were in Litrite and Second Reighba tried to kill me while I was in interrogation—"

"He tried to *kill* you?" Lee exclaimed. "You didn't tell us that."

Elise tilted her head. "Didn't I? Anyway, it doesn't matter. Second Reighba tried to kill me and he got pretty close, I think, but before he could, something happened."

Lee's dark gaze fixed on her face, riddled with worry.

"I somehow got into his mind. Like, I started seeing his memories. But then, he started seeing mine, too, because I don't know how to control it yet."

"Control what?" Laleitha interrupted again, before leaning forward intensely. "Are you saying we can do this with the Lumire?"

Elise shook her head. "I can, apparently. Talious said they thought one of us might be like this—different from the others, I mean. But whatever is different about me, the rest of you don't have it, meaning I have to learn to control it on my own."

Lee leaned back, studying Elise curiously. "So what is it, exactly?"

She shrugged. "I don't know, really. The Lumerians call it semerisee. It just means I can get into people's minds. The other day, when I asked to talk to Ms. Kilodrist alone, that was what I was telling her. Then, she went and got Talious, and he had me try to get in his mind—"

"Did you do it?"

Elise nodded. "Not at first, but he started putting these pin things in my hand. Not normal pins. They hurt far too much to be normal. They made my whole hand hurt and my entire arm tingle. He said he had to do this because when my body is under stress, the Lumire engages."

Lee frowned. "He hurt you?"

"He didn't want to," Elise said, defending him. "But apparently, if I have this semerisee thing, it's really important that I learn how to use it. He didn't give a reason *why* it's so important, but after what happened with Second Reighba, I can see what it's like to not have any control over it . . . and I don't want to do that again."

"Why didn't you tell us?" Lee asked, her voice quiet, refusing to meet Elise's eyes.

Elise swallowed the lump in her throat. "Because it scared me. I didn't want to think about it. And I think that's how Talious figured out we're up to something. I think he saw it in my head while I was in his. He said he wouldn't tell Kilodrist as long as I didn't tell anyone what I saw in his head."

Laleitha looked at her, confused. "Why wouldn't he want you to tell anyone what you saw? Did you see something bad?"

Elise nodded gravely. "I don't know what the things I saw mean, but I don't think any of it was good. That's the thing about this semerisee, I think. I never see random memories; it's always the kind we feel very strongly about. The kind that stick with us. I don't like it."

Lee looked back out at the people passing by. "Can you promise me one thing, Mont? Never look in my mind without asking me first, okay?"

Elise nodded. "I promise. I don't think I'll ever have to though."

Lee grinned, huffing out a small laugh, still not looking at Elise but down at her hands.

A few moments passed in silence between the two before Laleitha suddenly looked back up at Elise, a mischievous smile spreading slowly. "Watch this," she said, beginning to eye a passerby.

"Don't set someone's pants on fire!" Elise exclaimed, grabbing her sister's arm.

"Come on, Mont. It'll be hilarious."

"What the *hell* are you two doing?" a voice demanded from behind. They turned to see Gerald standing beside the bench, looking down at them with a half-amused, half-exasperated expression. "Terrorizing the public. Lee, were you actually going to set someone on fire?"

"Just in time," Laleitha said, ignoring his question. "Where're the guys?"

"I don't know," Gerald answered. "Anton and Darren aren't here yet."

"Obviously." Elise turned back to look at the doors of the hub. "What time is it?"

"One o'clock, last I checked," Gerald answered. "We can give them a few minutes, but if they don't turn up soon, we have no time to wait."

"Yeah, yeah," another voice said from behind. "We know all you have an iron fist on the curfew, *King.*"

The three looked back to find the last two approaching them.

"Where were you guys?" Lee demanded.

"I can't even begin to explain," said Darren.

Ж

The convenient thing about Lumeria was the several booths with unclosing portals hanging within them set up in several places around the city. There were many at the front entrances of buildings or next to bus stops, but the Arc City's downtown transportation hub had more than they could imagine. Open portals flanked hallway after hallway, organized by destination region. The Pallain section was on the left wing of the first floor, beside a small section entitled, *Orphian City,* with rows and clusters leading to every major city in Pallain and various spots within each city. According to the directory, the Elevis and Lestin sections made up the second floor, the Ikollis and

Staris sections made up the third, and "The Other Society and beyond" made up the fourth.

In the "America" section of the fourth floor, they quickly located the portal labeled *the Port, Chicago, Illinois*. Apparently, there were also locations in New York, Virginia Beach, Sioux Falls, Salt Lake City, and Phoenix, which Elise had several questions about but no time to answer them.

When they stepped through, they found themselves in the strange but vaguely familiar place they at first came upon, back when they were confused and scared. The basin shape was easy to recall, and it didn't take them long to find the door to the old bank they had first come through.

Outside, the streets of Chicago were at a busy hour, seven in the evening. Elise looked around, her eyes settling on the nearest parking garage. Gerald had spotted it as well and led the others toward it.

Elise scanned the area, searching for a car big enough to hold all of them.

"Truck," Darren said. "We want a truck."

"Ha." Gerald laughed. "So three of us can cram into the back seat? I don't think so."

"I can only hijack trucks."

"Nice try," Elise muttered, walking past him to a van. "Let's take this one. It's big."

The other four approached it, Gerald placing his hands on the door. "I got this," he muttered, closing his eyes. In an instant, the door's lock popped, and Gerald shot a playful smirk Elise's way as he pulled it open. "You're up, Darren."

They piled in, the girls and Anton in the backseat, Darren in the driver's seat, and Gerald on the passenger side. Darren excitedly removed the plastic cover on the steering column, revealing a stream of wires.

"Okay, I'll need directions," he muttered as he worked.

"East Dundee is about an hour from here," Laleitha said.

"That is where we are going," Elise went on. "King Avenue."

It wasn't long before the car started and Darren looked around with a mischievous smile. "This takes me back," he said, shifting into gear. "Sophomore year, went to a party with Angelina Denver, drove away at midnight in Jackson Marten's car with Angelina, Jenna Erickson, and Sophia Moore."

"You dog," Gerald said playfully.

Elise rolled her eyes.

"Sophia went off with Jackson again, though, after he tried to fight me for stealing his car," Darren continued with a shrug.

Gerald laughed. "Who won?"

Darren smiled. "We played dirty, he picked up a rock, I went for the balls, and it all evened out." He pulled out of the parking garage, taking his turns rather fast. "Junior year, stole my teacher's car and took Jenna to the beach during third and fourth period. We had started dating the beginning of that year." He shook his head, still smiling. "I probably would have been expelled if Mr. Wilson didn't love me. He was sympathetic to my cause."

"Your cause?" Elise repeated. Darren started to explain before she shook her head. "I change my mind. I don't want to know. Take a right here."

Darren jerked the car right, getting a few honks from other drivers.

"Where did you learn to drive?" Laleitha exclaimed.

Darren laughed. "In my defense, I failed my driver's test six times. If we crash, I'm not completely to blame since you let me be the driver."

Elise and Laleitha directed him through several Chicago suburbs to King Avenue, as Darren went on about stories from his high school.

It was dark by the time they reached King Avenue. "It's this house here," Elise said, pointing at 8741. "This is his house."

The five Majors stepped out of the car, closing their doors behind them. The house was deathly still, the windows dark and shrouded. Elise almost expected to see the door open for them, revealing the smiling face of Hank Martinez, beckoning her in to have some tea and tinker with whatever material he had on hand. The sad realization crossed her mind once more that he never was the well-respected man he pretended to be but a criminal. She found herself cursing him for his deception, wishing he had never come to King Avenue so she would have never met him.

Laleitha led them around to the side door, which was still unlocked. Elise trailed behind, surveying the entire house with keen eyes. She was the last to step into the dusty living room, which still smelled of books and sawdust.

"It has to be downstairs," Laleitha said.

Elise nodded. "I've only been in one room downstairs. There could be anything down there."

The girls led them through the dark, silent house until they reached the basement door, which Gerald pulled open to reveal an eerie and unwelcoming staircase of concrete. Elise felt around the wall for a light switch, but when she found it, no light flickered on.

"Great," Darren muttered. "If this isn't creepy enough—"

"Save it," Gerald snapped. He looked back down the dark staircase, gathering all of his courage. "Okay, I'll lead. There's probably nothing bad down there, but if there is . . ." He didn't bother finishing.

Gerald started down the row of blackness, Elise following closely behind. Their footsteps and breath were the only sounds in the entire house, seemingly echoing across the hall.

There was a small *whoosh* from behind and an orange glow illuminated the area. Elise turned to see Laleitha's entire hand engulfed in flames, lighting the way. Anton held up his own hand, and his fingertips crackled as another flame burst to life and spread down his skin. Darren and Gerald did the same. Elise held out her own arm and focused on the very energy of the particles that formed her fingertips. Engaging the Lumire, a small, controlled light grew from her as the feel of her skin began to numb.

They reached the last stair, and the room opened into the only one Elise knew. The table, counter, and benches were scattered with dusty tools, as always, and the barrels and boxes were stacked neatly in the corner, untouched. If the dust were removed, it would almost look like somebody had been in here yesterday.

"Okay, spread out," Gerald said.

Elise set aside her bag and followed the left wall until she found another doorway. She entered cautiously, almost expecting to find a human skull staring at her. A rancid smell hit her like a brick wall and she stumbled backward, repulsed at the horrible odor. She went numb when she realized what she was smelling. A cold, dreadful ice cube seemed to be sinking down her spine. "Guys?" she called. "I think I found something dead."

"Some*thing* dead?" Gerald said from behind as several footsteps drew nearer.

"I don't see it," she explained. "I just smell it."

When Gerald reached her side, he reacted the same way she did, drawing back and crinkling his nose, threatening to vomit.

Laleitha choked behind her. "Definitely dead."

Elise braved forward, the light from her hand guiding her, until she found the body in the corner, sitting upright against the wall, his throat cut and his entire torso maimed.

She gasped silently, staring at the awful sight. His intestines spilled from his open stomach, and dried, reddish-black blood crusted the ends of the giant open wound. The entire side of his neck had been coated with blood as if it had been painted on, and his head hung from the body like a door sagging on hinges, the wall keeping it almost upright. Vomit pitched up Elise's throat once again, but she caught it quickly and forced it back down. Darren didn't catch his in time, turning toward the nearest corner and choking out the contents of his stomach.

Anton approached the body, quenching the fire on his hands and kneeling at the remains of a torn shirt that lay just next to it. He pulled a small ID card out of what used to be a breast pocket.

"Special Agent Levile Portute," he read quietly, "of the LSE."

"He's Lumerian," Gerald said, also letting the fire die on his fingers. His voice was steady, but when Elise turned to look at him, his face reflected the same sickly reaction to the sight Elise felt in her gut.

"What's he doing here?" Elise asked, looking around at the blank faces of her friends as the fire went out on her hand as well.

"Seems like he's been here awhile," Gerald remarked, squatting to inspect the body.

"He was probably killed by the cut to the throat," Elise said. "Judging by the blood loss from the neck versus the . . . other wound, and if he was already dead, there would be no reason to cut the throat unless it was some sort of ritualistic thing."

Laleitha shook her head. "This isn't one of those detective books you're obsessed with, Mont."

"It sounds like fair reasoning," Gerald said with a shrug.

Darren turned away, almost losing it at the sight of the mauled man.

Anton touched the man's pant leg. It seemed stiff but somehow damp and speckled with small flecks of—ice?

"What the hell?" King murmured. "It almost looks like he was recently frozen."

"Recently thawed out, you mean," Laleitha said.

"Why does he smell, then?" Darren asked.

Laleitah shrugged. "Maybe this was done after he thawed out." She gestured to the gaping wound in his torso.

"But the wound on his neck looks like it happened before he was frozen," Gerald remarked.

Darren shook his head. "This doesn't make any sense."

"What is this?" Anton murmured, carefully reaching into the open wound at the bottom and picking a small green fiber from the crusted blood.

"It looks like some sort of . . . *creature* did this," Gerald speculated.

Elise's eyes trailed to the dead man's hands. "What is that he's holding?" She pointed to what looked like a crumpled up piece of paper balled in his fist.

Gerald unraveled the man's stiff fingers, sliding the paper from them. It was a small, crinkled slip, no bigger than a credit card. He read aloud words that made Elise's heart sink. "The Way is closed. The Son of Orphia is dead."

"The Way can't be closed," Elise said. "The tower is still there. Isn't the tower the indicator?"

"Is it still there?" Laleitha wondered. "We haven't seen it since the night we were abducted."

Gerald stood. "Laleitha and I will go check. Until we get back, you three stay here and look for an entrance of some sort."

Laleitha turned and headed toward the stairs, Gerald following. Elise, Darren, and Anton began inspecting the walls, looking for any sign of an abnormality.

Darren sighed, frustration cutting his patience thin. "What are we even supposed to be looking for?"

"I don't know," Elise replied. "Anything out of the ordinary."

"You mean besides the dead body in the corner, the tower a few blocks away, the fact that we are looking for a secret passage that nobody knows how to get into or even what it looks like, and the aroma in this freaking house that makes me feel like I'm about to be mauled by Hannibal Lecter?" he exclaimed, growing more and more flustered with every word, his temper flickering like the fire that now remained only on Anton's hands.

"Besides those," Elise answered, restraining the comments about his temper that tried to work their way up her throat.

"Great," he said. "That's just great, because the only productive thing we're doing right now is waiting for King and Lee to get back just so we can know if The Way is even open at all! We can go around feeling up the wall all night but we all know we aren't going to find anything."

"You think that man died for nothing?" Elise snapped, turning to face him. "You think Marty died for nothing?" Her voice was cold, quiet, and low. "The only reason you are here at all is because *we* are. You don't believe any of this; you have no reason to. Well, I do have a reason to believe and I'm holding onto this chance to understand why Marty died, why we are who we are—and if you don't want to be a part of that, then you can leave."

"Found something," Anton exclaimed from the other side of the room.

Darren shot Elise a cold stare before turning to approach Anton.

Elise followed. She suddenly regretted her outburst. Her calm had returned quickly, but she bitterly wished she could have held on to it. Something about being in Marty's house wound her up like a coil.

They found Anton closely inspecting a hole in the wall with several cracks across the entire surface of the concrete. He tapped the wall with his knuckles, the sound echoing backward through the cement. "Hollow."

This was followed by footsteps coming down the stairs. "It's still there," Gerald said. "The Way is still open. Did you guys find anything?"

Elise nodded. "We think so."

"Behind this wall," Darren added.

Gerald cracked his knuckles. "Let's knock it down." He approached it, placing his hands on the stone. Everything began to rumble, the cement slowly falling apart, tumbling out of place.

"King, stop," Laleitha said. "You're going to take the whole house down."

She was right. King had nearly torn the wall apart, with a large crevice stretching down the middle revealing some sort of black marble. They cleared away the rest of the loose rock to find themselves standing in front of a large black circle embedded in the stone. A golden knob protruded from the very center, strange designs stretching across the entire door, while a silver band ran across the side.

"This is the door," Elise said. "The entrance to The Way."

Gerald tried the knob, pushing and pulling, but the door did not budge. Each of them attempted to open it using the Lumire, but they couldn't even gain control of it, as if it were resistant to the Majors' power.

"Maybe we should blow it up," Laleitha suggested.

"Too risky," Gerald said. "We'd probably bring the roof down."

"Do we have any other options?" she argued.

"I can try to contain the blast," Elise offered, "and focus it on the door."

"We all can," Gerald corrected. "Lee, you can try to blow it down."

Elise backed up, Anton beside her, while Gerald and Darren stood on the other side of the door, braced for an explosion. Laleitha stood facing the door, in the very middle of the room. She took a deep breath, the veins in her arms beginning to glow with orange heat. She raised her hands, focusing herself completely on the black marble.

Suddenly, the door erupted into an inferno. Elise's palms shot up as she tried to roll the flame back toward the door, pushing it with an immense amount of concentration. The fire continued to rage, bulging with heat with every pulse of Laleitha's heart.

Finally, the fire subsided, and Laleitha was left bent over as she panted. Elise almost choked, trying to catch her breath. She looked back and realized the door was still intact, not even scathed.

"Okay," Darren said, "I think it is pretty clear we aren't getting through this door."

"We need to consider all of our options," Elise said.

"We need to *get* some options," Gerald said. "What time is it?"

"I don't know," Laleitha replied. "But I'm sure they've realized we're gone by now."

Elise looked back at the door. It was obviously not as "normal" as they had anticipated and wouldn't open except for Orphia or his council. She cursed herself for being so thoughtless. If Orphia could live centuries without death, if his Omenescents could use the Lumire to obtain godly powers, if they had the ability to move an entire place in and out of existence at their own free will, why wouldn't the door display the same magical aspects? *If we can't penetrate from the outside, how else could we possibly get in?*

The answer hit Elise like a truck. Wordlessly, for fear her idea would prove to be ineffective, she walked back over to the body of the dead man. Kneeling at his stomach, she examined the open wound closely, inspecting the small green fibers embedded in his blood.

Between two fibers, she found a small, almost microscopic chunk of dirt. Not daring to hold it in her fingers, she touched it with the Lumire, carefully swallowing it with her control and pulling it from its place in the man's rotting corpse.

"What's that?" Gerald asked, sounding confused and a little disturbed.

"What are you doing, Mont?" Laleitha also questioned in the same tone as Gerald.

Elise stood, the small piece of soil floating just above her fingers, a silver glow beginning to twirl and flicker around it ever so faintly. "Can we assume," she said, "that whatever mauled this man came from within The Way?"

Darren shrugged. "There's a good chance."

Gerald nodded. "That's probably where the green hairs came from too—whatever attacked him."

"His body," Anton corrected. "He was already dead."

"So whatever did this did it for fun?" Darren said, cringing.

"Or for food," Laleitha added.

"That's an even more disturbing thought," Darren remarked.

"Yeah, okay," Elise interjected. "My point is, it could have carried this piece of dirt with it, which means this dirt was in The Way."

"That's your point?" Gerald raised his eyebrows. "Because I don't think any of us follow."

"Transportation rods," Elise said. "In order to build one, you have to have particles from the exact spot you want to go. It was in the book Kilodrist gave us. We can build a transportation rod using this chunk of dirt and use it to get into The Way."

"You know how to build a transportation rod?" Gerald said, almost challengingly.

"No," Elise answered, "but I have a book that can tell me how."

CHAPTER TWENTY-SEVEN

Into The Way

Elise could do nothing but pray as she and her friends approached the house across the street of 8741, her heart sinking as they got closer. She punched in the garage door code and the door rolled upward as a near-empty garage was revealed. Only one car remained in its stall, Percy's. *What is Percy doing home? Even stranger, what is Mom doing away from home?*

She opened the door to find the lights on in the kitchen. "Percy?" she called.

"Elise?" Her brother's voice echoed through the hall as he came rushing down the stairs.

Suddenly, Elise found herself crushed to her brother's chest, his arms tightly enveloping her.

She returned his embrace gladly, burying her face into his shoulder and her hands fisted in the back of his shirt. "I missed you," she managed, but it came out muffled against his shoulder.

Percy paused when he noticed their sister and the three strangers. "Who are they?"

"They're my friends," Elise explained. "And we need your help."

Percy looked between his sister and the others. "Tell me everything."

⅍

The six gathered in the kitchen. Elise and Gerald sat at the counter across from Percy, who listened to them explain. Laleitha and Anton snacked on crackers at the table as Darren looked over the pictures on the fridge.

After explaining what she could to Percy, Elise pulled the book from her bag, flipping through the pages of sketches and instructions on how to build various devices and structures. When she finally reached the page she needed, she found herself looking at thousands of words, with a diagram of a rod dominating the right side of the page. She turned the book to face her brother. "We need to build this, but we don't have the supplies."

"What do you need? I could probably get them for you if I can find them in the stores around here," Percy said.

Elise traced her fingers across the listed supplies. "We need a glass tube, a lot of the materials found in lightbulbs, a high powered battery . . . Holy crap, this list is long. Give me a minute. I'll write it down."

As Elise began scribbling words on a notepad, Gerald spoke. "Elise tells us you're going to the navy?"

Percy nodded. "Yeah, they've been working us hard, but I like it. I had to come home for a few days because . . ." He hesitated, his voice becoming softer. "Uh, our dad is presumed dead."

Elise's pencil paused. "They think he's dead?" She looked up with wide, startled eyes.

"He's been missing for months, and there has been no sign of him anywhere," Percy explained quietly, grim sorrow filling his voice. "They haven't even found a body. Nobody's seen him. There's no trace at all."

Laleitha was quiet, staring down at her hands. Elise turned back to the list, despite the heaviness in her chest. She refused to think about it; she refused to let it sink in. Not now.

After Elise had finished the list and Percy had headed out the door with it, Gerald said to her, "I'm sorry about your dad."

Elise shook her head. "Let's not talk about it. I need to focus."

Gerald nodded. "Right."

Darren remained at the fridge, trailing his fingers along the pictures. "You played soccer," he remarked upon seeing her rugby pictures.

Elise nodded. "So did Percy. We would practice together at the park all the time."

Darren turned back to the fridge. "That seems nice," he said. "I never had any siblings—never wanted one either."

King snorted. "You know what? Neither did I."

"Why don't you want siblings?" Elise directed the question to Darren.

He shrugged. "Our house is screwed up enough. I don't think a second child is what we need. Mom and Dad are too busy fighting anyway. They've always been like that. I could never tell what they were arguing about though—something I never understood."

Percy arrived back home almost an hour later, carrying everything they needed. Elise set to work, attempting to spread out the pieces on the table, but when the table proved too small, she moved to the living room floor.

She worked for hours. Each time she became too confused to continue, she'd start over, almost crushing the pieces in frustration. Her nimble fingers grew numb as the time passed. Her friends would attempt to help but only grow as confused as her.

"How is it coming?" Percy asked after a while.

Elise shook her head, not even looking up from her work. "This is really advanced stuff, Perce. It even specifies at the top of the page that this is fundamental level sixty, which as I understand is part of Lumeria's weird education system, but I can assume it's really high up there. Having the Lumire makes it easier though. It cuts out a lot of the procedures that require big machinery and lots of prep."

"You really want to go through with this?"

"We don't have any other options, Percy," Elise said, closing her eyes and shaking her head once again.

In the kitchen, Laleitha had taken an interest in the other two books Elise had stuffed in her bag. She first removed Hank Martinez's notebook then the Old Lat dictionary.

"What is that?" Darren asked, looking over her shoulder at the strange drawing on the notebook page Laleitha was translating.

"A mind stone," she replied simply.

"A what?" Percy asked.

"Apparently someone can trap their consciousness in a stone when they die," she explained. "But nobody can access it unless they have an interpreter."

"How do you get an interpreter?"

Laleitha shrugged. "Hasn't been figured out yet. Nobody has ever communicated with a mind trapped in a mind stone before."

Darren flipped through a few more pages of the journal. "This guy just explains a bunch of devices in here?"

Laleitha shook her head. "No, he has a lot of personal experiences recorded, too, but it's all addressed to Elise and whenever he brings up something she wouldn't understand, he describes it on the next page."

"What the hell is this?" Darren stopped on a page with a large sketch dominating the space. It displayed a large cylindrical machine that opened at the top, with several components on the inside topped with a small bulb. Just before the walls opened above it, Marty had drawn a small tornado.

Laleitha frowned. "I have no idea. I haven't gotten that far yet."

Darren shrugged and continued on.

Finally, after hours of strenuous work, Elise emerged with a glowing silver rod, complete with a metal cap on the bottom.

Everyone stood when they saw her.

"You finished," Gerald remarked.

"I hope this works." She sighed.

The girls hugged Percy goodbye before standing tensely, facing the hall, mentally preparing themselves for what they might see.

"Ready?" Gerald, who held the rod, asked while looking around.

They nodded and he tossed the rod. With a crack, a silver band formed in the air, outlining the circumference of a portal. Elise's breath caught in her throat. *I was successful.* On the other side of the portal was a dark area, with dirt and dust covering the floor and a faint light above them, out of sight.

Gerald was the first to leap through, followed by Laleitha, then Anton, then Darren. Elise examined the rod hanging from the top of the portal and took it in her hands. She leapt through, her grip on the rod sucking the portal back into it as she passed between one place and The Way.

Darkness swallowed them, all except the faint glow of the rod. Elise handed it to Darren to stuff in his jacket pocket before they looked around. They appeared to be in some sort of garden. As Elise's eyes adjusted to the darkness, more and more of the picture came into place. They were on one of several garden platforms suspended in a cylindrical gorge, a small stream running from one to the other, passing over the gap that separated them with narrow wooden bridges. Elise walked to the side of the dirt platform, looking over the edge at the maze of layers below, following the stream with her gaze as it spiraled its way down the ginormous abyss, running from garden to garden. At the bottom, the rest of the water was dumped into a deep, dark pool.

Elise opened her mouth to speak, but before she could, there was a snap from behind.

Darren let out a cry as he stumbled. Elise whipped around to see a series of vine-like limbs reeling upward like a snake about to strike. They all were clustered in the center, extending from a single origin and lashing outward.

"What the hell?" Darren exclaimed from the ground, sounding mortally terrified.

The vine lashed at Gerald, who frantically dove away before the plant caught his foot. At the same time, Darren was attacked once again, this time with a blow to the ribs.

Elise shrieked as the vine lashed at her as well. Her first reaction compelled her to attempt to get away, but the vine had already struck her. The force of the blow sent her flying, almost falling from the ledge where the garden ended. If she hadn't caught hold of a loose root, she probably would have plummeted off the side. Fear gripped her as her eyes stared downward. Suddenly, the vine found her wrist that grabbed the root and pulled her upward, tossing her into the air. She would have screamed, but the only noise that escaped her lips was a brief yell. She wasn't halfway into the air before the vine released her, flinging her upward. A sharp pain shot through her as the same vine struck her again, this time in the stomach with much more force. She let out a cry and flopped to the ground, her body bouncing on the impact. She had no time to let the pain ease through her muscles; she had to move before the vine could take hold of her once more.

Stumbling to her feet, she broke into a run. Laleitha had already begun fighting back, her hands engulfed in fire as she bent the flame toward the reeling and thrashing vine. Anton was wrestling in a tangle of greenery that had wrapped around him. Gerald and Darren used sticks they had broken off of the nearest tree to slap away vines that attempted to strike them.

Another vine lashed at Elise, but her hands shot up in time to catch it in her Lumire. She tried to manipulate the vine to her will, but though she could grip it with her power, it resisted and slithered from her grasp.

A silver mist began to weave around her fingertips like an energy current she moved with her mind—the physical manifestation of the Lumire. Her hand shot out at the vine; she felt it within her power's reach, and she took hold of it. Raising her other hand, she tore the limb in half, using an immense amount of effort as it resisted.

She released the torn plant, letting it flop to the ground. Laleitha shrieked from the other end as the vine knocked her backward. Anton had broken loose from the greenery and was scrambling for something to use as a weapon.

Elise advanced, preparing herself to strike again until every vine was torn from its foundation, when something from behind her jabbed at her back, sending her lurching forward.

She let out a cry of shock as the vine she had initially been approaching lashed around her waist. The piece she had torn was beginning to extend itself into the soil, lacing small roots into the dirt. Once it had secured itself, it rose back into the air, still very much alive.

The other vine wound around her, strangling her as the new plant licked against her ankles.

Elise struggled against them, her hands heating with orange fire as the Lumire instinctively engaged from the pain.

Suddenly, the vine released her as it began to burn. Elise thudded to the ground, too breathless to move. The furious vine retaliated, thrusting her away.

Elise somehow found the breath to scream as she flew from the edge, plummeting toward the waters at least a mile below, before the vine caught her ankle, crudely pulling her from her momentum and jerking her into a stop. The terror caught in her throat and a relentless pain crushed her lungs. Her skin almost burned where she had been struck, and now, as she dangled in the middle of an abyss, she was truly convinced she was going to die. The thought hardly had time to process before the vine snapped back. Elise's body was flung into the dirt with terrible impact, leaving her skidding across the other plants until her momentum slowed.

The only thing that kept Elise's ribs from cracking was the Lumire. She lay with her face in the dirt, briefly considering faking dead so she could be spared any pain to come if she fought on, but the fear lingered within her that if she did so, her friends would die. That was when her hands found something peculiar in the dirt. Despite the fact that every shift in her bones caused aching pain, despite the question of how it got there and her cluelessness on what to do with it, her fingers closed around the hilt of a knife.

Sluggishly, she sat up, lifting the knife so she could examine it. It was golden but dull and plastered with dirt. Frankly, she was transfixed.

"Elise!" Gerald's shout drew her attention from the knife to him.

He was scrambling away from three vines, looking around at his friends desperately. Anton was in the process of climbing to his feet a few paces behind him.

"Lee, Darren!" Gerald continued.

Pushing herself to her feet, she hurried in his direction, dodging a vine as it tried to snap at her again. Gerald had found another tree, evidently out of the creature's reach, and was bracing himself against it, Anton at his side.

"This isn't working." Gerald panted. "We're just running around aimlessly."

By then, Laleitha and Darren had approached as well.

Gerald pushed himself from the trunk. "We need a strategy."

"We can't cut any of them off," Elise said. "I tried. The section you cut off just sprouts roots and becomes another one."

"Then we try going for the cluster in the center," Laleitha suggested. "That's probably its heart."

"I saw it," Anton panted. "Its mouth is at the center. It's got rows of teeth and everything . . . it's horrifying . . . but I think the heart's there, too, in the bulge below it."

"How are we going to get there?" Darren asked.

"We keep the limbs occupied," Gerald said. "Anton can go for the center. Elise go on the right, Darren, the left. I'll be helping whoever needs help. Lee, you got the fire—try to light up the center as Anton approaches. You probably won't be successful but it will keep their attention on you. An—" He cut off abruptly. "Where'd you get that?" he asked, staring at Elise's knife.

"Hmm?" She looked down at it, having briefly forgotten about her latest discovery. "Oh, I found it."

"Give it to Anton. He can attack the heart with it," Gerald said.

She did so.

"Okay," King said. "You ready?"

They nodded.

"All right. Let's go. Elise and Darren, swing wide on your sides," he said.

Elise turned her attention back to the vine creature. Every limb had drooped to the ground but still writhed gently. She paced to the right, her eyes fixed on a single vine she seemed to have caught the attention of. She readied herself as she slowly worked her away around the creature. Several vines had lifted themselves by now, predators having just found some prey.

Briefly, her eyes trailed back to where Anton stood by the tree. Laleitha and Gerald had snuck to the other end by now, and a flame began to flicker on her sister's fingers.

Elise wasn't sure which happened first, but with a flick of Laleitha's wrist, a fire burst forth toward the center while at the same time, the vine lashed out at Elise. The first jab was quick, giving Elise little time to react. It struck her hip, sending her stumbling a few steps backward, before it immediately pulled back and prepared itself for another blow. Across from her, two vines had engaged Darren.

Elise would be ready this time. She would try to hit it or grab it—whatever she had time for before it slithered from her grip. However, when the vine flew at her at an even quicker speed, she resolved to dive away. She tumbled, quickly finding her feet and bouncing back up. The vine-creature flew at her again, this time grasping her around her chest. Instinctively, she grabbed the vine with both hands. Then, a sudden thought came to her. The Lumire engaged and she felt the energy flow from the creature to her. An almost uncontrollable energy surged through her, causing her hands to tremble as the life drained from the creature she grasped. The vine shriveled up, its green beginning to fade to a sickly gray. Her hand suddenly released the greenery, causing it to drop to the ground. The pale, shriveled vine flopped to the dirt and slowly drew back to the central tangle they all sprang from. She felt renewed, the silver energy glowing as it ran through her veins.

A cry from Anton suddenly caught her attention. It appeared, as he dove toward the center tangle, a vine had taken its attention away from Laleitha and now hoisted the boy high into the air. The knife fell from his hands and landed on the ground with a muffled bump.

"Anton!" Elise exclaimed, diving toward the knife.

She scooped it up, regripping it in her hands so she could attack the heart with it, but the minute she did so, a limb swiped her from the ground. Suddenly, she was once again lifted high into the air, the vine's grip tightening under her ribs as she thrashed. Caught by surprise, she fumbled the knife, desperately trying to catch it before it fell to the ground again. To her astonishment, Gerald appeared beneath her and snatched the knife from the air. She was about to exclaim something, but the vine creature then tossed her and her words were replaced with a shriek. Her head was fuzzy. It was becoming incredibly difficult to process what was happening. Another vine creature pulled her from the air, her momentum being jerked away from her flying body.

Her hands clasped the vine that wrapped around her, beginning to pull energy from it again. It began to droop, withering quickly as it lost the strength to hold Elise. She plopped to the ground, newly energized but still panting.

To her left, one plant tentacle suddenly became completely engulfed in flames. It writhed in fury before smacking away its attacker, Laleitha. Two vines had grabbed Darren, wrapping around either end of him and pulling. He yelled in pain as the vines threatened to tear him apart. Anton tried to free him. Gerald still had the knife and was hacking and tussling with several limbs as he sprinted for the heart. Elise started toward her friends before the creature wrapped itself around her ankle and hoisted her up into the air, preparing to slam her back down. She swung at the creature, prompting it to drop her again. The impact almost shattered her bones. Gerald lunged, plunging the knife into the tangle. There was a squish and a yellow liquid spurted wildly from the heart, causing Gerald to stumble away to avoid it.

Suddenly, the vines released their captives, dropping them to the ground as they shriveled meekly back to their severed center. Gerald let out a breathless sigh of relief. Elise rolled onto her stomach, swallowing the groan that attempted to escape her, and pushed herself to her feet.

The vines, however, slowly slid from the tangle in the center, beginning to mount themselves in the ground, still very alive and now very plentiful.

Gerald, when he had realized what he had done, scrambled backward.

Darren cursed in frustration.

"What do we do?" Anton cried, backing away as the vines began to reel backward, preparing to strike.

"Jump!" Darren yelled, throwing himself off the ledge.

Elise turned and ran, along with the rest of her friends. Gerald flew from the edge, Anton following. Laleitha skidded to a stop at the edge, her eyes first laying upon the distance that she hadn't yet seen.

"Wait, *what?*" she shrieked.

"*Go!*" Elise placed a hand square on her sister's back and shoved. She balanced herself on the ledge before taking a deep breath and letting herself fall.

Gerald extended a hand toward them, securing them with them Lumire as he slowed their descent. Still, it was the Lumire again that kept her from dying when she hit the water, as she almost passed out from the excruciating pain. The water slapped her, turning her skin red and the dirt on her face to mud. The air was pulled from her lungs the moment she cried out in silent pain under the surface.

A strong hand grasped her back and hoisted her upward as she struggled to the surface. Her face broke into the air and the hand released. She turned to see Gerald struggling in the water beside her. Finding the strength to kick, she pushed forward toward shore. Her hands finally found something stable when they hit the hard, chilly rock. With a single, extremely painful thrust, she pulled herself onto the cold surface of land.

She sat there for a moment, her chest heaving, her body trembling, trying to catch her breath before she braved the darkness that surrounded her.

Darren was the last to pull himself from the water, flopping onto the rock and sprawling out, groaning in pain.

Gerald still held the golden knife, covered with the creature's strange yellow blood.

Laleitha was the first to speak, her voice quivering. "What was that?"

"I think that was the thing that mauled that man," Gerald said. "It has green bristles just like the one we found."

"Wouldn't surprise me," Darren grunted. "To think, we could have been dismembered!" he added in a nervous laugh.

Anton pulled himself to his feet. "We have to go on," he said. "This was only one of several corridors."

"Where do you think the drive would be?" Elise asked, climbing to her feet.

"Drive?" Darren said. "We're not here for the drive. The Prime Devise probably already has it."

"Then what are we looking for?" Gerald questioned, looking at Darren challengingly.

"For what"—he gestured to Elise—"what's-his-face was looking for when he died."

Gerald sighed helplessly. "We don't even know what that is."

"A mind stone," Laleitha suddenly said. "In Hank's journal, he said he was looking for a mind stone and thought he was close."

"The mind stone of Orphia's lost son?" Anton went on, his voice sounding hopeful.

Elise looked from her sister to the faces of her friends. "How do you know?"

"Hank wrote about it in his journal," Darren explained. "Lee translated it while you were building the transportation rod. He was looking for a mind stone, and he thought it was hidden in The Way to Orphia's Tower."

Elise nodded, catching on. "That must have been the information he was hiding from the council."

Gerald stood. "Yeah, okay, it all makes sense, but how do we find it?"

They stood at the mouth of the hall and looked into it, all in silent agreement on what to do.

"Okay," Gerald said. "No matter what, we stick together. No splitting up in a place like this. I don't care how efficient we are that way; it's too dangerous."

"Agreed," Elise and Laleitha said together as Darren grunted his approval and Anton nodded.

Gerald nodded too. "I got the knife. I'll lead," he said, spinning the knife in his hand as he entered the dark cavern.

※

Once they had gathered enough energy to use the Lumire again, they filled the hall with the flickering light of the fire on their hands.

They walked on, with Gerald at the front and Laleitha at the back, until they spotted a light in the distance. As they approached it, they noticed the room was filled with busy people and clacking machinery. They took to the sides of the walls, concealing themselves from anyone looking in their direction. The tunnel ended at a suspended balcony overlooking what Elise assumed to be some sort of factory, judging by the machinery. Lights hung in rows at the high ceiling and water poured in from one wall, turning a hydroelectric wheel.

Anton was the first to find the courage to creep forward, peeking his head out of the tunnel to check left and right. Gerald followed, and it was Elise's curiosity alone that pushed her out of the dark tunnel.

Gerald silently climbed up into the supports that lined the perimeter of the ceiling, concealing himself in the darkness. He offered a hand down to Elise, pulling her up, and they both helped lift Anton, Laleitha, and Darren.

They stared down at the commotion below. Elise's heart pounded as she watched what was happening. At the edge of the room, lines of men and women were bound tightly, heads lolling on their shoulders, barely conscious. The workers took the bindings of a man and half-led, half-dragged him to a glass chamber, where they strapped him in and hooked up wires to him, one on his forehead, one over his heart, four lining his waist and two on his back. The glass tube closed, and the machine that the wires were connected to fired up. Though the glass silenced the sound, the man was obviously screaming, fully conscious now. After ten painful seconds, the man went limp as he was removed from the chamber.

From the machine the wires connected to, a tube on the side filled with a red liquid, which the workers drained into small vials before placing the vials onto a conveyor belt. On the other side of the room, sand, iron, and a strange blue stone sat in large vats connected to another machine. When the machine engaged, a raging inferno opened beneath each vat. A small tube ran across the room, filled with a peculiar liquid, presumably coming from the melted sand, iron, and blue goo. This was poured into another machine, which slowly transferred the mixture into a humanoid mold of wires, gears, and metal rods before the mold was lifted from the structure, revealing a hard blue body.

The red vials from the first machine were slipped into a device, turning the liquid into a mist, then the mist was sprayed down the throat of the blue body. Moments later, yellow eyes opened when the blue body awoke, eerily transparent but very alive. It marched from its stand, where another worker attached a mechanical collar to it and led it away.

Laleitha put a hand over her mouth. "Oh my God."

Elise stared down at the factory, her body cold. It was almost as if they were turning people into machines. In the book Kilodrist had given her, it explained how the impulses of neurons could be analyzed and replicated using pieces of microscopic machinery called imitators, which first had to draw from the original example. That was when her eyes trailed to the sign on the wall, a white tree in a navy blue circle.

"Is that the seal of the Prime Devise?" she whispered to Gerald beside her.

"Yeah, didn't you see it all painted all over that base in Litrite?" he responded.

"No," she said. "I was a bit preoccupied."

"What is the Prime Devise doing in The Way?" Gerald wondered.

"How do they have access?" Laleitha added.

Elise shook her head. "I'm an idiot. How didn't I see this coming? If they are hiding something they might need immediately, they wouldn't leave it in a hidden place that opens every few centuries at random, *unless* they have a way to open it."

"The only way to open it is in Orphia's tower," Gerald said. "How would they have access to Orphia's tower?"

Elise swallowed. "Something is wrong here."

"Besides the fact that they are putting human lives into blue hosts?" Anton, who hadn't taken his eyes from the machines, remarked.

"This is fucked up," Darren agreed, shaking his head.

"We can only assume that they have this whole place explored," Gerald said.

"The stone would be in the oldest part," Lee speculated.

"What do you want us to do? Carbon date the walls?" Darren scoffed.

Elise hardly listened. A terrible idea had come to mind, but it was the only way she saw that would get them to the stones. "Guys," she said, in the midst of their arguing, "I know what we can do, but we have to fight."

CHAPTER TWENTY-EIGHT

The Race and the Chase

Elise watched in painful anticipation as her sister crept to the edge of the ledge, ready to make a dramatic entrance. Taking a deep breath, swallowing her anxiety, the girl jumped, soaring down to the bottommost layer, the fire already igniting on her hands. The minute she landed, the flame shot from her palms until she was surrounded by a heated haze of rolling and raging protection.

There were shouts of surprise as all attention turned to the girl in the middle. Gerald hopped from his perch onto the ledge, throwing his hand out toward the man nearest to him, sending him flying back into the wall with a horrible *slam* before he crumpled to the ground.

Elise, Darren, and Anton dropped as well. Elise grasped the rails to the platform and launched herself over it, feeling the flight of the fall that had become rather familiar to her by now. She landed on her feet, taking special care to bend her knees as she landed to avoid destroying her ankles.

Gunfire exploded from either side of the room and, in a risky attempt at a new strategy, Elise extended her hand and engaged the Lumire. She had to be quick, catching the bullets the minute she felt them touch her power's limits. The bullets halted immediately, as if they had impaled an invisible wall, sending a silver ripple through the air. For a moment, they hung there, stiller than stone.

Impressed and rather proud of her own work, Elise drew the bullets near to her so they were almost hovering over her fingertips. One man ran at her, wielding a crowbar, and Elise clenched her fist, sending a single bullet flying toward him. The moment Elise realized what she had done, her hand shot out and directed the bullet downward, and it flashed through his knee, sending the man tumbling to the ground.

She sent the rest of the bullets toward the men above her who were dueling the boys, but she hardly had time to watch them fall before she was tackled from behind. A large body rolled over her, flying with her as she slammed to the ground hard. The minute they skidded to a stop, a metal chunk slammed into her forehead. Her vision immediately blurred, the pain oozing through her bones like poison. The man pinning her wound up again, raising his makeshift metal weapon high above his head. Elise needed to react, she knew she needed to react, but her head hurt too much to focus the Lumire on anything. The man struck again, renewing the pain with something much greater. Instinct took over, the Lumire rushing to protect its host, and the weapon flew from the man's hand, launched backward until it was out of sight. Elise's hand shot up and grasped his arm. Fresh, rejuvenating energy glowed in her veins, cooler and sweeter than water. The man let out an agonized cry as his skin began to pale, the veins standing out in his flesh. Elise released him, pushing his body from hers as she struggled against the pain in her head with her new energy.

Staggering to her feet, she attempted to aim her mind at anything, but the world around her refused to come into focus. Shaking her head furiously, she turned in circles, ready to engage the Lumire, only to find that no more opponents rushed to fight them.

"You all good down there?" Gerald called to them.

"Yep," Laleitha replied.

"We got the package," Darren said, gesturing to a man tied up in wires next to him, with a fabric gag tied around his head.

"Send him down," Elise said.

Darren lifted the man, who now struggled in fear, over the edge of the rails, then released him, letting him drop. Both Elise and Laleitha extended their hands and the Lumire touched the man as he approached. The man's fall slowed as the girls worked together to guide him to the ground.

Gerald, Darren, and Anton hoisted themselves over the edge, falling to join the girls. Anton shifted over to the prisoners in the corner to free them as the others handled the man.

Laleitha pulled the gag from his mouth.

"Where is the stone?" Gerald said, his voice dangerously serious.

The bewildered man sputtered, trying to find his words. "St-stone?"

Elise exchanged glances with Gerald; they both knew what this meant. "Stone" was rather self-explanatory to somebody who knew of it and its importance, but they could not reveal their purpose to somebody who could possibly report back to Reighba, not if they were already oblivious.

Elise turned to face the man, taking a deep breath. She thought back to that day she entered Talious's head, the pain she endured in order to penetrate his mind, and then the concentration she had to maintain so she could stay in his mind. She closed her eyes and the Lumire extended her senses. The man in front of her trembled with fear. His mind already buzzed, she could easily tell. She focused on the buzzing, the storm of thoughts, the hurricane of confusion, then suddenly delved into it.

"What's she doing?" she distantly heard Gerald ask from behind her.

Laleitha began to reply, then suddenly, all of Elise's awareness of the outside world fell away.

A thousand images flew through her mind at once, igniting a fire in her own head. She almost pulled out instinctively before she regripped control, forcing herself to slow the images, to make sense of the sounds. She was seeing his memories, which she didn't need. Elise needed to zero in on something, but navigating a mind was far beyond anything she'd ever done before. Trying desperately to stop the rush of thoughts in his head, she focused all her attention on the image, which refused to slow in front of her. Some parts of it began to glow brightly, while other parts began to vibrate uncontrollably with sheer panic, distorting the image in his mind beyond recognition. Several other thoughts, visions, and sounds rushed past her as she tried to navigate through his mind, his attachments, what he experienced currently, what happened subconsciously, his mind's control over the body, everything within him.

A headache grew within her, but she pushed on, wading through the ocean of information she found, willing the man to produce the stone in his mind. Then, an image crossed her eyes, a dark room with a single stand in the middle. Atop the stand was a small chest, and within it a glowing stone with strange encryptions carved into each of its faces. The picture pulled away from the room, retreating backward through the halls until it reached the very room he was in. Elise's mind snapped back into her own, the excruciating pain she had almost forgotten returning to her temples.

She backed away, unaware of the fact that she trembled. "I got it," she managed. "I know where the stone is."

"Are you sure?" Gerald asked.

She nodded. "I'm sure."

Suddenly, alarms began to blare, red lights flickering all around them.

"That's our cue," Darren grunted.

"We have to go!" Elise cried, running right toward the large hall that would lead them to the stone.

A voice sounded from the speakers above. "There has been an intrusion. Initiate code Eleven A. Evacuate products of interest, clean up the expendables, find the intruders."

"Products of interest—that means the stone," Gerald exclaimed as they ran along the steel-walled hall.

"And the drive," Elise added.

"And whatever the hell else they're hiding here!" Darren yelled.

The hall opened into a large hub, where jets were parked and uniformed men and women rushed along various raised platforms frantically. The five faced a large waterfall that covered the wall in the distance, probably a hidden exit.

"Right," Elise exclaimed. "Go, right."

"There!" one woman screamed, pointing directly at them.

They stood out, being among the youngest and the only people who did not wear a gray uniform. A man in the corner held a device to his mouth and began to speak into it before Gerald impulsively threw the golden knife at him. The dagger impaled him in the shoulder, causing him to lurch in pain. Elise winced, but ran on as Gerald snatched the knife from the man's wound. People were screaming and rushing now, a few armed guards fruitlessly shooting at them.

One lunged at Elise, tackling her to the ground, but Elise's momentum kept her rolling, throwing the man off. With a single thrust of Elise's hand, he shot backward across the floor.

Laleitha pulled her sister to her feet. "They know we're going for the stone!"

"We have to get there first!" Gerald yelled as they charged on.

They had ducked back into another hall now, this one narrow and unlit. Far shorter than the others, it soon opened up into a looming cavern with polished, perfectly level black floors and a few trees that spotted the room in neat, small beds here and there.

Gerald let out a cry as he skidded to a stop, pulling Anton by the shirt to a halt as well. Elise's heart leapt into her throat as she found her toes on the edge of a giant rift in the floor. A raging river flowed at the bottom of the canyon, so far below.

Elise had hardly taken in the sight when she realized Darren hadn't stopped and was tumbling down. Laleitha's hand shot out and grabbed his wrist, only to be pulled down with him. Elise cried her sister's name as she watched her fall, reaching after her as if she still expected to catch her Laleitha's fingers. Her heart almost stopped as the two plunged into the water below.

"We have to go after them!" Anton cried.

"Elise, you get the stone," Gerald said. "We'll get Darren and Lee."

Elise nodded, her heart still screaming at her to go after her sister. At the other end of the ginormous hall was a bridge over the canyon; Elise sprinted toward it. Over the bridge she went, rushing across the cavern to an opening on the other side, one that would lead to a corridor like the one they first entered, except the gardens were replaced by huge tanks of water that were suspended in the air, filled with strange sea creatures. This she had seen in the man's mind.

When the passage opened into the vast room, however, she was caught by surprise when she saw streams of water rushing from the ceiling directly above the tanks, which were threatening to overflow by now. *This is the work of the Prime Devise.* She ran along the narrow bridge at the bottom. *They're destroying this room.*

Suddenly, one of the tanks gave way, pouring tons upon tons of water down to the marble floor below. Elise shrieked and ducked as the water splashed over the bridge, threatening to sweep her away. The liquid dampened her shirt and socks and she winced, clutching the railing as the heavy fluid passed over her. A few strange fish lay dying on the path in front of her; some she could have sworn were luminous, but she had no time to observe. She had to run. As she dashed across the path, more and more tanks began to dump their load to the floor, seemingly miles below, sometimes splashing Elise's bridge halfway through their journey.

When the walls finally pulled the room to an end, Elise passed through a narrow doorway that opened into a hall so dark and vast that the walls to her left and right were out of sight. She looked down and faced a shallow slope of stairs, one so wide it spread across the entire hall, many other exits feeding into this single staircase.

A bang came from Elise's right, and a bullet bounced off her cheek. She turned to see a man pointing a gun at her from a distance. Pulling the bullet from the ground with the Lumire, she shot it back at the man, who dove to avoid it.

The man rolled, stupidly preparing for another shot, before he passed out with no warning, flopping limply onto the top stair, his limbs sprawling haphazardly. Startled, Elise stared at the unconscious man, then she realized she wasn't alone in this room.

In the middle of the dark, endless hall stood a shriveled old man with sunken eyes. His back was hunched and his teeth looked like fangs, but his eyes glowed a pale blue like shining diamonds. Elise found herself face to face with Thentis, the mind-reading Omenescent.

"I'm surprised to see you here, despite Clair's predictions," he said, his voice almost challenging and cunning, as chilling as it was the first time she heard it in Orphia's courtroom. "She told me you would come, but I only saw the will in you, not the initiative."

Elise said nothing but looked at the man, probably with a puzzled and slightly terrified expression. *Clair?* She vaguely remembered Ellington saying the name. She was another Omenescent. She was the Omenescent who could see the future. She was one of the Omenescents nobody had even seen—that might not even exist. The idea of Clair unsettled Elise, but the sight of Thentis in front of her unsettled her more.

"You are frightened by me," he said. "Everybody is. They know I can see them for who they really are—a horrifying thought, especially to someone with demons. Like you."

The night in Litrite flashed through her mind, the men she killed, Reigha, the things she saw in Peter's mind. She realized then that Thentis was in her mind. She felt him, his presence poking at her very thoughts. Engaging the Lumire, she closed her eyes and shut her mind from his reach, pushing him out of her head like a splinter out of her skin.

Thentis blinked. "I see you've discovered that you're a semeric. This one thing distinguishes you from the other Majors, and all others before you, with the exception of few."

"Why am I different?" she asked, her voice hard.

"Because you serve a purpose in this world that is different from the Majors before you. You are meant for something more, something terrifying."

Elise's heart began to sink as he spoke.

"And that is why I am here, to help you realize that and to warn you. Clair sees terrible things to come for you and your friends. She sees you walking in handcuffs down an aisle of betrayed and disappointed Lumerians. She sees you tearing yourself and your friends apart in loyalty to a man who isn't who you believed. She sees you bringing down a mantle that has reigned for years."

Elise was frozen now, her entire body icy. Maybe it was her telepathy, or maybe just a gut feeling, but something told her Thentis was not making this up. Clair really was an Omenescent who could see into the future and really did see Elise doing these things.

"But she is rooting for you," Thentis added, confusing Elise further. "She sees that what you are doing is necessary. As do I."

"Necessary to what?" Elise aksed.

"Everything," Thentis answered. "To the good of Lumeria, of Inseana, of the Prime Devise, and the Lumerian Council. She sees that what you are doing is upholding the purpose of the Majors, but, unfortunately, Orphia doesn't see that."

Elise swallowed. "Should I be concerned?"

"As of right now, no. But when the time comes that you find Clair's words to be true, remember your purpose." He held out a silver baton that almost seemed to materialize out of nowhere in his hand.

Elise hesitated before slowly stepping down the remaining stairs to take it from him. The metal was cold to her touch. In her hand, she held Axis, the centuries-old weapon of the Majors. She braced her hands on both ends and turned. With a click, it snapped open at incredible speed, revealing the curved ax blades at each end.

"How did you get this?" she inquired.

"Orphia has many agents spread across many nations," Thentis responded. "They are not friends or enemies to anyone but Orphia. Unlike me."

Elise looked up at the man. "I thought you weren't supposed to choose sides."

"I'm not," he replied. "But Orphia is not the master of my mind. He only controls what I do, not what I think."

"Does he know you are here?" Elise said, closing Axis with another turn of the hilt.

"Of course," Thentis said, extending his arms. "He designed these halls for me and Clair and Antedal and Avisil, so it is not a crime for me to wander down here," he explained. "We don't venture down here often, as you can imagine. Orphia never intended the way to his tower to be this frightening. He meant it to be our own piece of the world, a chrysalis of all the natural wonders we could ever wish for, to satisfy any desire we might find within ourselves to leave our home. It might have been that way when he built it, but his imagination twisted it as his mind aged, and these beautiful shards of the world above are now mingled with the horrors of the human mind. No, we don't often come down here anymore, but sometimes it does get rather lonely in Orphia's tower. If you are lucky, you may even meet the others one day. I think you'll find them more pleasant than you find me."

Elise looked back at the man lying on the steps, his gun just hanging from his fingers. "How does the Prime Devise have access to this place?" she demanded.

"They have infiltrated The Way to Orphia's tower," Thentis said simply. "Much like you have. Not even their own people know. This is a crime punishable by anything, up to and including execution, but only if somebody testifies against them. I feel enough people have already been executed by the order the man gave over the speaker: *Eleven A*. They are now killing the laborers, the ones they consider to be expendable."

His statement suddenly reminded Elise of her mission. "Have they moved the stone yet?"

Thentis smiled. "The mind stone of the lost son of Orphia? I believe not, but they are headed there now. Hurry, Elise Montason, and remember my words."

Elise wasted no time rushing past Thentis and down the dark hall, his words chasing her like a ghost as she sprinted. Finally, she reached the door she was looking for. It was black and perfectly round, like the one at the entrance that they could not penetrate, but this one was unlocked. She took the silver rod on the right of it and turned it along the circumference of the circular door, listening to gears click and snap behind it as she did so. It popped open and she clambered through, straining her eyes against the blackness ahead of her. This hall was narrow and the ceiling was so low, Elise almost had to duck as she walked along cautiously.

When this passageway opened into a room, it was the very one she saw in the man's mind—small, dim, and with only a table in the middle. She opened the chest on the table, staring down at the glowing stone within. Picking it up, she examined the engravings that covered it. Despite the glow and the odd characters carved into it, the stone seemed perfectly normal, as if Orphia's son had picked it up off his lawn and decided to put his consciousness in when he died. Slipping the stone into her pocket, she turned back to the narrow hall and began her escape.

⚹

When Elise reached the room where Laleitha and Darren had fallen, she faced the very thing she dreaded. An entire squadron of guards, clad in the Prime Devise uniform of black and navy blue, squared off against her. She paused on seeing them, her eyes wide and her heart beating rapidly. Some pointed guns at her before their commander waved his hand. They drew blades from their belts, double-edged knives that shimmered unusually in the light. It dawned on Elise that the Prime Devise must know about the procedure that could be done to metals to make the Majors vulnerable to them. The dreadful suspicion these blades were crafted with the sole purpose of killing her crossed her mind as well.

Her thumb pressed the rod she held behind her, twisting it ever so slightly. Axis thinned in her hand as the blade extended, suddenly becoming a terrifying weapon. She counted ten men, each armed. *What if I kill them? What if there is no way around it?*

They all began to move toward her, though some came quicker than others. One man approached, swinging at Elise with his blade. Out of instinct, fear, and the Lumire pushing her on, Axis shot up, the blade catching on the metal rod. The man withdrew, preparing a wildly skillful maneuver. Elise had no idea how to fight with a weapon like this and no training that could possibly match that of her opponent's. Rather sloppily, she swung the left end at his torso, but he quickly avoided it. Placing both hands on the rod, she prepared herself to defend against the man's attack. Another man flew at her, and she bit back a shriek as she swung around to deflect his knife with Axis's left blade. The first man came at her as well, and she whipped the weapon around to slash at him—a mistake she realized only when the second man knocked the hilt of his knife against her head then slashed at her cheek. She stumbled backward, almost crying out in pain as warm blood began to ooze from the burning cut on her cheek.

Both men jumped on her, a third and fourth approaching. She swung Axis, successfully knocking the blade from the hand of the second man but only as the first swiped his across her side. She screamed in pain, jerking away from him as she fell to her knees. Desperate and furious, she wildly whipped Axis back toward him in vain. The third man snatched the blade from her hands. Elise was almost sobbing now as the pain in her side became overwhelming. Her blood spilled, saturating her torn shirt. They were all around her now, grabbing her by the arms and hoisting her upward until they were carrying her. One reached into her pocket and slipped the stone from its place.

"So, this is what they were after," he muttered. "No harm done after all."

Panic rose in her chest. She had to move, she had to fight, she had to get the stone back, but she couldn't with the pain that coursed through her, making her limbs feel heavy as lead.

"Bring her to Reighba," the man commanded.

The man holding her left arm redrew his knife and pressed it to her throat. "Don't try anything," he hissed, digging the edge into her skin slightly. At the very moment the blade began to pierce her skin, the Lumire suddenly burst from her. Excruciating pain ricocheted through her bones as the impact of her Lumire-fueled blast knocked every man backward until they were a good distance from her.

Elise hit the ground hard. Trembling, she rolled over, feeling for the wound in her side. Her shaking fingers touched the open cut, still seeping with blood. Bracing herself for more intense pain, she touched the wound, choking down the vomit that nearly erupted up her throat when the pain shot through her. She traced her fingers along the cut, the Lumire beginning to heat it. It wouldn't help much, she guessed, but it would stop the bleeding.

She let out an agonized yell when the heat slowly fused the wound back together. The scream echoed through the hall, leaving an eerie silence in its wake. Whimpering, Elise lay on the ground, searching for anything to draw energy from. The men who had attacked her were still breathing, but many were unconscious. One stirred, but a terrible gash across his stomach ensured he would not be mobile any time soon.

Elise closed her eyes, trying to swallow back the pain and clear her mind. The Lumire still crackled around her, allowing her to feel the very floor shake when something crashed several corridors away. Focusing further, the energy of the very particles in the air began to seep into her skin, refueling her until she felt strong enough to fight past the pain in her side.

Standing up, she extended a hand toward Axis, which still lay in the limp hand of one of the unconscious men. At first, the blade refused to conform to her will and the Lumire snapped back into her, triggering a terrible headache that faded within seconds. She winced then focused harder on the blade, extending the Lumire to it once again and pulling it into her hand. She trudged over and took the stone from the man's pocket.

Suddenly, a distressed voice came from behind. "Elise!" Gerald yelled.

She turned to see him running toward her from a hall leading to a place she did not know.

"Go!" he exclaimed, rushing past her with a brief tug on the arm.

Alarmed, she snapped her head back to see what he was running from. Another squadron of Prime Devise guards pursued him, this one much larger, all wielding the shimmering blades. She wasted no time in charging after her friend, not even bothering to note they were sprinting into another corridor unfamiliar to both of them.

Entering this corridor confused them at first, almost as if they had exited The Way. The room was ginormous, nearly to the point of appearing endless, not unlike the hall in which Elise encountered Thentis. This one, in contrast, was a forest. Where the clouds would be in the outdoors, a cave ceiling hung, stretching to the rocky walls that were almost out of sight to the two as they ran. The floor was of dirt and grass, sloping and buckling like a real forest floor, as dense deciduous trees blanketed the entire room. A forest contained by cave walls.

The two skidded along the leafy path, leaping over the bushes and fallen trees, ducking under low-hanging branches. Alarms began to scream in the distance once again.

They pushed faster, Elise fighting against the aching pain in her side, until there was a sudden explosion in front of them. Elise dived away, her eyes immediately finding the man with the cannon-like instrument who perched on the rocks that made up the wall in the distance.

She had no time to look for Gerald. He had dashed to the trees to the left of the explosion, so she took off once more, darting under branches and weaving around trunks.

It wasn't long before another rocket flew from the barrel of the gunman, letting out a faint hiss as it soared. Elise hardly had time to dive away from the explosion as the trees only a short distance away from her burst into a raging inferno. The flames licked her as she tumbled away from them. Gerald sprang to the cover of a bush.

She stumbled to her feet, extending a hand toward the flames. The fire dimmed as the heat and energy flowed into her hand, but she could not linger there long. As much as she needed the energy the flame could provide, there would only be a narrow few seconds before the gunman resumed firing. She retracted her hand from the energy flow and turned away to make her escape.

She bounded across the forest floor to rejoin Gerald, who had emerged from the cover of the bush shortly after the explosion hit.

"This way!" he exclaimed, leading her left.

They continued their escape, strange darts skidding through the leaves around them from the gunners who lurked in the forest.

As she ran, Elise scanned the landscape, noticing to her horror there were troops on either side of them. Gerald scooped up a stick, which began to glow and crackle as he ignited a flame on it. He whipped it at them, not even bothering to watch it soar. When it finally reached the men, it struck one in the chest, exploding on contact.

They hurtled through the forest, picking up even more speed as Elise's pain finally began to pass. Suddenly, Gerald let out a cry and stumbled to the ground. A dart had shot right into his ankle, one of the same darts used by the assassins on the night they were presented to the Lumerian people. Elise stooped to help him, quickly plucking the dart from his skin and sealing the hole with fire before either of them had time to think. The skin sizzled blood red and already began to swell, but Elise refused to let him look at it.

"They're getting close. We have to move!" she exclaimed. "Can you run?"

He stood, wincing from the pain. "Yeah, I can try," he grunted, his voice reflecting the same fear as hers.

They took off again, this time with Elise behind Gerald, frantically trying to deflect incoming darts and urge Gerald forward when he stumbled.

Finally, the trees began to thin and the entrance to the next hall opened in the form of a stone archway. In her plight against the gunmen, Elise had forgotten their other pursuers, the Prime Devise squadron. They were close now; one dived behind her, his blade catching her ankle. She fell and rolled, Gerald pulling her arm hard, jerking her upright. The minute they crossed through the stone archway, Gerald's hand extended out at the stones, sending them tumbling down behind them. The leading man let out a cry as he scrambled away from the falling rocks, the other men skidding to a halt before they could reach the collapsing exit.

Elise finally allowed herself to rest, sliding down until her bottom was against the cold stone floor, Axis clattering from her grip. For a moment, the only sound was their heavy breathing and a distant ruckus behind the stones.

When she caught her breath, she looked up at her friend. "Where are the others?" she asked, her voice weak as the pain in her side lurched back into the forefront of her mind again. The pain in her ankle where the blade caught her was barely a scratch, long forgotten about next to the sting of the wound in her side.

"They're fine," he said. "I got separated from them before the Prime Devise found me. This place is the most confusing—"

"Don't try making sense of it," Elise said before he could finish. "None of it makes any logical sense, not the fact that there is a forest, a man-made canyon, a room with hanging tanks filled with glowing fish and floating gardens that grow living vine-creatures. It makes no sense at all."

Gerald nodded, beginning to walk on down the cavern. "The canyon led to a network of waterways," he said. "There are underwater passages that lead everywhere. Some of the rooms we found could only be entered through the water."

"Are any of them safe?" she asked, walking beside him.

"I don't think anywhere is safe in here, Elise," he said. "The Prime Devise has the entire place mapped out. That was one of the rooms we found, a small room with a map of the entire Way carved into the wall. It was huge. We couldn't find any exits. Darren still has the transportation rod, though we agreed we wouldn't leave until we were all together."

Elise said nothing, a disturbing thought tugging at her mind. *Not all of us may make it. Some of us might die here.* She immediately regretted coming, cursing herself for being so determined before. Then, she remembered Clair had told Thentis she would come, and she wondered if some twist of fate was at work.

"I met Thentis," she said quietly after a moment.

Gerald looked at her, puzzled. "The mind reader? Here? Did he say anything?"

"He said the Prime Devise infiltrated Orphia's tower," she replied. "That even though we will betray and disappoint the Lumerian people, he believes in us."

"Betray and disappoint? Where did that come from?" Gerald asked, his face twisted incredulously.

"Clair, the Omenescent who sees the future—she's apparently seen a lot about us," Elise explained. "He also said we'd tear ourselves apart and bring down a mantle that stood for years."

"What a great pep talk."

"But do you know what that means?" Elise exclaimed. "I think the mantle we'd be tearing down is ourselves—the Majors. I think it means we'll be the last Majors, that we're going to screw up somehow and all die, ending the line of Majors in the process."

"How'd you come to that conclusion?"

"Are there any other mantles that stood for years that we could tear down?" she said.

He shrugged. "The Lumerian Council? Orphia? Who knows?"

"He also gave me this." Elise extended a closed Axis.

Gerald took the rod from her. "Axis?" he said, running his hand along the metal as he inspected it. "How did he get this?"

"I don't know," Elise responded. "He said Orphia has several agents."

"Orphia stole this?"

"I don't know. I'm not sure that's a conclusion we can come to. None of this adds up."

Gerald once again fell silent. Elise had resolved to keep quiet about what Thentis said about her purpose, about what made her different. *Purpose!* The word almost seemed sinister and scornful now.

The cavern ended at an open cave with a waterfall running down the left wall to a small pool in a deep crevice in the floor.

Gerald peered into the dark water. "This is one of the passages," he said.

"Where are we going?" Elise asked.

"To the small room with the map," he replied. "That was where I saw Lee, Darren, and Anton last. We can only get there through the waterways."

"And you know how to get there?"

"I can figure it out."

"King, we'll be holding our breath underwater. I don't think we'll have time to figure it out," Elise argued.

"Once we get to the places I'm familiar with, I can get us there easily." He prepared to slip into the water.

"But we don't know how far we are from your familiar places," Elise pointed out, but Gerald had already submerged himself, sending up a splash.

Elise sighed and dove in after him. The water was icy cold, but Gerald hardly seemed to be bothered. His hands glowed with the same orange heat they had used so many times, creating a dim light in the murky waters, as well as keeping him from dying of hypothermia.

Following his lead, Elise's hands began to sizzle with the heat of the Lumire as she kicked after him, plunging downward, the only way the walls permitted. Her eyes, surprisingly did not sting, nor were they at all bothered by the water. This must be the work of the Lumire, she assumed.

When the narrow passage they traveled down opened, the two found themselves looking at an entire hall of possible networks to embark through. Gerald moved toward one to their right and Elise was slow to follow, her eyes scanning the other dark tunnels and open halls. It wasn't long before a clouding tension began in her head as the carbon dioxide in her blood began to panic her brain. She let out a tiny squeak of distress, looking around for an exit. A dim light poured in from the surface at a distance, and she kicked toward that, giving Gerald's arm a tug. With seconds to spare before she thought she'd pass out, she burst from the water, gasping as she took in the cold air.

Elise groped for land, but her hands reached only smooth black walls with a few small holes her fingers locked into.

"This is where Lee and Darren fell," Gerald said, emerging next to her.

They scanned the familiar place from an unfamiliar angle. This was the canyon they had fallen down, which meant Gerald would know the way, hopefully.

"Gerald?" she asked, her voice weak from the effort it took to stay in one place above the rushing waters.

"Yeah?"

"Picture the waterways you traveled through," she said.

"What?"

"Please," she pressed.

He paused before saying, "Okay."

"Brace yourself," she said, closing her eyes.

Reengaging the Lumire—and the headache—she delved into his mind. A sharp pain ricocheted through her head as Gerald instinctively resisted. On seeing Elise wince, he eased his mind, letting her peer into his thoughts. *What is she looking for?*

Elise heard the thought and she responded by thinking, *"I'm looking for your path through the waterways."*

A sudden understanding spread through his body and, once more, images of the underwater tunnels passed across his closed eyes. Elise watched, attempting to memorize what she saw. Down below the canyon but further forward, he and Anton had reached a fork and had gone right, before discovering a hole in the tunnel ceiling—that they watched Darren swim through from a distance—and followed him up into that. Trailing their friends, they reached a small, dark room that they would later discover to have a map carved into its back wall.

Elise pulled from his mind, her head hurting even more than it did when she lacked oxygen.

"How do you do that?" Gerald asked. "Are you okay?"

Elise grunted. "It hurts." Pulling away from him, she ran a cold, wet hand over her forehead. "It hurts."

"It's not far from here. Can you swim?" Gerald pressed.

Elise nodded, taking a deep breath and submerging herself once more.

CHAPTER TWENTY-NINE

The Way Is Closing

When they emerged from the water, gasping and spitting, they found themselves in an empty room. It was only a bit bigger than the one that contained the mind stone. Half of the floor was dominated by the water, and cement walls closed the tiny space. When Elise caught her breath, her eyes laid upon the map.

Pulling her wet body and sopping clothes from the water, she stood and gazed at the map. Gerald was not exaggerating when he told her the map was huge; it covered the entire wall from ceiling to floor. It took the form of a series of lines connecting boxes and circles, but the entire thing was more intricate than the labyrinth. Each of the boxes was labeled with a number, and the number was listed at the side next to a title.

"See the stars?" Gerald said, tracing a finger along a tiny star carved next to the number in one room. Elise scanned the board to notice several more of these stars. "They're the rooms that the Prime Devise has renovated, made completely theirs."

Elise turned away, scanning the rest of the room. "There's nobody here," she said. "Where else do you think they'd be?"

"I told them to stay here," Gerald replied.

"Are we in the right room?"

Gerald nodded. "Maybe the Prime Devise found them."

Elise would have preferred not to think about that possibility. She gazed around and discovered a small imperfection in the cement. Wordlessly, she approached it and saw something else had been carved into the wall. Kneeling next to it, she recognized the familiar handwriting immediately.

Meet in 87 - AH

"They left," Gerald said from over her shoulder.

"Where is room eighty-seven?" Elise asked, turning back to the map.

She scanned the wall, finding room eighty-seven at the very edge. It was a large rectangle with two halls leading to it on either end.

"Okay, I found it," she said. "And it's the forest room we were just in."

"But since we blocked off the other entrance, the only way back to it would be through the room with the canyon. We can't get back there; we wouldn't be able to get out of the waterway."

Elise grimaced. "Right, I forgot about that. Well, I guess we know the general area it's in."

He shrugged. "Good enough. You ready to swim?"

She nodded, and they slipped back into the liquid abyss. Elise's skin tightened as the freezing water swallowed her. Opening her eyes and letting the Lumire rush under her skin, her hands began to glow.

Pushing downward, they delved once more into the network of underwater tunnels. When the tunnel they were retreating from opened up, a wide basin with rocky walls lay in front of them, more tunnels opening in several areas along the basin's edge. Looking up toward the surface, there was nothing above them but a wall of rocks and a metal door facing downward.

Suddenly, the door slid open, and a strange device floated downward into the water. Headlights flickered on and an engine began to run, pushing the one-man water vehicle down into one of the tunnels. Elise concealed herself behind a large rock that protruded from the wall, but she was beginning to lose her breath as their time underwater became prolonged. Kicking off from the wall, Elise rushed furiously for the door, slipping herself between its silver flaps before they pulled shut. Gerald remained right beside her the entire time.

When the door locked, they found themselves in a blue basin with the door situated at the bottom. She stood and began to climb up the side of the strange basin then noticed the near-empty hall was full of them. Circular dips in the floor lined the entire passage, a door to the water at the very bottom of each. Along the long side of the walls, the small submarine vehicles were held by crane-like structures, ready to plop into the water below.

Then, she noticed the sickening scene. Bodies scattered the floor in pools of blood. With the memory of the mechanical voice ringing in her ears, Elise remembered the command: *Eleven A . . . evacuate items of interest, clean up expendables . . .* As Thentis had mentioned, "clean up expendables" meant "kill the workers." A sick feeling sat in Elise's stomach when her eyes rested on the corpses. The body count deeply disturbed her.

"Come on," Gerald said. "There's a door this way."

The door he found was small and regular looking, which was probably the most absurd thing about the area. When they opened it, they found themselves in a vertical room with a spiral staircase extending upward for what seemed like forever.

"I feel like we're in some sort of twisted game like chutes and ladders," Gerald muttered as they began climbing upward.

Suddenly, a rumble shook the room. The two paused, taking hold of the railing and gripping it with white knuckles as the quake passed. After a moment of silent listening, they gathered the courage to move forward.

They stopped at the first door they found, which wasn't far from their starting point. Exiting through there, they stood on a balcony of rocks.

Gerald breathed a sigh of relief. "Found it."

"This wasn't on the map," Elise remarked with a frown.

As she walked forward, she realized they were back in the forest room, except on a ledge carved into the rocky wall. The forest was laid out before them, the tips of the trees just reaching the ledge on which they stood. Evidently, there were more than just two entries to this room. This might have been the ledge on which one of the gunmen was perched when she and Gerald were pursued through this room earlier. However, there was no sign of any Prime Devise officers. There was no sign of anyone. Then, she heard a familiar voice from below.

"Elise?"

She looked down to spot the mess of brown curls looking up at her. Laleitha stood just below the ledge, the golden knife clutched in her hand and Anton at her side.

"Lee, thank God."

"Where's Darren?" Lee asked.

"Gerald said he was with you."

"Elise," she said, taking a deep breath, her voice more grim and terrified than Elise had ever heard it. "We have to get out of here. The Way is closing."

Elise's heart sank. "Darren has the transportation rod."

Suddenly, there was another rumble, this one much more intense. Rocks slowly tipped from their place on the wall, tumbling downward with echoing crashes. With no warning, the balcony fell from Elise's feet, sending her and Gerald tumbling down to the ground below. Elise landed hard, the impact ricocheting through her bones. Lee rushed to Elise's side, helping her sit up. When she looked back up at her ledge, she realized it was still there, then it suddenly shimmered and disappeared once more. "Wha—"

"The Way is flickering in and out of existence," Anton explained softly.

"We have to get out of here," Gerald agreed.

The two scrambled to their feet and took off with their friends toward the nearest exit. The quake resumed, once more spilling stones from the wall. Elise shrieked as one of the ginormous rocks smashed into the ground right beside them, sending dust, dirt, and tiny shards of stone flying into the air.

They flew through the trees, sprinting for their lives, fearful of being crushed by the falling rocks. Elise tore through a bush and ducked under a low-hanging branch, her eyes moving up to the walls as she ran, watching in horror as the rocks fell.

Suddenly, Laleitha let out a cry as a huge piece of the rocky ceiling broke from its suspensions. Elise prepared to dive out of the way as she charged from its path until suddenly, it disappeared. The four paused, looking up at the ceiling with amazed, frightened confusion.

Between breaths, Gerald quietly asked, "Where did it go?"

Then it reappeared, only a few feet above the treetops, threatening to crush them in a matter of seconds. Several let out cries of shock as they dived out of the way, hiding their faces as the stone shattered on the ground, sending dirt flying into the air like fog.

Elise trembled in place while the dirt settled, the ground beneath her still shaking.

There was a harsh tug on her arm as Anton shot past her, pulling her with him. She stumbled to her feet and followed, her ears ringing furiously and her side still throbbing from her earlier injury. The exit was close now, only about a hundred feet.

Sprinting as hard as she could, she weaved between the trees, her eyes focused on the opening in the stone wall. The trembling ground sent shivers through her very bones.

Finally, they tore through the last of the trees and down into a vaguely familiar hall. The ground still rippled and shrugged with the constant quake as cracks opened up in the walls and ceiling.

"Where is Darren?" Gerald shouted over the ruckus, his voice angry and panicked.

Nobody had a response, but they kept running, searching desperately for a place that didn't shake terribly.

They had reached the room with the polished black floor and the canyon as chunks of the floor were beginning to break off and descend to the raging water below. Anton, who led the pack, turned left down the way back to the place where the Prime Devise made the blue stone people.

The minute they darted back into the room, the tank that held the mixture of melted materials evaporated into nothingness, sending a searing hot liquid running across the floor, burning through the tiles. Elise scrambled away from the rapidly approaching blue fluid that shimmered as the lights above them flickered. One of the suspended lights broke from its cord and crashed to the floor.

Then, with no warning or reason, the shaking paused. Elise's breath caught in her throat, waiting frightfully for something—*anything*—to happen, but everything was still. She looked around at her friends. Laleitha had her back against the wall, her cheeks flushed and sweat dripping from her chin. Gerald clung to a machine, skin speckled with sweat as he trembled in place. And then there was Anton, leaning against the wall with genuine, horrified fear in his eyes—but only his eyes.

A small meow sounded from a distance, and the party looked up to see Emperor Evanstin's silver cat pacing above them on the supports in the room.

"What," Elise squeaked, "the hell is—"

Abruptly, the entire earth lurched underneath her, the boom almost shattering her eardrums. She fell forward onto the ground that was shaking once more, the terror resuming.

A familiar yelp caught her attention, and when she looked up, she spotted none other than Darren Nosia on the second floor, desperately clutching the railing.

Gerald let out an incoherent shout of relief as he reached for the nearest ladder.

"What the hell is going on?" an utterly confused Darren shouted.

Elise sped up the ladder, all of them sprinting toward their terrified friend.

"The transportation rod," Gerald exclaimed. *"Now!"*

Darren nodded frantically and took the rod from its hiding place in his jacket. It broke into a portal the moment it left his hand, revealing an empty yard surrounded by a dark forest. Elise wasted no time in jumping through. Gerald was the last to go, closing it behind him.

They slammed into the grass, the moisture immediately cooling their burning skin. The new atmosphere was silent, still, and regular, making the change from chaotic and confusing almost painful.

Darren groaned, rolling in place to face the stars. Elise could hardly do so; exhaustion hit her like a truck. Suddenly, a blinding green flash burst to life, lasting only one painful millisecond before it was gone again.

Elise finally gathered the strength to lift her head and found herself in the small clearing of 9551 West. The tower, however, was absent, as The Way was now closed.

Letting her eyes fall shut and her head rest on the grass, she engaged the Lumire. Frost began to crackle as it formed on the grass around her, all of its thermal energy flowing into Elise's muscles. She once again found the initiative to move, something that had been becoming increasingly difficult to do lately. She stood, brushing the grass from herself and wearily looking around.

"Did you get the stone?" Laleitha asked, sitting up.

Elise revealed the stone from her pocket. "Yeah."

"Good," Darren said. "It wasn't all for nothing."

"It never is," Gerald said, offering a hand to help him up. "But now, we're bringing home the son of Orphia, like we said we would."

"We should get going," Laleitha said. "Let's get back before the council issues an empire-wide search for us."

"Right," Gerald agreed. "Lead the way."

Elise and Laleitha walked side by side as they guided the boys back to the Montason house. They were silent, pondering what had just happened, letting the fear ease out of them.

I wonder why the rod led us back to the tower instead of Marty's house. Elise hardly cared about finding the answer.

When they arrived back at Elise's house, they opened the door to find Percy waiting for them. "Elise, Lee, thank God. I thought you were dead." He breathed as he embraced his sisters. "You were gone for hours."

"We were gone for that long?" Gerald asked, puzzled.

"You were gone the entire day," he said, looking back at Gerald blankly. "You left last night."

Gerald looked at the faces of his friends, who shared in his bewilderment. "That's not what it felt like."

"It makes sense," Anton said quietly. "Time must move differently in The Way."

Elise shrugged. "Regardless, Percy, we're here to say goodbye. We need to go back to Lumeria now and face the . . . the consequences of our actions."

Percy looked at her with wide eyes, like he always did when slightly upset and rather confused. Besides this, his face showed nothing more than expectancy and curiosity.

Elise stepped forward to embrace her brother once more, and he hugged her tightly, both of them fearing it might be the last time in years they would do so. Neither let this worry surface, though, and when she stepped back, he only looked at her with a sense of pride. He was proud of who his sister was, even if he could never possibly understand her situation fully. For that, Elise felt a swell of gratitude and affection toward him rising in her chest.

"I'll be back soon," Elise said. "I think. Eventually."

Gerald gave him a playful salute and the five turned to leave the Montason house, preparing themselves for whatever the Lumerian Council had in mind for them.

CHAPTER THIRTY

If You Want to Protect These People

It was late evening when the five stepped through the portal and onto the doorstep of Fort Kingshold. They rushed across the street and into the adjacent building, retreating back into their living quarters before another eye could rest upon them. They had agreed to discuss their next move there before making any other decisions—such as who to come clean to first, who to give the mind stone and Axis to, and how and when to do any of this. An eerie but expected silence settled on their familiar living quarters when they arrived back.

"I need to check something," Anton muttered as he made his way over to the computer.

"What?" Laleitha asked.

"You know that snake that Mont built?" Anton said. "I kinda . . . slipped that into Ellington's case before he left."

Elise stared at him. *What if Ellington found it? What if he thinks we're up to something? Why did Anton do this without asking us? Or at least telling us?*

Lee, however, was not as bothered by this but found it amusing. "You did?"

Gerald's brow furrowed. "Why?"

Anton shrugged. "My initial plan was to keep tabs on Ellington so we could guess how much time we had left, but then I realized we'd only be able to access the feed from this computer so it would only help us before and after we left," he explained. "And, also, for fun."

Darren nearly laughed. "I love this kid."

He nodded, typing furiously on the keyboard.

"Anton, why didn't you tell us about this?" Gerald asked, walking up behind him.

The boy shrugged and said, "I didn't want—" then froze completely.

Gerald grew silent, too, staring at the screen with almost bulging eyes.

"What is it?" Elise asked as she and her sister joined them.

On the screen in front of them, through a small hole, they saw two men holding guns to the heads of Lumerian diplomats. One man, who paced in and out of view, was speaking, and they didn't need to get a good look at him to recognize the cunning, intelligent movements of Alfred Reighba. He had the diplomats in Insenea.

"Well." Darren gulped. "Shit."

"We have to get to the emperor's office," Gerald said, starting back toward the door.

The rest followed, leaving Axis and the mind stone behind, the urgency in their movements soon turning into a run as they hurried over to Fort Kingshold and up to the top floor. They navigated to the emperor's wing, where the entire security team was absent for some mysterious reason. They made their way to a dimly lit office, the only one they saw occupied.

Gerald opened the door quickly, freezing when a roomful of people jumped. Emperor Evanstin and several Arc Leaders crowded in the small room, facing a large screen that depicted the same room they had seen on their computer.

Reighba's face on the screen smiled. "Well, it looks like your problems are solved, Your Grace."

"Where *were* you five?" one of the Arc Leaders spat.

"Not now, Harold," Emperor Evanstin said with clipped tones. "We have a different problem at hand."

"Ah," Reighba said. "So it wasn't a Lumerian scheme."

Gerald slowly entered the room. "What's going on?"

Emperor Evanstin beckoned the five in, lining them up toward the side of the room. "We've been trapped. Chancellor Reighba has taken our group of diplomats hostage and will agree to send them home only if we hand you five over to the Prime Devise."

Elise's heart sank. The way he explained that almost made Elise suspect he was considering it. She could only imagine what the Prime Devise would want to do with her. Kill her? Experiment on her? Put her into one of those blue stonemen?

"And if you don't?" Laleitha questioned.

"They die," Reighba said simply from the screen. "For all that you Majors have done. For all the times that you've betrayed the Lumerian Council then hid behind it once again so they'd save your skin. I speak for all of these diplomats, your people here, when I say, if you truly want to protect these people, you will exchange places with them now."

"They are not going anywhere," Emperor Evanstin shot back at the man on the screen. "What do you want with them? What can we give you instead?"

Reighba smiled again. "Ah, but you see, Emperor, these *Majors* have only been here for three months and they have caused more trouble for us than you have without them in decades. How can we ensure, regardless of what you give us instead, that this trend will not continue?"

"The attack in Litrite was issued by a rogue officer who acted on his own authority against the council's wishes. The Majors only followed the orders of their superior," Emperor Evanstin explained, the anger in his voice quivering threateningly.

"And tonight's attack?" Reighba inquired on.

The Emperor's words faltered and, instead of quickly firing back as usual, his eyes drifted over to the five.

"It wasn't an attack," Darren said defensively.

"Then what would you call it, Mr. Nosia?" Reighba said.

"What were you doing in The Way?" Gerald spat.

"The Way?" one Arc Leader with a fat nose and a stout frame repeated. "That place doesn't exist. And even if it did, it wouldn't be accessible to neither Lumerians or Inseanans."

"It exists," Elise insisted. "We were there."

"And guess who else was there," Laleitha added, staring at Reighba's face on the screen.

The Arc Leader looked between the Majors and Reighba. "How?"

Darren removed the transportation rod from his pocket and dropped it on the table in front of them.

Emperor Evanstin regarded the rod for a moment before glancing sternly at the Majors, then lifted his eyes back to the screen. "What were you doing in The Way, Mr. Reighba?"

There was silence.

Elise wanted to scream. *She* knew what he was doing there. She saw the Prime Devise manufacture blue stone creatures and grow killer vines and glowing fish. She saw them harvesting resources she couldn't begin to describe from The Way. She saw them use that place as a weapons manufacturer, then she watched them kill their own people when they thought they were discovered.

"Your Majors seem to know," Reighba said, as if reading Elise's expression. "Perhaps you should ask them."

The emperor once again looked toward the five, a stony expression on his face.

"I fear," Reighba said, folding his hands behind his back, "that your diplomats would have returned home safely if your Majors had remained in Lumeria. I had no malicious intentions when I offered to host your representatives—I was even considering a partnership with Lumeria, regardless of your cowardly absence. But when I received word that your Majors had infiltrated our most treasured and vital facility, I knew I couldn't let this go without the threat to my people being handled. Surely, you can understand."

Emperor Evanstin studied the Majors with an unreadable expression, and Elise tried to swallow her guilt under his pressing gaze. After a long moment, he turned back to Reighba and spoke calmly. "Chancellor, I assure you the Majors had no evil intentions in their actions tonight, though the Lumerian Council will need time to discuss these events in order to decide how to handle them."

"It's simple," Reighba said. "You give them to me and *save* several members of your council."

"And what would you do if you got them?"

"Continue what we were doing before the Majors entered Lumeria," Reighba answered. "It's rather obvious life was more peaceful without them. They're magnets to danger and disputes. My people have called for remedy and, as their chancellor, it is my duty to answer them."

"That could be so, but if your people are concerned, it's solely because of your attempts to assassinate the Majors," Emperor Evanstin pointed out.

"My attempts?" Reighba repeated, innocently. "Your Grace, I'm afraid you have no proof. In fact, most of the evidence indicates it was one of the works of the Stormy City's—"

"I don't need to try you in front of Orphia to make you answer for what you've done, Chancellor," Evanstin interrupted. "But it is my choice not to for the sake of your people and my own."

"If you want to do something for your people and mine, you will comply," Reighba responded. "I have run out of patience, Your Grace. I will give you until midnight, your time. You will come via jet plane carrying the Majors and whatever nonmilitary personnel necessary. When the Majors have arrived and are in my custody, I will lead your diplomats out into that same jet and permit you to leave. At midnight exactly, all of your diplomats will be executed. If you bring anything other than a single jet plane, your diplomats will be executed, and your plane will be shot out of the sky. If you give me any indication that you are preparing an attack, your diplomats will be executed and my legions will be ready. I hope I have made myself clear." With that, the screen flickered to black.

"Ellington's in there," Gerald whispered to Elise.

She did not reply. Her mind hung on Reighba's words.

The emperor turned angrily to the Arc Leaders. "Try to get him back online. Our negotiations are not finished," he said to one at the computer. "We need a plan."

"We cannot attack," the one named Harold said. "They are expecting a single jet."

"They would kill our diplomats if we even attempted an attack," another added.

"So you send us," Gerald interrupted.

All eyes turned to him.

"King—" Darren began.

"It's the only logical option," Gerald said. "We have limited time, we can't organize a plan, an attack is out of the question, and he made it clear there was no other negotiable solution."

Elise nodded. Gerald was right. The only way to get Ellington out of there was for them to go. The realization made her go numb, the only feeling under her skin being the chill of fear. *I deserve it. After I killed those men, after I endangered people who were just trying to clean up my mess, I deserve this.*

"They'll kill you," Emperor Evanstin said. "There is no question about that. But I feel you're right. I feel our only hope is to hand you over to them." He approached the five. "But listen to me. The minute that jet leaves with our diplomats flying to safety, you do whatever you can to get out of there. You have done it before; I have faith you can do it again. Do you understand me?"

Elise swallowed. She had been prepared the last time she broke in and out of that base in Litrite. She had trained with Westbecker, memorized the floor layout, and had a week to mentally prepare for whatever the Prime Devise was hiding behind its walls. Even that attack had had an effect on her. Though her injuries were minor, she felt hollowed. She had lost her innocence, she had taken lives, and now there were demons that followed her around every second of the day for it. *I deserve this.*

"We'll send a fleet to retrieve you," the emperor said.

"All due respect, Your Grace," another Arc Leader said. This one was lanky and painfully thin, with a carefully styled sweep of red hair on his head. "But these are children. Sending them to die—regardless of our reasons—is morally wrong."

"We are not sending them to die!" the emperor snapped.

"We can't send a fleet to retrieve them; they'll be expecting that and waiting with one of their own," Harold pointed out.

"I have confidence in our pilots and camouflage technology. The extraction will be quick and evasive."

"There's a transportation rod!" Darren blurted. "One that Westbecker used to get us into Litrite. It opens right by the base there. You can use that to get over the border."

All eyes paused on Darren, confused.

"Where is this transportation rod?" the fat one asked.

The Majors exchanged confused glances. "Um . . . in a shed, in the woods," Elise answered slowly, realizing it wasn't much help.

One of the Arc Leaders, a petite woman with dark brown hair tied in a neat ponytail and a mass of freckles covering her face, turned to the emperor. "I know the shed she's referring to," she said. "He used to conduct training exercises in the woods half an hour outside city limits." The woman looked back at Elise. "Does that sound right?"

Elise nodded earnestly.

"So, we retrieve the transportation rod," another Arc Leader said, this one old, dark-skinned, and graying. "Even if we extend it, we'll only be able to fit one-man birds through one at a time, who'll then have a twenty-minute flight from Litrite to Hiseroth minimum."

"It's still a better bet than trying to cross the border with an entire fleet," the tall redheaded Arc Leader pointed out. "They'd shoot us down immediately if we tried that."

The one the emperor assigned to get Reighba back online spoke up. "We can't get him back online, Your Grace."

"We have no way to monitor the scenario besides the information the Majors can supply us with, which will hardly be sufficient," the graying man said. "We are working with almost no information here."

"There is a way," Elise blurted. "There's a device hidden Stanford Ellington's case. It's currently feeding information to the computer in our living quarters."

Harold shot the emperor a look of exasperation before the emperor raised his hands. "When this is over, we'll have to ask you a few questions about that, but seeing as it is necessary to use in this situation, we will use it thusly."

"This is ridiculous!" the fat one exclaimed. "We can't seriously be considering doing exactly what Westbecker did."

"Westbecker didn't send them in to save diplomats," the freckled female argued.

"We don't have time for a debate," Emperor Evanstin growled. "These kids are our five Majors and our only chance at saving those people." He turned to an Arc Leader beside him. "Get them prepared for takeoff."

)(

Impending doom approached as Elise slipped on the appropriate clothes—which had been supplied by someone in the armory and fitted exactly to their sizes—and set off for the jet. She wore a thick black top with padding in the chest and stomach and the golden Lumerian crown crest sewn on the left breast, along with long gray pants littered with compartments and straps for weapons or tools.

The Arc Leader named Harold led them to a small room with a wall covered completely with different colored transportation rods, rambling as he did so. "This room is used only by Arc Leaders and can take them any place in the city and any major city in the entire Lumerian empire." He took a rod from the wall and tossed it outward. It opened with a familiar *crack*. "Come with me."

On the other side of the portal was a wide hall with light gray brick walls and stone floors. "We are in the LSE private airport; your jet is in terminal one. I was given instructions to pass to you, so listen closely. You will arrive at a Prime Devise base in Hiseroth, Inseana. This base is operating as their central command base until the repairs to the one in Litrite are finished. We will be monitoring your heart rate, and a small camera embedded in the Lumerian seal on your shirt will be transmitting a video feed. On the jet there, you will be given medical attention if necessary and a map of the base to study so you may grow familiar with the layout. It is likely that you will be escorted into the building by Prime Devise officers.

"When we give you the signal, you will have to disarm them and escape quickly, by any means necessary. We will give you the signal through the camera in your shirt; it will send an electrical shock into you that doesn't inflict any pain or damage but gets the message across. This signal will be given when the diplomats are in the clear. Emperor Evanstin will meanwhile be attempting to contact and negotiate with Reighba in order to divert him from direct involvement in the exchange. Assuming we can get them there through the transportation rod without being shot out of the sky, there will be cloaked Lumerian birds circling the perimeter, waiting for us to give them your location and the okay. They will retrieve you and get you home. Understand?"

Elise nodded tentatively, hoping she retained that much information. The frantic quickness of his voice only made her muscles tense as she followed him to terminal one.

They entered a large area with a single jet parked on the cement. The walls extended up into the second story, where people watched from their computers through glass windows. The jet was sleek and silver with the Lumerian flag painted on wings that curved backward, giving it the shape of a bird mid-dive.

Their escort led them up to the stairs that lowered from the bird's body. "Good luck, Majors," he said, stopping in place with his hands folded formally behind his back. "We will be with you every step of the way."

"Right." Darren snorted from behind Elise as they climbed the stairs into the jet plane.

The inside of the jet was dimly lit, but rows of four chairs lined the walls, with a few seats all turned to face the middle. In the very back and the front, two computers were stationed; only two of them were occupied, however, with one person in the back and one in the front. There was a circular entrance to the pilot's cabin, and both the pilot and the copilot were set to take off.

Elise sat nearest the door, ready to step off when the time came and face what she had coming. Her sister did the exact opposite and positioned herself farthest from the door, farthest from everyone—she wanted to be alone. Gerald and Darren sat next to each other on the other side of the aisle, two seats down from Elise's. Anton, however, sat directly next to Elise, wordless and grim.

"Straps yourselves in," one of the people by the computers said as the door rolled shut.

Elise did as she was told, crisscrossing the straps on her body so she was tightly secured in her seat.

The jet lifted from the ground, lurching upward as it did so. The doors in the building's roof opened, allowing the plane to rise between them. When the bird had climbed high enough, the back thrusters engaged and the silver body shot forward, still gaining altitude as it did so. Elise watched the city shrink below her as they approached the clouds. The strangely shaped buildings had become almost familiar, the ones like giant arrowheads and pointed pillars. The reddish haze that the stars cast over the buildings seemed so warm now, like a balmy hearth that engulfed the city. As the Arc City passed from sight, Elise's eyes traced the silver line of the monorail tracks that ran through every large city in the empire.

There were so many people down below her, so oblivious to this new horror that had come to life right before Elise's eyes. They didn't know of the new tower that had been built on all of Elise's guilt, fear, and ignorance, a tower of Elise's reputation as a Major, the only part of her the people saw, one that would soon come crumbling down due to her failure. How would the rest of the empire respond when they found out? What would Ellington say? Would there be mourning for the last Majors? The last Majors whose only acts for Lumeria were to attack a Prime Devise base under a rogue officer's orders and betray the Lumerian Council just to see what a personal friend died for? Elise suddenly realized just how much she cared about how the Lumerian people saw her. It was almost as if they were presenting her with a chance to become the person they saw her as, which she had let slip away without a second thought.

Thentis was right. They'd be the ones to bring down a mantle that stood for years; they'd be the ones to end the endless line of Majors.

A sudden, heart-lifting epiphany touched Elise's mind. Thentis had also told her she would walk in handcuffs down an aisle of betrayed and disappointed Lumerians and tear herself and her friends apart in her righteous fight for what she believed in. Both things she had not yet done. He was told this by Clair, the Omenescent who saw the very future, the absolute and inevitable future, fate's future. This was not the end for Elise yet; Clair foresaw her living on.

One woman who was originally next to a computer approached. "Do you have any injuries that need treating?" she asked.

She's almost forgotten about the wound in her side, which still ached dully but not enough for her to focus on over the more pressing concerns since she exited The Way. Vaguely, Elise explained what happened to her side, that she'd been slashed by a Prime Devise officer, and the woman kneeled beside her to inspect it, awkwardly poking and prodding at the flesh while holding the straps aside.

"It doesn't look like there's any internal damage. Given what's happened, it's remarkable how quickly this is healing. I was told that can happen with the Lumire." She lightly pressed on the burn marks. "These probably won't go away, unless the Lumire can heal them too."

Elise thanked the woman, who moved on to treat Anton behind her.

The bird sped on. Elise's gaze frequently trailed to the digital clock above the pilot's cabin, with red numbers glaring out at them. She counted the hours until the time would run out. It had been around nine o'clock in the evening when they had returned to Lumeria. Now, it was eleven and they had only an hour left. Elise closed her eyes, running a million possibilities through her mind, trying to develop a ploy for each one in an attempt to be prepared.

"Elise," a voice said behind her.

She turned to see the rest of her friends gathered with Gerald and Darren. She unstrapped herself and stood, joining them in their cluster.

"I'm not going to talk plans or anything with you guys," King said. "Because, honestly, I'm sick of that. I just—" He cut off, shaking his head. "I don't think we're anywhere near our end. Think about it. We escaped the Prime Devise twice, three times if you include the night we were abducted; we took out the Inseanan's strategic heart with only a few months of training and *alone*; we got in and out of a place that a shitload of people have been searching for over the course of centuries. I genuinely don't believe anything bad's gonna happen tonight. By tomorrow, we are going to come back here and give the Lumerian people something to cheer for. This is what we, the Majors, are supposed to be all about. I don't care what Thentis thinks. I mean, he's probably right about some things because he was in our heads, but I think we've already done a damn good job of proving him wrong. If there is anything that I've learned in the past month, it's that if we have a motive and a method and the Lumire, anything we put our minds to is in reach. We're going to prove that today, right? And we'll do it again when we have to. Whatever it takes."

Darren's face broke into a smile and he looked around at the rest of his friends.

Elise couldn't help but grin as well.

"How was that for my first pep talk?" Gerald asked, a cracking a grin of his own.

"Not too bad, actually," Elise said.

"Got me fired up," Darren remarked.

Minutes later, Elise's ears popped as the bird began to descend below the clouds once again. They touched down not long after, the plane settling slowly into its new position. Elise closed her eyes, readying herself to face the Prime Devise once again. This time, a steel layer of reassurance sat under her skin; this time, she knew she was going to be okay.

The door opened as the stairs lowered to the ground, revealing a troop of Prime Devise officers awaiting them. They all held shimmering knives—knives deadly to the Majors.

Gerald was the first to stand, walking to the very front of the aisle and facing the stairs before Elise, Darren, Anton, and finally Laleitha followed his lead. The air changed as Elise stepped out of the bird, leaving behind the cloud of apprehension as she entered the new atmosphere that buzzed with stiff electricity and cautious anticipation.

The guards held their blades across their chest, the sharp edge facing the five that filed between the two lines the troops had formed. A woman stood in front of them, one Elise had never seen before. The woman carried herself high, giving Elise the sense she was important.

The woman gave the first two officers a nod and they began to search Gerald, one holding his blade at Gerald's throat while the other patted him up and down. Then, they proceeded to put him in handcuffs. They moved on to Elise, who made herself as stiff as possible as the threatening hands moved over her. Even when they handcuffed her and moved on to Darren, she could feel their every movement, her muscles tensing every time they stood up too sharply or took hold of something.

After a tense minute, the Majors were left weaponless and the Prime Devise officers appeared confident enough to lead the Majors onward. Elise's eyes drilled holes into the woman's back, waiting for her to do something threatening. She had briefly considered the possibility the Prime Devise wouldn't let the diplomats go even when the Majors were handed over, but something inside told her otherwise, something she had picked up from Peter Reighba's head. Peter, the Second Reighba, the son of this sinister leader had been raised to be honorable, honest even, and his father was much too proud to give up his reputation of being noble just for a few diplomats. It was the Majors he really wanted, and he didn't have to violate whatever honor code he lived by in order to get them.

A black gate guarding a wide, dimly lit hall opened as they walked on. The guards were visibly on edge, expecting the Majors to do something at any moment.

Elise scowled. Emperor Evanstin's plan was predictable; it basically followed the lines of the precautions the officers were trained for. Of course, they had no opportunity to devise something elaborate, which was exactly Reighba's intention when he limited their time.

Lights flicked on when they detected the group's movement, guiding them to a large elevator with glass walls and polished wooden floors.

The officers lined the perimeter of the box, forcing the Majors into the middle. The leading woman had stepped aside as the Majors were prodded into the elevator, entering last and facing the five.

The doors slid shut behind her and she opened her mouth to speak. "You are about to stand before our chancellor, Alfred Reighba. You are to treat him with the utmost respect and obey his orders silently. If you try to leave, display disrespect toward our leader, or attempt to inflict any harm on our chancellor or your escorts, you will be punished then killed. On Chancellor Reighba's dismissal, you will be escorted to our experimental wing, where you will be put in containment. Again, any attempts to resist us will lead to your *certain* and immediate death."

Certain death. The phrase essentially acknowledged the experimentation might kill them. It was just a question of when they would die and for what. Elise shivered.

Her eyes trailed to the glass walls. Stone was rolling by on either side, but behind them, behind the glass, was an open field of cement that later fed into the city. This city was much different than the one of Lumerian structure. Many of the buildings looked to have a hexagonal base, each with sharp, jagged edges and bright, reflective surfaces that stretched high into the sky.

The officer to her right shifted his blade toward her threateningly as she attempted to turn her head further. The message came across clearly, so she slowly returned her gaze forward.

The elevator slowed until it stopped, and the door reeled open once more. The woman finally permitted herself to turn her back on the Majors again as she led them out into a new room.

Here, Reighba stood with his back to a large screen as gunmen around the perimeter held their weapons to their chest. The Lumerian diplomats remained in their seats, heads down, looking too terrified to move. Reighba appeared positively relaxed as the Majors were led to stand in front of him, as if he were only accompanying houseguests on a peaceful Sunday.

"Kneel to our chancellor," the woman ordered.

Elise swallowed, refusing, spite building up in her chest. Gerald stiffened next to her as not one of the five knelt.

With a harsh jab between her shoulder blades, the officer behind her dug the hilt of his blade into her, grabbing her by the neck and forcing her to the ground.

Reighba grinned. "Usually unnecessary, but it is rather flattering to see the Majors kneel before me."

Elise's fists clenched behind her back.

Reighba cast a glance at the officers lining the room, one for each Lumerian diplomat in the room. "It appears we'll have to send you home now. You may thank your Majors before you leave, if you wish," he said.

Elise's gaze finally found Ellington, whose entire face was flushed with red. The very way he looked at them spoke volumes of how desperately he wanted to send the Majors—his students—back home.

Shoving their captives forward, the guards began to file the diplomats into the elevator. They said nothing, but many cast glances their way. Elise refused to meet any of their eyes, especially not Ellington's.

The woman left the room with them, leaving the Majors kneeling in front of their guards as they faced Alfred Reighba.

"The emperor is wise," he chuckled. "And you thought he would never give them up, Peter."

Elise's head whipped to the corner where Reighba had looked and, sure enough, Second Reighba leaned against the wall, clad in his usual black uniform and his distinct navy and white mask.

"He's either wise or crazy," he remarked with a snort.

His voice was familiar, as if Elise had known him for years. It had echoed through her head so often when his memories once again flashed through her mind. This troubled Elise even further.

Reighba turned back to them. "I could believe either. Regardless, I'm grateful he did what he did. You five will be very helpful to us."

"You think your experiments will do anything?" Gerald spat.

His guard slammed the hilt of his blade against the back of Gerald's head, causing him to lurch forward, before pulling him back upright again and sliding his blade around his throat, challenging him to continue speaking.

"The Lumerian Council isn't done with you," Gerald went on through gritted teeth.

Elise remained inhumanly still, her very heartbeat apparently paused. They all awaited the same thing. The guards suspected it, but the Majors knew it. The Lumire was already flowing from her, feeling around the room for points of leverage.

Elise's only real concern was Second Reighba . . . there was something special about him too. She'd seen him turn his skin to steel, and she knew he could do much more. The impossible question of *how* tugged at her brain relentlessly.

Reighba hardly seemed bothered by Gerald's threats, even though Elise sensed Reighba knew they were true. There was something terrifyingly casual about him, something that made him seem so completely at home in a room full of gunmen and hostages. Elise was the only one among the Majors who hadn't witnessed his wrath, but her friends had described his ferocity, the terrifying look in his eyes as he beat Darren relentlessly out of sheer anger and spite. She found it hard to imagine the calm, composed man in front of her could show such viciousness.

But her friends had seen it. Darren had felt it.

Reighba strode forward. "I feel like you will serve us as especially useful, Gerald Rodum. I thank you in advance." Turning, he paced back to his original place, still speaking as he did so. "No matter what your Lumerian Council can do, I fear they've lost a valuable asset—"

Suddenly, a small jolt of electricity shot through Elise. *The signal!*

The blade at Gerald's throat shot forward, impaling the ground with amazing speed.

Elise thrust her guard backward, slamming him into the wall and releasing him to crumple to the ground. In a split second, she was climbed to her feet, then suddenly she dived back down as an explosion of fire erupted from her sister.

Peter Reighba moved as quickly as them, however, leaping onto Darren and bringing him to the ground.

They had no time to help him, however, and Laleitha darted to the window, shouting to Elise as she did so. The two girls, made fearless with adrenaline and the Lumire, threw themselves through the glass, tucking their heads before the impact. The window shattered around them, scratching their skin like the claws of a cat. The shards fell away quickly as the girls tumbled downward.

Elise let her gaze trail to the ground and her heart dropped when she noticed what was down there. A tangle of vine-like limbs stirred then lashed out quicker than lightning itself.

The first vine smacked Laleitha sideways, sending her busting through another window. Elise let out a cry as the vine creature took hold of her, whipping her in the other direction before snapping around and tossing her back through the glass, sending her tumbling into a new room.

She crashed to the floor, quickly rolling over and scrambling away from the shattered window, out of the vine-creature's reach. Then, she let her body ache from the impact.

They knew we'd try. They're guarding every door and window.

Picking herself up, she cast another glance at the creature before deciding she had better chances *anywhere* else. She turned and slipped out the door, continuing cautiously. She was in a hall that was plain and quiet, simple and dead empty. She found an elevator and stepped inside. *What a ridiculous method of escape.*

The thought then occurred to her the Prime Devise might be watching her, sending guards to any location she headed to. Her eyes drifted up to the security camera at the top corner of the elevator. She thrust a hand toward it and the Lumire pierced the lens.

She lowered her hand so it was in front of her then extended her fingers. Her palm faced the ground, and the silver mist that once twisted around her fingers began to form a hazy string stretching in either direction. Elise's breath quivered; using the Lumire this frequently was beginning to take a toll on her, especially as the pressure built and the energy rose.

The doors clicked open and Elise released the silver mist, letting it shoot outwards and soar down the hall. To her relief, nobody was there to receive the blow. She stepped out into the hall, which was again empty, and the doors closed behind her. This confused Elise at first, before it dawned on her the Prime Devise must have evacuated the base of all those who weren't fit to fight the Majors. Good.

Suddenly, there was a painfully loud beep, followed by distant clicks, before tons upon tons of water burst from every room along the hall. Elise had no time to react before she was swept off her feet, plunging into the water that raged into the corridor. Her breath caught in her throat as she fought her momentum to get back to the surface. Elise's feet brushed the bottom, giving her the perfect opportunity to push off from the floor and break into the air. Her head nearly hit the ceiling when she did so, and the water rose at an exponential rate, engulfing her once again before she could get more than a single breath. *A trap! They knew we'd try. They set a trap.*

A muffled crack sounded as one of the windows began to cave under the pressure of containing the furious waters. Elise kicked frantically toward the nearest door, tugging on it harshly to find that it was locked. The window behind her shattered and water began to spill out of the room, tugging fiercely on Elise, who still clung to the door handle.

The Lumire once again engaged instinctively, and the door handle snapped from its place and disintegrated in Elise's hand. The door popped open and water immediately spilled out, this time taking Elise with it.

The pressure lifted from her as she flopped to the floor, water still rushing by her. She sputtered and gasped for air, which was, once again, in abundant supply. The Prime Devise was growing more and more creative in their attempts to kill them.

Climbing to her feet, she took in her surroundings, an incredibly large, square room with rows of small, square doors lining the walls—some sort of strange containment unit. And she no longer stood alone but was accompanied by the one person she wanted most to avoid—Peter Reighba.

He waited in the corner for her to notice him, silently challenging her to fight him with an icy stare through his mask.

Fear rippled through her, the silver mist instinctively forming at her fingers again, before her opponent lunged with inhuman speed. Her hand jerked up, his arm meeting her palm as he attempted to punch. A jolt of energy shot through her on the contact, but in a split second he was punching with the other arm. She staggered away before the blow hit her, moving with an instinctive speed that impressed even her. He kicked her right knee and it collapsed as she let out a cry of pain. His arm came down hard, but both of Elise's hands shot up to stop the blow. Pain rippled under her muscles but the adrenaline and the Lumire kept her sharp. Second Reighba kicked her in the chest, sending her tumbling backward but giving her enough space to roll to her feet and prepare for the next blow.

His hand reached to the device in his left arm, his skin beginning to change into a dull-colored steel. Elise gulped, internally screaming at herself to think. *A plan, I need a plan!*

Peter advanced, throwing a punch, before the silver mist bolted toward his fist, catching it in midair. Elise held it there for a minute, waiting for her opponent to move again, but something else within him stirred, a silent, burning frustration.

As if all of his anger was let loose at once, he flashed forward, drilling his other fist into her side and coming at her once more with his fist before she slipped from his grip and backed away. His assault continued, Elise deflecting several of his blows, to her own amazement, but never finding the opportunities to fight back. He kept advancing and she kept evading. Peter only grew angrier as Elise grew more worn.

Finally, Peter found what he wanted, slamming Elise in the stomach and continuing his blows before Elise could even attempt to respond. Her very bones were beginning to burn as his metal fists beat her. Each time Peter reeled back, more blood stained his steel knuckles.

If Elise could have, she would have screamed in agony, then the world around her suddenly changed. She was back in the dark room in Fort Kingshold, Talious in front of her as she nearly sobbed. That day she recalled easily—the day when Talious had stuck long, torturous pins into her fingers until she got into his mind.

"You can do it, Elise," he said calmly.

"It hurts!" she cried, the agonizing pain bringing tears to her eyes.

"You can do it," he told her again.

"No, I can't!"

Elise snapped back to reality, the Lumire bursting from her uncontrollably, sending her opponent flying backward. She lay there for a moment, feeling the cold floor against her hot, flushed skin as a trickle of blood from the gash on her forehead dripped down her temple to the smooth surface below. Her chest steadily heaved up and down, but her breathing was quiet and calm. Peter rolled over with a groan, the surprise draining from him, replaced by renewed frustration as he stood.

Taking a deep breath, Elise summoned all her energy and hoisted herself to her feet, staggering, blinking, turning in confusion as the world refused to stop spinning around her. She had steadied herself by the time Peter managed to climb to his feet as well, but the image of him in front of her was still blurry, the lights around her too bright.

The Lumire floated around the room without her control, moved by instinct alone, taking hold of the small doors that lined the walls and ripping them from their hinges.

Collecting herself, Elise thrust them toward him, but he knocked them away with renewed strength. Charging at her again, this attack much more furious, Peter raged. Elise could hardly deflect the first two blows before he knocked her backward. Her body flew, smashing into the wall behind her, sending dust and rubble into the air.

Suddenly, a body crashed into Peter before he could strike again, tossing both figures out of Elise's view. The entire world around her was hazy, a terrible headache clouding her senses.

She pulled herself from where she had collapsed on the ground, not even realizing that she had fallen until she did so, stumbling when her feet tried to carry her. As she braced herself against the wall, the scene in front of her slowly came into focus. Darren Nosia dueled with Peter, but Peter had the upper hand with his inhuman speed and amazing strength. The glinting instrument that first caught Elise's eye was the duel blades of Axis that Darren fought with.

Peter knocked Axis aside, the ends automatically closing back into the baton that clattered to the ground. Darren fought on, still having no advantage over the Peter's many years of training.

Slowly, Elise extended her hand and Axis quickly flew into it. To her distress, just that small use of the Lumire intensified the pain in her head. Her cold fist pressed against her forehead as she tried to force the pain away for Darren's sake.

Axis opened in her hand, snapping into a thin rod with thick, curved blades at either end.

Darren staggered to a corner after one of Second Reighba's blows, jerking away to avoid another one. Peter's momentum took him to the corner momentarily, and that was when Elise shot into action. Lunging forward, the blade impaled the wall just centimeters away from Peter's throat.

Her enemy paused wisely, his eyes staring through his mask at the blade. Elise pulled it from the wall, keeping it at his throat threateningly. His frightened eyes trailed to her, begging her not to do it. She had him trapped between the wall and her blade, and it would be so easy to end him and all of the pain he could bring to them right there.

She couldn't. She would not willingly kill again. She had seen his thoughts and memories, felt his pain and witnessed his sorrows. She had seen his compassion and regrets, his fears and his fondest memories. His life was just as real and vivid as hers, but it was the only reality he knew. Who was she to take that away from him?

"Run, Darren," she said through gritted teeth, her chest still heaving. *"Run."*

Darren hesitated, looking between her and Second Reighba with stunned confusion. Darren looked directly at her face, seeing how serious she was, her fear, pain, and anger alike all reflecting in her hard, brown eyes. He complied.

Elise briefly closed her eyes when the pain in her head raged once again as she held Axis in place with the Lumire, stepping away, still threatening to press it into his throat.

Second Reighba stared at her as she backed away, Axis still levitating in front of him. He did not dare move.

Elise turned and ran, fighting through the pain all over her body. The moment she stepped into the hallway, Axis flew back into her hand. She tore after Darren, knowing at any moment Second Reighba would come charging after her.

The two sprinted through the facility, taking every turn they could in a desperate attempt to escape the threat of Reighba's son.

Minutes later, Elise found herself on a metal balcony that overlooked the waterworks. She and Darren had slowed to a walk, catching their breath as they softly tread on the noisy metal. The headache was beginning to fade, but the gash on her temple from Peter's punches still bled down her face, burning as if a branding iron was pressed to her skin. She tore a piece of her sock off and pressed it to the wound. She wasn't about to fuse it with fire again; that would have made her scream like the earth was crushing her, and Second Reighba would locate them in seconds.

Darren's eyes drew back to Axis, which Elise closed with a turn of the hilt.

"Which way do you think is out?" he asked, still breathing heavily.

"I don't know," Elise said. "But once we find it, we can't wait for the others. Otherwise, we'll just get captured again."

He nodded, grimly. "I know. I hope they're all right."

Suddenly, a figure burst from the shadows, smashing Elise with immense force, sending her flying from the ledge. She let out a cry and landed hard on a cylindrical silver tank.

Darren shouted her name from behind.

When her eyes found the figure again, she saw it was Second Reighba, his skin covered with strange brown and green scales. *Snakeskin. For stealth purposes.* He had flown over the rails as he attacked her, but he had landed far from Elise.

She scrambled backward, feeling for Axis before realizing it had clattered to the floor. She rolled sideways, tumbling off the tank and landing on the floor with both feet and taking up the rod once again. Reighba lunged at her, but she darted away, weaving between the tanks and around the controls. *Think! I need a plan!*

"Elise!" Darren shouted from the balcony. His eyes scanned the entire room, unable to see either Elise or Second Reighba. Both of them were lost in the maze of water tanks.

Suddenly, Elise heard a muffled shout followed by a series of hard footsteps and painful grunts. *Darren.*

Maneuvering through the wide room, she broke from the line of tanks to see Darren frantically dodging Second Reighba, who apparently had climbed back up on the platform. The moment her eyes found him was the same moment Darren threw himself over the rail.

He landed hard but on his feet, though not before Peter could launch himself off the balcony as well, landing quietly and gracefully.

They took to the cover of the tanks, Elise whispering, "I have an idea." She led him to the other end of the rows.

They waited in dead silence; even their heavy breathing was soundless. Turning in circles, their keen eyes inspected every inch of their view in an attempt to locate Second Reighba.

Something shimmered in front of Darren before disappearing. Then, with no warning, Second Reighba began to appear in bits at a time as he turned from clear glass to normal flesh.

Elise shrieked in surprise before engaging the Lumire and rupturing the tank beside her, ripping it open. Hot, burning water burst from the cylinder. The two Majors took no time to witness the outcome, seizing the time they had bought to dart behind the other tanks and race through the nearest exit as the water exploded from behind them.

There was a shout from the other end of the hall they dashed down, echoing against the walls. "Mont!"

Elise quickened her pace, having no voice to yell back with.

The two finally burst into the next room to find themselves face to face with Laleitha and Gerald.

"What happened to you?" Lee cried when she saw the blood at Elise's forehead.

"Second Reighba," she explained briefly between breaths. "Where's Anton?"

"That's the thing," Gerald said. "He's with Reighba."

"And," Lee went on, "Reighba's holding a gun to our father's head."

CHAPTER THIRTY-ONE

The Inside Men

"Our birth father?" Elise cried, appalled.

Laleitha nodded grimly.

"As in Lucious Ataliarma."

Laleitha nodded again. "I have no idea how he got here or what he's doing here, but Reighba has him and Anton's with him."

Elise looked around at her friends, exchanging glances with Gerald and casting a worried look in Darren's direction. "We have to go."

Gerald led the way, Laleitha at his heels. A million thoughts stormed in Elise's mind as she followed, the pain in her forehead becoming excruciating. They weaved through the halls, dashing up a large spiral staircase and sprinting down hall after hall, passage after passage.

Finally, Gerald slowed, creeping to the windows of the room. Reighba spun a knife in his hand with a charismatic grin on his face as he paced around the room. He held a gun in his other hand, his finger lightly tapping on the trigger, but it was pointed at the floor almost casually.

Anton had shoved himself into a shadowy corner, his fearful eyes watching Reighba spin the knife intently. Anton looked as if he had been rendered catatonic, standing inhumanly stiff.

Indeed, in the very middle of the room, Lucious Ataliarma knelt. His built but stocky figure—with a sharply angled face and scruffy black facial hair—was extremely distinct. He clutched his leg, which gushed blood onto the floor as his face scrunched into an expression of sheer pain.

Elise's entire body went numb. Her heartbeat and the image in front of her were the only things that seemed real as a terrible sickness began to stir in her stomach. She didn't even notice her sister's icy grip on her arm, so tight it nearly tore through Elise's skin.

That was her father in there. Her father, the man everybody thought had died a lying, cheating lunatic. She was beginning to doubt anything she'd previously heard about her father was true—perhaps it truly wasn't a coincidence that two of his daughters were Majors. Had Reighba captured him to use as a mechanism for controlling the Majors, a means of blackmail? Or was her father involved in much different business than she expected?

A snakeskin hand whizzed just centimeters from her face and smashed the glass they peered through. Shrieks echoed through the hall as the four whirled around to see the mask of Second Reighba. Elise fell backward against the wall in a stunned instinct to evade. Second Reighba stood right in front of her, towering over her as his skin slowly began to change back to steel.

He wound up again and she put up her arms in defense. A bone-shaking blow from an indestructible hand rippled through her muscles when his fist landed on her forearm. Before she could even react, his other fist struck her ribcage from underneath. Balling his fists in the shirt fabric covering her shoulders, he shoved her away from him.

Elise stumbled backward as Second Reighba turned from her to her friends. She had no time to notice the door next to her before it slammed open, revealing Alfred Reighba. Pointing his gun at Lucious still, he reached toward her and pulled her into the room, thrusting her inside.

She scrambled away from the man, joining Anton against the back wall. Her father's gaze nearly burned her skin when it turned to her, but she refused to look at him.

"Elise!" he cried. Elise refused to acknowledge him. Not now, while her friends were in danger and there wasn't time to unravel his secrets.

The commotion outside the room could be caught only through the narrow windows. The five were no match against Second Reighba, not even Gerald, not even when they worked together. The father of Second Reighba stood in the doorway, his gun still pointing at Elise's father. Then, his voice echoed through the hall. "Stop immediately or he dies." He hadn't yelled it loudly, but it compelled each one of them to freeze.

Second Reighba released his grip on Darren, who he had been engaged with in a fierce tussle at the time of the interruption, then strolled to the back, folding his arms behind him.

Reighba grinned. "How wonderful. You listened. Now, enter the room slowly and join your friends."

They complied, Laleitha staring only at her father as she entered, while Gerald eyed Reighba challengingly as he passed. Darren, however, could not be still and controlled, jumping at each of Reighba's movements, eyes darting everywhere in the room.

Peter Reighba entered last, his arms still folded behind his back, until he reached for the device on his arm and his skin slowly began to change back to flesh.

Reighba smiled again. "What a familiar environment," he remarked. "Though, now we have an exciting twist," he added, casting a glance at their father in the center.

"Why is he here?" Laleitha demanded, her voice somewhere between threatening and horrified.

"I have rather helpful resources," Reighba explained. "And it turns out that I have had a spy under my nose the entire time." He cast a fond look in Lucious's direction, as if he were providing him with the highest form of entertainment.

A sudden understanding dawned on Elise. He was the Lumerian Council's inside man. He never went missing. He never died. He was here, watching the Prime Devise attempt to murder his daughters.

Why him? Why couldn't it have been anyone but him?

"He didn't crack under pressure. I was rather impressed," Reighba went on. "But I always get the truth eventually. I was surprised to learn that he has two daughters with the Lumire. Ironic how the life of the life-giving father is now in the hands of his children." He laughed. "I love irony, so I thought I'd share the experience with you."

Spite built in Elise's chest for this man. His good-natured smile betrayed his sinister words.

"Well," Reighba said, "Mr. Ataliarma, it appears I have to kill you now. In order for the noble justice of the Prime Devise to prevail, mercy will have to wait." He raised the gun, pointing it directly at Ataliarma's head, before the voice of Anton Hystar rang out through the room.

"Don't touch him!"

Reighba paused, his eyes fixing on the small boy, then to the object he held in his hand. A large, dull gray drive was clutched in his shaking fingers. *The* drive. The Prime Devise's backup plans all crammed into one single device.

Elise almost smiled, admiration for the sneaky boy flooding through her.

"If you shoot him," Anton said, his voice quivering slightly, "I'll crush it."

Reighba paused, staring at the boy, before he moved. In a split second, a silver object flew from his hand. Elise didn't realize it was the knife until it had impaled Anton in the stomach.

The entire room froze, all eyes on Anton as he collapsed to the ground. As he fell, Gerald caught the drive before it left his hand. The small boy tumbled to the floor, a grunt escaping him as he did so. Elise could only watch in shock as the front of his shirt began to grow a deep shade of scarlet.

Then, Gerald looked Reighba directly in the eye and crushed the drive in his fist, letting the shards rain to the ground.

They did it. They successfully took out the heart of the dragon, just as Westbecker knew they could. This hardly computed for Elise, as it seemed a Pyrrhic victory while Anton was bleeding out on the floor.

Elise's eyes darted back to Reighba when she realized time was still moving. For a moment, Reighba was silent, his eyes following the shards of what once was his backup database fall to the floor. Then, he pulled the trigger to his gun, but Lucious had already dived, apparently preparing himself during Anton's distraction. He was not able to fully escape the shot, however, and the bullet tore through his left leg, the one that already had the bullet wound at the knee. He let out an agonized cry as his blood sprayed across the floor.

Gerald lunged at Reighba, who instinctively turned the gun to him. The bullets clattered to the ground, having no effect on Gerald.

At the same time, Peter rushed to Gerald, and Elise's Lumire-fueled instinct sent her flying to intercept the masked man. Her body crashed into him, making him stumble, then his hand grabbed her wrist and thrust her across his body. Laleitha did not hesitate to join the brawl, attacking Peter from the other side. Darren had joined as well, but Elise had no time to take notice of his struggle.

Lee jabbed at Peter's face before he grabbed her wrist, maneuvering himself around her as he twisted her arm behind her back. Elise flew at him from the other side, shoving him away from her sister. He used Elise's momentum against her, throwing her off and leaving her skidding. She grabbed his wrist as he turned around, preparing to strike him with her other hand. He whipped about, his other fist flying around him at terrifying speed. She frantically eluded his blow, then her sister came from the other side of him and his attention turned back to the younger girl.

The silver mist flew from Elise as the Lumire activated, binding his ankles while her sister attacked him and gripped his waist. With a swing of her fingers, Elise drove him against the wall with the Lumire, rather out of control with her power. The pain in her head again renewed, but then and there, she didn't give a thought to the torment. She thrust her hand in the other direction, still completely aimless. Peter flew from the new impression in the wall, being launched across the room and smashing through the enormous window. It shattered into several shards, only large pieces at the corner still intact. His body then hung limply in the air, completely at the mercy of the Lumire.

When Laleitha's startled yelp reached Elise's ears, she realized what she was doing. She wasn't going to let anyone die by her hand, especially not Peter Reighba. Breathing deeply, she slowly pulled the limp body back into the building, dropping her grip on him and letting him crumple to the floor, unconscious.

Her attention snapped immediately to Darren when he suddenly went up in flames, the room filling with an orange glow and a horrible cry. Alfred Reighba, Laleitha, and Elise all scrambled away from Darren as he fell to the floor, screaming in agony. She hadn't realized how dim the room was until the bonfire that was Darren Nosia began to rage in the center of it. Her mouth fell open and her eyes went wide as they fixed on the horrible sight. His skin began to scar and become distorted; his mouth was agape as cries erupted from him. His body writhed in sheer torture. It was cripplingly painful for Elise to watch.

Gerald alone rushed to Darren, putting his hands on Darren's shoulders and draining the fire's heat by pulling the energy back into Gerald. The flame on Darren's skin slowly faded, sinking from a raging blaze to a dancing flame to a contorted burn, then to only strings of steam rising from scarred, mottled skin. Elise looked away as Darren's entire body collapsed to the floor, quivering.

Even Reighba sat still, taking in the horrible sight. Darren's skin was raw and crinkled, his clothes were singed, and his body suddenly looked frail as he quivered on the floor in sheer agony.

At this moment, when it seemed the entire earth was still, something cold and excruciatingly painful snuck between Elise's shoulder blades.

It felt as if her heart stopped, her head beginning to swim feverishly as the very life seemed to drain from her. She gasped, struggling to take in a breath as her throat constricted. Her eyes filled with liquid, causing the world around her to blur, and she collapsed to the floor.

Even Anton sat a little straighter in his position against the wall, and Elise could see the shocked looks of Laleitha and Gerald before the face of Ella Evanstin, the emperor's daughter, came into view, gripping the bloody knife she had just stuck into Elise's back.

"Ella." Gerald could hardly whisper, his anger making his voice strained.

"I'm sorry," she said, sounding like she was choking back a sob. "I really didn't want to. I swear I never wanted to hurt anybody."

"Put the knife down," King ordered her. His voice was not hard or angry, but a little bit of danger flickered in his tone.

"I can't let you live now," she said, shaking her head and biting her lip. "Not after what you've done."

"It was you," Lee spat. "You—*you're* the traitor."

"They came to me when I was young," she said, tears in her eyes. "They knew everything about me, about my family. They showed me how they would kill my father if I disobeyed. They described in detail the very pain he would feel." She shook her head. "He's the only one I've ever had."

Elise could barely hear anymore as hazy blackness began to swallow her. She couldn't move, she couldn't speak, and the very thoughts that flew through her mind brought pain. Her chest heaved against the floor, pain shooting through her with every breath. Her cheek was pressed to the freezing tile, letting the tears from her eyes and sweat from her forehead pool beneath her.

"You were the Prime Devise's spy," Gerald repeated, unable to wrap his head around it.

She shook her head, the tears rolling down her face. "I didn't want to be."

"You didn't have to be," Laleitha responded coldly.

"Ella," Gerald said, taking a step forward, one hand outstretched. "This place is not your home. Come back with us now. We'll make it right. We can protect you and your dad from them."

There was a long pause as her eyes fixed on him. Reighba watched from the corner, silent, observing. This was unnerving, begging the question of what he was thinking, what he could possibly be planning.

"This isn't how it has to go," Gerald assured her once more.

Then, without warning, a silver Lumerian jet swooped in front of the window. What was left of the glass shattered as bullets sprayed from the bird. Several of them pelted Ella, ripping through her skin. Her body fell to the floor, her blood already beginning to pool around her. The rapid fire forced Reighba to flee to the safety of the corner but not before a few bullets could tear through his leg and hip. Lucious had taken cover as well, ducking in the far corner with his eyes set upon the dead body of Ella Evanstin.

Gerald and Lee dived to the floor, probably out of instinct, as the bullets merely bounced off them, leaving no marks in their place.

By then, Elise could hang on no longer. The blackness that had been consuming her finally swallowed her mind. Only the image of the silver bird remained as she became completely numb to the bedlam around her.

CHAPTER THIRTY-TWO

Explanations

A million voices echoed in Elise's skull as her consciousness returned. Voices she knew but couldn't identify. Some were barely distinguishable, except for when a soft woman's voice whispered, "Your father loves you, Peter."

She opened her eyes. The room around her was extremely bright, making her immediately regret waking up, but when her eyes adjusted, she realized where she was and what had happened.

The walls of the hospital were royal blue. For some reason she had known that beforehand, maybe Anton or Darren mentioned it. Elise reached up to rub her face, only to realize she had white wrappings around her forehead where the gash had been.

Becoming bored with staring at the ceiling, she braced her hands on the mattress and pushed herself up into a sitting position. Brown curls in the corner of her gaze caught her attention. Laleitha sat next to Elise, her head resting on her elbow, asleep.

"Lee," Elise said quietly, trying to gently wake her. Her sister remained soundly dreaming. "Laleitha," she said again.

No response.

"Lee, we're out of food."

"Huh?" Her sister raised her head groggily.

Elise snickered, but the pain in her chest and back prohibited any further laughter.

Laleitha's sleepy gaze slowly brightened as she focused on her sister. "You're alive."

"Yeah."

Lee nodded happily, searching for more words.

Elise swallowed, resting her head back on the pillow. "What happened after I blacked out?" she asked. "And before? Some of it's a bit fuzzy."

That wasn't entirely true, but Elise just wanted to hear Laleitha explain it. She wanted to confirm that none of it was the work of her imagination, or a pain-induced hallucination, or some freaky nightmare she just woke from.

Her sister drew in a deep breath. "Well, we were fighting Reighba and his son, do you remember that?"

Elise nodded.

"And then Darren got fried."

Lee stopped when Elise winced. Yeah, she remembered that.

Shifting in her spot, Laleitha continued, "Well, when that happened, everybody just kinda stopped fighting. It was like we were too shocked to do anything. You were standing with your back to the door, and everybody was looking at Darren. Apparently, Ella Evanstin had been creeping around outside during most of it, and when we were all staring at Darren, Reighba spotted her and gestured for her to make a move. She snuck up behind you and stuck a knife in your back, and I guess that pulled us out of the trance. We talked to her, really not sure what else to do, but before we could figure it out, Talious came flying one of those Lumerian birds and shot her down. Apparently, the minute the diplomats got within the safety of our borders, the fleet came to get us. We had to wait for a while for another plane big enough to seat more than one person to arrive and bring us home, but in that time, Talious landed and tried to give us all some help. We were able to keep Anton conscious but not you."

Elise sighed, remaining silent for a moment to take it all in. After a few beats, she sighed again and shifted slowly in her spot. "So it was Ella the whole time. She was the traitor. No wonder she wasn't suspected."

"And our dad was Lumeria's spy," Lee added quietly. "It's almost perfect. How it all worked out, I mean."

Elise nodded, understanding what Lee meant. Though Elise despised nearly every aspect of this whole mess, it all fit together, answering every question she had in perfect irony. Her father's absence put into play the most pivotal developments of her life. The Prime Device's continued attempts to kill the Majors caused the council to struggle to control them, ultimately bringing about the destruction of what the Prime Devise wanted to protect in the first place. Reighba would have loved it had he been Lumerian.

"Where is Dad now?" she asked.

"They gave him a leave of absence," Lee explained. "Nobody knows where he is now. He's probably going back home. Not sure what he's going to do about the gunshot wounds. I mean, they fixed him up pretty well, but he still isn't totally healed up yet."

"Did this happen after I blacked out?"

Lee nodded. "They got us on the plane, gave us some emergency medical attention, brought us back here and took you, Darren, and Anton to get proper treatment. You're the second to wake up."

"Darren's still out?" Elise asked. Last she'd seen of him, he was on the ground barely moving.

"Yeah. Anton was the first to wake; he was up three days ago. He's healing now," Laleitha said.

"How long was I out?"

Her sister shrugged. "A week?"

Elise closed her eyes. "Darren . . ." she murmured.

"He's alive. He's healthy," Lee assured her. "It's just . . ."

Elise raised her eyebrows.

"He's kind of . . . deformed," she said.

Elise had no response. She tried to picture the boy, his cocky grin, swept-up blond hair, and tan skin. He had always been rather good-looking, and obviously enjoyed that about himself, but now Elise's imagination was torturing her. Each image of what he could possibly look like ran through her mind. Knowing her and Laleitha, they wouldn't care how he looked, but Darren himself would be gripped with revulsion.

"How did it happen?" Elise asked. "Do you know?"

Her sister nodded, her eyes trailing to the floor. "Gerald."

Elise's heart sank.

"He was aiming for Reighba. He told me on the way back."

Elise didn't respond.

There was a gentle knock on the door, instantly remedying Elise's wish for a different topic, then the grinning face of Stanford Ellington poked into the room. "Hello, Miss Montason. I'm happy to see you're awake."

Behind him entered Anton, who grinned when his eyes fell upon the sisters, and Gerald, who greeted them quietly. They each sat in a chair against the back wall, facing the bed that Elise sat in.

"It appears we are obliged to provide you with an explanation or two," Ellington said.

"That'd be nice," she responded. "Let's start with my dad. He was the spy?"

"Yes, your father was our council's spy. He has been working for us since he was twenty. Best deep-cover operative we have."

His tone was troubling to Elise. He stated the information with such straightforwardness that one would almost believe it was just another day in transitioning.

"I'm going to guess it's no coincidence that the two people he had children with were Majors," Elise said, flatly.

Ellington gave an admitting shrug. "We tracked your parents before we tracked you, but they were too old to be suddenly introduced into Lumerian society, so we had to take matters into our own hands."

"So it was a lie then," Lee said. "Before. When Kilodrist told us you just *happened* to be investigating Silver Industries when you stumbled upon us. The emperor said something about it, too, but he said you were just 'keeping tabs on us for a while.' What, did the council also agree to lie to us about it?"

Ellington opened his mouth, letting it hang there for a moment as he tried to articulate a sentence. "We . . . did not plan to tell you anything. I can't speak for Ms. Kilodrist or the emperor about why they lied to you. We had to speed up the natural process just so we could introduce you to Lumerian society before the Prime Devise got ahold of the Majors. We would have contacted you earlier, but we wanted to make sure everything was prepared so transitioning would run smoothly."

"So you thought it was a good idea to screw with their lives just so you could get what you wanted?" Elise asserted, her temper beginning to flicker slightly. "Us. A weapon."

"You have to understand." Ellington seemed to be growing agitated, his tone becoming graver with the more resistence he saw. "There are many things in play here. Things that I don't have the authority to know nor disclose."

Elise shook her head, closing her eyes.

Perhaps there was a reason why Eleanor shut herself in so often, why she refused to be seen when she cried. This was something Elise hadn't thought about, but now that she had the idea, it couldn't be more obvious.

She distantly wondered if the others were in the same situation. Had Lumerian agents ever come into contact with their parents? She also wondered if her Marty knew her father was Lumerian. If her father was a Lumerian agent and Marty was a Lumerian fugitive, could their friendship have been another of the council's scams?

"Elise, you *have* to understand," Ellington pleaded. "We took the measures we had to in order to restore a symbol of peace and security to an empire. You are so much more than just weapons, more than just *human beings* at that. You are Lumeria's prosperity. My dear, you have to think about the big picture."

"It doesn't exactly sound like you thought it through either," Elise argued. "It affected us in ways that you didn't account for, didn't it? My mother was a mess after Dad left and gave me a shitty childhood because of it. I grew up feeling more alone when I was with my family than when I was locked in my room. I-I could have been a different person if my dad was actually there because he loved us."

Ellington shook his head. "It wasn't my decision."

Elise looked at King, who had his head down, then at Lee, who had fixed her eyes on Elise's bedsheets. "Lee?" she asked, prompting her sister to say something, perhaps fight Ellington alongside her.

Her sister shook her head. "Just don't, Elise. There's nothing to argue," she said so quietly Elise could barely hear her.

Something told Elise that Ellington had already had this conversation with Laleitha.

Ellington cleared his throat promptly. "Regardless," he went on, "his location is unknown at the moment. We feel he deserves that privilege. There is talk of him resigning his duties, but nothing is official yet."

Elise wasn't surprised, nor was she very disappointed. Just numb. All she knew was her father's absence; this was no change from the familiar. Also, she didn't know what she would say to her father if she saw him again. There would be too much to say, so she would likely say none of it and just stare at him, drink in the reality that he never truly loved her, that he never truly was her dad.

"On a different note," Ellington continued, "one that I'm sure you are aware of, the spy in the Lumerian Council was, in fact, the emperor's daughter. She was killed by the bullets from the bird that Talious piloted to save you."

"Talious came to save us," Elise remarked distantly. "Again . . ."

King's face broke into a grin as she asked this. "Hell yeah, he did," he exclaimed. "You should have seen him. He agreed to teach me how to fly one of those things sometime."

Elise managed a small snicker before turning her attention back to Ellington. "So he killed her? Talious killed Ella Evanstin?"

Ellington nodded. "The emperor will be hosting a funeral tomorrow night."

"And Reighba?" she pressed. "What happened to him?"

The man shifted his weight. "Reighba and his son are still live. However, perhaps that is for the better. The death of Inseana's chancellor is not something Lumeria should be responsible for, even in circumstances like that of last week's. Reighba will definitely be busy the next couple of months. The Inseanan public was oblivious to their attempts to assassinate you, which means that Reighba has quite a bit of either explaining or cleaning up to do. As I've told you before, the Prime Devise builds much of their success off of public opinion."

"What happens now?" Gerald asked. "I mean, two countries attacked each other. Where we come from, that usually means war."

Ellington let out a clipped, "Ha!" before going on with an explanation. "War doesn't seem very likely at this point. In order for there to be a war, there has to be a foreseeable end goal that both countries are trying to attain through military action. For Inseana, that seemed to be the death of the Majors, but you have proven to them that such a goal would not be reached." Ellington stood, beginning to stroll around to Elise's bedside. "A council meeting will be convened today at four o'clock in which we will discuss your . . . *actions*. Regarding The Way, that is. You will be expected to recite the entire experience. By the emperor's orders, your punishment will be dropped. He sees the sacrifice you made for the diplomats as an act of redemption, though there is still controversy surrounding the matter. Negotiation attempts are still being made with the Prime Devise, but we suspect that this will be the end of their schemes for now. The council is attempting to build enough confidence to just call the last month a 'series of tensions.'"

"Like the Cold War," Laleitha added.

"The what?" Ellington asked.

"It's a historical reference to things that happened in the Other Society; don't bother yourself with it," Gerald explained quickly.

Ellington nodded. "Ah. Well, back to the impending council meeting. Ms. Kilodrist, Mr. Talious, and I have conferred, and we think it would be beneficial that you inform us of the events in The Way before the council. Would you be comfortable with that?"

They nodded.

After taking turns describing what happened while Ellington listened closely, he gave a stiff nod, thinking intently. "I think," he said when they were finished, "you'd better leave out the part including Thentis. The council would be incredulous."

Elise lowered her eyebrows. "Do you believe me?"

"I can supply you with several explanations as to what you saw so that perhaps you can use this information when you explain it to the council," Ellington said, conveniently forgetting Elise's question. "The vine-creature is called a *marcedor* vine, a creature that the Prime Devise is known for genetically engineering. They thrive on the blood of any living thing, absorbing it through their small fibers, which is why they attacked you. As for the blue figures they were manufacturing, those are called stonemen, and they can be used as soldiers but programed like machines. They do so by replicating bodily and cognitive functions using machines called imitators. They are soldiers that can be programed, but have the same primal instincts as humans. This confirms our suspicion that they're building an army. As to the army's purpose, we do not yet know. We pray we never find out."

There were a few murmurs of agreement before Ellington pulled out a small case, continuing on with his words. "As for the golden knife you found"—he opened the case, revealing the knife itself—"it is called Bane and was a weapon passed down from Major to Major before it went missing some time ago. I believe the emperor mentioned this to you when you met with him. One can only guess how it ended up in The Way."

Elise was about to continue when the door opened once more. A nurse stuck her head into the room, asking, "Mr. Ellington?"

"Yes?" he said, mildly confused.

"Darren Nosia is awake."

Anton, Laleitha, and Ellington jumped to their feet. Laleitha cast a glance to her sister, who nodded her on as she followed the others out of the room. Elise slowly shifted her weight, trying to disregard the pain in her back and the dizziness that clouded her mind as she moved.

Gerald still sat in his chair, a dark expression on his face as he stared at the floor.

"You're not going to see him?" Elise asked, as she kicked her feet over the side of the bed.

"I don't think he wants to see me," Gerald replied, shaking his head. "I don't think I can face him."

Elise slipped off the bed, wobbled a bit as she reached for something to steady herself with. "You didn't do it on purpose," she said once she was balanced.

He stood to help her. "But I still did it. Lee and I were the only ones to walk away without scars."

Elise shook her head. "I don't think that's true."

She found walking easier than she expected, but still did so slowly to avoid testing her limits. Gerald accompanied her, prolonging the walk to see Darren as much as possible.

"Do you wish you could have seen your dad before he left?" Gerald asked.

Elise thought about that for a moment before shaking her head. "I don't want to face him now that I know how deep his lies really ran. I feel like if I were to face him again with all cards on the table . . . I feel like it would finally sink in that he kind of destroyed my life."

"He was following orders," Gerald said. "It doesn't make him a bad person. I think the council did what they had to for the good of their people, even if it was inhumane. That's how a lot of tough calls are made."

Elise bit the inside of her lip. "My mom should have been given a choice, King," she said. "*We* should have. What good could we have done if we didn't want to be here?"

"I don't think any of us would have agreed to it if we did have a choice," he pointed out.

"I might have," Elise said. "Peter Ginagenus Reighba is no older than us, and *he* was given a choice. Look what he's accomplished."

Gerald stared at her. "Elise?"

She met his eyes, confused.

"How do you know that?" he demanded. "How do you even know his middle name?"

Elise abruptly looked away. "That was a damn good question, King. I . . ." She stammered. "I don't . . . know." She hadn't even realized she shouldn't have known that. "I must have picked it up from when I saw his memories."

Gerald's eyes remained on her. "It sounds like you saw a lot more than just his memories, Elise."

"I don't know what happened," she said firmly. "And I don't know how I know this stuff. Something happened in that interrogation room. I don't know what it was, but I just want to forget about it."

He dropped the subject.

When they finally made their way to Darren's room, Gerald waited outside with Ellington, leaning against the wall as his friends entered.

When Elise approached Darren's bed and more of him came into view, her heart began to wrench. His skin was covered entirely with scars, hard flesh of varying shades all the way up to his head, where his hair was gone. His open blue-gray eyes stood out on his face strangely. It was like seeing a zombie open its eyes.

"You all right, Darren?" Anton said quietly.

The beginnings of a tired smile tugged at his cheeks. "Yeah, little man, I'm alive. Probably still the best-looking too," he murmured.

"How do you feel?" Elise asked.

He grunted. "Like shit."

Lee shrugged. "That's understandable."

"Where is Gerald?" Darren asked.

"Outside," Anton answered. "I imagine you have a lot to say to him?"

Darren grunted again. "The bastard won't even come see me. I would spit if I could." His voice was quiet and serious, filled with bitter loathing.

"He didn't mean to, Darren," Laleitha said.

"Don't tell me I can't be angry," he snarled. "Look what he did. I don't care if he wanted to or not. I was the only one who suffered out of the two of us."

That's not true. But Darren was too gripped with anger. He wouldn't want to believe Gerald regretted what he did.

They were silent as Anton went to the door, cracking it open and muttering to Gerald, "Darren wants to see you."

The concerned boy followed his friend into the dim room, looking down at the scarred figure with a pained expression.

Darren's gaze was fixed on Gerald, a calm flame burning in his eyes. "Don't look at me like that," he snapped, and Gerald quickly turned his head away.

"I'm sorry, Darren," he whispered.

Darren's nose crinkled. "No, you're not. You don't know what *this* is like. How could you *possibly* be sorry? You're *King*. All you ever get is respect and that's all you're used to. I saw you in the crowd when we were going to be presented. The people were all over you and you loved it. Look at *me* now. I won't be able to be in a crowd without people quickly looking away or staring. People will look at me like a freak while you enjoy their applause. This is because of *you*, Gerald, so why should you get to be sorry?"

"Because you're my friend," Gerald responded, meekly.

Darren paused. "Look at me," he said, his voice dangerously low. He waited for Gerald's eyes to reach his face. "I'm something else now, because of you. I'm not your friend."

Elise had seen Darren get angry before, but this was new. Now, his words were calm but backed by wild emotion. His lip curled as he spoke. His eyes burned as he did so. Something had changed in Darren, something awful.

Ellington knocked on the door. "Not to intrude, but we should think about preparing for the council meeting soon. I suggest you finish with Darren."

Gerald hastily made for the door while the rest turned back to Darren.

"Ms. Kilodrist told me we'd be given the chance to visit home for a bit soon," Anton said, ignoring the entire situation that had just ended. "What are you going to do?"

Darren closed his eyes. "Sort things out with my family," he said. "Then, I don't care what they say—I'm going to Vegas."

Elise almost chuckled before remembering the pain she'd feel. "You're going to Vegas? *Why?*"

He shrugged. "I like blackjack. And I'll fit in with the other freaks there."

"Perfect," Lee said. She looked up at her sister. "Should we go get ready for the council meeting?"

Elise nodded. "Bye, Darren," she said.

"Bye."

The three filed out, joining Gerald as Ellington went in to explain everything to Darren.

"If you have any vacation plans, I don't advise Vegas," Elise muttered to Gerald.

They made their way back to their living quarters, changing into fresh clothes and Elise removing the bandages on her head. The gash didn't look too terrible when it wasn't bleeding, but it still slightly frazzled her.

She paused for a moment, staring into the mirror. Her mind trailed back to the people who died on that day in Litrite. Shame swept over her once again, her heart heavier this time. She didn't expect this feeling to go away soon.

Slipping out the door, she headed across the room to the bedroom Anton stayed in. Lightly pushing open the door, she realized he was not there. King had told her Anton carved up the walls, but now that she witnessed it in person, she was overcome with a strange sense of awe for the boy. At every side of the room, he had decorated the entire wall with intricate designs and little scenes. Her gaze traced the wall to her left, lingering on a picture of a small headstone with a rose laid gingerly on top of it. Moving on, she spotted five figures in the very middle of the wall. The first held a book, wavy hair swept over her shoulders; the next had curly hair and fire dancing on her fingers. The third was the smallest but had a completely blank face with no detail. The fourth was the tallest, a grin spread across his face and a small crown on his head. The last appeared to be laughing, a crooked grin on his face and a hand on his friend's shoulder. Beneath the five figures, "family" was carved in Anton's handwriting.

A wistful smile crossed Elise's face, a sudden feeling of affection for Anton pacing through her.

Turning, she spotted the knife on his nightstand and took it back to her own room. On the wall, she carved three stars, one for each who died on that day in Litrite.

CHAPTER THIRTY-THREE

Goodbye for Now

The council meeting was incredibly stressful for Elise. The four of them sat next to Ellington at their assigned desk in the tall council room. Darren was obviously unable to attend, but he was given access to the livestream recording so he could listen in. Knowing Darren, he would probably have tried to spring to his feet several times. According to the nurses, he yelled at the speakers relentlessly, disregarding the fact that nobody in the meeting could hear him. Gerald had a hard time keeping his mouth shut as well.

After reciting their experience in The Way to the Arc Leaders, they listened for what seemed like hours to people arguing about their punishment, the debate growing increasingly heated. The emperor did not back down, however, and they walked away from the meeting with a full pardon but at the same time, very dubious respect from the majority of the council members. The diplomats they had exchanged places with vouched for them adamantly, but there remained a great number who refused to let go of the fact that they had deliberately deceived the council, went against orders, and triggered the entire mess with the diplomats being held hostage in the first place.

As they retreated from the council room, they were approached by the emperor himself. "Could I have a moment with you four, please?" he asked.

He led them back to his office, the luxurious place with polished wooden walls and golden floorboards. When they entered, Gerald froze to see Darren lying on one of the couches. Elise gave him an encouraging pat on the shoulder as she passed, exchanging glances with him.

Emperor Evanstin sank into a chair, gesturing for the others to do the same. Cautiously, they sat, just like they did the first time they were here, full of secrets and lies. Elise sat next to Laleitha, across from Anton and Gerald.

"You five have been on quite an adventure," the emperor began. "Despite what the Arc Leaders say, they are undeniably impressed with you. You have, in fact, completed your first patriot's labor, now you only have two more to complete before you are officially inducted."

"*Only* two?" Gerald grunted.

"No, that's too easy," Darren muttered at the same time.

A soft meow sounded as the silver cat with its ruby collar entered the room. Darren's eyes shot to the cat, staring at it intently. This subtle action confused Elise at first, before the memory came crashing back to her that this cat had somehow made it into The Way with them.

"I can only thank you," the emperor went on, not noticing their alarmed expressions at the cat's arrival. "It seemed your actions were the only possible escape from Reighba's ploy. You have proven that the empire needs you, which is why I granted you a full pardon."

"Thank you for that," Gerald said sincerely.

"*But.*" The emperor stood, walking to his desk and picking up with delicate fingers the mind stone of Orphia's son. "A rather disturbing realization has come to light regarding the stone."

"Is that not the mind stone of Orphia's son?" Elise asked, a sudden concern filling her.

"Well, we'd never know for certain until we build an interpreter; that is the only way to access the consciousness inside of the stone. However, an interpreter has not been invented yet, so it will be quite a while before we are able to find out."

"So what is the problem?" Laleitha inquired.

"Do you know the Arc Leader Harold Alvenice?" the emperor asked.

They nodded.

"I know the name," Gerald said.

"He pointed out to me, in private, that a key characteristic of minds stones is that they glow only in the dark. This stone glows in both the dark and light, suggesting it is not a real mind stone at all."

The Majors were silent, their eyes fixed on the stone.

"It appears," the Emperor went on, "that you have retrieved a decoy. One can only guess that Reighba has the real one."

"So we went to The Way for nothing," Darren growled.

"Oh, no, of course you did not go to The Way for nothing. You brought us the information that the Prime Devise has infiltrated The Way. Usually, no empire can testify against another unless they are in possession of the person they wish to testify against and can *make* them attend. This only applies to the normal crimes against the empire, but when the laws of the Ancient Convention are violated, matters are taken much more seriously. Our Arc Leaders can testify against the leaders of the Prime Devise, and all of Inseana will be affected."

"What exactly *are* the laws of the Ancient Convention?" Gerald asked.

The emperor shifted in his seat. "It is a series of laws, mostly pertaining to Orphia, that keep the stable system in check. They are the very laws that explain the Trials of Orphia and even state that all those with the Lumire must train to become Majors. They are usually very general rules but are set up so it is difficult to find loopholes. The Ancient Convention was the basis of all the empires and Trials of Orphia since the beginning. They are the documents that outline the protocols pertaining to Orphia that apply to every government in his jurisdiction."

"And what happens if one is proven to have violated the laws?" Elise asked.

"In these kinds of cases, Orphia both decides the punishment and issues it. He can deny them trade resources and strip the leaders of their power, all things that can greatly affect how the empire operates. He does, in fact, have access to a workforce that can enforce this punishment, and to disobey or inflict harm on any of his workforce can result in similarly serious punishments. This force is called Orphia's Legion. Not much is known about it. Never has anybody outside the Orphian City been given the opportunity to gain any knowledge of it, other than its recruiting process. Anyway, we can testify now because of the information you brought us; we can even look to the Omenescents as witnesses. This is our way of making the Prime Devise pay for threatening our people."

Laleitha stroked the silver cat tentatively, scratching its back as it purred contentedly, keeping a close eye on it, as if it were about to sprout demon wings at any minute. She then looked up at the emperor and asked, "What happens to the Prime Devise then?"

"One cannot tell for sure," Emperor Evanstin said. "But when empires really piss him off"—he gave a wry chuckle—"he has a tendency to respond by forbidding any person or vehicle to cross their borders, coming in or going out.

This cuts off both imports and exports, isolating them within their own borders. If he does this, the Inseanan economy will plummet. We will have paid Inseana back with something that cannot be easily restored. All this because of you."

Elise raised her eyebrows.

"Whoa," Gerald remarked. "Not exactly what we had in mind when we left, but I guess we're flexible."

"Who would've thought we'd be fighting Inseana with economics?" Darren snorted.

Elise snickered. "When's the hearing going to take place?"

"That's yet to be determined," the Emperor replied. "We plan to wait so negotiations can cool down. I greatly look forward to it, I must admit. It is only the council's wishes that negotiations continue. If there was no council at all, I would order a heavy infantry attack, but that would be unwise and the council knows it."

Elise frowned, puzzled by the man's words.

He looked back up at them. "They took my daughter's life," he said, his voice filled with pain. "First, they took the meaning from it, turning her against me just so she could protect me, then she was killed for the position they put her in. That, I can never forgive."

※

"Lots to investigate," Ellington said as he paced around their living quarters the next day. The Majors had retreated back to their rooms to begin packing, preparing to visit home to finally explain everything to their families. "We have the Prime Devise, the mind stone, Mr. Westbecker's predicament, *why* the Prime Devise was looking for the lost son of Orphia . . . so many unanswered questions," he remarked.

Elise pushed the rest of her belongings deeper into the bag. "And I'm assuming we are allowed to participate in none of it."

"You are to focus on training," he said, pointing to Elise before moving his gaze around to the others. "All of you. You are not Majors yet, and until the day comes when you are inducted, you will still be my students."

"And mine," Talious added as he entered the room. "I'm not an advocate for keeping track of debts, but you five owe me."

King groaned. "That can't be good."

"Yes," Ellington said. "He was the one who piloted the jet that saved you. Quite a maneuver that was; even the Arc Leaders were impressed."

Talious shrugged, a fond grin almost—*almost*—reaching his lips.

Elise zipped up her bag, set to go when the time came. She walked across the room, ignoring the vocal commotion that consisted of Ellington's stress, Gerald's increasing flippancy, Anton's side remarks, and Talious just saying whatever he felt like saying. She pushed open the unlocked bathroom door to see Darren standing in front of the mirror. He stared at himself, his eyes tracing every scar and misshapen piece of skin. The noise behind her seemed to fade, everything becoming heavy and still once again.

"The doctor said that this isn't how a normal person would look if this happened to them," he said quietly, his eyes not leaving the mirror. "Apparently the Lumire was fighting back when I went up in flames. In some places it succeeded and my skin was protected, but in most places, it didn't. That's what made the scars."

"Honestly," Elise said, standing next to him, "I don't think a normal person would have survived that."

"I can't even recognize myself," he whispered. "What will Dad say?"

"They're your family," Elise said. "They don't care how you look."

"You guys are my family," he said. "I know you don't care, but my parents . . . we've never really been able to get along. Sometimes I wondered if they cared about me at all. And that was before . . ." He looked down at himself. "All this."

Elise didn't know what to say. Something told her his parents really did love him but he could just never realize it. Maybe seeing him like this would make them realize how much they cared about him. "Well, if things don't get better," she said, "you always have us to come back to."

He nodded. "Yeah."

"Are you going to fix things up with King?"

"Eventually. Maybe. Maybe when I get used to . . . what he did," Darren replied. It seemed incredibly hard for him to say it out loud: *the scars.*

Elise was content with his answer. "Good."

Darren exited the bathroom, letting Elise relieve herself. When she left the room, she found her sister had joined the others in the main area as well, her bag placed next to Elise's.

"Well, it appears you are all set to leave," Ellington said. "Talious has volunteered to drive all of you home from the Port, so you can say goodbye to him when you thank him. As for my goodbyes . . ." He stood in front of them, a wide smile opening on his face. "Don't get into any trouble. I'll see you in a week or two."

They beamed back at him then followed Talious out.

"And be responsible in Las Vegas, Darren," Ellington called after them.

"Right. Yup," Darren responded without looking back.

The minute the doors to Fort Kingshold opened, Elise found herself stunned. A cheer erupted from a large crowd that had gathered in the entry hall of Fort Kingshold, all the council members, the Arc Ledaers, the League of Lumeria members, and all others who worked in the fort, it seemed, had come together, clapping for them. Elise's heart leapt into her throat as she looked out at them. In a daze, Elise looked toward Darren, who let out a gleeful laugh, forgetting his scars for a moment.

"I told you," Gerald said, turning to his friends. Elise could barely hear him amid the clapping. "I told you we'd give them something to cheer for."

Elise looked at Anton to her left. His mouth had twisted into a smile, something she hadn't seen much from the boy. Next to Anton, Laleitha looked out at the crowd with a blank face, but in her eyes, Elise saw contentedness, pride even.

Then, Elise finally found it in her to laugh.

"They're hosting a party for you," Talious told them quietly, leaning down toward them so the crowd couldn't hear. "All the Arc Leaders and the council members, I mean."

"Do they know we're leaving today?" Elise asked over her shoulder.

"Yes, yes they do," Talious said. "But I doubt they really care. They like excuses to celebrate, even if the people they're celebrating can't attend."

"I thought half these people hated us," Lee said. "Why are they clapping for us now?"

Talious shrugged. "Sign of respect, I guess. The Majors have returned to Lumeria and proved themselves to not be worthless duds. Even if I hated them, I'd want to celebrate that."

Lee exchanged glances with Elise before they both shrugged, deciding that was reasonable enough.

"Keep moving," Talious told them softly. "Our transport is this way."

The crowd cleared the way for them as they made their way through, maneuvering to the private room of transportation rods, which they had been granted one-time-only access to by Emperor Evanstin. It didn't take long for Talious to locate the rod labeled *the Port*, which he promptly opened before them.

Laleitha was the first to enter, then Darren, then Anton, then Elise. Gerald paused for a minute before stepping through, turning his head to look back at Fort Kingshold. Finally, he sighed and stepped into the Port. Talious followed.

After stepping through the portal to the Port, they walked casually from the small bank and hopped into a new black Ford, with Talious at the driver's seat, Darren in the passenger seat, and the others stuffed in the back. Elise couldn't help but think back to the night when she was captured by Sar Prague and taken to Second Reighba. She thought back to the chase through Silver Industries, the first time she used the Lumire to set a man on fire. She made a mental note to carve another cross on the wall for that man, and perhaps one for the girl who was taken by mistake and shot in the head. She shuddered at the memory of the poor girl.

"So, where are we going?" Talious asked them.

"East Dundee," the sisters said together.

"Santa Rosa, so airport," Darren said.

"Brooklyn," Gerald answered. "So, yeah, airport."

Darren didn't look at Gerald, keeping his eyes forward, burning holes into the back of Talious's seat.

"And you, kid?" Talious asked Anton.

The small boy shrugged. "Aberdeen, South Dakota. So probably airport."

"Anyone have cash?" Darren asked.

"Don't worry, kid," Talious said. "They gave me enough to send all of you home."

"Can we agree," Laleitha said as Talious began to drive, "that we're going to leave out the part where we all almost die when we tell this story to our families?"

"*All* almost die?" Elise laughed. "What happened to you and Gerald? Were you stabbed between the shoulder blades or something?"

"Yeah, we're not putting that out there," Gerald agreed, disregarding Elise's statement. "The last thing my siblings need to worry out is me dying horribly."

Lee looked at her sister. "And your mom is probably already stressing about Percy. I think it would be better if they didn't know."

"So you guys plan to lie to them?" Anton said. "What if you do die? What would they think?"

Elise exchanged glances with her sister and then with Gerald.

"Well, I think as long as we just do what we are told to do for a while, we'll stay out of danger," Gerald said.

"And dying without warning is kind of our family's thing," Laleitha added referring to Marty and the fact that their father had been presumed dead.

Darren smiled. "Yeah, the only real reason we were in danger at all was because we escaped to The Way."

"That's arguable," Anton grunted.

"Still," Gerald said, "Ellington is probably just going to have us training for a while, until the council is in any real danger, but by the time that comes, we'll already be done with our training."

"Don't say that here," Darren said. "There's no wood to knock on."

Elise enjoyed the ride home immensely, knowing it would be the last time she'd see her friends for a few weeks. It seemed strange when she suddenly realized who these people were in her life. She had always wanted a life that was eventful and interesting, full of adventure and the inevitable danger that came with it, and that wish had been granted it such a way that she didn't even realize her life had changed for the better.

When Talious arrived at the Montason house at 8742 King Avenue, Elise and Laleitha turned to their friends to say goodbye.

"You staying with me tonight?" Elise asked Lee as they climbed from the car.

Lee nodded. "I'll go home tomorrow. My mom can survive one more day."

"Great, you can try to reconcile with my mom, then," Elise remarked. "Once we break the news about our dad. After me, I mean. I have some things to clear up with my family."

Laleitha snorted. "That's not new."

The garage door was closed, so Elise decided to take a different approach. Stepping up to the front door, she knocked three times.

Her face spread into a grin when the confused and mildly worried face of her mother answered the door. "Hey, Mom," Elise said. "I guess I owe you an explanation."

Epilogue

Reighba adjusted the bandages on his leg and stomach. The bullet wounds hurt no more than any other he'd ever endured, but these bullet wounds meant something to him. They would remind him every day of his failure, of his hatred, making these bullet wounds his greatest weapon. Between his fingers, he held a small piece of paper, one he toyed with mindlessly, folding it over and over again in his hand.

His son paced around in front of him, the distress from not being able to remember what had happened making him restless. "Calm down, Peter," Reighba muttered to his son as he folded the paper in his fingers. "It is only a concussion. You will remember what happened in time."

"It was Montason," he growled. "That much, I do know."

"The Montason girl paid for it," Reighba said soothingly, creasing the fold in the paper in his hands. "Miss Evanstin made sure of that. Now we ponder our next move."

"Initiate the stonemen company," Peter said.

Reighba shook his head. "After what has happened and what is at stake, we can't operate in the open anymore."

"So you plan to put the lives of our own people at risk?" Peter was on edge today.

"Or course not," Reighba scoffed, turning his gaze away from the paper in his hand and looking down at the other papers on his desk. "Peter, are you familiar with the Gray Army in Stormy City?"

Peter shrugged. "I've heard people talk. Most of the rumors I hear about it are wild enough to pass as an urban myth."

Reighba shook his head. "No, no, no. I'm talking about the actual rings, the chains of drugs, weapons, information . . . Though it all begins in the Stormy City, it has spread everywhere, mainly to Lumeria, perhaps even to our domain, anywhere with resources and buyers."

Peter lowered his eyebrows as he paced. "And you want to get involved?"

"No, I want to control it."

"How do you plan to do that? The Vortex Queen and the Stormy City's Royal Court controls it," Peter said flatly. "Ever since the public became suspicious that *we* were the ones attacking the Majors, we've become unpopular in Trimeterous. If you want to do under-the-table business with anybody over there, you have to give them some justification."

Reighba slapped the paper in his hand downward and looked at his son with raised eyebrows. "Are you suggesting that I disclose the Clandestine Drawings to the public?"

"Not all of it," the boy responded. "Just the fact that you had an agreement with Lumeria that essentially *proves* most of their council is corrupt. They failed to uphold it and are now blackmailing us. This gives us reason to attack the Majors. Such an imbalance of power would eventually lead to Lumeria gaining the upper hand over us in ways that the public could pick up on *without* access to classified information. By justifying ourselves, we can assure the public that we are fighting for them and that Lumeria is the enemy."

Reighba threw up his hands. "Just the fact that we are involved in the Clandestine Drawings at all would lead the people to believe that we aren't fighting for them," he snapped. "That agreement will remain secret to parliament, remain secret to the cabinet, remain secret to the courts, and *especially* remain secret to the people. My God, boy, I could demote you for even suggesting we make those details public."

"If it justifies our attacks on Lumeria, then the public deserves to know," his son argued.

"The maintenance of positive public opinion is rarely the result of complete honesty, boy."

"So, now what? We're reading from Lumeria's playbook?"

"If you think Lumeria is a political bear trap, then you haven't dipped your toes into what really goes on in our parliament. That's shameful coming from the chancellor's son." He leaned forward, his voice growing dangerously quiet.

"Listen to me closely, boy. You do not bring up the Clandestine Drawings again, or I will have to teach you a *very* hands-on lesson about it."

Peter was silent. He stopped pacing, staring out the window of his father's office. His father had chosen this room for his own because of the view itself. It overlooked Hangar C, where a fleet of small ships that they fondly referred to as "stingrays" sat on platforms of varying height and size, protruding from the wall like peeling bark on a birch tree. Below the platforms, a long waterfall tumbled down the polished walls to the river at the bottom of the gorge. This river would take them to Starlight Lake, where the stone called palsalt would be harvested by the stingrays. It was always quite a sight to watch the stingrays fly from the platform, joining the waterfall as they were swept into the river.

"Peter," Reighba said, picking up the paper again.

He turned to face his father.

"You know I can always tell when you are hiding something from me, as I have for the last six months when your skin began to change. I still don't know how you do that or how you obtained that power. I assume that as long as I don't ask, you won't tell, and as long as you won't tell, you won't lie. I will let you tell me when you are ready."

A guilty and rather frightened feeling coursed through Peter. Slowly, he crossed the room to sit across from his father at his desk. "What is that?" Peter asked, nodding to the paper Reighba had been holding.

"It's the note from Hank Martinez to the Montason girl, the one I had Sar Prague retrieve for me," the older man explained. He chuckled. "Oh, the knowledge she would have if she had known how to read it."

"Why won't you tell me what it says?"

Reighba looked Peter in the eye then shrugged. "I guess we're both hiding things from each other, just as all functional families do."

Peter snorted, decidedly ignoring the fact that his father was trying to bait him into revealing his secret.

"When do you plan to make your next move?" he asked his father.

"Tonight," Reighba told him darkly. "Now, here is what I want you to do. You will send Quinn Deritomy to lead her officers to the Stormy City. She is to work them into the system. We need eyes everywhere. She will wait in the Stormy City until I give her further instruction to leave."

Peter raised his eyebrows. "How long is this expected to take?"

"The saying in the Stormy City's network is 'Time is the best cover.' We have to carefully spread out our advances in the plan. Of course, the plan is not yet finalized since that Rodum boy crushed our backup drive," Reighba said bitterly. "Now, leave. Carry these instructions to Quinn."

Peter obeyed, leaving the room.

When Reighba was alone, he let out a sigh. These Majors would be more trouble for him than he had anticipated. His son was right about one thing. Once the Majors were officially inducted, Lumeria would have significantly more power than them—much more to blackmail them with and much more to expand the parameters of the Clandestine Drawings with. Even right now, they were a threat. Their rebellious nature made them unpredictable, a valuable asset to the Lumerian Council, even though the Lumerian Council no longer appreciated it.

It was time to move his domain to a more secretive culture, so he could eventually penetrate the Lumerian Council from inside the council. The Majors had no power in the Stormy City, and, in enough time, he would have it at his fingertips . . .

TO BE CONTINUED IN
The Vortex Queen